ARTHUR KOESTLER

THE GHOST
IN THE MACHINE

UNABRIDGED

PAN BOOKS LTD : LONDON

THE GHOST
IN THE MACHINE

First published 1967 by
Hutchinson Publishing Group Ltd.
This edition published 1970 by Pan Books Ltd,
33 Tothill Street, London, S.W.1

2nd Printing 1971

ISBN 0 330 02476 0

Printed by Hazell Watson & Viney Ltd,
Aylesbury, Bucks

To the Fellows and Staff
1964-5
at the Centre for Advanced Study
in the Behavioural Sciences

CONTENTS

PART TWO

BECOMING

PART THREE

DISORDER

APPENDIX I

APPENDIX II

PREFACE

IN a previous book, *The Act of Creation*, I discussed art and discovery, the glory of man. The present volume ends with a discussion of the predicament of man, and thus completes a cycle. The creativity and pathology of the human mind are, after all, two sides of the same medal coined in the evolutionary mint. The first is responsible for the splendour of our cathedrals, the second for the gargoyles that decorate them to remind us that the world is full of monsters, devils and succubi. They reflect the streak of insanity which runs through the history of our species, and which indicates that somewhere along the line of its ascent to prominence something has gone wrong. Evolution has been compared to a labyrinth of blind alleys, and there is nothing very strange or improbable in the assumption that man's native equipment, though superior to that of any other living species, nevertheless contains some built-in error or deficiency which predisposes him towards self-destruction.

The search for the causes of that deficiency starts with the Book of Genesis and has continued ever since. Every age had its own diagnosis to offer, from the doctrine of the Fall to the hypothesis of the Death Instinct. Though the answers were inconclusive, the questions were still worth asking. They were formulated in the specific terminology of each period and culture, and thus it is inevitable that in our time they should be formulated in the language of science. But, paradoxical as it sounds, in the course of the last century science has become so dizzy with its own successes, that it has forgotten to ask the pertinent questions – or refused to ask them under the pretext that they are meaningless, and in any case not the scientist's concern.

This generalization refers, of course, not to individual scientists, but to the dominant, orthodox trend in the contemporary sciences of life, from evolutionary genetics to experimental psychology. One cannot hope to arrive at a diagnosis of the predicament of man so long as one's image of man is that of a conditioned reflex-automaton produced by chance mutations; one cannot use a stethoscope on a slot machine. One eminent biologist, Sir Alister Hardy, wrote recently: 'I have come to believe, and I hope to convince you, that this present-day view of evolution is inadequate.'[1] Another eminent zoologist, W. H. Thorpe, speaks of 'an undercurrent of thought in the minds of scores, perhaps hundreds, of biologists over the past twenty-five years', who are sceptical regarding the current orthodox doctrine.[2] Such heretical tendencies are equally in evidence in the other life-sciences, from the study of genetics to the study of the nervous system, and so to the study of perception, language and thought. However, these diverse non-conformist movements, each with a particular axe to grind in its particular field, do not as yet add up to a new coherent philosophy.

In the pages that follow I have attempted to pick up these loose ends, the threads of ideas trailing on the fringes of orthodoxy, and to weave them into a comprehensive pattern in a unified frame. This means taking the reader on a long and sometimes devious journey before we arrive at our destination, the problem of man's predicament. The journey leads through Part One, mainly concerned with psychology, and Part Two, which is concerned with evolution; and, though it must of necessity include excursions into domains seemingly remote from the central subject, I hope that these may be of some interest in themselves. Perhaps some readers, firmly entrenched on the humanist side in the cold war between the two cultures, will be dismayed by this apparent desertion into the enemy camp. It is embarrassing to have to repeat, over and again, that two half-truths do not make a truth, and two half-cultures do not make a culture. Science cannot provide the ultimate answers, but it can provide pertinent questions. And I do not believe that we can formulate even the simplest questions, much less arrive at a diagnosis, without the help of the sciences of life. But it must be a true science of life, not the antiquated slot-machine model based on the naïvely mechanistic world-view of the nineteenth century. We shall not be able to ask the right questions until we have replaced that rusty idol by a new, broader conception of the living organism.

I was much comforted to discover that other writers who try to talk across the frontier between the two cultures find themselves in the same quandary. In the first paragraph of his book *On Aggression*[3] Konrad Lorenz quotes a letter from a friend whom he had asked to read critically through the manuscript. 'This', his friend writes, 'is the second chapter I have read with keen interest but a mounting feeling of uncertainty. Why? Because I cannot see its exact connection with the book as a whole. You must make this easier for me.' Should the gentle reader of these pages occasionally feel the same reaction, all I can say is that I have tried my best to make it easier for him. I do not think there are many passages in this volume which he will find too technical; but wherever that is the case, he can safely skip them and pick up the thread further down.

While writing this book, I was greatly encouraged and helped by a Fellowship at the Centre for Advanced Study in the Behavioural Sciences in Stanford, California. This rather unique institution, more familiarly known as the 'Think-Tank', annually assembles fifty Fellows elected from varied academic disciplines, and provides them, on its hill-top campus, with the facilities for a whole year's interdisciplinary discussions and research, free from administrative and teaching duties. This proved a most beneficial opportunity for the clarification and testing of ideas in workshops and seminars, attended by specialists in various fields, ranging from neurology to linguistics. I can only hope that the stimulation – and friction – which they generously provided in the course of our sometimes heated discussions have not been wasted.

Some of the subjects discussed in this volume are dealt with in greater detail in *The Act of Creation*, and in my earlier books. I have had to quote from these fairly often; where a quotation appears in the text without mentioning the author by name, it is from these earlier books.

*   *   *   *

I am very grateful to Prof. Sir Alister Hardy (Oxford), Prof. James Jenkins (Univ. of Minnesota), Prof. Alvin Liberman (Haskins Laboratories, New York) and Dr Paul MacLean (NIMH, Bethesda) for their critical reading of parts of the manuscript; and to Prof. Ludwig v. Bertalanffy (Univ. of Alberta), Prof. Holger Hydén (Univ. of Goeteborg), Prof. Karl Pribram (Stanford Univ.), Prof. Paul Weiss (Rockefeller Institute) and L. L. Whyte (CAS, Wesleyan Univ.) for many stimulating discussions on the subject of this book.

A.K.

PART ONE

ORDER

I

THE POVERTY OF PSYCHOLOGY

He had been eight years upon a project for extracting sun-beams out of cucumbers, which were to be put into vials hermetically sealed, and let out to warm the air in raw inclement summers.

SWIFT *Voyage to Laputa*

The Four Pillars of Unwisdom

PROVERBS ix, 1, says that the house of wisdom rests on seven pillars, but unfortunately does not name them. The citadel of orthodoxy which the sciences of life have built in the first half of our century rests on a number of impressive pillars, some of which are beginning to show cracks and to reveal themselves as monumental superstitions. The four principal ones, summarized in a simplified form, are the doctrines

(a) that biological evolution is the result of random mutations preserved by natural selection;

(b) that mental evolution is the result of random tries preserved by 'reinforcements' (rewards);

(c) that all organisms, including man, are essentially passive automata controlled by the environment, whose sole purpose in life is the reduction of tensions by adaptive responses;

(d) that the only scientific method worth that name is quantitative measurement; and, consequently, that complex phenomena must be reduced to simple elements accessible to such treatment, without undue worry whether the specific characteristics of a complex phenomenon, for instance man, may be lost in the process.

These four pillars of unwisdom will loom up repeatedly in the chapters that follow. They provide the background, the contemporary landscape, against which any attempt to design a new image of man must be silhouetted. One cannot operate in a vacuum; only by starting from the existing frame of reference can the outline of the new design be set off clearly, by way of comparison and contrast. This is a point of some importance, and I must insert here a personal remark to forestall a line of criticism which past experience has taught me to expect.

If one attacks the dominant school in psychology – as I did in my last book and as I shall do again in the present chapter – one is up against two opposite types of criticism. The first is the natural reaction of the defenders of orthodoxy, who believe that they are in the right and that you are in the wrong – which is only fair and to be expected. The second category of critics belongs to the opposite camp. They argue that, since the pillars of the citadel are already cracked and revealing themselves as hollow, one ought to ignore them and dispense with polemics. Or, to put it more bluntly, why flog a dead horse?*

This type of criticism is frequently voiced by psychologists who believe that they have outgrown the orthodox doctrines. But this belief is often based on self-deception, because the crude slot-machine model, in its modernized, more sophisticated versions, has had a profounder influence on them – and on our whole culture – than they realize. It has permeated our attitudes to philosophy, social science, education, psychiatry. Even orthodoxy recognizes today the limitations and short-comings of Pavlov's experiments; but in the imagination of the masses, the dog on the laboratory table, predictably salivating at the sound of a gong, has become a paradigm of existence, a kind of anti-Promethean myth; and the word 'conditioning', with its rigid deterministic connotations, has

* See Appendix Two: 'On Not Flogging Dead Horses.'

become a key-formula for explaining why we are what we are, and for explaining away moral responsibility. There has never been a dead horse with such a vicious kick.

The Rise of Behaviourism

Looking back at the last fifty years through the historian's inverted telescope, one would see all branches of science, except one, expanding at an unprecedented rate. The one exception is psychology, which seems to lie plunged into a modern version of the dark ages. By psychology I mean in the present context academic or 'experimental' psychology, as it is taught at the great majority of our contemporary universities, and as distinct from clinical psychiatry, psychotherapy or psychosomatic medicine. Freud and, to a lesser degree Jung, are, of course, immensely influential, but their influence is more strongly felt in the humanities – in literature, art and philosophy – than in the citadel of official science. By far the most powerful school in academic psychology, which at the same time determined the climate in all other sciences of life, was, and still is, a pseudo-science called Behaviourism. Its doctrines have invaded psychology like a virus which first causes convulsions, then slowly paralyses the victim. Let us see how this improbable situation came about.

It started just before the outbreak of the First World War when a professor at Johns Hopkins University in Baltimore, named John Broadus Watson, published a paper in which he proclaimed: *'the time has come when psychology must discard all reference to consciousness ... Its sole task is the prediction and control of behaviour; and introspection can form no part of its method.'*[1] By 'behaviour' Watson meant observable activities – what the physicist calls 'public events', such as the motions of a dial on a machine. Since all mental events are private events which cannot be observed by others, and which can only be made public through statements based on introspection, they had to be excluded from the domain of science. On the strength of this doctrine, the Behaviourists proceeded to purge psychology of all 'intangibles and unapproachables'². The terms 'consciousness', 'mind', 'imagination' and 'purpose', together with a score of others, were declared to be unscientific, treated as dirty words, and banned from the vocabulary. In Watson's own words, the Behaviourist must exclude 'from his scientific vocabulary all subjective terms such as sensation, perception, image, desire, purpose, and even thinking and emotion as they were subjectively defined'.³

It was the first ideological purge of such a radical kind in the domain of science, predating the ideological purges in totalitarian politics, but inspired by the same single-mindedness of true fanatics. It was summed up in a classic dictum by Sir Cyril Burt: 'Nearly half a century has passed since Watson proclaimed his manifesto. Today, apart from a few minor reservations, the vast majority of psychologists, both in this country and in America, still follow his lead. The result, as a cynical onlooker might be tempted to say, is that psychology, having first bargained away its soul and then gone out of its mind, seems now, as it faces an untimely end, to have lost all consciousness.'⁴

Watsonian Behaviourism became the dominant school, first in American academic psychology and subsequently in Europe. Psychology used to be defined in dictionaries as the science of the mind; Behaviourism did away with the concept of mind and put in its place the conditioned-reflex chain. The consequences were disastrous not only for experimental psychology itself; they also made themselves felt, in clinical psychiatry, social science, philosophy, ethics, and the graduate student's general outlook on life. Although his name was less familiar to the public, Watson in fact became, next to Freud, and Pavlov in Russia, one of the most influential figures of the twentieth century. For, unfortunately, Watsonian Behaviourism is not a historical curiosity, but the foundation on which the more sophisticated and immensely influential neo-Behaviourist systems – such as Clark Hull's and B. F. Skinner's – were built. The more painful absurdities in Watson's books are forgotten or conveniently slurred over, but the philosophy, programme and strategy of Behaviourism have remained essentially the same. The next few pages are intended to demonstrate this – regardless of what the members of the Society for the Prevention of Cruelty to Dead Horses say.

Watson's book *Behaviourism*, in which he rejected the concepts of consciousness and mind, was published in 1913. Half a century later, Professor Skinner of Harvard University, who is probably the most influential contemporary academic psychologist, proclaims the same views in even more extreme form. In his standard work *Science and Human Behaviour* the hopeful student of psychology is firmly told from the very outset that 'mind' and 'ideas' are non-existent entities, 'invented for the sole purpose of providing spurious explanations ... Since mental or psychic events are asserted to lack the dimensions of physical science, we have an additional reason for rejecting them'.[5] By the same logic, the physicist may, of course, reject the existence of radio waves, because they are propagated through a so-called 'field' which lacks the properties of ordinary physical media. In fact, few of the theories and concepts of modern physics would survive an ideological purge on Behaviourist principles – for the simple reason that the scientific outlook of Behaviourism is modelled on the mechanistic physics of the nineteenth century.

The 'cynical onlooker' might now ask: if mental events are to be excluded from the study of psychology – what is there left for the psychologist to study? The short answer is: rats. For the last fifty years the main preoccupation of the Behaviourist school has been the study of certain measurable aspects of the behaviour of rats, and the bulk of Behaviourist literature is devoted to that study. This development, odd as it seems, was in fact an unavoidable consequence of the Behaviourist's definition of scientific method (the 'fourth pillar' mentioned above). According to his self-imposed limitations, the Behaviourist is only permitted to study objective, measurable aspects of behaviour. However, there are few relevant aspects of human behaviour which lend themselves to quantitative measurement under laboratory conditions, and which the experimenter can investigate without relying on introspective statements about private events experienced by the subject. Thus, if he wanted to remain faithful to his principles, the Behaviourist had to choose as objects of his study animals in preference to humans, and among animals rats and pigeons in preference to monkeys or chimpanzees, because the behaviour of primates is still too complex.

Rats and pigeons, on the other hand, can, under appropriately-designed experimental conditions, be made to behave as if they were indeed conditioned reflex automata, or almost so. There is hardly a self-respecting psychological faculty in the Western world without some white albino rats disporting themselves in so-called Skinner boxes, invented by that eminent Harvard authority. The box is equipped with a food tray, an electric bulb, and a bar which can be pushed down like the lever of a slot machine, whereupon a food pellet drops into the tray. When a rat is placed into the box, it will sooner or later press the lever down with its paw, and will be automatically rewarded by a pellet; and it will soon learn that to get food it must press the bar. This experimental procedure is called 'operant conditioning' because the rat 'operates' on the environment (as distinct from Pavlovian 'classical' or 'respondant' conditioning, where it does not). Pressing the bar is called 'emitting an operant response'; the food pellet is called a 'reinforcing stimulus' or 'reinforcer'; withholding the food pellet is a 'negative reinforcer'; the alternation of the two procedures is 'intermittent reinforcement'. The rat's 'rate of response' – ie, the number of times it presses the bar in a given period of time – is automatically recorded, plotted on charts, and regarded as a measure of 'operant strength'.* The purpose of the box is to enable the Behaviourist to realize his cherished ambition: the measurement of behaviour by quantitative methods, and the control of behaviour by the manipulation of stimuli.

The Skinner box did produce some technically interesting results. The most interesting was that 'intermittent reinforcement' – when pressing the bar was only sometimes rewarded by a pellet – could be as effective, and even more effective than when it was always rewarded; the rat, which had been trained not to expect a reward after every try, is less discouraged, and goes on trying much longer after the supply of pellets has been stopped, than the rat which had previously been rewarded after every try. (The words 'expect' and 'discouraged' which I have used would, of course, be disallowed by the Behaviourist because they imply mental events.) This proudest achievement of some thirty years of bar-pressing experiments is a measure of their relevance as a contribution to psychology. As one eminent critic, Harlow, wrote already in 1953: 'a strong case can be made for the proposition that the importance of the psychological problems studied during the last fifteen years has decreased as a negatively accelerated function approaching an asymptote of complete indifference'.[6] Looking back at the further fifteen years that have passed since this was written, one would come much to the same conclusion. The attempt to reduce the complex activities of man to the hypothetical 'atoms of behaviour' found in lower mammals produced next to nothing that is relevant – just as the chemical analysis of bricks and mortar will tell you next to nothing about the architecture of a building. Yet throughout the dark ages of psychology most of the work done in the laboratories

* Operant strength is usually measured, for technical reasons, by the 'rate of extinction' – how long the rat will persist in pressing the lever after the supply of pellets has been stopped.

consisted of analysing bricks and mortar in the hope that by patient effort somehow one day it would tell you what a cathedral looked like.

The De-Humanization of Man

However, if the futility of these experiments would be the only reason for criticism, then one would indeed be flogging indignantly a dead horse. But, incredible as it may seem, the Skinnerians claim that the bar-pressing experiments with rats, and the training of pigeons (about which more presently), provide *all the necessary elements to describe, predict and control human behaviour* – including language ('verbal behaviour'), science and art. Skinner's two best-known books are called *The Behaviour of Organisms* and *Science and Human Behaviour*. Nothing in their resounding titles indicates that the data in them are almost exclusively derived from conditioning experiments on rats and pigeons – and then converted by crude analogies into confident assertions about the political, religious and ethical problems of man. The motivational drive of the rat is measured by the number of hours it has been deprived of food before being put into the box; human behaviour, according to Skinner, can be described in the same terms:

> Behaviour which has been strengthened by a conditioned reinforcer varies with the deprivation appropriate to the primary reinforcer. The behaviour of going to a restaurant is composed of a sequence of responses, early members of which (for example, going along a certain street) are reinforced by the appearance of discriminative stimuli which control later responses (the appearance of the restaurant, which we then enter). The whole sequence is ultimately reinforced by food, and the probability varies with food deprivation. We increase the chances that someone will go to a restaurant, or even walk along a particular street, by making him hungry.[7]

Next in importance to Skinner of Harvard in shaping academic psychology was the late Clark Hull of Yale; his pupils still occupy key positions in the academic world. His system differed on technical points from Skinner's, but his basic outlook was the same: he, too, expressly postulated that the differences between the processes of learning in man and rat are merely of a quantitative, not of a qualitative, order:

> The natural-science theory of behaviour being developed by the present author and his associates assumes that all behaviour of the individuals of a given species and that of all species of mammals, including man, occurs according to the same set of primary laws.[8]

The unique attributes of man, verbal communication and written records, science, art, and so forth, are considered to differ only in degree, not in kind, from the learning achievements of the lower animals – once more epitomized, for Hull as for Skinner, in the bar-pressing activities of the rat. Pavlov counted the number of drops which his dogs salivated through their artificial fistulae, and distilled them into a philosophy of man; Professors Skinner, Hull and their followers took an equally heroic short cut from the rat in the box to the human condition.

Skinner's most impressive experiment in the 'prediction and control of behaviour' is to train pigeons, by operant conditioning, to strut about with their heads held unnaturally high. He turns on a light; then food appears in a place where the pigeon can only reach it by stretching its neck; after a while, each time the light is turned on, the pigeon stretches its neck, expecting the food. How does one extrapolate from this to the prediction and control of human behaviour? Skinner explains (his italics):

> We describe the contingency by saying that a *stimulus* (the light) is the occasion upon which a *response* (stretching the neck) is followed by *reinforcement* (with food). We must specify all three terms. The effect upon the pigeon is that eventually the response is more likely to occur when the light is on. The process through which this comes about is called *discrimination*. Its importance in a theoretical analysis, as well as in the practical control of behaviour, is obvious ... For example, in an orchard in which red apples are

sweet and all others sour, the behaviour of picking and eating comes to be controlled by the redness of the stimulus ... The social environment contains vast numbers of such contingencies. A smile is an occasion upon which social approach will meet with approval. A frown is an occasion upon which the same approach will not meet with approval. Insofar as this is generally true, approach comes to depend to some extent upon the facial expression of the person approached. We use this fact when by smiling or frowning we control to some extent the behaviour of those approaching us ... The verbal stimulus 'Come to dinner' is an occasion upon which going to a table and sitting down is usually reinforced by food. The stimulus comes to be effective in increasing the probability of that behaviour and is produced by the speaker because it does so.[9]

How to Manipulate Tautologies

Skinner did not intend to write a parody.* He means it seriously. Less obvious, however, than the monumental triviality of its pronouncements is the fact that the pedantic jargon of Behaviourism is based on ill-defined verbal concepts which willingly lend themselves to circular arguments and tautological statements. A 'response', the layman would imagine, is an answer to a stimulus; but 'operant responses' are 'emitted' to *produce* a stimulus which occurs *after* the response; the response 'acts upon the environment in such a way that a reinforcing stimulus is produced'.[10] In other words, the response responds to a stimulus which is still in the future – which, if taken literally, is nonsensical. An 'operant response' is not in fact a response, but an act initiated by the animal; but, as organisms are supposed to be controlled by the environment, the passive term 'response' is mandatory in the whole literature. Behaviourism is based on *S-R theory* (stimulus-

---

* In a memorable essay, 'Pavlov and his Bad Dog' (*Encounter*, London, Sept 1964), attacking the English brand of Behaviourism, Kathleen Nott pointed out three main characteristics of this kind of jargon: '(1) *Grandiose-inflationary* or "*Bullfrog*" (B.f.); (2) *Disguise by obviousness* or "*Poe*" (E.A.P.) and (3) *Pejorative reference to unacceptable concepts or other psychological theories*, or *Giving a Name a Bad Dog* (B.D.).'

response theory) as first defined by Watson: 'The rule or measuring rod, which the Behaviourist puts in front of him always is: can I describe this bit of behaviour I see in terms of "stimulus and response"?'[11] These S-R bits are regarded as the 'elements' or 'atoms' of the chain of behaviour; if the R for 'response' were eliminated from the terminology, the chain would fall to pieces, and the whole theory collapse.

Another omnipresent term in contemporary psychological jargon – which has even found its way into political jargon – is the ugly word 'reinforcement'. What exactly does it mean? According to Skinner's 'law of conditioning': 'if the occurrence of an operant is followed by presentation of a *reinforcing stimulus,* the strength [of that operant] is increased'.[12] And how is a 'reinforcing stimulus' defined? 'A reinforcing stimulus is defined as such by its power to produce the resulting change [in strength].'[13] Translated into human language, we arrive at the tautology: the probability of repeating an action is increased by reinforcement, where 'reinforcement' means something which increases that probability.* As one of Skinner's critics wrote: 'Examining the instances of what Skinner calls *reinforcement,* we find that not even the requirement that a reinforcer be an identifiable stimulus is taken seriously' (Chomsky).[15] According to Skinner, 'a man talks to himself ... because of the reinforcement he receives';[16] thinking is 'behaving which automatically affects the behaviour and is reinforcing because it does so';[17] 'just as the musician plays or composes what he is reinforced by hearing, or as the artist paints what reinforces him visually, so the speaker engaged in verbal fantasy says what he is reinforced by hearing or writes what he is reinforced by reading';[18] and the creative artist is 'controlled entirely by the contingencies of reinforcement'.[18a] Fortunately, in Skinnerian parlance, the word 'control' is as

---

* The 'strength' of an operant is measured by the probability of it being repeated in similar conditions.[14] The tautological nature of the so-called law of conditioning has been repeatedly pointed out before.

empty as 'reinforcement'. Originally, in talking of pigeons and rats, 'prediction and control of behaviour' had a concrete meaning: by giving and withholding rewards, the animal's behaviour could be drastically shaped by the experimenter. But in the case of the writer who is controlled by the 'contingencies of reinforcement', the word 'control' refers to the fact that his 'verbal behaviour may reach over centuries or to thousands of listeners or readers at the same time. The writer may not be reinforced often or immediately, but his net reinforcement may be great'[19] (which accounts for the great 'strength' of his behaviour, whatever that means). Thus the environment which 'controls entirely' the writer's verbal behaviour includes stimuli centuries ahead; and determines whether he should hammer out on his typewriter a tragedy or a limerick.

This brings us to the Behaviourist's attitude to human creativity. How can scientific discovery and artistic originality be explained or described without reference to mind and imagination? The following two quotations will indicate the answer. The first is again from Watson's *Behaviourism*, published in 1925; the second from Skinner's *Science and Human Behaviour*, published thirty years later; thus they enable us to judge whether there is any substantial difference between the paleo-Behaviourist and neo-Behaviourist attitudes. (Some readers will perhaps notice that I have already used the same passage from Watson in *The Act of Creation*, for it happens to be the *only* passage in his fundamental book in which creative activities are discussed):

> One natural question often raised is, how do we ever get new verbal creations such as a poem or a brilliant essay? The answer is that we get them by manipulating words, shifting them about until a new pattern is hit upon . . . How do you suppose Patou builds a new gown? Has he any 'picture in his mind' of what the gown is to look like when it is finished? He has not . . . He calls his model in,

picks up a new piece of silk, throws it around her, he pulls it in here, he pulls it out there . . . He manipulates the material until it takes on the semblance of a dress . . . Not until the new creation aroused admiration and commendation, both his own and others, would manipulation be complete – the equivalent of the rat's finding food . . . The painter plies his trade in the same way, nor can the poet boast of any other method.[19a]

In the article on 'Behaviourism' in the 1955 edition of the *Encyclopaedia Britannica* you will find five columns of eulogy for Watson. His books, we are told, 'demonstrate the possibility of writing an adequate, comprehensive account of human and animal behaviour without the use of the philosophical concept of mind or consciousness'. One wonders whether the author of the *Encyclopaedia Britannica* article (Professor Hunter of Brown College) would really regard the above quotation as 'an adequate and comprehensive account' of how *Hamlet* or the Sistine Chapel came into being.

Thirty years after Watson, Skinner summed up the Behaviourist's views on how original discoveries are made in *Science and Human Behaviour*: 'The result of solving a problem is the appearance of a solution in the form of a response . . . The relation between the preliminary behaviour and the appearance of the solution is simply the relation between the manipulation of variables and the emission of a response . . . The appearance of the response in the individual's behaviour is no more surprising than the appearance of any response in the behaviour of any organism. The question of originality can be disposed of . . .'[20]

Needless to say, the 'organisms' referred to are once more his rats and pigeons. Compared with Watson's, the language of the Skinnerians has become more dehydrated and esoteric. Watson talks of manipulating words until a new pattern is 'hit upon', Skinner of manipulating 'variables' until 'a response is emitted'. Both are engaged in question-begging on a heroic scale, apparently driven by an almost fanatical urge to deny, at all costs, the existence of properties which account for the humanity of man and the rattiness of the rat.

The Philosophy of Ratomorphism

Behaviourism started as a kind of puritan revolt against the excessive use of introspectionist methods in some older schools of psychology which held – in James' definition – that the business of the psychologist was 'the description and explanation of states of consciousness'. Consciousness, Watson objected, is 'neither a definable nor a usable concept, it is merely another word for the "soul" of more ancient times ... No one has ever touched a soul or seen one in a test-tube. Consciousness is just as unprovable, as unapproachable as the old concept of the soul ... The Behaviourists reached the conclusion that they could no longer be content to work with intangibles and unapproachables. They decided either to give up psychology or else to make it a natural science ...'[21]

This 'clean and fresh programme', as Watson himself called it, was based on the naïve idea that psychology could be studied with the methods and concepts of classical physics. Watson and his successors were quite explicit about this; their efforts to carry out their programme became a truly procrustean operation. But while that legendary malefactor merely stretched, or cut off, the legs of his victim to make him fit his bed, Behaviourism first cut off his head, then chopped him up into 'bits of behaviour in terms of stimulus and response'. The theory is based on the atomistic concepts of the last century, which have been abandoned in all other branches of contemporary science. Its basic assumptions – that all activities of man, including language and thought, can be analysed into elementary S-R units – were originally founded on the physiological concept of the reflex arc. The new-born organism came into the world equipped with a number of simple, 'unconditioned' reflexes, and what it learnt and did in its lifetime was acquired by Pavlovian conditioning. But this simplicist schema soon went out of fashion among physiologists. The greatest among them in his time, Sir Charles Sherrington, wrote already in 1906: 'The simple reflex is probably a purely abstract conception, because all parts of the nervous system are connected together and no part of it is probably ever capable of reaction without affecting and being affected by various other parts ... The simple reflex is a convenient, if not a probable, fiction.'[22]

More recently, a leading neurologist, Judson Herrick, summed up the situation:

> During the past half-century an ambitious programme of reflexology was elaborated, notably by Pavlov and the American school of Behaviourism. The avowed objective was to reduce all animal and human behaviour to systems of interlocking reflexes of various grades of complexity. The conditioning of these reflexes by personal experience was invoked as the mechanism of learning. The simple reflex was regarded as the unit of behaviour, and all other kinds of behaviour were conceived as brought about by the linkage of these units in successively more complicated patterns.
>
> The simplicity of this scheme is attractive but illusory. In the first place, the simple reflex is a pure abstraction. There is no such thing in any living body. A more serious defect is that all the information we have about the embryology and phylogenetic development of behaviour shows clearly that local reflexes are not the primary units of behaviour. They are secondary acquisitions.[23]

With the decline of the reflex, the physiological foundations on which S-R psychology was built, had ceased to exist. But that did not unduly worry the Behaviourists. They shifted their terminology from conditioned *reflexes* to conditioned *responses*, and kept manipulating their ambiguous terms, in the manner we have seen, until responses became controlled by stimuli still in the womb of the future, reinforcement turned into a kind of phlogiston, and the atoms of behaviour evaporated in the psychologist's hands even as the physicist's hard little lumps of matter had evaporated long ago.

Historically, Behaviourism started as a reaction against the excesses of introspective techniques, as practised particularly by German psychologists of the so-called Würzburg school. At first its intention was merely to exclude consciousness, images and other non-public phenomena as *objects of study* from the field of psychology; but later on this came to imply that the excluded phenomena *did not exist*. A programme for a methodology, which had its arguable points, became transformed into a philosophy which had no point at all. One might as well tell a team of land surveyors that for the purpose of mapping a limited area they could treat the earth as if it were flat – and then subtly instil the dogma that the whole earth *is* flat.

Behaviourism is indeed a kind of flat-earth view of the mind. Or, to change the metaphor: it has replaced the anthropomorphic fallacy – ascribing to animals human faculties and sentiments – with the opposite fallacy: denying man faculties not found in lower animals; it has substituted for the erstwhile anthropomorphic view of the rat, a ratomorphic view of man. It has even re-named psychology, because it was derived from the Greek word for 'mind', and called it the 'science of behaviour'. It was a demonstrative act of semantic self-castration, in keeping with Skinner's references to education as 'behavioural engineering'. Its declared aim, 'to predict and to control human activity as physical scientists control and manipulate other natural phenomena',[24] sounds as nasty as it is naïve. Werner Heisenberg, one of the greatest living physical scientists, has laconically declared: 'Nature is unpredictable'; it seems rather absurd to deny the living organism even that degree of unpredictability which quantum physics accords to inanimate nature.

Behaviourism has dominated the stage throughout the dark ages of psychology, and is still, in the 1960s, dominant in our universities; but it never had the stage all to itself. In the first place there have always been 'voices in the wilderness', mostly belonging to an older generation which had come to maturity before the Great Purge. In the second place, there was Gestalt psychology, which at one time looked like a serious rival to Behaviourism. But the great expectations which the Gestalt school aroused were only partly fulfilled, and its limitations soon became apparent. The Behaviourists managed to incorporate some of their opponents' experimental results into their own theories, and continued to hold the stage. The interested reader can find this controversy outlined in *The Act of Creation*, and there is no need to go into it here.* But the net result was a kind of abortive Renaissance followed by a Counter-Reformation. Lastly, to round off the picture, there is a younger generation of neurophysiologists and communication theorists who regard orthodox S-R psychology as senile, but are often forced to pay lip-service to it, if they want to get on in their academic careers and get their papers published in the right sort of technical journal – and who become in varying degrees infected in the process by the doctrines of flat-earth psychology.

It is impossible to arrive at a diagnosis of man's predicament – and by implication at a therapy – by starting from a psychology which denies the existence of mind, and lives on specious analogies derived from the bar-pressing activities of rats. The record of fifty years of ratomorphic psychology is comparable in its sterile pedantry to that of scholasticism in its period of decline, when it had fallen to counting angels on pin-heads – although this sounds a more attractive pastime than counting the number of bar-pressings in the box.

* Particularly in Book Two, Chapter Twelve, 'The Pitfalls of Learning Theory', and Chapter Thirteen, 'The Pitfalls of Gestalt'.

THE CHAIN OF WORDS
AND THE TREE OF LANGUAGE

*On an occasion of this kind it becomes more than a moral duty to speak
one's mind. It becomes a pleasure.*

OSCAR WILDE

THE emergence of symbolic language, first spoken, then
written, represents the sharpest break between animal and
man. Many social animals have some system of communication by signs and signals, but language is a species-specific,
exclusive property of man. Even 'mongolian' idiots, incapable
of looking after themselves in the most primitive ways, are
capable of acquiring the rudiments of symbolic speech – but
not dolphins and chimpanzees, highly intelligent as they are
in other respects. Nor rats and pigeons.

Language, then, one would expect, is a phenomenon whose
study more than any other would show up the absurdity of
the ratomorphic approach. It not only does that; it also provides the best opportunity for introducing, by way of contrast,
some of the basic concepts of the new synthesis in the making.
This contrast between the orthodox and the new approach can
be summed up by two key words: the chain versus the tree.

The Chain

The long extract which follows is representative of the orthodox Behaviourist approach to language. It is taken from a
textbook for college students to which various professors at

distinguished American universities have contributed.[1] The author of the extract is himself chairman of a psychology department. It was published in 1961; the dialogue featured in the extract is adapted from an earlier textbook. I mention these details to show that this text, fed to thousands of students, is in the most respectable academic tradition. It is headed 'Complex Activities' and it is the *only* passage devoted to the glories of human language in this entire textbook:*

We have said that learning either may be of the respondant [classical Pavlovian] or of the operant [Skinner, Hull] conditioning type . . . The experimental data that we have presented in connection with our conditioning studies have, however, been limited to rather simple responses such as salivation [in dogs] and bar-pressing [by rats]. In our everyday life we seldom spend much time in thinking about such isolated responses, usually thinking of more gross activities, such as learning a poem, carrying on a conversation, solving a mechanical puzzle, learning our way around a new city, to name only a few. While the psychologist could study these more complicated activities, as is done to some extent, the general approach of psychology is to bring simpler responses into the laboratory for study. Once the psychologist discovers the principles of learning for simpler phenomena under the more ideal conditions of the laboratory, it is likely that he can apply these principles to the more complex activities as they occur in everyday life. The more complex phenomena are, after all, nothing but a series of simpler responses [sic.]. Speaking to a friend is a good example of this. Suppose we have a conversation such as the following:

He: 'What time is it?'
She: 'Twelve o'clock.'
He: 'Thank you.'
She: 'Don't mention it.'
He: 'What about lunch?'
She: 'Fine.'

Now this conversation can be analysed into separate S-R units. 'He' makes the *first response*, which is emitted probably to the stimulus of the sight of 'She'. When 'He' emits the operant, 'What time is it?', the muscular activity, of course, produces a sound, which also serves as a stimulus for 'She'. On the receipt of this stimulus, she emits an operant herself: 'Twelve o'clock', which in

* An extract from this text also appeared in *The Act of Creation*, p. 603.

turn produces a stimulus to 'He'. And so on. The entire conversation may thus be diagrammed as:

$$S_I \longrightarrow R_A \leadsto S_A \quad R_C \leadsto S_C \quad R_E \leadsto S_E$$
$$R_B \leadsto S_B \quad R_D \leadsto S_D \quad R_F$$

In such complex activity, then, we can see that what we really have is a series of S-R connections. The phenomenon of connecting a series of such S-R units is known as *chaining*, a process that should be apparent in any complex activity. We might note that there are a number of sources of reinforcement throughout the chaining process, in this example the most obvious being the reinforcement of 'She' by receiving an invitation for lunch and of 'He' by having the invitation accepted. In addition, as Keller and Schoenfeld point out, there are such sources of reinforcement as the hearer 'encouraging' the speaker to continue, the use that the conversationalists make of the information received (he finds out what time it is), etc.

This example of the analysis of a complex activity is but one of numerous activities that we could discuss. You should continue to think of others yourself and try to diagram the chaining process for them. For instance, what would a diagram look like for a football end running downfield and catching a pass, for a pianist playing a piano, or for a girl knitting a sweater?[2]

And this is the end of what the student learns about 'complex human activities'. The rest of this chapter, entitled 'Learning, Retention and Motivation', is concerned, in the author's own words, with 'salivation and bar-pressing'.

Reading this dialogue one has the vision of two cute automatic slot-machines facing each other on the college campus, feeding each other with stimulus coins and popping out prepackaged verbal responses. Yet this inane exchange between He and She is not a random improvisation by the author – he adapted it reverently from another textbook, Keller and Schoenfeld's *Principles of Psychology*, and other writers have done the same, as if it were a classic example of human conversation.

The diagram represents the application to language of the

Behaviourist credo: that all human activities can be reduced to a linear chain of S-R units. At a first glance, the diagram might impress one as a simplified but plausible schematization – until one takes a closer look at it. It is based on Skinner's book *Verbal Behaviour* – the first large-scale attempt to tackle human language in terms of Behaviourist theory. According to Skinner, speech sounds are emitted as any other 'bits of behaviour'; and the process of conditioning which determines verbal behaviour (including thinking) is essentially the same as the conditioning of rats and pigeons; the methods of these experiments, Skinner claims, 'can be extended to human behaviour without serious modification'.[3] Thus when our author speaks of the psychologist's preference for studying 'simpler responses', he means the responses of salivation and bar-pressing, as the context shows. But what on earth have the S-R symbols in the diagram in common with bar-pressing? What justification is there to call 'Don't mention it – What about lunch?' a 'conditioned response unit'? A conditioned response is a response controlled by the stimulus; and a 'unit' in experimental science must have definable properties. Are we to believe that He was conditioned to answer each 'Don't mention it' with a lunch invitation? And in what conceivable sense are we to call 'Don't mention it – What about lunch?' a *unit* of behaviour?

I seem to be labouring points which are obvious to the non-psychologist, but the purpose will soon become apparent. Obviously, then, the phrase 'Don't mention it' might also produce the response 'Well, goodbye' or 'You have got a ladder in your stocking' or a number of alternative 'bits of verbal behaviour', according to whether She uttered the phrase lingeringly with a sexy smile, or as a brisk brush-off, or hovering between the two; and further depending on whether or not He finds her attractive, whether He is free for lunch, and if so whether He has the cash to pay for it. The simple S-R unit is neither simple nor a unit. It is difficult for the layman to believe that the textbook author is not aware of the complex, multi-levelled mental processes which go on in the two people's heads during and in between the emission of sounds. Surely these 'private processes' must be implied, taken for granted, in what the author is saying? Perhaps they are; but by denying that private events have a place in psychology, he has denied himself the possibility, and even the vocabulary to discuss them. The Behaviourist's way to get around this difficulty is to lump all these unmentionable private processes together in the nondescript term 'intervening variables' (or 'hypothetical mechanisms') which 'mediate between stimulus and response'.* These terms are then used as a kind of garbage bin for the disposal of all embarrassing questions about the intentions, desires, thoughts and dreams of the organisms called He and She. An occasional reference to 'intervening variables' serves as a face-saving device, since everything that goes on in a person's mind is covered by it, and need not be discussed. Yet in the absence of any discussion of the mental events behind the dialogue, the comments of our textbook author are reduced to utter triviality, and the neat diagram is empty of meaning. A diagram is meant to give a graphic representation of essential aspects of a process; in this case both text and diagram pretend to do so, but in fact give no indication of what is really happening. The same dialogue could have taken place between casual acquaintances, or shy lovers, or it could record the picking up of a prostitute. The pseudo-scientific balderdash: 'When He emits the operant, "What time is it?", the muscular activity produces a sound which also serves as a stimulus,' and so on, is totally irrelevant to the episode it pretends to describe and explain. And this applies generally to any attempt to describe the language of man in terms of S-R theory.

* See Appendix Two.

The Tree

The strategic advantage gained from labouring the obvious absurdity of a theory is that it makes the proposed alternative appear as almost self-evident. The alternative, set out in the pages that follow, proposes to replace the concept of the linear S-R chain by the concept of multi-levelled, hierarchically ordered systems, which can be conveniently represented in the form of an inverted tree, branching downward:

FIGURE I

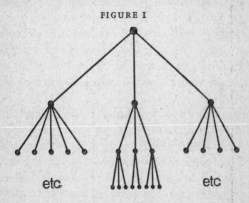

We find such tree diagrams of hierarchic organization applied to the most varied fields: genealogical tables; the classification of animals and plants; the evolutionist's 'tree of life'; charts indicating the branching structures of government departments or industrial enterprises; physiological charts of the nervous system, and of the circulation of the blood. The word 'hierarchy' is of ecclesiastical origin and is often wrongly used to refer merely to order of rank – the rungs on a ladder, so to speak. I shall use it to refer not to a ladder but to the tree-like structure of a system, branching into sub-systems, and so on, as indicated in the diagram. The concept of hierarchic order plays a central part in this book; and the most convenient way to introduce it is by means of the hierarchic organization of language.

The young science of psycholinguistics has shown that the analysis of speech presents problems of which the speaker is blissfully unaware. One of the main problems arises from the deceptively simple fact that we write from left to right, producing a single string of letters, and that we speak by uttering one sound after the other, also in a single string, along the axis of time. This is what lends the Behaviourist's concept of a linear chain its superficial plausibility. The eye takes in a whole three-dimensional picture, embracing many shapes and colours simultaneously; but the ear only receives linear pulses one at a time, serially, and this fact may lead one to the fallacious conclusion that we also *respond* to each speech-sound, bit by bit, one at a time. This is the bait which the S-R theorist has swallowed, and on which he has been dangling ever since.

The elementary speech sounds are called phonemes; they correspond roughly to the written alphabet; in English there are forty-five of them. If listening to speech consisted in the chaining of separately perceived phonemes by the listener, he would literally not understand a word of what is said to him. Let me explain this paradox. If we were to translate the process of listening to speech from acoustical into optical terms, this would mean flashing on to a screen before the subject's eye printed letters one by one, at the rate of twenty letters per second. The result would be something like a nervous breakdown. The ear of the listener has to take in about twenty phonemes per second. If he tried to analyse each phoneme as a separate 'bit' – or atom, or segment of language – all he would perceive would be a steady buzz. I owe this illustration to Alvin Liberman of the Haskins Laboratories – a pioneer in the field of speech-perception, and a participant in the Think-Tank seminar mentioned in the preface. He also commented wryly that if we go on labouring the point with the methods of the S-R theorist, 'we risk arriving at the conviction that human speech is an impossibility'.

The solution of the paradox becomes apparent when we revert from spoken to written language. When we read, we do not perceive the shape of one letter at a time (as in the screen-experiment just mentioned), but the patterns of one or several words at a time; the individual letters are perceived integrated into larger units. Similarly, when listening, we do not perceive separate phonemes in a serial order; perception combines them into higher units of approximately syllabic size. The speech sounds unite into patterns as musical sounds unite into melodies. But unlike the three-dimensional patterns perceived by the eye, speech and music form patterns in the single dimension of time – which seems mysterious and baffling. We shall see, however, that the recognition of patterns in time is no more – and no less – baffling than the recognition of patterns in space, because the brain constantly transforms temporal sequences into spatial patterns and vice versa (page 102). If you look at a gramophone record through a magnifying glass, you only see a single, wavy spiral curve, which, however, contains in coded form the infinitely complex patterns produced by an orchestra of fifty instruments performing a symphony. The airwaves which it sets in motion form, like the curve on the groove, a sequence with a single variable function – the variation of pressure on the eardrum. But a single variable in time is sufficient to convey the most complex messages – the Ninth Symphony or the Ancient Mariner – provided there is a human brain to decode it, to retrieve the patterns hidden in the linear sequences of pressure waves. This is done by a series of operations, the nature of which is as yet little understood, but which can be represented as a multi-levelled hierarchy of processes. It has three main sub-divisions: the phonological, syntactic and semantic.

'What Did You Say?'

We may regard as the first step in decoding the spoken message – the first step up the hierarchic tree – the integration by the listener of phonemes into morphemes. Phonemes are just sounds; morphemes are the simplest meaningful units of language (short words, prefixes, suffixes, etc.); they form the next higher level of the hierarchy. Phonemes do not qualify as elementary units of language, first because they come in much too fast to be individually discriminated and recognized, but also for a second important reason: they are ambiguous. One and the same consonant sounds different, depending on the vowel which follows it, and vice versa, different consonants sometimes sound the same in front of the same vowel. Whether you hear 'big' or 'pig', 'map' or 'nap', depends, as the Haskins Laboratory experiments[4] show, largely *on the context*. Thus the S-R chain theory breaks down even on the lowest level of speech, because the phonemic stimuli vary with the context, and can only be identified in the context. But as we move upward to higher levels of the hierarchy we again meet the same phenomenon: the 'response' to a syllable (its interpretation) depends on the word in which it occurs; and individual words occupy the same subordinate position relative to the sentence as phonemes relative to words. Their interpretation depends on the context, and must be referred to the next higher level in the hierarchy. The late K. S. Lashley – a Behaviourist turned renegade – has given an amusing illustration of this:

> Words stand in relation to the sentence as letters do to the word; the words themselves have no intrinsic temporal 'valence'. The word 'right', for example, is noun, adjective, adverb, and verb, and has four spellings and at least ten meanings. In such a sentence as 'the mill-wright on my right thinks it right that some conventional rite should symbolize the right of every man to write as he pleases',

word arrangement is obviously not due to any direct associations of the word 'right' itself with other words, but to meanings which are determined by some broader relations ... Any theory of grammatical form which ascribes it to direct associative linkage of the words of the sentence overlooks the essential structure of speech.[5]

This is of course an extreme example of contrived ambiguity, but it makes its point with a vengeance against the S-R theorist who contends that speech sounds are 'like other bits of behaviour', and that language calls for no principles of explanation other than those employed in the operant conditioning of lower animals.

The ideal situation from the S-R theorist's point of view is a typist – let's call her Miss Resp – taking dictation from her boss, Mr Stims. Here, one would think, we have a perfect example for a linear chain of sound stimuli controlling a string of key-pressing responses (Miss Resp being reinforced by Stims with the prospect of a salary). Since complex behaviour is supposedly the result of the chaining of simple S-R links, we must assume that each sound emitted by Stims will cause Miss Resp to type the corresponding letter (provided he dictates at the same speed at which she types, which is assumed). But we know of course that something quite different happens. Miss Resp waits expectantly, doing nothing, until at least half the sentence is completed, then, like a sprinter at the starter's shot, races ahead until she has caught up with Stims; then waits expectantly with an admiring expression on her face. The phenomenon is known to experimental psychologists as 'lagging behind'; it also occurs in Morse telegraphy and has been studied in great detail.* Miss Resp was lagging behind because she was mentally engaged in climbing the tree of language: first up, from sound level to word level to phrase level, then down again. The downward

* For a more detailed treatment see *The Act of Creation*, Chapter, 'Motor Skills', pp. 544–6.

climb in the case of a skilled typist leads from 'phrase habit' through 'word habit' to 'letter habit'. The letter habits (hitting the correct key) are part of the word habits (a pre-set patterned sequence of movements triggered off as a single unit), which are part of the phrase habit (familiar turns of phrase which activate 'sweeps' of movements as integrated wholes). Although the performance is to a large extent as 'automatic' or 'mechanical' as any Behaviourist could wish for, it is nevertheless impossible to represent it as a linear chain of conditioned responses, because it is a multi-dimensional operation constantly oscillating between various levels, from the phonological to the semantic. No typist can be conditioned to take dictation in a language she does not know. It is this very complex knowledge, and not the chaining of simple S-R connections, which makes Miss Resp's fingers dance on the keyboard to Mr Stim's reinforcing voice. And, oh wonder, she can even type a letter *without* dictation, for instance to her fiancé in Birmingham. In this case her behaviour is presumably controlled by S-R links which, like gravity, are capable of action-at-a-distance.

The Postman and the Dog

So far I have touched on only a few of the difficulties of explaining how we convert pressure variations on the eardrum into ideas. Even more formidable is the problem how we convert ideas into air-pressure waves. Take a simple example: the farmer's little boy of about three, leaning out of the window, sees the dog snapping at the postman, and the postman retaliating with a vicious kick. All this happens in a flash, so fast that his vocal chords have not even had the time to get innervated; yet he knows quite clearly what happened and feels the urgent need to communicate this as yet unverbalized event, image, idea, thought, or what-have-you, to his mum. So he bursts into the kitchen and shouts breath-

lessly: 'The postman kicked the dog.' Now the first remarkable fact about this is that he does *not* say, 'The dog kicked
the postman', though he *might* say, 'Doggy *was* kicked *by*
the postman'; and again, he will *not* say, 'Was the dog kicked
by the postman?', and least of all, 'Dog the by was the kicked
postman'.

This was an example of a very simple sentence consisting of
four words only ('the' being used twice). Yet a change of the
order of two words gave a totally different meaning; a more
radical reshuffling, with two new words added, left the
meaning unaltered; and most of the ninety-five possible
permutations of the original words give no meaning at all.
The problem is how a child ever learns the several thousand
abstract rules and corollaries necessary to generate and com-
prehend meaningful sentences – rules which his parents would
be unable to name and define; which you and I are equally
unable to define; and which nevertheless unfalteringly guide
our speech. The few rules of grammar which the child learns
at school – long *after* it has learned to speak correctly – and
which it promptly forgets, are descriptive statements about
language, not recipes to generate language. These recipes, or
formulae, the child somehow discovers by intuitive processes
– probably not unlike the unconscious inferences which go
into scientific discovery – by the time it has reached the age
of four. By that time 'he will have mastered very nearly the
entire complex and abstract structure of the English language.
In slightly more than two years, therefore [starting at about
the age of two] children acquire full knowledge of the grammatical system of their native tongue. This stunning intellectual achievement is routinely performed by every pre-school
child (McNeill[6]'. As another renegade Behaviourist, Professor
James Jenkins, remarked at our Stanford seminar: 'The fact
that we can freely produce sentences we had never heard
before is amazing. The fact that we can understand them when
produced is nothing short of miraculous ... A child never

has a look at the machinery that produces English sentences. He *could* never have a look at that machinery. Nor is he being told about it since most speakers are completely unaware of it.'

The facts must indeed appear miraculous so long as we persist in confusing the string of words which is speech, with the silent machinery which generates speech. The difficulty is that the machinery is invisible, its working mostly unconscious, beyond the reach of inspection *and* introspection. But at least psycholinguistics has shown that the only conceivable model to represent the generation of a sentence does not work 'from left to right', but hierarchically, branching from the top downward.

The diagram below is a slightly modified version of Noam Chomsky's so-called 'phrase-structure generating grammar'.*

FIGURE 2

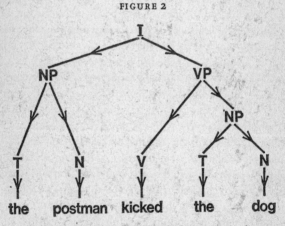

(modified after Chomsky). I: idea. NP: noun phrase. VP: verb phrase. T: article. N: noun. V: verb.

* Chomsky did not claim that it shows how a sentence is actually produced, but observational analysis of how small children learn to speak (by Roger Brown,[7] McNeill[8] and others) has confirmed that the model represents the basic principles involved.

This is about the simplest schema for generating a sentence. At the apex of the inverted tree is /I/ – it might be an Idea, a visual Image, the Intention of saying something – which *is not yet verbally articulated*. Let us call this the /I/ stage.* Then the two main branches of the tree shoot out: the doer and his doing, which at the /I/ stage were still experienced as an indivisible unit, are split up into different speech categories: noun-phrase and verb-phrase.† This separation must be a tremendous feat of abstraction for the child – how can you separate the cat from the grin, or the kick from the postman? – yet it is a universal property of all known languages; and it is precisely with this feat of 'abstract thinking' that the child starts its adventures in language at a very early age – in languages as different as Japanese and English.[9]

The verb-phrase in its turn splits immediately into the doing and its object. Lastly, the noun, and the article which previously was somehow implied in the noun, are spelt out separately. Deciding at which point of the rapid, predominantly unconscious working of the machinery the actual words pop up and fall into their places on the moving conveyor belt of speech – along the bottom line of the diagram – is a delicate problem for the introspectionist. We all are familiar with the frustrating experience – shared by semi-illiterates and professional writers alike – of knowing what we want to say, but not knowing how to express it, searching for the right words that will exactly fit the empty spaces on the conveyor belt. The opposite phenomenon occurs when the message to be conveyed is very simple and can be put into a ready-made turn of phrase like 'How do you do?' or 'Don't mention it'. The living tree of language is weighed down heavily by these clichés, which hang from its branches like

* Chomsky calls the apex S, standing for the whole sentence, which makes the model appear as a sentence-analysing, rather than a sentence-generating, model.

† The NP-VP division is more expressive and easier to handle than the related categories of subject and predicate.

clusters of bananas that can be picked a whole bunch at a time. They are the Behaviourist's delight. In a famous speech, from which I have just quoted, Lashley said: 'A Behaviourist colleague once remarked to me that he had reached a stage where he could rise before an audience, turn his mouth loose, and go to sleep. He believed in the chain theory of language.' This, Lashley concluded ironically, 'clearly demonstrates the superiority of Behaviourist over introspective psychology'.

But classical introspectionism did not fare much better. Lashley went on to quote Titchener (the grand old man of introspective psychology at the turn of the century) who, describing the role of imagery (which might be visual or verbal), had written: 'When there is any difficulty in exposition, a point to be argued pro and con, I hear my own words just ahead of me.'[10] This may be a boon to the timid lecturer, but from the theoretical point of view it is not much help – because the question how words arise in consciousness is merely pushed one step back, and thus becomes the question how word-images arise in consciousness.

Both answers – the Behaviourist's and the introspectionist's – avoid the basic issue of how thought is parcelled out into language, how the shapeless rocks of ideas are cunningly split into crystalline fragments of distinctive form, and put on the moving belt to be carried from left to right along the single dimension of time. The reverse operation is performed by the listener, who takes the string as his baseline to reconstruct the tree, converting sounds into patterns, words into phrases, and so on. When one listens to a speaker, the string of syllables itself hardly ever reaches consciousness; the words of the previous sentence, too, are rapidly effaced and only their meaning remains; the actual sentences suffer the same fate, and by the next day the twigs and branches of the tree have wilted away so that only the trunk survives – a shadowy generalized schema. We can represent both processes diagrammatically, indicating how 'imagination bodies forth the forms of things unknown', and how the pen 'turns them to shapes, and gives to airy nothings a local habitation and a name'; and we can also go through the operation in reverse gear to show how the traces left by the pen lose their shape and revert to airy nothings. But while these diagrams yield reliable formulae and rules, they provide only a superficial kind of understanding of how a child attains mastery of language, and how adults convert thoughts into airwaves, and back. A complete understanding of these phenomena will probably always elude our grasp because the operations which generate language include processes which cannot be expressed by language: the attempt to analyse speech leaves us speechless. To quote Wittgenstein: 'the thing which expresses *itself* in language, *we* cannot represent by language'.* This paradox is one of the many aspects of the mind-body problem, to which we shall return; for the moment let me merely point out that, in contrast to the rigid concept of the chain which drags the organism along its predetermined path, the dynamic concept of the growing tree implies an *open-ended hierarchy*. The meaning of 'openness' in this context will become evident as we go along.

'What do you mean by that?'

Let me return for a moment to the ambiguity of language, which will provide a first example of 'open-endedness'.

There are different kinds of ambiguities on different levels of the hierarchy. On the lowest level, as we saw, is the purely acoustic ambiguity of phonemes, revealed by their sound-spectrograms (sounds transformed into visible patterns as on the sound-track of a film). They show that the transitions between /bay/, /day/ and /gay/ are continuous, like the colours of a rainbow, and that whether we hear /day/ or /gay/ depends mainly on the context.

* Was *sich* in der Sprache ausdrückt, können wir nicht durch *sie* ausdrücken.

On the next level we find, in addition to sound ambiguity, the subtler indeterminacies of the meaning of words, of which several types are shown in Lashley's mill-wright example. They can be put to deliberate use in the pun, in the play of words, in assonance and rhyme.

The next level of ambiguity is less common, but has great theoretical importance for linguists, because it shows up nicely the fallacies of the chain concept. 'Young boys and girls are fond of sweets' sounds simple and unambiguous enough. But what happens if this is immediately followed by 'Young boys and girls have no hair on their chests'? If we follow the S-R schema, we shall very likely come to the conclusion that older girls do have hair on their chests. The reason is that in the first sentence we have parcelled out our 'verbal stimuli' thus: ((Young) (boys and girls)). So we tend to do the same thing in the second sentence. Only later do we realize that in the second sentence we must package the stimuli differently: ((Young boys) (and) (girls)). But if the stimuli can only be discriminated after completion of the chain allegedly based on discriminated stimuli, then we are moving in a vicious circle and the S-R model breaks down.*

Translated into neurophysiological terms, the hierarchic approach indicates that speaking and listening are both multi-levelled processes, which involve constant interactions and feedbacks between higher and lower levels of the nervous system (such as receptor and effector organs, the projection areas in the brain, other areas involving memory and association, etc.). Even Behaviourists must realize that man has a more complex brain than the rat, although they do not like to be reminded of it. Only by this multi-levelled activity of the nervous system is the mind enabled to transform linear

* In the terms of symbolic logic we would have to say that the response R to the whole sentence implies the responses r to its elements, which in turn imply the response R to the whole sentence: $R < r < R < r < R \ldots$ etc. – a variant of the paradox of the Cretan liar.

sequences along the single dimension of time into complex patterns of meaning – and back again.

The ambiguities so far discussed relate to the phonological and syntactic domains. They are resolved in a relatively simple way by reference to context on the next higher level of the hierarchy. But this analysis merely ensures intelligibility in the literal sense; it is no more than the first step upward into the vast, multi-layered hierarchies of the semantic domain. A sentence taken in isolation conveys no information as to whether it should be interpreted at face value, or metaphorically, or ironically, ie, meaning the opposite of what it seems to mean; or perhaps containing a veiled message – as the 'Don't mention it' in our dialogue. Such ambiguities of an isolated sentence can once more only be resolved by reference to its context – ie, to the next higher level in the hierarchy. This is exemplified when we ask at the end of a perfectly intelligible sentence: 'What do you mean by that?' Thus sentences stand in the same relation to their context as words to the sentence and phonemes to words. With each step upward in the hierarchy the peak seems to recede. In discourse concerned with relatively trivial matters the hierarchy comprises only a few levels, and the climber comes to rest. But we have seen that even that trivial dialogue between He and She tapers into a whole pyramid of overt messages, implicit meaning, the motivation behind it, and the motivation behind the motivation. Some psychoanalysts use the term 'metalanguage' for these higher levels of communication, where the real meaning of the message can only be got at through a whole series of de-coding operations.

But the series can also lead to an infinite regress. There are many examples of this in the more technical papers of both Freud and Jung setting out the details of individual case histories, where the ultimate meaning of the patient's messages – often conveyed in the language of dreams – recedes more and more into the elusive domain of archetypal symbols or the eternal struggle between Eros and Thanatos. The hierarchy is 'open-ended': its apex recedes with each step towards it, until it dissolves in the clouds of mythology.

Depth-psychology provides one example of an infinite receding series, starting with the ambiguity of the patient's verbal communications and receding towards the ultimate ambiguity of the existential riddle. But each step upward in the hierarchy has a clarifying and cathartic effect, providing limited answers to limited problems, or re-formulating in a more meaningful way those questions which cannot be answered.

Other examples of open hierarchies are provided by various 'universes of discourse' – such as certain branches of mathematics, the theory of knowledge, and all branches of natural science which have to manipulate infinite magnitudes in space or time. When the physicist talks of an 'asymptotic approach' to truth, he implicitly admits that science moves along an infinitely regressing series.

And so does the philosopher concerned with meaning, and the meaning of meaning; with knowledge and belief, and the analysis of the structure of knowledge and belief. It is, as we have seen, already a remarkable achievement that we can produce – and understand – grammatically correct sentences, although we cannot define the rules which enable us to do it. But just as a grammatically correct sentence conveys no information as to whether it should be taken at face value or in some twisted way, so it also conveys no information regarding its veridity. Thus, when the message has been received, the question arises whether it is true or false. Here again, so long as we talk of trivial matters, the question may be settled with relative ease; but in more complex universes of discourse the next question must inevitably be what we mean by true and false; and there we go again, up the spiral staircase into the rarified atmosphere of the epistemologist's domain – only to find that there is no end to the climb. To quote Sir Karl Popper (his italics):

> The old scientific ideal of *epistēmē* – of absolutely certain, demonstrable knowledge – has proved to be an idol. The demand for scientific objectivity makes it inevitable that every scientific statement must remain *tentative for ever*. It may indeed be corroborated, but every corroboration is relative to other statements which, again, are tentative . . .'[11]

Rules, Strategies and Feedbacks

This chapter was not intended as an introduction to linguistics, but as an introduction to the concept of hierarchic organization as exemplified in the structure of language. I have accordingly left out of account several factors which are important to linguistic theory, but not directly relevant to our purpose. The most important of these omissions is the class of *transformation rules* (Chomsky) which must be added to the 'structure-generating rules' to account for the speaker's ability to manipulate the branches of the tree in such a way as to produce a variety of related meanings (for instance, 'the postman kicked the dog', 'the dog was kicked by the postman', 'did the postman kick the dog?', 'was the dog not kicked by the postman?'). It all seems so simple, but consider for a moment how children ever acquire all the rules and corollaries needed to achieve even these simple transformations in a grammatically correct way.

I have mentioned Chomsky's 'transformation rules' merely for the sake of completeness. However, there are other aspects of 'verbal behaviour' directly pertinent to our subject which I have so far not mentioned; it will be simplest to point them out by way of a concrete example.

Let us return for a moment to the two opposite recipes for giving a lecture, quoted by Lashley. Perhaps the politician on a whistle-stop tour can indeed 'turn his mouth loose and go to sleep'. A bar pianist, too, can turn his fingers loose and do the same. But these are routines which have become automatized by practice and are hardly relevant to the question of how to compose a lecture which tries to say something new. Nor can we rely on the opposite recipe, and listen to the inner voice to guide us – like a medium engaged in automatic writing. How, then, does our lecturer manage in fact to produce a paper?

Let us assume that he is a history don who has been invited to give a guest lecture at an American university. Further assuming that he is free to choose the subject he likes, he will choose the subject he likes – let us leave it at that, to avoid another infinite regress into motivation, personality, and the influences which moulded his personality. He chooses as his subject 'Unsolved Problems of the Dead Sea Scrolls', because he is convinced that he alone has the key to the solution. But how is he going to convince his audience? First of all he must decide whether he should present his pet theory in a straightforward, non-polemical manner, or else show why and where all other theories went wrong. This is a matter of *strategy*, of choosing one among several alternative courses of putting the same message across; and at each further step he will be faced with other strategic choices.

He decides on the straightforward, non-polemical method, because he knows the kind of audience he will have to face, and does not wish to antagonize them. In other words, his strategy is guided by *feedback* – by the echo of his words from the audience, even if for the time being it is merely an anticipated echo from an imaginary audience.

Let us note that all this wavering and decision-making need not at this stage involve any verbal formulations; it may have taken the form of vague visual images. (For instance, the polemical method may be represented in his imagination by a white shape highlighted on a black surface – the Gestalt theorists' figure-background paradigm, and the straightforward method represented by a uniform grey. Questionnaires to scientists have revealed that in the decisive stages of creative thinking, visual and even muscular imagery predominates over verbal thinking.*)

Next comes the vexed problem of the 'organization of material'; vexed, because the different aspects of the problem, the welter of evidence and the welter of interpretations, are all interconnected like threads in a Persian carpet. Our lecturer is keenly aware of the pattern they form; but how can he convey that pattern if he has to unpick the threads in order to explain them one at a time? Here the problem of temporal order begins to intrude, although his mind may still be functioning in the partly or wholly non-verbal regions of images and intimations.

At last he arrives at a tentative arrangement of his material, under a series of headings and sub-headings, which he shuffles about as if they were compact building blocks. They are probably each represented by a mere jotted key-word. This again sounds simple enough, but the longer you think about it the more puzzling the nature of these building blocks appears to be. William James expressed this puzzlement in a memorable passage (his italics):

> ... And has the reader never asked himself what kind of a mental fact is his *intention of saying a thing* before he has said it? It is an entirely definite intention, distinct from all other intentions, an absolutely distinct state of consciousness, therefore; and yet how much of it consists of definite sensorial images, either of words or of things? Hardly anything! ... Yet what can we say about it without using words that belong to the later mental facts that replace it? The intention *to say so and so* is the only name it can receive. One may admit that a good third of our psychic life consists in these rapid premonitory perspective views of schemes of thought not yet articulate.[12]

But now the time has come for these intentional seeds to start growing into saplings which will branch out into sections, sub-sections, and so on: the selection of evidence to be quoted,

* See below, Chapter XIII.

of illustrations, comment and anecdotes, each of them neces-
sitating further strategic choices. At each node – branching
point – of the growing tree, more details are filled in, until at
last the syntactic level is reached, the phrase-generating
machine takes over, the individual words are lined up – some
effortlessly, some after a painful search, and are finally transformed into patterns of contractions of finger muscles guiding
a pen: the logos has become incarnate.

But of course the process is never quite as neat and orderly
as that; trees do not grow in this rigidly symmetrical way. In
our schematized account, the selection of the actual words
occurs only at an advanced stage of the process, after the
general plan and the ordering of the material have been decided
on, and the buds of the tree are ready to burst open in their
proper left-to-right order. In reality, however, one branch
somewhere in the middle might blossom into words, while
others have as yet hardly started to grow. And while it is true
that the idea or 'intention of saying a thing' precedes the actual
process of verbalization, it is also true that ideas are often airy
nothings until they crystallize into verbal concepts and acquire
tangible shape. Therein, of course, lies the incomparable
superiority of language over more primitive forms of mental
activity; but that does not justify the fallacy of identifying
language with thought and of denying the importance of non-
verbal images and symbols, particularly in the creative thinking of artists and scientists (Chapter XIII). Thus our lecturer
sometimes knows what he means, but cannot formulate it;
whereas at other times he can only find out what exactly he
means by explicit, precise verbal formulations. When Alice in
Wonderland was admonished to think carefully before speaking, she explained: 'How can I know what I think till I see
what I say?' Often some promising intuition is nipped in the
bud by prematurely exposing it to the acid bath of verbal
definitions; others may never develop without such verbal
exposure.

Thus we have to amend our over-simplified schema: instead of the symmetrically-growing tree, with branches steadily progressing downward, we have irregular growth and constant oscillations between levels. Transforming thought into language is not a one-way process; the sap flows in both directions, up and down the branches of the tree. The operation is further complicated, and sometimes brought to the verge of a breakdown, by our lecturer's deplorable tendency to correct, erase, chop off entire flowering branches from the tree and start growing them afresh. The Behaviourist calls this Trial-and-Error behaviour and compares it to the behaviour of rats running at random into the blind alleys of a maze; but the search for the *mot juste* is, of course, anything but random.

Matters would be even more complicated if our subject were a poet, instead of being a historian. If he were a poet, he would have to serve two masters – operate in two interlocking hierarchies at the same time: one governed by meaning and the second governed by rhythm, metre, euphony. But even though the lecturer writes in prose, his choice of words and phrasing is influenced by the demands of style. Complex activities are often dependent on more than one hierarchic order – trees with intertwining branches – each controlled by its own rules and value-criteria: meaning and euphony, form and function, melody and orchestration, and so on.

I have said enough to indicate some of the problems which human speech presents. Now Behaviourists, too, are in the habit of preparing papers, and even of writing books, so they must no doubt also be aware of the difficulties and complexities of the process. But when they discuss 'verbal behaviour', they manage to forget or repress them. They confine the discussion to such embarrassing trivialities as: 'The verbal stimulus "Come to dinner" is usually reinforced by food.' They demonstrate how the experimenter can 'control a subject's verbal behaviour' by placing 'a large and unusual pencil in an unusual place clearly in sight – under such circumstances it is highly probable that our subject will say *pencil*'[13] (both examples are from Skinner's *Verbal Behaviour*, a treasure-house of similar profundities). By these methods they can, as we have seen, go on talking about S-R atoms forming chains extending in a vacuum – without having to bother to define what the S's and the R's consist of.

Summary

Where indeed shall we look for the atoms of language – in the phoneme /e/? In the digram /en/? In the morpheme /men/? In the word /mention/? Or in the phrase /don't mention it/? Each of these entities has two aspects. It is a *whole* relative to its own constituent parts, and at the same time a *part* of the larger whole on the next level of the hier-archy. It is both a part and a whole – a sub-whole. It is one of the characteristic features of *all* hierarchic systems, as we shall see, that they are not aggregations of elementary bits, but are composed of sub-wholes branching into sub-sub-wholes, and so on. This is the first point of general validity to retain from the preceding discussion. I must now mention a few more characteristics of language which have the same universal validity for hierarchic systems of all types.

'Active speech' (in contrast to 'passive speech', ie, listening) consists in the stepwise elaboration, articulation, concretiza-tion, of originally inarticulate generalized intents. The branch-ing of the tree symbolizes this step-by-step, hierarchic process of spelling out the implicit idea in explicit terms, of converting the potentialities of an idea into the actual motion-patterns of the vocal chords. The process has been compared to the development of the embryo: the fertilized egg contains all the potentialities of the future individual; these are then 'spelled out' in successive stages of differentiation. It could also be compared to the way a military command is executed: the generalized order 'Eighth Army will advance in direction of Tobruk', issued from the apex of the hierarchy, is concretized in more detail at each of the lower echelons. Furthermore we shall see that the exercise of any skilled action, whether instinctive, like the nest-building of birds, or acquired, as most human skills are, follows the same pattern of spelling out a 'roughed-in' command by a hierarchic sequence of steps.

The next point to note is that each step in our imaginary lecturer's progress was governed by *fixed rules*, which, however, leave room for *flexible strategies*, guided by *feedbacks*. On the highest levels operate the rather esoteric rules of academic discourse; on the next lower level the rules of generating grammatically correct sentences; lastly, the rules which govern the activities of the vocal chords. But on each level there is a variety of strategic choices: from the selection and ordering of the material, through the choice of metaphors and adjectives, down to the variety of possible intonations of individual vowels.*

When we speak of fixed rules and flexible strategies, it is important to make a further distinction between these two factors. The *rules* on every level function more or less automatically, ie, unconsciously, or at least pre-consciously in the

---

* Once more it is interesting to note the intense reluctance of academic psychologists – even those who have outgrown the cruder forms of S-R theory – to come to grips with reality. Thus Professor G. Miller writes in an article on psycholinguistics: 'As psychologists have learnt to appreciate the complexities of language, the prospect of reducing it to the laws of behaviour so carefully studied in lower animals has grown increasingly remote. We have been forced more and more into a position that non-psychologists probably take for granted, namely, that language is rule-governed behaviour characterized by enormous flexibility and freedom of choice. Obvious as this conclusion may seem, it has important implications for any scientific theory of language. If rules involve the concepts of right and wrong, they introduce a normative aspect that has always been avoided in the natural sciences . . . To admit that language follows rules seems to put it outside the range of phenomena accessible to scientific investigation'.[14] What a very odd notion of the purpose and methods of 'scientific investigation'!

twilight zones of awareness, whereas the *strategic choices* are mostly aided by the bright beam of focal consciousness. The machinery which canalizes inarticulate thought into grammatically correct channels operates hidden from sight; so does the machinery which ensures the correct innervation of the vocal tracts, and also the machinery which controls the logic of 'commonsense' reasoning, and our habits of thought. We hardly ever bother to have a look at these silent machineries, and even if we try, we are unable to describe their modes of operation, unable to define the rules embodied in them; and yet these are the rules of language and thought which we blindly obey. If they contain hidden axioms and built-in prejudices – so much the worse for us. But at least we know that those rules which both discipline and distort thinking are only binding for the individual who acquired them, and subject to historical change.

Nevertheless, as far as the individual is concerned, his language and thought are rule-governed, and to that extent determined by automatisms beyond conscious control. But only to that extent. The rules which govern a game like chess or bridge do not exhaust its possibilities, but leave the player at practically each step with a number of strategical choices. These choices, of course, are also determined by considerations of a higher order – but the emphasis is on 'higher order'. Each choice is 'free' in the sense of not being determined by the rules of the game itself, but by a different order of 'strategic precepts' on a higher level of the hierarchy; and these precepts have an even larger margin of indeterminacy. We are once more in an infinite regress – comparable to the endless types of ambiguities of language, each of which can only be resolved by reference to the next higher level of the open-ended hierarchy. This line of argument evidently leads to the problem of freedom of choice, to be further discussed in Chapter XIV.

To conclude, let me revert once more to that Behaviourist

lecturer who turns his mouth loose and goes to sleep. I have compared him to a bar pianist reeling off a popular tune. In both cases a single command from a higher level of the hierarchy 'triggers off' a pre-set, more or less automatized performance. The process is comparable to pressing a button on a jukebox, the pianist merely has to say to himself: 'La Cucaracha' or 'Pop goes the Weasel', and let his fingers look after the rest. But even in this routine he is *not* simply unfolding an S-R chain, where depressing one piano key acts as a stimulus to depress the next. For, as a skilled bar pianist, he is perfectly capable, again at a single trigger command, of transposing the whole piece from C Major into B Flat Major, where the keys and intervals form *a totally different chain*. The fixed 'rule of the game' in this case is represented by the melodic pattern; the scale – and the rhythm, phrasing, syncopation, etc, – are again a matter of flexible strategies.

The 'spelling out' of an implicit command in explicit terms often involves such trigger-releaser operations, where a relatively simple command from 'higher quarters' activates complex, pre-set action-patterns. These, however, are not rigid automatisms, but flexible patterns offering a variety of alternative choices. To shake hands, to light a cigarette, to pick up a pencil, are routines often performed quite unconsciously and mechanically, but also capable of infinite variations. I would only have to press a single mental button to continue writing this page in French – or Hungarian; but that does not necessarily mean that I am to be regarded as a jukebox.

III

THE HOLON

I ask the reader to remember that what is most obvious may be most worth of analysis. Fertile vistas may open out when commonplace facts are examined from a fresh point of view.

L. L. WHYTE

THE concept of hierarchic order occupies a central place in this book, and lest the reader should think that I am riding a private hobby horse, let me reassure him that this concept has a long and respectable ancestry. So much so, that defenders of orthodoxy are inclined to dismiss it as 'old hat' – and often in the same breath to deny its validity. Yet I hope to show as we go along that this old hat, handled with some affection, can produce lively rabbits.*

The Parable of the Two Watchmakers

Let me start with a parable. I owe it to Professor H. A. Simon, designer of logic computers and chess-playing machines, but I have taken the liberty of elaborating on it.[2]

There were once two Swiss watchmakers, named Bios and Mekhos, who made very fine and expensive watches. Their names may sound a little strange, but their fathers had a smattering of Greek and were fond of riddles. Although their watches were in equal demand, Bios prospered, while Mekhos

---

* More than thirty years ago, Needham wrote: 'Whatever the nature of organizing relations may be, they form the central problem of biology, and biology will be fruitful in the future only if this is recognized. The hierarchy of relations, from the molecular structure of carbon compounds to the equilibrium of species and ecological wholes, will perhaps be the leading idea of the future'.[1] Yet the word 'hierarchy' does not even appear in the index of most modern textbooks of psychology or biology.

just struggled along; in the end he had to close his shop and take a job as a mechanic with Bios. The people in the town argued for a long time over the reasons for this development and each had a different theory to offer, until the true explanation leaked out and proved to be both simple and surprising.

The watches they made consisted of about one thousand parts each, but the two rivals had used different methods to put them together. Mekhos had assembled his watches bit by bit – rather like making a mosaic floor out of small coloured stones. Thus each time when he was disturbed in his work and had to put down a partly assembled watch, it fell to pieces and he had to start again from scratch.

Bios, on the other hand, had designed a method of making watches by constructing, for a start, sub-assemblies of about ten components, each of which held together as an independent unit. Ten of these sub-assemblies could then be fitted together into a sub-system of a higher order; and ten of these sub-systems constituted the whole watch. This method proved to have two immense advantages.

In the first place, each time there was an interruption or a disturbance, and Bios had to put down, or even drop, the watch he was working on, it did not decompose into its elementary bits; instead of starting all over again, he merely had to reassemble that particular sub-assembly on which he was working at the time; so that at worst (if the disturbance came when he had nearly finished the sub-assembly in hand) he had to repeat nine assembling operations, and at best none at all. Now it is easy to show mathematically that if a watch consists of a thousand bits, and if some disturbance occurs at an average of once in every hundred assembling operations – then Mekhos will take four thousand times longer to assemble a watch than Bios. Instead of a single day, it will take him eleven years. And if for mechanical bits, we substitute amino acids, protein molecules, organelles, and so on, the ratio between the time-scales becomes astronomical; some calculations[3] indicate that the whole lifetime of the earth would be insufficient for producing even an amoeba – unless he becomes converted to Bios' method and proceeds hierarchically, from simple sub-assemblies to more complex ones. Simon concludes: 'Complex systems will evolve from simple systems much more rapidly if there are stable intermediate forms than if there are not. The resulting complex forms in the former case will be hierarchic. We have only to turn the argument around to explain the observed predominance of hierarchies among the complex systems Nature presents to us. Among possible complex forms, hierarchies are the ones that have the time to evolve.'[4]

A second advantage of Bios' method is of course that the finished product will be incomparably more resistant to damage, and much easier to maintain, regulate and repair, than Mekhos' unstable mosaic of atomic bits. We do not know what forms of life have evolved on other planets in the universe, but we can safely assume that *wherever there is life, it must be hierarchically organized.*

Enter Janus

If we look at any form of social organization with some degree of coherence and stability, from insect state to Pentagon, we shall find that it is hierarchically ordered. The same is true of the structure of living organisms and their ways of functioning – from instinctive behaviour to the sophisticated skills of piano-playing and talking. And it is equally true of the processes of becoming – phylogeny, ontogeny, the acquisition of knowledge. However, if the branching tree is to represent more than a superficial analogy, there must be certain principles or laws which apply to all levels of a given hierarchy, and to all the varied types of hierarchy just mentioned – in other words, which define the meaning of 'hierarchic order'. In the pages that follow I shall outline several of these principles. They may at first sight look a little abstract, yet taken together, they shed a new light on some old problems.

The first universal characteristic of hierarchies is the relativity, and indeed ambiguity, of the terms 'part' and 'whole' when applied to any of the sub-assemblies. Again it is the very obviousness of this feature which makes us overlook its implications. A 'part', as we generally use the word, means something fragmentary and incomplete, which by itself would have no legitimate existence. On the other hand, a 'whole' is considered as something complete in itself which needs no further explanation. But *'wholes' and 'parts' in this absolute sense just do not exist anywhere*, either in the domain of living organisms or of social organizations. What we find are intermediary structures on a series of levels in an ascending order of complexity: sub-wholes which display, according to the way you look at them, some of the characteristics commonly attributed to wholes and some of the characteristics commonly attributed to parts. We have seen the impossibility of the task of chopping up speech into elementary atoms or units, either on the phonetic or on the syntactic level. Phonemes, words, phrases, are wholes in their own right, but parts of a larger unit; so are cells, tissues, organs; families, clans, tribes. The members of a hierarchy, like the Roman god Janus, all have two faces looking in opposite directions: the face turned towards the subordinate levels is that of a self-contained whole; the face turned upward towards the apex, that of a dependent part. One is the face of the master, the other the face of the servant. This *'Janus effect'* is a fundamental characteristic of sub-wholes in all types of hierarchies.

But there is no satisfactory word in our vocabulary to refer to these Janus-faced entities: to talk of sub-wholes (or sub-assemblies, sub-structures, sub-skills, sub-systems) is awkward and tedious. It seems preferable to coin a new term to designate these nodes on the hierarchic tree which behave partly as wholes or wholly as parts, according to the way you look at them. The term I would propose is 'holon', from the Greek *holos* = whole, with the suffix *on* which, as in proto*n* or neutro*n*, suggests a particle or part.

'A man', wrote Ben Jonson, 'coins not a new word without some peril; for if it happens to be received, the praise is but moderate; if refused, the scorn is assured.' Yet I think the holon is worth the risk, because it fills a genuine need. It also symbolizes the missing link – or rather series of links – between the atomistic approach of the Behaviourist and the holistic approach of the Gestalt psychologist.

The Gestalt school has considerably enriched our knowledge of visual perception, and succeeded in softening up the rigid attitude of its opponents to some extent. But in spite of its lasting merits, 'holism' as a general attitude to psychology turned out to be as one-sided as atomism was, because both treated 'whole' and 'part' as absolutes, both failed to take into account the hierarchic scaffolding of intermediate structures of sub-wholes. If we replace for a moment the image of the inverted tree by that of a pyramid, we can say that the Behaviourist never gets higher up than the bottom layer of stones, and the holist never gets down from the apex. In fact, the concept of the 'whole' proved just as elusive as that of the elementary part, and when he discusses language, the Gestaltist finds himself in the same quandary as the Behaviourist. To quote James Jenkins again: 'There is an infinite set of sentences in English whose production and understanding is part of the daily commerce with language, and it is clear that neither the S-R nor the Gestalt approach is capable of coping with the problems involved in the generation and understanding of these sentences ... We can't regard a sentence as a holistic, unanalysable unit, as the Gestaltists might maintain one should. One cannot suppose that the sentence is regarded as a perceptual unity which has welded its elements together in some unique pattern, as is the usual Gestalt analysis of perceptual phenomena.'[5] Nor do we find wholes on levels lower than the sentence – phrases, words, syllables, and phonemes are not parts, and not wholes, but holons.

The two-term part-whole paradigm is deeply engrained in our unconscious habits of thought. It will make a great difference to our mental outlook when we succeed in breaking away from it.

Social Holons

In Chapter II I discussed the hierarchic structure of language. Let us now briefly turn to a quite different kind of hierarchy: social organization.

The individual, *qua* biological organism, constitutes a nicely integrated hierarchy of molecules, cells, organs, and organ systems. Looking inward into the space enclosed by the boundaries of his skin, he can rightly assert that he is something complete and unique, a whole. But facing outward, he is constantly – sometimes pleasantly, sometimes painfully – reminded that he is a part, an elementary unit in one or several social hierarchies.

The reason why any relatively stable society – whether of animals or humans – must be hierarchically structured, can again be illustrated by the watchmakers' parable: without stable sub-assemblies – social groupings and sub-groupings – the whole simply could not hold together.

In a military hierarchy the holons are companies, battalions, regiments, etc, and the branches of the tree stand for lines of communication and command. The number of levels which a hierarchy comprises (in this case from commanding general to individual soldier) determines whether it is 'shallow' or 'deep'; and the number of holons on any given level we shall call (after Simon) its 'span'. A primitive horde of tribesmen is a very shallow hierarchy with perhaps two or three levels (chieftain and lesser chieftains), and a large span to each. Conversely, some Latin-American armies of the past are said to have numbered one general to each private soldier – which would be the limit case of a hierarchy turning into a ladder (page 39). The efficient working of a complex hierarchy must obviously depend, among other things, on the proper ratio of depth to span – something analogous to the Greek sculptor's golden section, or rather to Le Corbusier's hierarchic 'modulator' theory.

A society without hierarchic structurings would be as chaotic as the random motions of gas molecules flying, colliding and rebounding in all directions. But the structuring is obscured by the fact that no advanced human society – not even the totalitarian state – is a monolithic structure, patterned into one single hierarchy. This may be the case in some very 'unspoilt' tribal societies, where the exigencies of the family-kinship-clan-tribe hierarchy completely control the individual's existence. The medieval church and modern totalitarian nations have tried to establish equally effective monolithic hierarchies, with only limited success. Complex societies are structured by several types of interlocking hierarchies, and control by higher authority is only one among them. I shall call these authority-yielding hierarchies 'control hierarchies'. Obvious examples are government administrations, military, ecclesiastic, academic, professional and business hierarchies. Control may be vested in individuals or in institutions – 'bosses' or anonymous treasury departments; it may be rigid or elastic; it may be guided to a greater or lesser extent by feedback from the lower echelons: electorate, employees, student-bodies; but each hierarchy must nevertheless display a well-articulated tree-structure, without which anarchy would result – as it does when some social upheaval puts an axe to the trunk of the tree.

Entwined with these control hierarchies are others, based on social cohesion, geographical distribution, etc. There are the family – clan – sub-caste – caste hierarchies, and their modern versions. Interlocking with them are the hierarchies based on geographical neighbourhood. Old towns like Paris, Vienna or

London have their *quartiers*, each of them relatively self-sufficient, with its local shops, familiar cafés, pubs, milkmen and sweeps. Each is a kind of local village, a social holon, which again is part of a larger division – Left Bank and Right Bank, City and West End, amusement centre and civic centre, parks, suburbs. Old towns, notwithstanding their architectural diversity, seem to have grown like organisms, and to have an individual life of their own. Towns which have mushroomed up too fast have a depressing amorphousness because they lack the hierarchic structure of organic development. They seem to have been built not by Bios but by Mekhos.

FIGURE 3

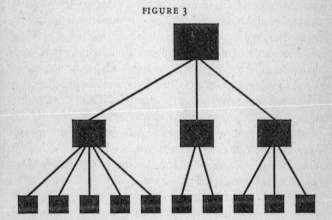

Thus the complex fabric of social life can be dissected into a variety of hierarchic scaffoldings, as anatomists dissect muscles, nerves and other correlated structures from the pulpy mess. Without this attribute of *dissectibility*,* the concept of the hierarchy would have a degree of arbitrariness. We are only justified to talk of trees if we are able to identify their nodes and branches. In the case of a government department or a business concern, dissection is easy: the branching tree-chart

* Simon (*op cit*) speaks of 'decomposable' hierarchies, but 'dissectibility' seems preferable.

may actually hang on the office wall. The simplest type of
chart (without cross-connections) will usually look something
like Figure 3.

Let this represent a government department, such as the
Home Office: then each holon – each box – in the second row
will represent a branch of it: Immigration – Scotland Yard –
Prison Commission, etc, and each box in the third row a
sub-department, etc. Now which are the criteria which
justify 'dissecting' the Home Office in this and no other way?
Or, to put it differently, how did the maker of the chart
define his holons? He may have been shown a town map
indicating Home Office buildings, and plans of each building;
but that would not be enough, and sometimes even misleading,
because some department may be housed in several buildings
in different parts of the town, and several departments may
share the same building. What defines each box as an entity is
the *function* or task assigned to it – the nature of the work
which the people in each department do. There is, of course,
in any efficient hierarchy a tendency to keep people working
on the same task in the same room or building, and to that
extent spatial distribution enters into the picture, but only to
that extent. Office boys and telephones bridge the distances
between functionally-related desks – as nerves and hormones
do in the control hierarchies of the living organism.

There is not only *cohesion* within each holon, but also
separation between different holons to lend precision to the
chart. The people who work within a given department
transact much more business with each other than with people
in other departments. Moreover, when one department
requests information or action from another department, this
is not as a rule done by direct person-to-person contact, but
through official channels, involving the heads of each department. In other words, the lines of control run along the
branches of the tree up and down; there are no horizontal
short cuts in an ideal control-hierarchy.

In other types of hierarchies the holons cannot be so easily defined by their 'function' or 'task'. We cannot define the 'function' of a family, clan, or tribe. Nevertheless, as in the previous example, the members of each of these holons function together, cohere, interact, much more with each other than with members of other holons. And if business is to be transacted between two clans or tribes, it is again done *via* the chieftains or elders.* These ties of cohesion and boundaries of separation are both the result of shared traditions, such as the laws of kinship and the resulting codes of behaviour. In their ensemble they form a pattern of *rule-governed behaviour*. It is this pattern which lends the group stability and cohesion, and which defines it as a social holon, with an individuality of its own.

We must distinguish, however, between the rules which govern individual behaviour and those which guide the activities of the group as a whole. The individual may even be unaware of the fact that his behaviour is rule-governed, and no more able to name the rules which guide his conduct than he is able to name those which guide his speech. The activities of the social holon, on the other hand, depend not only on the complex interactions between its parts, but also on its interaction as a whole with other holons on its own, higher level of the hierarchy; and these cannot be inferred from the lower level any more than the function of the nervous system can be inferred from the level of individual nerve cells, or the rules of syntax can be inferred from the rules of phonology. We can 'dissect' a complex whole into its com-

---

* Once these ties of cohesion begin to weaken and the boundaries of separation become blurred, the tribal hierarchy is decaying. The Indian frontier provinces provide a sad illustration of the consequences of a rash policy of 'de-tribalization' without offering a substitute structure of values. *Mutatis mutandis*, the emotional instability of Western society and particularly of its youth, is obviously a consequence of the breakdown of the traditional hierarchic structures without as yet any alternative in sight. But the discussion of social pathology must be postponed to Part Three of this book.

posite holons of the second and third order, and so on, but we cannot 'reduce' it to a sum of its parts, nor predict its properties from those of its parts. The hierarchy concept of 'levels of organization' in itself implies a rejection of the reductionist view that all phenomena of life (consciousness included) can be reduced to and explained by physico-chemical laws.

Thus a stable social holon has an individuality or 'profile' – whether it is a Papuan tribe or a Treasury department. Every closely-knit social body sharing a common territory and/or a code of explicit and implicit laws, customs and beliefs tends to preserve and assert its pattern – or else it could not qualify as a stable holon. In a primitive society the tribe might be the highest unit of the shallow hierarchy, a more or less self-contained whole. But in a complex society, with its many-levelled hierarchies, it is equally essential that each holon – whether an administrative department, a local government or the fire brigade – should operate as an autonomous, self-contained unit; without division of labour and delegation of powers, according to the hierarchic schema, no society can function effectively.

Let us revert for a moment to our Home Office example, and let one 'box' be the Department of Immigration. In order to operate as a self-reliant unit, the department must be equipped with a set of instructions and regulations enabling it to take routine contingencies in its stride, without having to consult higher authority in each particular case. In other words, what enables the department to function in this efficient way, as an autonomous holon, is once more a set of fixed rules, its *canon*. But here again there will be cases where the rules can be interpreted in this way or that, and so leave room for more than one decision. Whatever the nature of a hierarchic organization, its constituent holons are defined by *fixed rules* and *flexible strategies*.

In the present example, too, it is obvious that the individual codes which guide the conduct of the people who work in the department are not the same as the rules which determine the actions of the department. Mr Smith may be willing to grant a visa to an applicant on grounds of compassion, but the regulations say differently. And we find a further parallel to previous examples (p 60). When the rules allow more than one course of action, the matter must be referred to the head of the department, who might find it advisable to appeal for a decision to a higher level of the hierarchy. And there again, strategic considerations of a higher order may arise – such as the availability of housing, the colour problem, the labour situation. There may even be conflict between Home Office policy and the Ministry of Economics. Once more we are moving in a regressing series (although in this case, of course, it is not an infinite regress).

To repeat: it is essential for the stability and efficient functioning of the body social that each of its sub-divisions should operate as an autonomous, self-reliant unit which, though subject to control from above, must have a degree of independence and take routine contingencies in its stride, without asking higher authority for instructions. Otherwise the communication channels would become overloaded, the whole system clogged up, the higher echelons would be kept occupied with petty detail and unable to concentrate on more important factors.

The Basic Polarity

However, the rules, or codes, which govern a social holon act not merely as negative *constraints* imposed on its actions, but also as positive *precepts*, maxims of conduct or moral imperatives. As a consequence, every holon will tend to persist in and assert its particular pattern of activity. This *self-assertive tendency* is a fundamental and universal characteristic of holons, which manifests itself on every level of the social hierarchy (and, as we shall see, in every other type of hierarchy).

On the level of the individual, a certain amount of self-assertiveness – ambition, initiative, competition – is indispensable in a dynamic society. At the same time, of course, he is dependent on, and must be integrated into, his tribe or social group. If he is a well-adjusted person, the self-assertive tendency and its opposite, the *integrative tendency*, are more or less equally balanced; he lives, so long as things are normal, in a kind of dynamic equilibrium with his social environment. Under conditions of stress, however, the equilibrium is upset, leading to emotionally disordered behaviour.

No man is an island – he is a holon. A Janus-faced entity who, looking inward, sees himself as a self-contained unique whole, looking outward as a dependent part. His *self-assertive tendency* is the dynamic manifestation of his unique *wholeness*, his autonomy and independence as a holon. Its equally universal antagonist, the *integrative tendency*, expresses his dependence on the larger whole to which he belongs: his *'part-ness'*. The polarity of these two tendencies, or potentials, is one of the *leitmotivs* of the present theory. Empirically, it can be traced in all phenomena of life; theoretically, it is derived from the part-whole dichotomy inherent in the concept of the multi-layered hierarchy; its philosophical implications will be discussed in later chapters. For the time being let me repeat that *the self-assertive tendency is the dynamic expression of the holon's wholeness, the integrative tendency, the dynamic expression of its partness.**

The manifestations of the two tendencies on different levels go by different names, but they are expressions of the same polarity running through the whole series. The self-assertive tendencies of the individual are known as 'rugged individualism', competitiveness, etc; when we come to larger holons we speak of 'clannishness', 'cliquishness', 'class-consciousness',

---

* In *The Act of Creation* I talked of self-assertive and 'participatory' tendencies; but 'integrative' appears to be the more appropriate term.

'*esprit de corps*', 'local patriotism', 'nationalism', etc. The integrative tendencies, on the other hand, are manifested in 'cooperativeness', 'disciplined behaviour', 'loyalty', 'self-effacement', 'devotion to duty', 'internationalism', and so on.

Note, however, that most of the terms referring to higher levels of the hierarchy are ambiguous. The loyalty of individuals towards their clan reflects their integrative tendencies; but it enables the clan as a whole to behave in an aggressive, self-assertive way. The obedience and devotion to duty of the members of the Nazi SS Guard kept the gas chambers going. 'Patriotism' is the virtue of subordinating private interests to the higher interests of the nation; 'nationalism' is a synonym for the militant expression of those higher interests. The infernal dialectic of this process is reflected throughout human history. It is not accidental; the disposition towards such disturbances is inherent in the part-whole polarization of social hierarchies. It may be the unconscious reason why the Romans gave the god Janus such a prominent role in their Pantheon as the keeper of doorways, facing both inward and outward, and why they named the first month of the year after him. But it would be premature to go into this subject now; it will be one of our main preoccupations in Part Three of this volume.

For the time being we are only concerned with the normal, orderly functioning of the hierarchy, where each holon operates in accordance with its code of rules, without attempting to impose it on others, nor to lose its individuality by excessive subordination. It is only in times of stress that a holon may tend to get out of control, and its normal self-assertiveness changes into aggressiveness – whether the holon is an individual, or a social class, or a whole nation. The reverse process occurs when the dependence of a holon on its superior controls is so strong that it loses its identity.

Readers versed in contemporary psychology will have gathered, even from this incomplete preliminary outline, that in the theory proposed here there is no place for such a thing as a destructive instinct; nor does it admit the reification of the sexual instinct as the *only* integrative force in human or animal society. Freud's Eros and Thanatos are relative late-comers on the stage of evolution: a host of creatures that multiply by fission (or budding) are ignorant of both.* In our view, Eros is an offspring of the integrative, destructive Thanatos of the self-assertive tendency, and Janus the ultimate ancestor of both – the symbol of the dichotomy between partness and wholeness, which is inseparable from the open-ended hierarchies of life.

Summary

Organisms and societies are multi-levelled hierarchies of semi-autonomous sub-wholes branching into sub-wholes of a lower order, and so on. The term 'holon' has been introduced to refer to these intermediary entities which, relative to their subordinates in the hierarchy, function as self-contained wholes; relative to their superordinates as dependent parts. This dichotomy of 'wholeness' and 'partness', of autonomy and dependence, is inherent in the concept of hierarchic order, and is called here the 'Janus principle'. Its dynamic expression is the polarity of the Self-Assertive and Integrative Tendencies.

Hierarchies are 'dissectible' into their constituent branches, on which the holons form the 'nodes'. The number of levels which a hierarchy comprises is called its 'depth', and the number of holons on any given level its 'span'.

Holons are governed by fixed sets of rules and display more or less flexible strategies. The rules of conduct of a social holon are not reducible to the rules of conduct of its members.

The reader may find it helpful to consult from time to time Appendix I, which summarizes the general characteristics of hierarchic systems as proposed in this and subsequent chapters.

* For a discussion of Freudian metapsychology, see *Insight and Outlook*, Chapters XV, XVI.

IV

INDIVIDUALS AND DIVIDUALS

I have yet to see any problem, however complicated, which when you looked at it the right way did not become still more complicated.

POUL ANDERSON

A Note about Diagrams

BEFORE we turn from social organization to biological organisms, I must briefly remark on various types of hierarchies and their diagrammatic representation.

There have been several attempts to classify hierarchies into categories, none of them entirely successful, because unavoidably the categories overlap. Thus one can broadly distinguish between 'structural' hierarchies, which emphasize the spatial aspect (anatomy, topology) of a system, and 'functional' hierarchies, which emphasize process in time. Evidently, structure and function cannot be separated, and represent complementary aspects of an indivisible spatio-temporal process; but it is often convenient to focus attention on one or the other aspect. All hierarchies have a 'part within part' character, but this is more easily recognized in 'structural' than in 'functional' hierarchies – such as the skills of language and music which weave patterns within patterns in time.

In the type of administrative hierarchy we have just discussed, the tree diagram symbolizes both structure and function – the branches are lines of communication and control, the nodes or boxes each represent a group of physically real people (the department head, his assistants and secretaries).

But if we chart in a similar way a military establishment, the tree will only represent the functional aspect, because, strictly speaking, the boxes on each level – whether they are labelled 'battalion' or 'company' – will contain only officers or NCOs; the place for the other ranks which makes up the bulk of the battalion or company is in the bottom row of the chart. For our purposes this does not really matter, because what we are interested in is how the machinery is functioning, and the tree shows exactly that – it is the officers and NCOs who determine the operations of the holon as repositories of its fixed rules and makers of strategy. But people who are inclined to think in concrete images, rather than in abstract

FIGURE 4

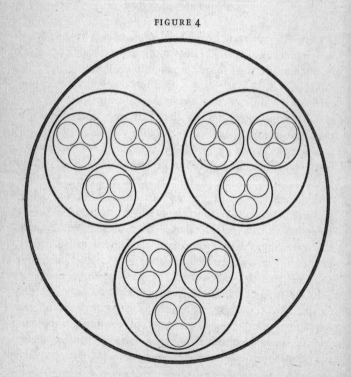

schemata, often find this rather confusing. If, however, we wanted to emphasize the *structural* aspect of an army, we might draw a diagram, such as Figure 4, which shows how platoons are 'encapsulated' into companies, companies into battalions, etc. But such structural diagrams are clumsy, and contain less information than the branching tree.

Some authors put *symbolic hierarchies* (language, music, mathematics) into a separate category; but they might just as well be classified as 'functional hierarchies', as they are produced by human operations. A book consists of chapters, consisting of paragraphs, consisting of sentences, etc; and a symphony can similarly be dissected into parts within parts. The hierarchic structure of the product reflects the hierarchic nature of the skills and sub-skills which brought it into being.

In a similar way, all *classificatory hierarchies*, unless they are purely descriptive, reflect the processes by which they came into being. Thus the species-genus-family-order-class-phylum classification of the animal kingdom is intended to reflect relations in evolutionary descent – here the tree diagram represents the archetypal 'tree of life'. Similarly, the hierarchically sub-divided subject-index in library catalogues reflects the hierarchic ordering of knowledge.

Lastly, phylogeny and ontogeny are *developmental hierarchies* in which the tree branches out along the axis of time, the different levels represent different stages of development, and the holons – as we shall see – reflect intermediary structures at these stages.

It may be useful to repeat at this point that the search for properties or laws which all these varied kinds of hierarchies have in common is more than a play on superficial analogies. It could rather be called an exercise in 'general systems theory' – a relatively recent branch of science, whose aim is to construct theoretical models and 'logically homologous laws' (v. Bertalanffy) which are universally applicable to inorganic, biological and social systems of any kind.

Inanimate Systems

As we move downward in the hierarchy which constitutes the living organism, from organs to tissues, cells, organelles, macromolecules, and so on, we nowhere strike rock bottom, find nowhere those ultimate constituents which the old mechanistic* approach to life led us to expect. *The hierarchy is open-ended in the downward, as it is in the upward direction.* The atom, itself, although its name is derived from the Greek for 'indivisible' has turned out to be a very complex, Janus-faced holon. Facing outward, it associates with other atoms as if it were a single unitary whole; and the regularity of the atomic weights of elements, closely approximating to integral numbers, seemed to confirm the belief in that indivisibility. But since we have learned to look inside it, we can observe the rule-governed interactions between nucleus and outer electron-shells, and of a variety of particles within the nucleus. The rules can be expressed in sets of mathematical equations which define each particular type of atom as a holon. But here again, the rules which govern the interactions of the sub-nuclear particles in the hierarchy are not the same rules which govern the chemical interactions between atoms as wholes. The subject is too technical to be pursued here; the interested reader will find a good summary in H. Simon's paper, which I have quoted before.[1]

When we turn from the universe in miniature to the universe at large, we again find hierarchic order. Moons go round planets, planets round stars, stars round the centres of their galaxies, galaxies form clusters. Wherever we find orderly, stable systems in Nature, we find that they are hierarchically structured, for the simple reason that without such structuring of complex systems into sub-assemblies, there

---

* Throughout this book, the term 'mechanistic' is used in its general sense, and not in the technical sense of an alternative to 'vitalistic' theories in biology.

could be no order and stability – except the order of a dead universe filled with a uniformly distributed gas. And even so, each discrete gas molecule would be a microscopic hierarchy. If this sounds by now like a tautology, all the better.*

It would, of course, be grossly anthropomorphic to speak of 'self-assertive' and 'integrative' tendencies in inanimate nature, or of 'flexible strategies'. It is nevertheless true that in all stable dynamic systems, stability is maintained by the equilibration of opposite forces, one of which may be centrifugal or separative or inertial, representing the quasi-independent, holistic properties of the part, and the other a centripetal or attractive or cohesive force which keeps the part in its place in the larger whole, and holds it together. On different levels of the inorganic and organic hierarchies, the polarization of 'particularistic' and 'holistic' forces takes different forms, but it is observable on every level. This is not the reflection of any metaphysical dualism, but rather of Newton's Third Law of Motion ('to every action there is an equal and opposite reaction') applied to hierarchic systems.

There is also a significant analogy in physics to the distinction between fixed rules and flexible strategies. The geometrical structure of a crystal is represented by fixed rules; but crystals growing in a saturated solution will reach the same final shape by different pathways, ie, although their growth processes differ in detail; and even if artificially damaged in the process, the growing crystal may correct the blemish. In this and many other well-known phenomena we find the self-regulatory properties of biological holons foreshadowed on an elementary level.

* Often, however, we fail to recognize hierarchic structure, for example in a crystal, because it has a very shallow hierarchy consisting of only three levels (as far as our knowledge goes) – molecules – atoms – sub-atomic particles; and also because the molecular level has an enormous 'span' of near-identical holons.

The Organism and its Spares

As we ascend to the hierarchies of living matter, we find, even on the lowest level observable through the electron microscope, sub-cellular structures – organelles – of staggering complexity. And the most striking fact is that these minuscule parts of the cell function as self-governing wholes in their own right, each following its own statute-book of rules. One type of organelles look as quasi-independent agencies after the cell's growth; others after its energy supply, reproduction, communications, and so on. The *ribosomes*, for instance, which manufacture proteins, rival in complexity any chemical factory. The *mitochondria* are power plants which extract energy from food by a complicated chain of chemical reactions involving some fifty different steps; a single cell may have up to five thousand such power plants. Then there are the *centrosomes*, with their spindle apparatus, which organizes the incredible choreography of the cell dividing into two; and the DNA spirals of heredity, coiled up in the inner sanctum of the *chromosomes*, working their even more potent magic.

I do not intend to wax lyrical about matters which can be found in any popular science book; I am trying to stress a point which they do not sufficiently emphasize, or tend to overlook altogether – namely, that the organism is not a mosaic aggregate of elementary physico-chemical processes, but a hierarchy in which each member, from the sub-cellular level upward, is a closely integrated structure, equipped with self-regulatory devices, and enjoys an advanced form of self-government. The activity of an organelle, such as the mitochondrion, can be switched on and off; but once triggered into action it will follow its own course. No higher echelon in the hierarchy can interfere with the order of its operations, laid down by its own canon of rules. The organelle is a law unto itself, an autonomous holon with its characteristic pattern of structure and function, which it tends to assert, even if the cell around it is dying.

The same observations apply to the larger units in the organism. Cells, tissues, nerves, muscles, organs, all have their intrinsic rhythm and pattern, often manifested spontaneously without external stimulation. When the physiologist looks at any organ from 'above', from the apex of the hierarchy, he sees it as a dependent part. When he looks at it from 'below', from the level of its constituents, he sees a whole of remarkable self-sufficiency. The heart has its own 'pacemakers' – in fact three pacemakers, capable of taking over from each other when the need arises. Other major organs have different types of coordinating centres and self-regulating devices. Their character as autonomous holons is most convincingly demonstrated by culture experiments and spare-part surgery. Since Carrell demonstrated in a famous experiment that a strip of tissue from the heart of a chicken embryo will go on beating indefinitely *in vitro*, we have learnt that whole organs – kidneys, hearts, even brains – are capable of continued functioning as quasi-independent wholes when isolated from the organism and supplied with the proper nutrients, or transplanted into another organism. At the time of writing, Russian and American experimenters have succeeded in keeping the brains of dogs and monkeys alive (judged by the brain's electrical activities) in apparatus outside the animal – and in transplanting one dog's brain into another live animal's tissues. The Frankensteinian horror of these experiments need not be stressed – and they are only a beginning.

Yet spare-part surgery has, of course, its beneficial uses, and from a theoretical point of view it is a striking confirmation of the hierarchic concept. It demonstrates, in a rather literal sense, the 'dissectibility' of the organism – viewed in its bodily aspect – into autonomous sub-assemblies which function as wholes in their own right. It also sheds added light on the evolutionary process – on the principles which guided Bios in putting together the sub-assemblies of his watches.

The Integrative Powers of Life

Let us go back for a moment to the organelles which operate inside the cell. The mitochondria transform food – glucose, fat, proteins – into the chemical substance *adrenosin-triphosphate*, ATP for short, which all animal cells utilize as fuel. It is the *only* type of fuel used throughout the animal kingdom to provide the necessary energy for muscle cells, nerve cells and so on; and there is only this *one* type of organelle throughout the animal kingdom which produces it. The mitochondria have been called 'the power plants of all life on earth'. Moreover, each mitochondrion carries not only its set of instructions how to make ATP, but also its own hereditary blueprint, which enables it to reproduce itself independently from the reproduction of the cell as a whole.

Until a few years ago, it was thought that the only carriers of heredity were the chromosomes in the nucleus of the cell. At present we know that the mitochondria, and also some other organelles located in the cytoplasm (the fluid surrounding the nucleus) are equipped with their own genetic apparatus, which enables them to reproduce independently. In view of this, it has been suggested that these organelles may have evolved independently from each other at the dawn of life on this planet, but at a later stage had entered into a kind of symbiosis.

This plausible hypothesis sounds like another illustration of the watchmakers' parable; we may regard the stepwise building up of complex hierarchies out of simpler holons as a basic manifestation of the integrative tendency of living matter. It seems indeed very likely that the single cell, once considered the atom of life, originated in the coming together of molecular structures which were the primitive forerunners of the organelles, and which had come into existence independently, each endowed with a different characteristic property of life – such as self-replication, metabolism, motility. When they entered into symbiotic partnership, the emergent whole – perhaps some ancestral form of amoeba – proved to be an incomparably more stable, versatile and adaptable entity than a mere summation of the parts would imply. To quote Ruth Sager:

> Life began, I would speculate, with the emergence of a stabilized tri-partite system: nucleic acids for replication, a photosynthetic or chemosynthetic system for energy conversion, and protein enzymes to catalyse the two processes. Such a tripartite system could have been the ancestor of chloroplasts and mitochondria and perhaps of the cell itself. In the course of evolution, these primitive systems might have coalesced into the larger framework of the cell . . .[2]

The hypothesis is in keeping with all we know about that ubiquitous manifestation of the integrative tendency: symbiosis, the varied forms of partnership between organisms. It ranges from the mutually indispensable association of algae and fungi in lichens, to the less intimate but no less vital inter-dependence of animals, plants and bacteria in ecological communities (biocoenosis). Where different species are involved, the partnership may take the form of 'commensualism' – barnacles travelling on the sides of the whale; or of 'mutualism', as between flowering plant and pollinating insects, or between ants and aphides – a kind of insect 'cattle' which the ants protect and 'milk' for their secretions in return. Equally varied are the forms of cooperation within the same species, from colonial animals upward. The Portuguese man-of-war is a colony of polyps, each specialized for a particular function; but to decide whether its tentacles, floats and reproductive units are individual animals, or mere organs, is a matter of semantics; every polyp is a holon, combining the characteristics of independent wholes and dependent parts.

The same dilemma confronts us, on a higher turn of the spiral, in the insect societies of ants, bees, termites. Social insects are physically separate entities, but none can survive if separated from its group; their existence is completely controlled by the interests of the group as a whole; all members of the group are descendants from the same pair of parents, interchangeable and indistinguishable, not only to the human eye but also probably to the insects themselves, which are supposed to recognize members of their group by their smell, but not to discriminate between individuals. Moreover, many social insects exchange their secretions, which form some kind of chemical bond between them.

An individual is usually defined as an indivisible, self-contained unit, with a separate, independent existence of its own. But individuals in this absolute sense are nowhere found in Nature or society, just as we nowhere find absolute wholes. Instead of separateness and independence, there is cooperation and interdependence, running through the whole gamut, from physical symbiosis to the cohesive bonds of the swarm, hive, shoal, flock, herd, family, society. The picture becomes even more blurred when we consider the criterion of 'indivisibility'. The word 'individual' originally means just that; it is derived from the Latin *in-dividuus* – as atom is derived from the Greek *a-tomos*. But on every level, indivisibility turns out to be a relative affair. Protozoa, sponges, hydra and flatworms can multiply by simple fission or budding: that is, by the breaking up of one individual into two or more, and so on, *ad infinitum*. As von Bertalanffy wrote: 'How can we call these creatures individuals when they are in fact "dividua", and their multiplication arises precisely from division? ... Can we insist on calling a hydra or a turbelerian flatworm an individual, when these animals can be cut into as many pieces as we like, each capable of growing into a complete organism? ... The notion of the individual is, biologically, only to be defined as a limiting concept.'[3]

A flatworm, cut into six slices, will actually regenerate a complete individual from each slice within a matter of weeks.

If the wheel of rebirth transforms me into a flatworm meeting a similar fate, must I then assume that my immortal soul has split into six immortal solons? Christian theologians will find an easy way out of this dilemma by denying that animals have souls; but Hindus and Buddhists take a different view. And secular-minded philosophers, who do not talk about souls, but affirm the existence of a conscious ego, also refuse to draw a boundary line between creatures with and without consciousness. But if we assume that there exists a continuous scale of gradations, from the sentience of primitive creatures, through various degrees of consciousness, to full self-awareness, then the experimental biologist's challenge to the concept of individuality poses a genuine dilemma. The only solution seems to be (see Chapter XIV) to get away from the concept of the individual as a monolithic structure, and to replace it by the concept of the individual as an open hierarchy whose apex is forever receding, striving towards a state of complete integration which is never achieved.

The regeneration of a complete individual from a small fragment of a primitive animal is an impressive manifestation of the integrative powers of living matter. But there are even more striking examples. Nearly a generation ago, Wilson and Child showed that if the tissues of a living sponge – or a hydra – are crushed to pulp, passed through a fine filter, and the pulp is then poured into water, the dissociated cells will soon begin to associate, to aggregate first into flat sheets, then round up into a sphere, differentiate progressively and end up 'as adult individuals with characteristic mouth, tentacles and so forth' (Dunbar[4]). More recently, P. Weiss and his associates have demonstrated that the developing organs in animal embryos are also capable, just like sponges, of re-forming, after having been pulped. Weiss and James cut out bits of tissue from eight to fourteen day old chick embryos, minced and filtered the tissues through nylon sheets, re-compacted them by centrifuging, and transplanted them to the membrane of another growing embryo. After nine days, the scrambled liver cells had started forming a liver, the kidney cells a kidney, the skin cells to form feathers. More than that: the experimenters were also able to produce normal embryonic kidneys by mincing, pooling and scrambling kidney tissues from several *different* embryos. The holistic properties of these tissues survived not only disintegration but also fusion.[5]

Fusion can even be induced between different species. Thus Spemann combined two half newt-embryos in their early, gastrular stage – one a striped newt, the other a crested newt. The result was a well-formed animal, one side striped, the other crested. Even more spooky are recent experiments by Professor Harris at Oxford, who developed a technique for making human cells fuse with mouse cells. During mitosis, the cell-*nuclei* of man and mouse also fused, 'and the two sets of chromosomes were found to be growing and multiplying quite happily within the same nuclear membrane . . . Such phenomena', one commentator wrote, 'will surely affect our concept of organism in some degree . . . There are obviously sufficient possibilities along these lines to encourage or terrify everyone for some time to come' (Pollock[6]).

In the light of such experimental data, the homely concept of the individual vanishes in the mist. If the crushed and re-formed sponge possesses individuality, so does the embryonic kidney. From organelles to organs, from organisms living in symbiosis to societies with more complex forms of inter-dependence, we nowhere find completely self-contained wholes, only holons – double-faced entities which display the characteristics both of independent units and of inter-depen-dent parts.

In the previous pages I have emphasized the phenomena of inter-dependence and partnership, the *integrative* potential of holons to behave as parts of a more complex whole. The other side of the story reveals, instead of cooperation, competition between the parts of the whole, reflecting the *self-assertive* tendency of holons on every level. Even plants, which are mostly green and not 'red in tooth and claw', compete for light, water and soil. Animal species compete with each other for ecological niches, predator and prey compete for survival, and within each species there is competition for territory, food, mates and dominance.

There is also a less obvious competition between holons *within* the organism in times of stress, when the exposed or traumatized parts tend to assert themselves to the detriment of the whole. The pathology of hierarchic disorder will be discussed in Part Three.

Under normal conditions, however, when the organism or body social is functioning steadily, the integrative and self-assertive tendencies are in a state of dynamic equilibrium – symbolized by *Janus Patulcius*, the 'Opener', with a key in his left hand, and *Janus Clusius*, the 'Closer', jealous guardian of the gate, with a staff in his right.

To sum up, stable inorganic systems, from atoms to galaxies, display hierarchic order; the atom itself, formerly thought of as an indivisible unit, is a holon, and the rules which govern the interactions of sub-nuclear particles are not the same rules that govern the interactions between atoms as wholes.

The living organism is not a mosaic aggregate of elementary physico-chemical processes, but a hierarchy of parts within parts, in which each holon, from the sub-cellular organelles upward, is a closely integrated structure, equipped with self-regulatory devices, and enjoys a degree of self-government. Transplant surgery and experimental embryology provide striking illustrations for the autonomy of organismic holons.

The *integrative* powers of life are manifested in the phenomena of symbiosis between organelles, in the varied forms of partnership within the same species or between different species; in the phenomena of regeneration, in lower species, of complete individuals from their fragments; in the re-formation of scrambled embryonic organs, etc. The *self-assertive* tendency is equally ubiquitous in the competitive struggle for life.

V

TRIGGERS AND FILTERS

All the time the Guard was looking at her, first through a telescope, then through a microscope, and then through an opera-glass. At last he said, 'You're travelling the wrong way . . .'

Through the Looking-Glass

Triggers

YOU turn a switch or push a button on a machine, and this simple, effortless gesture releases the coordinated action of hundreds of wheels, pistons, levers, vacuum tubes or what have you. Such *trigger mechanisms*, where a relatively simple command or signal releases extremely complex, pre-set action-patterns, are a favourite device in biological and social organization. By this means the organism (or body social) is able to reap the full benefits of the autonomous, self-regulating character of its sub-divisions – its holons on lower levels. When the Cabinet decides to raise the Bank Rate from six per cent to seven per cent, or to send troops to a trouble-spot in the East, the decision is worded in brief, laconic terms, which merely imply, but do not specify, the intricate sequence of actions that will follow. The decision triggers various department heads and experts into activity; these will provide the first set of more specific instructions, and so on, down along the branching hierarchy to the termina units – bank clerks or paratroopers. At each step on its downward journey, the signal releases pre-set action-patterns which transform the implicit message into explicit terms, from the general into the particular. We have seen analogous processes at work in the production of articulate speech: the non-verbal, inarticulate intent of conveying a message triggers off the phrase-structuring mechanisms, which in turn bring the rules of syntax into play, and so on, down to the spelling out of the individual phonemes.

In the performance of manual skills we follow the same procedure: my conscious ego, at the apex of the hierarchy, gives out the laconic order: 'Light cigarette', and leaves it to the lower echelons in my nervous system to fill in the details by sending out a pattern of impulses, which activate sub-centres, which control the contractions of single muscles. This spelling-out process, from intention to execution, is rather like operating a series of combination locks, on different levels, in descending order. Every holon in the motor hierarchy has – like a government department – its rule-governed patterns for coordinating the motions of limbs, joints, muscles, according to the level which it occupies in the hierarchy; thus the command 'Light cigarette' does not have to specify what each of my finger muscles is supposed to do to strike a match. It merely has to trigger the appropriate centres into action, which will spell out the implicitly 'coded' command in explicit terms by activating their own sub-units in the appropriate strategic order, guided by local feedbacks. Generally speaking, *a holon on the /n/ level of the hierarchy is represented on the /n + 1/ level as a unit and triggered off as a unit.**

Like all our previous generalizations, this, too, is meant to apply to all types of hierarchies – including, for instance, the hierarchic sequence of embryonic development. This starts with a rather remarkable kind of trigger action: pricking the unfertilized egg of a virgin frog with a fine platinum needle is sufficient to initiate the growth of that egg into a normal adult frog. It has been shown that even in higher mammals like rabbits and sheep, simple mechanical or chemical stimuli can

* Or, to put it differently: the holon is a system of relations which is represented on the next higher level as a unit, ie, a relatum.

produce the same effect. Sexual reproduction is indispensable for creating variety; for mere propagation a simple trigger releaser will do.

The trigger is, of course, normally a sperm. The genetic code of the fertilized egg is said to contain the 'blueprint' of the future adult, but it would be more correct to say that it embodies a set of rules or instructions for manufacturing it. The rules are laid down in a chemical code, which comprises four letters: A, G, C and T (the initials stand for chemical substances whose long names are irrelevant to our purpose). The 'words' which these letters form on the long spirals of chromosomes in the cell nucleus contain the instructions which the cell has to follow. One of the main tasks of an embryonic cell is the manufacture of proteins required for growth. There are thousands of different proteins, but they are all made of the same building blocks: twenty different kinds of amino-acids, put together in different combinations; and each amino-acid corresponds to a 'word' of three letters in the genetic code. Thus the instructions of the implicit four-letter alphabet are 'spelled out' in the twenty-letter alphabet of amino-acids, which provides all the necessary combinations for the thousands of proteins which make an organism.

The differentiation of structures and their shaping into form in the growing embryo is a stepwise affair which has been compared to the way a sculptor carves a statue out of a piece of wood – but also to the child's acquisition of articulate and coherent speech. At each successive step, from the fertilized egg to the finished product, the overall instructions contained in the four-letter alphabet of the genetic code are first roughed in, then sketched in, and finally spelt out in elaborate detail; and each step is initiated by biochemical triggers (enzymes, inducers, hormones, and other catalysts).

How to Build a Nest

I shall have more to say about hierarchic order in embryonic development in Chapter IX; for the moment let us turn to the instinctive activities of the adult animal.* The growing organism is governed by its genetic code: in the adult organism a different type of code takes over, located in the nervous system. It incorporates the fixed 'rules of the game' which control the stereotyped rituals of courting, mating, duelling, and the much more flexible skills of building nests, hives or webs. Each of these skills can again be hierarchically 'dissected' into sub-skills, that is, functional holons, down to the level of 'fixed action-patterns' – to use Konrad Lorenz' term. In all these activities the trigger principle plays a dominant and conspicuous role. The triggers are certain stimulus patterns in the environment – sights, smells, sounds, which the ethologist calls 'releasers' or 'sign-releasers'. Thus, for instance, the nuptial colours of the stickleback (a fresh-water fish) are blue eyes and a red under-belly; and any object, regardless of its shape, that is red underneath, when brought near the territory of a male stickleback will act as a releaser for attack. The stickleback has five different methods of threatening and attacking, each triggered by a slightly different releaser. Similarly, animal species which engage in ritual tournaments – where the adversary acknowledging defeat is spared – have each a limited repertory of fighting moves, rather like the lunges, thrusts and ripostes of fencers.

W. H. Thorpe has made a detailed analysis of the functional holons which enter into the nest-building activity of the long-tailed tit. He enumerated fourteen different action-patterns (such as 'searching' and 'collecting' building materials; 'weaving', 'pressing', 'trampling', 'lining', etc), each of them

* Most activities which we call 'instinctive' are in fact partly acquired, or modified, by early learning.

consisting of simpler patterns, and triggered by at least eighteen different releasers. Instead of endlessly watching rats endlessly pressing the bar in the Skinner box, students of psychology would be well advised to study Thorpe's description, of which the following is a much abbreviated version.

The tit uses four different building materials: moss, spider's silk, lichens and feathers, each of which has a different function and requires a different kind of skilled manipulation. The activity starts with the search for a convenient site, a branch which forks in the right way. When the site is found, moss is collected and placed on the fork. Most of it falls off, but the bird persists until a few pieces have stuck. When this stage is reached, the bird switches from collecting moss to collecting spider's silk, which is rubbed on the moss until it sticks, then stretched and used for binding. These activities continue until a platform has taken shape. Now the bird switches back to moss and starts constructing the cup around it, first by 'sidewise weaving', later by 'vertical weaving' in a sitting position, steadily rotating its body as the curved rim of the cup begins to take shape. At this stage, new action-patterns make their appearance: 'breast-pressing' and 'trampling' with the feet. When the cup is about one-third complete, the bird starts collecting the third building material, lichens. These are used to cover the outside only of the nest, 'by stretching out over the rim from inside the nest and by hanging on the outside in various more or less acrobatic attitudes'. When the cup is about two-thirds completed, the building routine is changed in such a way as to leave a neat entrance-hole at the most convenient point of approach. The wall around the hole is strengthened, the dome of the nest completed, and now the furnishing can begin, using the fourth building material, feathers. Thorpe comments:

> So much for simplicity! But perhaps the most significant point of all is the evidence provided that the bird must have some 'conception' of what the completed nest should look like, and some sort

of 'conception' that the addition of a piece of moss or lichen here
and here will be a step towards the 'ideal' pattern, and that other
pieces there and there would detract from it ... Its actions are
directional and it 'knows when to stop' ...[1]

By comparing this description with Watson's description of
how Patou makes a gown ('Has he a picture in his mind? He
has not'), or with Skinner's method of conditioning pigeons,
one gets an idea of the contrast between the flat-earth view of
Behaviourism and living reality. Where, for instance, is the
indispensable 'reinforcement' – the stick and the carrot which,
according to the Behaviourist, would be required at each step
to make the bird persist in activities that include thirteen
different types of construction jobs? And yet the tit persists,
without any reward, until it has finished the nest. And how
could it be maintained that the tit is 'controlled by the contingencies of the environment' when it has to search the
environment, now for moss, now for spider's silk, now for
lichen and feathers; yet, however varied the 'contingencies of
environment', it succeeds in building the same kind of nest?
Or, take as another example, the common spider, who will
suspend its web from three, four or more points of attachment, according to the lie of the land, but will always arrive
at the same familiar symmetrical pattern, where the radial
threads bisect the laterals at equal angles, according to the
fixed canon of rules which controls its activities. How to apply
these rules to a particular environment – whether to make a
pentagonal or hexagonal web – is a matter of flexible strategy.

All instinctive activities consist of hierarchies of sub-skills –
in the spider's case the judging of angles and weaving of the
thread – controlled by fixed rules and guided by adaptable
strategies. It is this dual characteristic which justifies us in
calling a sub-skill a 'functional holon'. As such, it also has the
various other characteristics of holons previously discussed. A
skill can be exercised in the service of some larger activity and
as part of it; but virtually any skill can also become a habit

which brooks no interference and may be pursued for its own sake. In the first case, the functional holon serves the *integration* of behaviour; in the second case, it can display very marked *self-assertive* tendencies – the proverbial 'stubbornness of habits'. Whatever clever 'strategies' you use to disguise your handwriting, you cannot fool the expert and get away with it in court. The same goes for your gait, accent of speech, the use of favourite turns of phrase. Habits are behavioural holons, governed by rules which mostly operate unconsciously. Taken together, they constitute what we call personality or style. But each holon also has a margin of strategic choices, and that margin of choice increases in ascending order with the increasing complexity of higher levels. And if we ask what determines the conscious choices at the apex, we again find ourselves in a regressing series.

Filters

So far we have been concerned with 'output': the spelling out of intent into action, including the 'intent' of the fertilized egg to grow into an adult, and of a fertile idea to grow into articulate language. Before we turn to the 'input' side – sensations and perceptions – it might be useful to revert for a moment to the analogy of a military operation in old-fashioned, classical warfare.

The General in Command issues an order which contains the plan of action in broad outlines; this is transmitted from Divisional Headquarters to Brigade Headquarters to Battalion Headquarters, and so on; at each successive echelon in the hierarchy the plan is more elaborated until the last detail is filled in. The reverse process takes place in collecting information about the movements of the enemy and the lie of the land. The data are collected on the lowest, local levels by patrols reconnoitring the terrain. They are then stripped of irrelevant detail, condensed, filtered and combined with data from other sources at each higher echelon, as the stream of information flows upward along converging branches of the hierarchy. Here we have a very simplified model of the working of the sensory-motor nervous system.

On the motor side, we had a series of 'triggers'. On the perceptual side we have instead a series of 'filters' or 'scanners', through which the vital input traffic must pass on its ascent from sense-organ to cerebral cortex. Their function is to analyse, de-code, classify and abstract the information that the stream carries, until the chaotic multitude of sensations, which constantly bombard the senses, is transformed into meaningful messages.

Of most of these input-processing activities we are blissfully unaware. They are performed by a whole hierarchy of processing agencies built into the apparatus of perception. On the lowest level, there is the screening, or filtering out, of sensations that are irrelevant to the activity in hand or the mood of the moment. One is normally not aware of the pressure of the chair against one's backside, nor of the contact between skin and clothing. The eye and the ear are also equipped with such selective screening contrivances ('lateral inhibition', 'habituation', etc).

The next stage in processing is very striking – once one starts thinking about it. If you hold the index finger of the right hand ten inches, the same finger of the left hand twenty inches, in front of your eyes, you *see* them as being of equal size, although the image on the retina of one is *twice as large* as the other. People moving about in a room do not seem to shrink or grow in size – as they should – because we *know* that their size remains constant, and this knowledge somehow interferes with the visual input at some level of the nervous system, and falsifies it in the noble cause of making it conform to reality. The photographic lens has no such built-in mechanism; it will honestly show the left index finger twice as large as the right, and a sunbathing girl's foot stretched out towards the camera as a case of elephantiasis. 'Even our elementary perceptions', wrote Bartlett, 'are inferential constructs';[2] but the inferential process functions on unconscious levels of the hierarchy.

The tendency to see a familiar object as of its actual size, regardless of distance, is called by psychologists the 'size constancy phenomenon'. Not only the size but also the colour and shape of the retinal image of a moving object is all the time changing with its distance, illumination and angle of vision; yet we are mostly unaware of these changes. Accordingly, to the phenomenon of size constancy we have to add those of colour and shape constancy.

The constancies are only a part of our repertory of *perceptual skills*, which form the grammar of vision, and provide the 'rules of the game' that enable us to make sense out of the ever-changing mosaic of our sensations. Though they operate automatically and unconsciously, they can be modified by learning. When a subject in a psychological laboratory puts on inverting glasses which turn the world, including his own body, upside down, he is at first completely lost, unable to walk, and may also feel seasick. After a few days of constantly wearing the glasses he readjusts himself to living in a visually upside down world. The adjustment requires at first great conscious effort, but in the end the subject seems hardly aware that the world is upside down. The retinal image remains inverted, and so of course is its projection in the brain, but his mental image – there is no other word for it – is now the right way up; and when at this stage the glasses are taken off, it takes him some time to readjust to normality.*

Our perceptual habits are as stubborn as our motor habits. It is as difficult to alter our way of seeing the world as it is to alter our signature or accent of speech; each habit is governed by its own canon of rules. The mechanisms which determine

* This is a simplified account of a somewhat controversial subject. For details, see, for instance, Gregory[3] and Kottenhoff.[4]

our vision and hearing are part of our perceptual equipment, but operate as quasi-independent functional holons, hierarchically ordered along the entwined trees of the nervous system.

The next step upward in the hierarchy leads to the baffling phenomena of pattern-recognition – or, to put it differently, to the question how we abstract and recognize universals. When you listen to a gramophone record of an opera with, say, fifty instruments in the orchestra and four voices singing, and then look at the record with a magnifying glass, the whole magic is reduced to the single wavy, spiral curve of the groove. This poses a problem similar to that of how we interpret language (cf Chapter II). The airwaves, too, which carry the opera into the ear, have only a single variable: variations of pressure in time. The individual instruments and voices have all been superimposed on each other: violin, flute, soprano, and what have you, have been scrambled together into an acoustic porridge, and the mixture threaded out into a kind of long noodle – a single modulation pulse which makes the eardrum vibrate faster and slower with varying intensity. These vibrations are broken down in the inner ear into a sequence of pure tones, and that sequence is all that is transmitted to the brain. Any information regarding the individual instruments whose production has gone into the porridge seems to be irretrievably lost. Yet as we listen, we do not hear a succession of pure tones; we hear an ensemble of instruments and voices, each with its characteristic timbre. How this dismantling and reassembling operation is performed we understand only very imperfectly to date,* and no textbook of psychology seems to deem the matter worthy of discussion. But we know at least that the timbre of an instrument is determined by the series of partials which accompany the fundamental, and by the energy-distribution among them; together they provide the characteristic tonal

* See *The Act of Creation*, pp 516 ff.

spectrum of the instrument in question. We identify the sound of a violin or flute by reconstructing this spectrum – that is, by picking out and bracketing together its partials, which were drowned among thousands of other partials in the composite air-pulse. In other words, we abstract a stable pattern from the acoustic flux – we fish out of it the timbre of the flute – and of course the timbres of a number of other instruments. These are the listener's stable auditory holons. They in turn combine, on the higher levels of the hierarchy, into patterns of melody, harmony, counterpoint, according to more complex rules of the game. (Melody, for instance, is a pattern quite different from timbre, extracted from the same medley of sounds by tracing different variables: rhythm and pitch.)

Melody, timbre, counterpoint, are patterns in time – as phonemes, words and phrases are patterns in time. None of them makes sense – musical, linguistic, semantic sense – if considered as a linear chain of elementary units. The message of the air-pressure pulses can only be decoded by identifying the wheels within wheels, the simpler patterns integrated into more complex patterns like arabesques in an oriental carpet. The process, as already mentioned, is made to appear more mysterious by the fact that time has only a single dimension. But a single variable is sufficient to encode all music ever written – provided there is a human nervous system to de-code it. Without it the vibrations caused by the gramophone needle are just so much moving air.

However, the recognition of patterns in space presents a no less difficult problem. How does one recognize a face, a landscape, a printed word, at a glance? Even the identification of a single letter, written by various hands, in various sizes, and appearing in various positions on the retina, and hence on the optical cortex, presents an almost intractable problem for the physiologist. In order to identify the input, the brain must activate some memory-trace; but we cannot have memory-traces which match all and every conceivable variation of writing the letter /f/ – not to mention several thousand ideograms, if one happened to be Chinese. Some very complex scanning process must be involved which first identifies characteristic simpler features in the complex whole (visual holons like loops, triangles, etc); then abstracts the relations between these features; and then the relations between the relations. Our eyes are in fact constantly engaged in a variety of different types of scanning motions, of which we are unaware; and experiments show that when scanning activities are prevented, the visual field disintegrates. Scanning the visual field means translating what is simultaneously given in space into a succession of impulses in time – as the TV camera transcribes its visual field into a succession of impulses in time, which are then re-translated by the receiving set into the image on the screen. And vice versa, when we listen to speech or music, the nervous system extracts patterns in time by bracketing together the present with the reverberations of the immediate past, and with memories of the distant past, into one complex process occurring in the specious present in the three-dimensional brain. It constantly transposes temporal into spatial patterns, and spatial events into temporal sequences. In Lashley's classic dictum: 'spatial and temporal order appear to be almost completely interchangeable in cerebral action'.[5]

Thus at the series of relay stations through which the input-stream must pass, it is subjected to filtering, scanning and analysing processes, which strip it of irrelevancies, extract stable configurations from the flux of sensations, analyse and identify patterns of events in space and time. A decisive stage is the transition from the perceptual to the cognitive levels of the hierarchy – from sight and sound to meaning. The sounds of the syllables /fiu/ and /lañ/ mean nothing. They are nonsense-syllables, unrelated to each other. But a relation instantly emerges when we learn that /fiu/ means 'boy' in Hungarian, and /lañ/ means 'girl'. Once we have invested the sound of a syllable with meaning, it cannot be divested of it.

The meaning we attach to these sound-patterns is agreed by the conventions of language. But man has an irrepressible tendency to read meaning into the buzzing confusion of sights and sounds impinging on his senses; and where no agreed meaning can be found, he will provide it out of his own imagination. He sees a camel in the cloud, a face hidden in the foliage of a tree, a butterfly or an anatomical detail in the ink-blot of the Rohrschach test; he hears messages conveyed by the booming of the church bells or the rattling of carriage wheels. The sensorium extracts meaning from the chaotic environment as the digestive system extracts energy from food. If we look at a Byzantine mosaic floor, we do not perceive it as an assembly of individual stone-fragments; we automatically combine the fragments into sub-assemblies – ears, noses, draperies; and these sub-assemblies into individual figures; and these into a composite whole. And when the artist draws a human face, he follows the reverse procedure: he first roughs in the outline of the whole, then sketches in eyes, mouth, ears, as quasi-independent sub-structures, perceptual holons which can be schematized according to certain tricks and formulae.

The hierarchic principle is inherent in our modes of perception; but it can be refined by learning and practice. When an art student acquires an elementary knowledge of anatomy, it improves not the skill of his fingers, but the skill of his eye. Constable made a study of the various types of cloud formation and classified them into categories; he developed a visual 'cloud vocabulary' which enabled him to see and paint skies as nobody had done before. The trained eye of the bacteriologist or of the X-ray specialist enables him to identify the objects he is looking for, where the layman only sees shadowy blurs.

If Nature abhors the void, the mind abhors what is meaningless. Show a person an ink-blot, and he will start at once to organize it into a hierarchy of shapes, tentacles, wheels, masks, a dance of figures. When the Babylonians began to chart the stars, they first of all grouped them together into constellations of lions, virgins, archers and scorpions – shaped them into sub-assemblies, celestial holons. The first calendar-makers wove the linear thread of time into the hierarchic pattern of solar days, lunar months, stellar years, Olympic cycles. Similarly, the Greek astronomers broke up homogenous space into the hierarchy of the eight heavenly spheres, each equipped with its clockwork of epicycles.

We cannot help interpreting Nature as an organization of parts-within-parts, because all living matter and all stable inorganic systems have a part-within-part architecture, which lends them articulation, coherence and stability; and where the structure is not inherent or discernible, the mind provides it by projecting butterflies into the ink-blot and camels into the clouds.

To sum up: in motor hierarchies an implicit intention or generalized command is particularized, spelled out, step by step, in its descent to the periphery. In the perceptual hierarchy we have the opposite process: the input of the receptor organs on the organism's periphery is more and more 'de-particularized', stripped of irrelevancies during its ascent to the centre. The output hierarchy concretizes, the input hierarchy abstracts. The former operates by means of triggering devices, the latter by means of filtering or scanning devices. When I intend to write the letter R, a trigger activates a functional holon, an automatized pattern of muscle contractions which produces the letter R in my particular handwriting. When I read, a scanning device in my visual cortex identifies the letter R regardless of the particular hand that wrote it. Triggers release complex outputs by means of a simple coded signal. Scanners function the opposite way: they convert complex inputs into a simple coded signal.

VI

A MEMORY FOR FORGETTING

Mais où sont les neiges d'antan?
FRANÇOIS VILLON

'I'VE a grand memory for forgetting, David,' remarks Alan Breck in *Kidnapped*. He speaks for all of us. Our fond memories are the dregs left in the wineglass, the dehydrated sediments of perceptions whose flavour has gone. I hasten to add that there are of course exceptions to this – memories of almost hallucinatory vividness of scenes or episodes which have some special emotional significance. I shall call this the 'vivid fragment' or 'picture-strip' type of memory – as distinct from 'abstractive' memory – and come back to it later in this chapter.

Abstractive Memory

The bulk of what we are able to remember of our own life history, and of the knowledge we have acquired in its course, is of the 'abstractive' type. Take a simple example: you watch a television play. The exact words of each actor are forgotten by the time he speaks his next line, and only the meaning remains; the next morning you only remember the sequence of scenes which constituted the story; after a year you only remember that it was about a tangle between two men and a woman on a desert island. The original input has been stripped, skeletonized. Similarly with books one has read, and episodes one has lived through. As time passes, memory is more and more reduced to an outline, a condensed *abstract* of the original experience. The play you saw a month ago has been abstracted by a series of steps, each of which condenses particulars into more generalized schemata; it has been reduced to a formula. The playwright's imagination made an idea branch out into a structure divided into three acts, each divided into scenes, each consisting of smaller divisions – exchanges, phrases, words. Memory-formation reverses the process, makes the tree gradually shrink back into its roots, as in a trick film played backward.

The word 'abstract' has, in common usage, two main connotations: it is the opposite of 'concrete' in the sense that it refers to a general concept rather than a particular instance; and in the second place, an 'abstract' is a summary or condensation of the essence of a longer document, such as civil servants prepare for their superiors. Memory is abstractive in both senses.

This is, as I have already said, not the full story. If it were, we should be computers, not people. But for the moment let us consider this abstractive mechanism a little further. Memory-formation is a process continuous with perception. It has been said that if a visitor wanted to see Stalin, he had to pass through seventeen gates, from the outer Kremlin gates to the door of the innermost sanctum, and at each successive gate he was submitted to a more thorough screening. We have seen that the sensory intake is subjected to a similar scrutiny before being admitted to awareness. At every gateway of the perceptual hierarchy it is analysed, classified, stripped of all detail that is irrelevant for the purpose in hand. We recognize the letter R written in an almost illegible scrawl as 'the same thing' as a huge printed R in a newspaper headline, by a scanning process which disregards all details as irrelevant and only retains the basic geometrical R-design – the 'R-ness' of the R – as worth signalling to higher quarters. The signal can then be encoded in a kind of simple Morse. It contains all the information that matters – 'it's an R' – in condensed, skeleton-ized form, but the wealth of detail is of course lost. The scanning process is indeed the exact reverse of the triggering process.

Even those few among the multitude of stimuli constantly impinging on our senses, which have successfully passed all screenings and thus achieved the status of a consciously per-ceived event, must usually submit to a further rigorous stripping before deemed worthy to be admitted to permanent memory storage; and with the passing of time even this skeletonized abstract is subject to further decay. Anybody who tries to write a detailed chronicle of his doings during the week before last must be painfully surprised at the rate of decay, and the amount of detail irretrievably lost.

This impoverishment of lived experience is unavoidable. It is partly a matter of parsimony – although the storage capacity of the brain is probably much greater than most people make use of in their lifetime; but the decisive factor is that the processes of generalization and abstraction imply by definition the sacrifice of particulars. And if, instead of abstracting universals like 'R' or 'tree' or 'dog', memory were a collection of all our particular experiences of 'R's' and 'trees' and 'dogs' – a store of lantern-slides and tape-recordings – it would be completely useless: since no sensory input can be identical in all respects with any stored slide or recording, we would never be able to identify an R or recognize a dog or understand a spoken sentence. We could not even find our way through that immense store of particularized items. Abstractive memory, on the other hand, implies a system of stored knowledge, hierarchically ordered with headings, sub-headings and cross-references like the entries in a *Thesaurus* or the subject catalogue of a library. Some volume may have got into the wrong place, and some flashy jacket designs might stick out and catch the eye, but on the whole the order holds.

A Speculative View

Fortunately there are compensations for the unavoidable impoverishment of lived experience in the abstractive process.

In the first place the scanning process can acquire a higher degree of sophistication through learning and experience. To the novice, all red wines taste alike, and all Japanese males look the same. But he can train himself to superimpose more delicate scanners on the coarser ones, as Constable trained himself to discriminate between diverse types of clouds, and classified them into sub-categories. Thus we learn to abstract finer and finer nuances – to make the perceptual hierarchy grow new twigs, as it were.

In the second place, memory is not based on a single abstractive hierarchy, but on a variety of interlocking hierarchies – such as those of vision, taste and hearing. It is like a forest of separate trees but with entwined branches – or like our library catalogue with cross-references between different subjects. Thus the recognition of a taste is often dependent on cues provided by smell, though we may not be aware of it. But there are more subtle cross-connections. You can recognize a tune played on a violin although you have previously only heard it played on the piano; on the other hand, you can recognize the sound of a violin, although the last time a quite different tune was played on it. We must therefore assume that melody and timbre have been abstracted and *stored independently by separate hierarchies* within the same sense modality, but with different criteria of relevance. One abstracts melody and filters out everything else as irrelevant, the other abstracts the timbre of the instrument and treats melody as irrelevant. Thus not all the details discarded in the process of stripping the input are irretrievably lost, because details stripped off as irrelevant according to the criteria of one hierarchy may have been retained and stored by another hierarchy with different criteria of relevance.

The *recall* of the experience would then be made possible by the cooperation of several interlocking hierarchies, which may include different sense modalities, for instance sight and sound, or different branches within the same modality. Each by itself would provide one aspect only of the original experience – a drastic impoverishment. Thus you may remember the words only of the aria 'Your Tiny Hand is Frozen', but have lost the melody. Or you may remember the melody only, having forgotten the words. Finally, you may recognize Caruso's voice on a gramophone record, without remembering what you last heard him sing. But if two or all three of these factors are represented in the memory store, the reconstruction of the experience in recall will of course be more complete.

The process could be compared to multi-colour printing by the superimposition of several colour-blocks. The painting to be reproduced – the original experience – is photographed through different colour-filters on blue, red, and yellow plates, each of which retains only those features that are 'relevant' to it: ie, those which appear in its own colour, and ignores all other features; then they are recombined into a more or less faithful reconstruction of the original input. Each hierarchy would then have a different 'colour' attached to it, the colour symbolizing its *criteria of relevance*. Which memory-forming hierarchies will be active at any given time depends, of course, on the subject's general interests and momentary state of mind.

Memory cannot be a store of lantern-slides and tape-recordings, nor of S-R building-blocks; so much is evident. But the alternative hypothesis which I have suggested – that memory is 'dissectible' into hierarchies with different criteria of relevance – is, frankly, speculative. However, some modest evidence for it can be found in a series of experiments which

James Jenkins and I carried out in the psychological laboratory at Stanford University.*

Two Types of Memory

The 'colour-printing' hypothesis goes some way towards explaining the puzzling phenomena of recall, but it is based solely on the abstractive type of memory, which alone cannot account for the extreme vividness of the 'vivid fragments' or 'picture-strips' mentioned at the beginning of this chapter. After some forty years, I can still hear the voice of the great Austrian actor, Alexander Moissi, whispering the last words of a dying man: 'Give me the sun.' I have forgotten what the play was about, even its author – it may have been Strindberg, Ibsen or Tolstoy – except for the hallucinatory clarity of that one fragment, torn from its context. Such fragments that have survived the decay of the whole to which they once belonged – like the single lock of hair on the mummy of an Egyptian princess – have an uncanny evocative power. They may be auditory – a line from an otherwise forgotten poem, or a chance remark by a stranger overheard on a bus; or visual – a gesture of a child, a mole on a schoolmaster's face; or even refer to taste and smell, like Proust's celebrated *madeleine* (a French pastry, not a girl). 'There exists a method of retention which seems to be the opposite of memory-formation in abstractive hierarchies. It is characterized by the preservation of vivid details, which, from a purely logical point of view, are often irrelevant; and yet these quasi-cinematographic

* The results were published in a technical paper;[1] the gist of the experiment was to show to each subject for a fraction of a second only (by means of an apparatus called a tachistoscope) a number of eight or nine digits, and then let him try to repeat the sequence. The results of several hundred experiments show that a highly significant number of errors (approximately fifty per cent) consisted in the subject correctly identifying all numbers in the sequence, but inverting the order of two or three neighbouring digits. This seems to confirm that the identification of individual digits, and the determination of their sequential order, are carried out by separate branches of the perceptual hierarchy.

details, picture-strips or "close-ups", which seem to contradict the demands of parsimony, are both enduring and strikingly sharp, and add texture and flavour to memory.'[2]

But if these fragments are so irrelevant, why have they been preserved? The obvious answer is that while irrelevant from the point of view of logic, they must have some special *emotive* significance – which may be conscious or not. Indeed, such 'vivid fragments' are usually described as 'striking', 'evocative', 'nostalgic', 'frightening', or 'moving' – in a word, they are always emotionally coloured. Thus among the criteria of relevance which decide whether an experience is worth preserving, we have also to include *emotional relevance*. The reason why a particular experience should have this kind of relevance may be unknown to the subject himself; it may be symbolic or oblique.

Nobody – not even a computer theorist – thinks all the time in terms of abstractive hierarchies; emotion colours all our perceptions, and there is abundant evidence to show that emotional reactions also involve a hierarchy of levels, including some ancient structures in the brain which are phylogenetically much older than the modern structures concerned with abstract conceptualizations (see Chapter XVI). One might speculate that in the formation of picture-strip memories these older, primitive levels in the hierarchy play a dominant part. There are some further considerations in favour of such a hypothesis. Abstractive memory generalizes and schematizes, while the picture-strip particularizes and concretizes – which is a much more primitive method of storing information.*

* The term 'information' in modern communication-theory is used in a more general sense than in common parlance. It means any input which 'informs' the organism, ie, *reduces its uncertainty*. Thus information includes anything from the colour and taste of an apple to the Ninth Symphony of Beethoven. Irrelevant inputs – ie, those which do *not* reduce uncertainty – convey no information and are called 'noise' – on the analogy of a noisy telephone line.

Abstractive memory may be compared with insightful learning, the picture-strip with conditioning. It may also be related to so-called eidetic images. It has been experimentally established[3] that a considerable percentage of children have this faculty. The child is told to fixate his eyes on a picture for about fifteen seconds, and is afterwards able to see it 'projected' on an empty screen, to point out the exact location of each detail, its colour, etc. Eidetic images occupy an intermediary position between retinal after-images and what we commonly call 'memory images'; Kluever speaks of these three types or levels of visual memory, and seems to imply that they are hierarchically ordered. Unlike after-images, eidetic images can be produced at will, and after long intervals (even years). They are like hallucinations, except that the child knows that the picture he sees is not 'real'.

But though quite common in children, eidetic memory fades with the onset of puberty and is rare among adults. Children live in a world of vivid imagery: the eidetic child's way of 'imprinting' pictures on the mind may represent a phylogenetically and ontogenetically earlier form of memory-formation – which is lost when abstractive, conceptual thinking becomes dominant.

Images and Schemata

Leaving eidetics and picture-strips aside, when normal adults talk about their memory images and assert that they can literally 'see' a remembered scene or face in their mind's eye, they are usually victims of a subtle form of self-deception. One way of showing this is the Binet-Muller test. The subject is asked to concentrate on a letter-square of, say, five rows of five letters each, until he thinks that he has formed a visual image of the square which he can 'see' in his mind's eye. When the square is taken away, he can in fact fluently 'read' out the letters – or so he thinks. But when asked to 'read' the square back to front or diagonally, he will take up to ten times longer. He honestly believes that he has formed a visual image, whereas in fact he has learned the sequence by rote; if he could really 'see' the square, he could read it in all directions with equal speed and ease.

This fallacy has been known for a long time. One of the earliest students of the subject, Richard Semon (who coined the word 'mneme' for memory), wrote half a century ago that visual recall 'renders only the strongest lights and shadows'. In fact, even shadows are usually absent from visual memories, and all but the crudest shades of colour. An image is defined as 'a revived sense-experience in the absence of sensory stimulation';[4] but since most details of the experience were lost in the filtering process of memory-formation, our visual images are much vaguer and sketchier than we are wont to believe. They are skeletonized visual generalizations – outlines, patterns, schemata – abstracted from the original output by several interlocking visual hierarchies, much as the melody, the timbre of voice and the words are extracted from the Caruso aria.

We use various, often confusing, words for these optic schemata – confusing because visual configurations are not easily translated into verbal terms. Yet the caricaturist can evoke the face of Hitler or Mao by a surprisingly few strokes, which schematize what we call a 'general impression'; adding perhaps a 'vivid detail', by sticking a cigar in Churchill's mouth. When we try to describe a person's face, we use expressions like 'bony', 'humorous', 'brutal', 'sad'. Verbally, each of these attributes is extremely difficult to define; visually, they are generalizations stripped of detail, but each definable by a few strokes of a pencil: they are perceptual holons.

Recognizing a person does not mean matching his retinal image against a lantern-slide in the memory-store containing his photographic likeness; it means subjecting the input to a hierarchy of scanning devices which extract from it certain basic configurations – the 'R-nesses', so to speak. Several perceptual hierarchies may collaborate in the task. A face, or a landscape, may have a 'melody', a 'timbre', a 'message' and several other attributes. My attitude to the person or landscape will determine which aspects are to be considered as relevant to be abstracted and stored, and which to be filtered out. For purposes of *recognition*, the 'melody' alone may be sufficient. But the *recall* of the face in its absence will be the more complete the more branches of the perceptual hierarchy have participated in retaining it. The richer the network connecting them, the more effectively it will compensate for the impoverishment of experience in the process of storing it. The outstanding memories which some great men are said to have possessed may be due to this multi-dimensional way of analysing and storing experiences.*

But for the great majority of people, recall is much less of a pictorial nature than they believe – see the experiment with the letter square. We overestimate the precision of our imagery as we overestimate the precision of our verbal thinking; quite often we think that we know exactly what we want to say, but ah, when it comes to putting it on paper! We are unaware of the blurs and gaps in our verbal thinking, as we are unaware of the missing detail, the empty spaces between the visual schemata.

Learning by Rote

The dullest sort of memory, which I have not mentioned so far, consists of word-sequences which have been learned by rote. But even here we find hierarchic order. The items

* In the language of the information theorist: 'When information is put in outline form, it is easy to include information about the relations among the major parts and information about the internal relations of parts in each of the sub-outlines. Detailed information about the relations of sub-parts belonging to different parts has no place in the outline and is likely to be lost. The loss of such information and the preservation mainly of information about hierarchic order is a salient characteristic that distinguishes the drawings of a child or someone untrained in representation from the drawing of a trained artist' (Simon[5]).

memorized are not single elementary bits, but larger holons which tend to form patterns. A poem learned by heart is given coherence by patterns of rhyme, rhythm, syntax and meaning, superimposed on each other on the colour-print principle. The job of memorizing is thus reduced to fitting the patterns together and filling in the gaps they leave. The same applies to learning a piano sonata, where the structure of the musical holons – the architecture of movements, of themes and variations, development and recapitulation, rhythm and harmony – is equally obvious. Where the data to be stored show no apparent cohesion, as in the case of memorizing the dates of battles and reigns, or a string of nonsense syllables, all sorts of mnemonic devices or jingles will be invented to provide some structural pattern.

Thus even rote-learning is never purely mechanical. A certain amount of 'stamping in' by repetition is often indispensable to provide cohesion. How much 'stamping in' is needed depends on the meaningfulness of the task, and on the subject's capacity for comprehending it. At one extreme there is the dog in the Pavlovian laboratory, who needs days or weeks of monotonously repeated experiences to cotton on to the fact that the figure of an ellipse shown on a cardboard signals food, but a circle does not. No wonder – for outside the laboratory, food is not signalled by ellipses on cardboards, and the dog's perceptual hierarchies are not attuned to treating them as relevant events. Similar considerations apply to Thorndike's cats in puzzle-boxes and Skinner's pigeons. They are all given tasks to learn for which they lack the native equipment, and which they can only learn by 'stamping in'. To proclaim this procedure to be the paradigm of human learning was one of the grotesque aberrations of flat-earth psychology.*

Gestalt theorists, on the other hand, are inclined to equally extreme views of the opposite kind. They would maintain

* For a more detailed discussion, see *The Act of Creation*, Book Two, Chapter XII.

that true insightful learning excludes all trial and error and is based on a total understanding of the 'total situation'. In the present theory, insight and understanding are regarded as matters of degree, and not, as the Gestalt school holds, an all-or-nothing affair. Insight depends on the multi-dimensional analysis of the input in its various aspects, on extracting relevant messages from irrelevant noise, identifying patterns in the mosaic until it has become saturated, as it were, with meaning.

To sum up: we must assume the existence of multiple, interlocking hierarchies of perception which provide the multi-dimensionality or multi-colouration of experience. In the process of storing memories each hierarchy strips down the input to bare essentials, according to its own criteria of significance.

Recalling the experience requires dressing it up again. This is made possible, up to a point, by the cooperation of the hierarchies concerned, each of which contributes those factors which it has deemed worth preserving. The process is comparable to the superimposition of colour-plates in printing – or of the wallpaper-maker's several stencils. Added to this are touches of 'vivid detail', perhaps fragments of eidetic imagery, which carry a strong emotive charge – and the result is a kind of collage, with glass eyes and a strand of genuine hair stuck onto the hazy schematized figure.

It may also happen that fragments of different origin are mistakenly incorporated into the collage – included in the recall of experiences to which they do not belong. For memory is a vast archive of abstracts and curios, which are all the time being rearranged and revalued by the archivist; the past is constantly being re-made by the present. But most of the making and remaking is not consciously experienced. The canons of perception and memory operate instantaneously and unconsciously; we are always playing games without awareness of the rules.

VII

THE HELMSMAN

The human being is the highest self-regulating system.
IVAN PETROVICH PAVLOV

I HAVE used the terms 'interlocking' or 'interlacing' hierarchies. Of course hierarchies do not operate in a vacuum. The liver is part of the digestive, the heart of the circulatory system; but the heart is dependent on the glucose which the liver provides, and the liver depends on the correct functioning of the heart. This truism of the inter-dependence of the various processes in an organism is probably the main cause of the confusion which has obscured from view its hierarchic structure. It is as if the sight of the foliage of entwined branches in a dense forest made us forget that the branches originate in separate trees. The trees are vertical structures. The meeting points of branches from neighbouring trees form horizontal networks at several levels. Without the trees there could be no entwining, and no network. Without the network each tree would be isolated and there would be no integration of functions. Arborization and reticulation (from *reticulum* = net) seem to be complementary principles in the architecture of organisms.

To get a possible misunderstanding out of the way, I must insert here a rather obvious remark. A forest consists of a multitude of trees. A living organism is an integrated whole – a single tree. And yet I have been talking of perceptual and motor hierarchies as if they were separate entities. In fact, of course, they are merely main *branches* on the same tree, or 'sub-hierarchies'. But to call them that would be unnecessarily pedantic, as each branch of a hierarchy is itself hierarchically structured. Thus it is often convenient to regard the Foreign Office and the War Office as separate hierarchies, although they are branches of Government joined at Cabinet level.

Sensory-Motor Routines

The most obvious example of interlocking hierarchies is the sensory-motor system. The sensory hierarchy processes 'information' and transmits it in a steady flow to the conscious ego at the apex; the ego makes decisions which are spelled out by the downward stream of impulses in the motor hierarchy. But the apex is not the only point of contact between the two systems; they are connected by entwining 'networks' on various levels.

The network on the lowest level consists of so-called local reflexes. They are short-cuts between the ascending and descending flow, like loops connecting the opposite traffic streams on a motor highway: routine reactions to routine types of stimuli, like the knee-jerk, which do not require the intervention of higher mental processes. The level to which decision-making is referred depends on the complexity of the situation. The knee-jerk, or the blink-reflex, is usually completed before the stimulus has reached awareness.

One of the fundamental errors of the crude Watsonian brand of Behaviourism was the assumption that complex activities result from the summation of isolated local reflexes. We now know that the opposite is true, that local reflexes are the last to make their appearance in the development of the nervous system in the embryo: 'Behaviour develops in man ... by the expansion of a total pattern that is integrated as a whole from the beginning, and by individuation of partial patterns (reflexes) within the unitary whole' (Coghill[1]). Moreover, reflexes are influenced by higher levels of the hierarchy:

even the knee-reflex goes haywire if the patient knows what the doctor is up to. Human behaviour is not a succession of knee-jerks and eye-blinks, and any attempt to reduce it to these terms leads again to flat-earth psychology.

On the next higher level are the networks of sensory-motor skills and habits – such as touch-typing or driving a car, which are performed more or less mechanically, and do not require the attention of the highest centres – unless some disturbance throws them out of gear. Driving a car is a routine which includes, among its 'rules of the game' stepping on the brake pedal when there is an obstacle ahead. But on an icy road braking can be a risky affair, the steering wheel has a different feel, and the whole strategy of driving must be altered – transposed into a different key, as it were. After a while this, too, may become a semi-automatic routine; but let a little dog amble across the icy road in front of the driver, and he will have to make a 'top-level decision' whether to slam down the brake, risking the safety of his passengers, or run over the dog. And if, instead of a dog, the jaywalker is a child, he will probably resort to the brake, whatever the outcome. It is at this level, when the pros and cons are equally balanced, that the subjective experience of freedom and moral responsibility arises.

Feedbacks and Homeostasis

But the ordinary routines of existence do not require such moral decisions, and not even much conscious attention. The physiological processes – breathing, digestion, etc – look after themselves: they are self-regulating. And so are most routine activities: walking, bicycling, driving a car. The principle of self-regulation is in fact fundamental to the hierarchic concept. If a holon is to function as a semi-autonomous sub-whole, it must be equipped with self-regulatory devices. In other words, its operations must be guided, on the one hand, by its own fixed canon of rules and on the other hand by pointers from a variable environment. Thus there must be a constant flow of information concerning the progress of the operation back to the centre which controls it; and the controlling centre must constantly adjust the course of the operation according to the information fed back to it. This is the principle of *feedback control*.* The principle is old – James Watt had already used it in his steam-engine to keep its velocity steady under varying conditions of load. But its modern applications, under the name of *cybernetics*, have been remarkably successful in the most varied fields, from physiology to computing machines – another case of pulling lively rabbits out of an old hat.

The simplest illustration of feedback control is thermostatically regulated central heating. You set the thermostat in the living room at the desired temperature. If the temperature falls below it, the thermostat activates an electrical circuit, which in turn increases the rate of burning in the heating plant. If it gets too hot in the room, the opposite process takes place. The plant in the cellar controls the temperature in the room; but the information sent back to it by the thermostat in the room corrects the function of the plant, and keeps it steady. Another obvious example is the servo-mechanism which keeps a ship on a steady course by automatically counteracting any deviation from it. Hence the term 'cybernetics' – from the Greek *cybernitos* = helmsman.

The living organism is also controlled by a thermostatic device, which keeps its temperature at a stable level – with variations rarely exceeding one centigrade, more or less. The seat of the thermostat is in the hypothalamus, a vital structure in the brain-stem. One of its functions is to maintain *homeostasis* – a steady body temperature, pulse rate, and chemical balance of body fluids. The microscopic thermostat in the brain-stem has been shown to react to local temperature changes of a hundredth of a centigrade. When the temperature

* Feedback is generally defined as the coupling of the output to the input.

in its immediate vicinity – on the ear-drum – exceeds a critical level, sudden sweating sets in. Conversely, when the temperature falls, the muscles automatically start to shiver, converting energy into heat. Other 'homeostats' (a term coined on the analogy of the thermostat) control other physiological functions, and keep the organism's *milieu interieur* – its 'inner environment' – on a stable level.

We thus have precise evidence for self-regulating mechanisms operating at the basic levels of the hierarchy. The word 'homeostasis' was coined by Walter B. Cannon, the great Harvard physiologist, who had a clear grasp of its hierarchic implications. He wrote that homeostasis liberates the organism 'from the necessity of paying routine attention to the management of the details of bare existence. Without homeostatic devices, we should be in constant danger of disaster, unless we were always on the alert to correct voluntarily what normally is corrected automatically. With homeostatic devices, however, that keep essential bodily processes steady, we as individuals are free from such slavery – free to . . . explore and understand the wonders of the world about us, to develop new ideas and interests, and to work and play, untramelled by anxieties concerning our bodily affairs.'[2]

Self-regulating devices are found not only on the visceral level; they operate on every level of an organism's activities. A boy riding a bicycle, a tightrope-walker balancing himself with his bamboo stick, are perfect examples of *kinetic* homeostasis. But each depends on constant kinesthetic feedback – on sensations reporting the movements, tensions, postures of his own body. When the feedback stops, homeostasis breaks down. The next quotation is from Norbert Wiener, who coined the term 'cybernetics', and put the concept of feedback on the map:

A patient comes into a neurological clinic. He is not paralysed, and he can move his legs when he receives the order. Nevertheless, he suffers under a severe disability. He walks with a peculiar, uncertain gait, with eyes downcast, on the ground and on his legs. He starts each step with a kick, throwing each leg in succession in front of him. If blindfolded, he cannot stand up, and totters to the ground. What is the matter with him?

... [He] suffers from *tabes dorsalis*. The part of the spinal cord which ordinarily receives sensations has been damaged or destroyed by the late sequelae of syphilis. The incoming messages are blunted, if they have not totally disappeared. The receptors in the joints and tendons and muscles and the soles of his feet which ordinarily convey to him the position and state of motion of his legs send no messages which his central nervous system can pick up and transmit, and for information concerning his posture he is obliged to trust his eyes and the balancing organs of his inner ear. In the jargon of the physiologist, he has lost an important part of his proprioceptive or kinaesthetic sense.[3]

In other words, the patient's sensory hierarchy, which provides the feedback to the controlling centre, has been impaired. All sensory-motor skills, from riding a bicycle to touch-typing and piano-playing, operate by means of feedback loops, provided by the complex networks which connect the two branches of the hierarchy.

But let us beware of using the principle of feedback control as a magic formula which explains everything – as computer theoreticians occasionally tend to do. The concept of feedback, without the concept of hierarchic order, is like the grin without the cat. We have seen that the performance of a skill follows a pre-set pattern, according to certain rules of the game. These are fixed, but sufficiently elastic to permit constant adjustments to variable environmental conditions. Feedback can only operate within the limits of those fixed rules – the 'canon' of the skill. The part which feedback plays is to report back on every step in the progress of the operation, whether it is overshooting or falling short of the mark, how to keep it on an even keel, when to intensify the pace and when to stop. But it cannot alter the intrinsic pattern of the skill. The tit building its nest has a conception of its shape somehow represented in its nervous system – otherwise the nests of all tits would not be alike; the constant feedback it receives through eye and touch merely tells the bird when 'weaving' should stop and be followed by 'trampling', and when that should be followed by 'lining'. One of the vital differences between the S-R concept and the present theory is that according to the former, the environment determines behaviour, whereas according to the latter, feedback from the environment merely *guides or corrects or stabilizes* a pre-existing pattern of behaviour.

The primacy and autonomy of such patterns of instinct-behaviour have been strongly emphasized in recent years by ethologists like Lorenz, Tinbergen, Thorpe, etc, and by biologists like v. Bertalanffy and Paul Weiss.* Our acquired skills display the same autonomy. As I am writing these lines, I am getting a constant feedback of the pressure of pen against paper through my fingers, and of the progress of the script through my eyes. But these do not alter the pattern of my handwriting, they merely keep it on an even keel; for, even with closed eyes, my writing will merely get shaky, but its pattern will remain unmistakably the same.

Loops within Loops

So far I have talked about sensory feedback guiding motor activities. But the cross-traffic in the network works both ways, and perception is guided by the intervention of motor activities. Seeing is inextricably mixed up with motion – from the large motions of head and eyeballs, down to the involuntary minute eye motions – drift, flicker, tremor – without which we cannot see at all. Similarly with hearing: if you try

* eg, P. Weiss: 'The structure of the input does not produce the structure of the output, but merely modifies intrinsic nervous activities which have a structural organization of their own.'[4] Or, v. Bertalanffy: 'The stimulus (that is, an alteration of external conditions) does not cause a process in an internally inactive system, but rather modifies the process in an internally active system.'[5]

to recall a tune, to reconstruct its auditory image, what do you do? You hum it. The perceptual and motor hierarchies are so intimately correlated on every level that to draw a sharp distinction between 'stimulus' and 'response' becomes arbitrary and meaningless. Both have been swallowed up by feedback loops, along which impulses run in circles like kittens chasing their tails.*

Let me illustrate this by a celebrated experiment. A cat's auditory nerve was wired to an electric apparatus so that nerve impulses transmitted from the ear to the brain could be heard in a loudspeaker. A metronome was kept going in the room, and its clicks, as transmitted by the cat's auditory nerve, and amplified by the apparatus, were clearly audible. But when a mouse in a jar was brought into the room, the cat not only lost interest in the metronome, as one would expect, but the impulses in its auditory nerve became feebler or stopped altogether. This is a dramatic example of how the admission of stimuli at a peripheral receptor-organ – the outermost Kremlin gate – can be controlled from the centre.

The lesson taught by this and similar experiments can be best summed up by way of an anecdote. In the good old days before the turn of the century, Vienna had a mayor, called Lueger, who professed to a mild form of anti-semitism. But he also cultivated a number of Jewish friends. When taken to task over this by one of his cronies, Lueger gave the classic answer: '*I* am the Burgomaster, and *I* decide who is a Jew and who is not.' *Mutatis mutandum*, the cat watching the mouse and turning a deaf ear to the metronome may just as well have said: 'It's *I* who decide what is a stimulus and what is not.'

---

* 'Because stimulus and response are correlative and contemporaneous, the stimulus processes must be thought of not as preceding the response, but rather as guiding it to a successful [conclusion]. That is to say, stimulus and response must be considered as aspects of a feedback loop' (Miller et al.[6]).

A Holarchy of Holons

Let us carry this inquiry into the meaning of current terminology a step further, and ask just what that convenient word 'environment' is meant to signify.

When I am driving my car along a country road, the environment in contact with my right foot is the accelerator-pedal, and the environment in contact with my left foot is the clutch-pedal. The elastic resistance to pressure of the accelerator provides a tactile feedback which helps to keep the speed of the car steady, while the clutch controls another invisible environment, the gearbox. The feel of the wheel under my hands acts like a servo-mechanism to keep a straight course. But my eyes encompass a much larger environment than my feet and my hands; it determines the overall strategy of driving. Thus the hierarchically organized creature that I am is in fact functioning in a hierarchy of environments, guided by a hierarchy of feedbacks.

One advantage of this interpretation is that the hierarchy of environments can be extended indefinitely. When a chess player stares at the board in front of him, the environment in which his thoughts operate is determined by the distribution of chessmen on the board. Assume that the situation allows twenty possible moves permitted by the rules of the game, and that five of these look promising. He will consider each in turn. A good player may be able to think at least three moves ahead – by which time the game would have branched out into a great variety of possible situations, each of which the player must try to visualize in order to decide on his initial move. In other words, he is guided by feedbacks from an imagined board, in an imagined environment. Most of our thinking, planning and creating operates in imaginary environments.

We have seen, however, that *all* our perceptions are

coloured by imagination. Thus the difference between 'real' and 'imaginary' environments becomes a matter of degrees – or rather of levels, ranging from the unconscious phenomena of projecting figures into the Rohrschach blot, to the chess master's uncanny powers of inventing the future. Which is just another way of repeating that the hierarchy is open at the top.

To sum up this chapter in a formula, we may say that the organism in its structural and functional aspects is a hierarchy of self-regulating holons which function (a) as autonomous wholes in supra-ordination to their parts, (b) as dependent parts in sub-ordination to controls on higher levels, (c) in coordination with their local environment.

Such a hierarchy of holons should rightly be called a *holarchy* – but, remembering Ben Jonson's warning, I shall spare the reader this further neologism.

VIII

HABIT AND IMPROVIZATION

All good things which exist are the fruits of originality.
JOHN STUART MILL

THE somewhat technical character of the preceding chapters and the frequent use of engineering terms like 'input', 'output', 'triggers', 'scanners' and the rest, might have aroused in the reader the uneasy suspicion that the author is trying to replace one mechanistic model by another mechanistic model, the concept of man as a conditioned automaton by a concept of man as a hierarchic automaton. In fact, however, we are gradually – though perhaps rather painfully – moving towards a way out of the trap of mechanistic determinism. The escape hatch, so to speak, is at that 'open end' at the top of the hierarchy, to which I have repeatedly referred, although the meaning of this metaphor can emerge only gradually.

It will perhaps become a little clearer if we consider the appearance of more complex, more flexible and less predictable forms of behaviour on successively higher levels of a hierarchy. Conversely, with each step down to lower levels, we find increasingly mechanized, stereotyped and predictable behaviour-patterns. When one is writing a gossipy letter to a friend, it is difficult to foretell what will come into one's head next; the choice of possible alternatives is very large. Once you have decided what to say next, the number of alternative ways of saying it is still large, but nonetheless more restricted by the rules of grammar, the limits of one's vocabulary, etc.

Finally, the muscle-contractions, which depress the typewriter keys, are stereotyped and could as well be carried out by a robot. In the language of the physicist, we would say that *a sub-skill, or holon, on the n level of the hierarchy has more 'degrees of freedom'* (a larger variety of alternative choices permitted by the rules) *than a holon on the $(n-1)$ level.*

Let me briefly recapitulate some points from earlier chapters: every skill (or habit) has a fixed and a variable aspect. The former is determined by its canon, the 'rules of the game', which lend it its characteristic pattern – whether the game is making a spider's web, constructing a bird's nest, ice-skating, or playing chess. But the rules permit a certain variety by alternative choices: the web can be suspended from three or four points of attachment, the nest can be adjusted to the angle of the fork in the branch, the chess-player has a vast choice among permissible moves. These choices, having been left open by the rules, depend on the lie of the land, the local environment in which the holon operates – they are a matter of strategy, guided by feedbacks. Put in a different way, the fixed code of rules determines the permissible moves, flexible strategy determines the choice of the actual moves among the permissible ones. The larger the number of alternative choices, the more complex and flexible the skill. Vice versa, if there is no choice at all, we reach the limit case of the specialized reflex. Thus *rigidity* and *flexibility* are opposite ends of a scale which applies to every type of hierarchy; and in every case we shall find that flexibility increases, rigidity decreases, as we move upward to higher levels.

The Origins of Originality

In the *instinctive behaviour* of animals, we find at the bottom end of the scale monotonously repeated patterns of courting and threatening, mating and fighting – rigid, compulsive rituals. Sometimes, when the animal is frustrated, these rituals are performed pointlessly on the wrong occasion. Cats will go through the motion of burying their faeces on the kitchen tiles. Young squirrels, reared in captivity, when given nuts will go through the motions of burying them in the bottom of the wire cage, 'and then go away contented, even though the nuts are exposed to full view' (Thorpe[1]).

At the opposite end of the scale we find very complex and flexible skills displayed by mammalians like chimpanzees and dolphins – but also by insects and fishes. Ethologists have produced impressive evidence to show that under favourable circumstances even insects are capable of behaving in ways which could not be predicted from the creature's known repertory of skills, and which fully deserve to be called 'ingenious' or 'original'. Professor Baerends, for instance,* has spent years on an exhaustive study of the activities of the digger wasp.[1a] The female of this species lays her eggs in holes which she digs in the ground. She provisions the holes first with caterpillars then, when the eggs have hatched, with moth larvae; then with more caterpillars, until she finally closes the hole. Now the point is that each female has to look after several holes at the same time, the inhabitants of which are in different phases of development, and thus need different diets. She not only provides each according to its needs, but when a hole is robbed of its supplies by the experimenter, promptly replenishes it. Another wasp builds clusters of clay-cells, lays an egg in each, provides it with provisions for the future, then seals the cell – much as the Egyptians used to do with Pharaoh's burial chambers. If now the experimenter makes a hole in the cell – something quite unprecedented in the wasp's scheme of things – she will first pick up the cater-pillars which have fallen out, and stuff them back through the hole, then set about mending the cell with pellets of clay – a repair job which she has never done before. But that is not the end of it. Hingston has described the exploits of another type

* A participant in the Stanford Seminar.

of wasp in a crisis. He made a hole in a cell in a fiendish way, so that it could not be repaired from the outside. But this species of wasp always works from the outside. The wasp wrestled with the task for two hours, until night came and she had to give up. Next morning she flew straight to the damaged cell, and set about repairing it by a new method: 'she examines it from both sides and then, having made a choice, elects to do the repair from *within*.'[2]

I have deliberately chosen these examples of improvisation by *insects* because the flexible skills of the higher mammalians are more familiar. Even *fishes*, according to Thorpe, can change their habits: 'If their normal behaviour-pattern is continually interfered with, quite large modifications in the normal instinctive orientation may be made.'[3] As for *birds*, in some species the male, who normally never feeds the young, starts doing so in the absence of the female. Lastly, I must briefly mention Lindauer's study of the honey-bee. We all know about von Frisch's discovery of the dance-language of the bee, but this is something different. Under normal conditions, there is rigid division of labour in the hive, so that each worker is occupied on different jobs in different periods of her life. During her first three days she cleans the cells. For the next three days she feeds the older larvae with honey and pollen. After that she feeds the younger larvae (who require an additional diet). From the age of ten days she is engaged in building cells; at twenty days she takes over guard-duties at the entrance of the hive; finally she becomes a forager, and remains one for the rest of her life.

That is, if all goes well. However, if any of the specialized age groups is taken away from the colony by the experimenter, other age groups take over their duties 'and thus save the super-organism. When, for instance, all foragers are taken away – usually bees of twenty days or over – young bees of scarcely six days old, who normally would feed the larvae, fly out and become foragers. If all building workers are taken away, their task is taken on by older bees who have already been builders before, but who had gone on to the stage of forager. To this end they not only change their behaviour, but also regenerate the wax-glands. The mechanisms of these regulations are not known.'[4]

Thus at one end of the scale we find fixed action-patterns and rigid compulsive rituals; at the other end surprising improvizations, and the performance of feats which seem to go far beyond the animal's repertory of habitual skills.

The Mechanization of Habits

In man, innate instincts are merely the foundation on which learning will build. While learning a skill we must concentrate on every detail of what we are doing. We learn laboriously to recognize and name the printed letters of the alphabet, to ride a bicycle, to hit the right key on the typewriter or on the piano. Then learning begins to condense into habits: with increasing mastery we read, write, type 'automatically', which means that the rules which control the performance are now applied unconsciously. Like the invisible machinery which transforms inarticulate thoughts into grammatically correct sentences, so the canons of our manipulative and reasoning skills operate below the level of awareness, or in the twilight zones of awareness. We are obeying the rules without being able to define them. In so far as our reasoning skills are concerned, this situation has its obvious dangers: the axioms and prejudices built into the canon act as 'hidden persuaders'.

There are two sides to this tendency towards the progressive mechanization of skills. On the positive side, it conforms to the principle of parsimony or 'least action'. By manipulating the wheel of the car mechanically I can give all my attention to the traffic around me; and if the rules of grammar did not function automatically, like a programmed computer, we could not attend to meaning.

Mechanization, like *rigor mortis*, affects first the extremities – the lowest subordinate branches of the hierarchy. But it also has a tendency to spread upward. To be able to hit the right key of the typewriter 'by pure reflex' is extremely useful, and a rigid observance of the laws of grammar is an equally good thing; but a rigid style composed of clichés and prefabricated turns of phrases, although it enables civil servants to get through a greater volume of correspondence, is certainly a mixed blessing. And if mechanization spreads to the apex of the hierarchy, the result is the rigid pedant, slave of his habits – Bergson's *homme automate*. First, learning has condensed into habit as steam condenses into drops; then the drops have frozen into icicles. As v. Bertalanffy wrote: 'Organisms *are not* machines, but they can to a certain extent *become* machines, congeal into machines. Never completely, however, for a thoroughly mechanized organism would be incapable of reacting to the incessantly changing conditions of the outside world.'[5]

One Step at a Time

Thus the mechanization of habits can never transform even an 'organization man' into an automaton; but conversely, the conscious ego can interfere to only a limited extent with the automatic functioning of the subordinate units of his body and mind. The driver at the wheel can control the speed of his engine, but has no power to interfere with the order in which the cylinders fire, the valves open and close; and the conscious ego is in a similar position. It has no control whatsoever over functions on the sub-cellular or cellular level. It has no direct control over smooth muscles, viscerae and glands. Even the coordination of 'voluntary' skeletal muscles is only to a limited extent under conscious control: one cannot alter at will one's characteristic gait, gestures, handwriting.

We have seen that when a conscious intent is formed at the apex of the hierarchy, such as 'Unlock that door' or 'Sign that letter', it does not activate individual muscle contractions, but triggers off patterns of nerve impulses which activate sub-patterns, and so on, down to the single motor units. But this can only be done one step at a time. The higher centres in the hierarchy do not normally have direct dealings with lowly ones, and vice versa. Brigadiers do not concentrate their attention on individual soldiers, and do not give them direct orders; if they did, the whole operation would go haywire. Commands must be transmitted by what the army calls 'regulation channels' – ie, step by step down the levels of the hierarchy. Attempts to short-circuit the intermediary levels – to turn the focal beam of awareness on the obscure and anonymous routines of lowly holons – usually end in the paradox of the centipede. When the centipede was asked in which precise order he moved his hundred legs, he became paralysed and starved to death, because he had never thought of it before, and had left it to the legs to look after themselves. We would share a similar fate if asked to explain how we ride a bicycle.

The paradox of the centipede derives from a breach of what one might call the 'one step at a time rule'. On the face of it it looks trivial; but it leads to some unexpected consequences, if we try to go against it. Thus the pseudo-explanations of language as the manipulation of the vocal cords or the chaining of operants leave a gaping hole between thinking and spelling, between the apex of the tree and its terminal branches. The rule also has some applications to psychopathology – from the awkward condition we call (by a misnomer) self-consciousness, to psychosomatic disorders. Self-consciousness (gaucheness, stage fright) results when conscious attention interferes with routines which under normal conditions are performed unconsciously and automatically. More serious disorders can result when attention is concentrated on physiological processes which function on even more primitive levels of the hierarchy, such as digestion and sex, and which must be left 'to look after themselves' if they are to function smoothly. Psychological impotence or frigidity, and spastic colons, are distressing variations of the paradox of the centipede.

Loss of direct control over processes on lower levels of the body hierarchy is part of the price paid for differentiation and specialization. The price is of course worth paying so long as the individual lives under fairly normal conditions, and can safely rely on his more or less automatized routines. But conditions may arise when this is no longer the case, and it becomes imperative to break with routine.

The Challenge of Environment

This brings us to a point of vital importance which I have so far not mentioned: the influence of the environment on the flexibility or rigidity of behaviour.

If a skill is practised in the same unvarying conditions, following the same unvarying course, it tends to degenerate into stereotyped routine, and its degrees of freedom freeze up. Monotony accelerates enslavement to habit; it makes the *rigor mortis* of mechanization spread upward in the hierarchy.

Vice versa, a changing variable environment demands flexible behaviour, and reverses the trend towards mechanization. The skilled driver on the familiar road from his home to his office hands over to the automatic pilot in his nervous system, while his thoughts are somewhere else; but if he gets into a tricky traffic situation, he will suddenly concentrate on what he is doing – the man takes over from the computer. However, the challenge of the environment can exceed a critical limit where it can no longer be met by skilled routine, however flexible – because the customary 'rules of the game' are no longer adequate to cope with the situation. Then a crisis arises. The outcome is either a *breakdown* of behaviour –

'when in danger or in doubt, run in circles, scream and shout'. The hierarchy has disintegrated. The alternative possibility is the sudden emergence of *new* forms of behaviour, of original solutions – which, as we shall see, play a vital part in both biological evolution and mental progress.

The first possibility is demonstrated by the cat which, unable to comply with the strict rules of its canon of hygiene, goes through the pointless motions of trying to bury the mess under the hard kitchen tiles. Human beings in a crisis are capable of equally senseless behaviour, repeating the same hopeless attempts to get out of it.

The alternative possibility is demonstrated by the unexpected improvizations of the digger-wasp, the reorganization of labour in the mutilated beehive – or a chimpanzee breaking a branch from a tree to rake in a banana beyond the reach of its arm. 'Original adaptations' of this kind, to meet challenges of an exceptional nature, point to the existence of unsuspected potentials in the living organism, which are dormant in the normal routines of existence. They foreshadow the phenomena of human creativity, to be discussed in Chapter XIII.

Summary

On successively higher levels of the hierarchy we find more complex, flexible and less predictable patterns of activity, while on successively lower levels we find more and more mechanized, stereotyped and predictable patterns. In the language of the physicist, a holon on a higher level of the hierarchy has more degrees of freedom than a holon on a lower level.

All skills, whether derived from instinct or learning, tend with increasing practice to become mechanized routines. Monotonous environments facilitate enslavement to habit; while unexpected contingencies reverse the trend, and may result in ingenious improvisations. Critical challenges may lead to a break-down of behaviour or to the creation of new forms of behaviour.

The higher echelons in a hierarchy do not normally communicate directly with lowly ones, but through 'regulation channels', one step at a time. A short-circuiting of intermediary levels may cause disorders of various kinds.

PART TWO

BECOMING

IX

THE STRATEGY OF EMBRYOS

Benjamin Franklin's reply to a lady who queried the usefulness of his work on electricity: 'Madam, what use is a new-born baby?'

THE classical Darwinian answer to the question how man was created out of a blob of slime is much the same as Watson's answer to the question how Patou creates a gown out of a piece of silk: 'He pulls it in here, he pulls it out there, makes it tight or loose at the waist ... He manipulates his material until it takes on the semblance of a dress ...'. The evolutionary process is supposed to operate by similar random manipulations of its raw material – pulling it in here, pushing it out there, putting a tail on here, putting an antler there – until 'a pattern is hit upon', fit to survive.

Flat-earth science explains mental evolution by random tries, preserved by selective reinforcement (the stick and the carrot), and biological evolution by random mutations (the monkey at the typewriter) preserved by natural selection. *Mutations* are defined as spontaneous changes in the molecular structure of genes, and are said to be *random* in the sense that they have no relation whatsoever to the organism's adaptive needs. Accordingly the great majority of mutations must have harmful effects, but the few lucky hits are preserved because they happen to confer some small advantage on the individual; and given sufficient time, 'anything at all will turn up'. 'The hoary objection', Sir Julian Huxley wrote, 'of the improbability of an eye or a hand or a brain being evolved by "blind chance" has lost its force' – because 'natural selection operating over the stretches of geological time'[1] explains everything.

In fact, however, the hoary objection has been steadily gaining in force during the mid-century decades – so much so that there is hardly a prominent evolutionist alive who has not expressed some heretical views concerning some particular aspect of the orthodox doctrine – while staunchly rejecting the heresies of others. Although these criticisms and doubts have made numerous breaches in the walls, the citadel of neo-Darwinian orthodoxy still stands – mainly, one supposes, because nobody has had a satisfactory alternative to offer. The history of science indicates that a well-established theory can take a lot of battering and get into a tangle of absurdities and contradictions, yet still be upheld by the Establishment until an acceptable global alternative is offered.* But historically the only serious challenge to neo-Darwinism came from Lamarckism; and Lamarckism had much valid and scathing criticism, but no constructive alternative to offer.

Indeed, for nearly a hundred years, the theorists of evolution have been fighting an embittered Civil War of Lamarckian Roundheads versus Darwinist Cavaliers. The actual dispute was of a complex, technical character; but it was highly charged with metaphysical, emotional and even political implications. In the Soviet Union, the Darwinian Cavaliers were summarily sent to labour camps under Stalin, and the survivors summarily rehabilitated under Khrushchev: an episode known as the 'Lysenko affair'. The main issue – over-simplified and put in a nutshell – is this: Lamarck believed that the adaptive modifications of physique and ways of life, which an animal acquires to cope more effectively with its environment, are transmitted by heredity to the offspring ('inheritance of acquired characteristics'). Thus if a boxer develops strong muscles by training, then his son, according

---

* See Thomas Kuhn's thesis of 'Paradigm-Change'[16], and the chapter on 'The Evolution of Ideas' in *The Act of Creation*.

to Lamarck, ought to be born with strong muscles. This would provide a sensible and reassuring view of evolution as the cumulative result of learning through experience and training for a better life; but unfortunately, as so often happens, the commonsense view turned out to be inadequate. To this day, in spite of great efforts, Lamarckism has failed to produce conclusive evidence to prove that acquired characters are transmitted to the offspring; and it seems fairly certain that, while experience does affect heredity, it does not do so in this simple and direct way.

But the failure of Lamarckism in its primitive form does not mean that the monkey at the typewriter is the only alternative to choose. Random mutations, preserved by natural selection, without doubt play a part in the evolutionary process – just as lucky coincidences play a part in the evolution of science. The question is whether this is the whole truth, or even the most important part of the truth.

A number of corrections and amendments to neo-Darwinian theory have been proposed by evolutionists over a number of years; and if these were to be put together, there would be little left of the original theory – as amendments to a Parliamentary bill can reverse its emphasis and intent. But, as already said, each critic had his particular axe to grind, with the result that 'Tis all in pieces, all coherence gone' – as John Donne lamented when medieval cosmology was landed in a similar crisis. In this and the next three chapters I shall collect some of these bits and pieces, and attempt to fit them together.

Docility and Determination

It takes fifty-six generations of cells to produce a human being out of a single, fertilized egg-cell. This is done in a series of steps, each of which involves (a) the multiplication of cells by division, and the subsequent growth of the daughter-cells; (b) the structural and functional specialization of cells (differentiation); and (c) the shaping of the organism (morpho-genesis). Needless to say, all three are complementary aspects of a unitary process.

Morphogenesis proceeds in an unmistakably hierarchic fashion. The development of the embryo from a shapeless blob to a roughed-in form, and through successive stages of increasing articulation, follows the familiar pattern described in previous chapters; I have mentioned the analogies with the sculptor, who carves a figure out of a block of wood, and with the spelling out of an amorphous idea into articulate phonemes. The step-by-step differentiation of cell-groups up to their

FIGURE 5

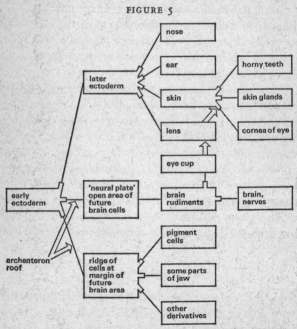

(after Clayton[2]). Diagram of some of the pathways open to early ectoderm in the amphibian embryo. Three only of the many inductive relationships are indicated by arrows

ultimate specialization presents the same hierarchically arborizing picture. See Figure 5.

The diagram schematizes some of the developmental possibilities of the ectoderm in the amphibian embryo. (The ectoderm is the outermost of the three layers of cell-populations into which the embryo differentiates at an early stage; the other two are mesoderm and endoderm.) The arrows on the left side of the diagram indicate the action of certain adjacent tissues ('inducers') which, when brought into contact with the ectoderm, act as *chemical triggers* on it. Those regions of the ectoderm which are in direct contact with the inducer-tissue will differentiate by stages into the animal's nervous system, including brain and eye-cups. Other regions of the ectoderm will, owing to their different surroundings, specialize in other ways. If a cell-population develops into 'skin', it may further specialize into sweat glands, horny layers, and so on. At each step biochemical *triggers* and *feedbacks* determine which of the alternative developmental pathways among several possibles a group of cells will actually follow.

Thus, when the eye-cups (the future retina), which grow out of the brain at the end of two stalks (the future optic nerves), make physical contact with the surface, the skin over the contact area folds into the concave cups and differentiates into transparent lenses (see arrows on the right of the diagram). The eye-cup induces the skin to form a lens, and the lens in its turn induces adjacent tissues to form a transparent horny membrane, the cornea. Moreover, if an eye-cup is transplanted under the skin on the belly of a frog embryo, the skin over it will obligingly differentiate into a lens. We may regard this obligingness or 'docility' of embryonic tissue, its readiness to differentiate into the kind of organ best suited to the tissue's position in the growing organism, as a manifestation of the *integrative tendency*, of the part's subordination to the interests of the whole.

But 'docility' is again only one side of the picture; the other is 'determination'. Both are technical terms. 'Docility' means the multipotential capacity of embryonic tissue to follow this or that branch of the developmental hierarchy according to circumstances. But along each branch there is a point of no return, where the next developmental stage of the tissue is 'determined' in an irreversible way. If, at the earliest, so-called 'cleavage stage' of its development, a frog-embryo is split into two, each half will develop into a complete frog, not, as it normally would, into a half frog. At this stage each cell, though it is a *part* of the embryo, has retained the genetic potential to grow, if need be, into a *whole* frog – it is a true, Janus-faced holon. But with each step of development along the branching tree, the successive cell-generations become more specialized, and the developmental 'choices' before a given cell-tissue – its genetic potential – become more and more restricted. Thus a piece of the ectoderm may still have the potentiality to develop into a cornea or skin-gland, but not into a liver or lung. Specialization, here as in other fields, leads to a decrease in flexibility. One might compare the process with the series of curricular choices which face the student, from the first broad alternative between Science and the Humanities, to the final 'determination' which turns him into a marine zoologist specializing in echinoderms. At each point of decision, where the pathways diverge, some minor hazard or incident may act as a trigger which 'induces' him to make this or that alternative choice. After a while, each decision becomes to a large extent irreversible. Once he has become a zoologist, there are still numerous pathways of specialization open to him; but he can hardly retrace his steps and become a barrister or a theoretical physicist. Here, too, the 'one-step rule' of hierarchies applies.

Once the future of a tissue's development is decided, it can behave in a strikingly 'determined' way. At the gastrular stage, when the embryo still looks like a partly infolded sac, it is nevertheless possible already to tell which organs each region will produce. If at this early stage a piece of tissue from an amphibian embryo, which would normally give rise to an eye, is transplanted onto the tail end of another, older embryo, it will become, not an eye, but a kidney-duct or some other organ characteristic of that region. But at a later stage in the embryo's growth, this docility of the presumptive eye-region is lost, and no matter to what location it is transplanted, it will develop into an eye – even on the host's thigh or belly. When a cell-group has reached this stage, it is called a morphogenetic field, organ primordium, or bud, as the case may be. Not only the future eye, but a limb-bud too, transplanted to a different position (on the same, or on another embryo), will form a complete organ; even a heart may be formed on the host's flank. This 'ruthless' determination of morphogenetic fields to assert their individuality reflects, in our terminology, the *self-assertive principle* in development.

Each morphogenetic field or organ primordium displays the holistic character of an autonomous unit, a self-regulating holon. If half of the field's tissue is cut away, the remainder will form not half an organ but a complete organ. If, at a certain stage of its development, the eye-cup is split into several isolated parts, each fragment will form a smaller, but normal, eye; and even the artificially scrambled and filtered cells of a tissue will, as we have seen (page 87), re-form again.

These autonomous, self-regulating properties of holons within the growing embryo are a vital safeguard; they ensure that whatever accidental hazards arise during development, the end-product will be according to norm. In view of the millions and millions of cells which divide, differentiate, and move about in the constantly changing environment of fluids and neighbouring tissues – Waddington called it 'the epigenetic landscape' – it must be assumed that no two embryos, not even identical twins, are formed in exactly the same way. The self-regulating mechanisms which correct deviations from the norm and guarantee, so to speak, the end-result, have been compared to the homeostatic feedback devices in the adult organism – so biologists speak of 'developmental homeostasis'. The future individual is potentially predetermined in the chromosomes of the fertilized egg; but to translate this blueprint into the finished product, billions of specialized cells have to be fabricated and moulded into an integrated structure. The mind boggles at the idea that the genes of that one fertilized egg should contain built-in provisions for each and every particular contingency which every single one of its fifty-six generations of daughter cells might encounter in the process. However, the problem becomes a little less baffling if we replace the concept of the 'genetic blueprint', which implies a plan to be rigidly copied, by the concept of a genetic *canon of rules* which are fixed, but leave room for alternative choices, ie, flexible strategies guided by feedbacks and pointers from the environment. But how can this formula be applied to the development of the embryo?

The Genetic Keyboard

The cells of an embryo, all of identical origin, differentiate into such diverse products as muscle cells, several varieties of blood cells, a great variety of nerve cells, and so on, in spite of the fact that each of them carries the same set of hereditary instructions in its chromosomes. The activities of the cell, whether in embryo or adult, are controlled by the genes located in the chromosomes.* But since we have evidence that *all* cells in the body, whatever their function, contain the *same* complete set of chromosomes, how can a nerve cell and a kidney cell fulfil such different tasks, if they are governed by the same set of laws?

A generation ago the answer to this question seemed to be simple. I shall put it into a somewhat frivolous analogy. Let

---

* To complicate matters, there also exist cytoplasmic carriers of heredity, but for our present purpose these can be left out of account.

the chromosomes be represented by the keyboard of a grand piano – a very grand piano with thousands of keys. Then each key will be a gene. Every cell in the body carries a microscopic but complete keyboard in its nucleus. But each specialized cell is only permitted to sound one chord, according to its speciality – the rest of its genetic keyboard has been inactivated by scotch tape. The fertilized egg, and the first few generations of its daughter cells, had the complete keyboard at their disposal. But successive generations have, at each 'point of no return', larger and larger areas of it covered by scotch tape. In the end, a muscle cell can only do one thing: contract – strike a single chord.

The scotch tape is known in the language of genetics as the 'repressor'. The agent which strikes the key and activates the gene is an 'inducer'. A mutated gene is a key which has gone out of tune. When quite a lot of keys have gone quite a lot out of tune, the result, we were asked to believe, was a much improved, wonderful new melody – a reptile transformed into a bird, or a monkey into a man. It seems that at some point the theory must have gone wrong.

The point where it went wrong was the atomistic concept of the gene. At the time when genetics got into its stride, atomism was in full bloom: reflexes were atoms of behaviour, and genes were atomic units of heredity. One gene was responsible for the colour of the eyes, a second for smooth or kinky hair, a third for causing bleeding sickness; and the organism was regarded as a collection of these mutually independent unitcharacters – a mosaic of elementary bits, put together in the manner of Mekhos' watches. But by the middle of our century, the rigidly atomistic concepts of Mendelian genetics had become considerably softened up. It was realized that a single gene may affect a wide range of different characteristics (pleiotropy); and vice versa, that a great number of genes may interact to produce a single characteristic (polygeny). Some trivial characters – like the colour of the eyes – may depend on a single gene, but polygeny is the rule, and the basic features of the organism depend on the totality of genes – the gene-complex or 'genome' as a whole.

In the early days of genetics, a gene could be 'dominant' or 'recessive', and that was about all there was to it; but gradually more and more terms had to be added to the vocabulary: repressors, apo-repressors, co-repressors, inducers, modifier genes, switch genes, operator genes which activate other genes, and even genes which regulate the rate of mutations in genes. Thus the action of the gene-complex was originally conceived as the unfolding of a simple linear sequence like that on a tape-recorder or the Behaviourist's conditioned-reflex chain; whereas it is now gradually becoming apparent that *the genetic controls operate as a self-regulating micro-hierarchy*, equipped with feedback devices which guide their flexible strategies.* This not only protects the growing embryo against the hazards of ontogeny; it would also protect it against the evolutionary hazards of phylogeny, or random mutations in its own hereditary materials – the blind antics of the monkey at the typewriter.

At the time of writing, this kind of suggestion still meets with scepticism among the hard core of orthodox geneticists – mainly, perhaps, because its acceptance must lead to a decisive shift of emphasis in our conception of the evolutionary process, as we shall see in the next chapter. But atomism, at least, is on its way out; it is encouraging to read, for instance, a passage like the following, quoted from a recent textbook for college students:

> All genes in the total inherited message tend to act together as an integrated whole in the control of [embryonic] development ... It is easy to fall into the habit of thinking that an organism has a set number of characteristics with one gene controlling each character. This is quite incorrect. The experimental evidence indicates clearly

* Significantly, Waddington calls his important book on theoretical biology *The Strategy of the Genes* (1957).

that genes never work altogether separately. Organisms are not patchworks with one gene controlling each of the patches. They are integrated wholes, whose development is controlled by the entire set of genes acting cooperatively.[3]

Since differentiation and morphogenesis proceed in hierarchic steps, this cooperative activity of the gene-complex must also proceed in a hierarchic order. The gene-complex is enclosed in the nucleus of the cell. The nucleus is surrounded by the cell-body. The cell-body is enclosed by a membrane, which is surrounded by body fluids and by other cells, forming a tissue; this, in turn, is in contact with other tissues. In other words, the gene complex operates in a *hierarchy of environments* (page 125).

Different types of cells (brain cells, muscle cells, etc) differ from each other in the structure and chemistry of their cell-bodies. The differences are due to the interaction between gene-complex, cell-body and the cell's environment. In each growing and differentiating tissue a different portion of the total gene-complex is active – only that branch of the gene-hierarchy which is concerned with the functions assigned to the tissue in question; the remainder of the genes is 'switched off'. And if we inquire into the nature of the agency which switches genes on and off, we find once more the familiar devices of triggers and feedbacks. The 'triggers' are the chemical 'inducers', 'organizers', 'operators' and 'repressors', etc, already mentioned. Needless to say, the way they work is only very imperfectly understood, and the proliferation of new terms is sometimes just a convenient method to mask our ignorance of details. But we know at least the broad principles involved. It is a process running in circles – in circles which get narrower, like the coils of a spiral, as the cell becomes more and more specialized. The genes control the activities of the cell by relatively simple coded instructions which are spelt out in the complex operations of the cell-body. But the activities of the genes are in turn guided by feedbacks from the cell-body, which is exposed to the hierarchy of environments. This contains, apart from chemical triggers, a number of other factors in the 'epigenetic landscape' which are relevant to the cell's future, and about which the genes must be informed. To use a term proposed by James Bonner,[4] the cell must be able to 'test' its neighbours 'for strangeness or similarity, and in many other ways'. By feeding back information on the lie of the land to the gene-complex, the cytoplasm thus co-determines which genes should be active and which should be temporarily or permanently switched off.

Thus ultimately a cell's fate depends on its position in the growing embryo – its exact location in the epigenetic landscape. Cells which are members of the same morphogenetic field (for instance, a future arm) must have the same genetic orchestration and behave like parts of a coherent unit; and their further specialization into 'solo players' (individual fingers) will again depend on their position *within* the field. Each organ-bud is a Janus-faced holon: relative to its earlier stages of development its destiny as a whole is irrevocably determined; but relative to the future, its parts are still 'docile' and will differentiate along the developmental pathway best suited to their local environments. 'Determination' and 'docility', self-assertive and integrative potential, are two sides of one medal (and so are, in the terminology of a hoary controversy among biologists, 'regulative' and 'mosaic' development).

In the types of hierarchies discussed before, the time factor played a relatively subordinate part. In the developmental hierarchy, the apex is the fertilized egg, the axis of the branching tree is the progress of time, and the levels of the hierarchy are successive stages of development. The structure of the growing embryo at any given moment is a cross-section at right angles to the time axis, and the two faces of Janus are turned towards the past and the future.

Summary

The purpose of this chapter was not to give a description of embryonic development, but to point out the basic principles which this development has in common with other forms of hierarchic processes discussed in previous chapters. J. Needham once coined a phrase about 'the striving of the blastula to grow into a chicken'. One might call the ensemble of devices which make it succeed the organism's 'pre-natal skills'. To quote James Bonner again: 'We know that nature, like man, accomplishes complex tasks by breaking them up into many simple sub-tasks.'[5] Development, maturation, learning and acting are continuous processes, and we must expect therefore that pre-natal and post-natal skills are governed by the same general principles.

Some of these principles,* which we found reflected in embryonic development, were: the hierarchically branching order of differentiation and morphogenesis; the 'dissectibility' of that order into self-regulating holons at various levels (stages); their Janus character (autonomy versus dependence, determination versus docility); their fixed genetic canons and adaptable strategies guided by feedbacks from the hierarchy of environments; the action of triggers (inducers, etc), which release pre-set mechanisms, and of scanners ('tests') which process information; the decrease of flexibility with increasing differentiation and specialization. Lastly, we found earlier on that the canon of fixed rules which governs a skill is a 'hidden persuader', which operates automatically or instinctively. *Mutatis mutandis*, we may say that an analogous relation prevails between the genetic code of ancient origin and the 'pre-natal skills' of the growing embryo.

* I would like to remind the reader that a summary of these principles can be found in Appendix I.

X

EVOLUTION:
THEME AND VARIATIONS

I refuse to believe that God plays dice with the world.
ALBERT EINSTEIN

IN THE last chapter we were concerned with ontogeny – the development of the individual. We can now turn to phylogeny, and the crucial problem of evolutionary progress.

The orthodox ('neo-Darwinian' or 'synthetic') theory attempts to explain all evolutionary changes by random mutations (and re-combinations) of genes; most mutations are harmful, but a very small proportion happens to be useful and is retained by natural selection. As already mentioned, 'randomness' means in this context that the hereditary changes wrought by mutation are totally unrelated to the animal's adaptive needs – that they may alter its physique and behaviour 'in any and every direction'. In this view, evolution appears as a game of blind man's buff. Or, in the words of Professor Waddington – a quasi-Trotskyite member of the Establishment whom I shall have occasion to quote repeatedly in this chapter: 'To suppose that the evolution of the wonderfully adapted biological mechanisms has depended only on a selection out of a haphazard set of variations, each produced by blind chance, is like suggesting that if we went on throwing bricks together into heaps, we should eventually be able to choose ourselves the most desirable house.'[1]

To illustrate the point, here is a simple example. The giant panda – mascot of the World Wildlife Fund – has on its forelimbs an added sixth finger, which comes in very 'handy' for manipulating the bamboo-shoots which are its principal food. But that added finger would be a useless appendage without the proper muscles and nerves. The chances that among all possible mutations those which produced the additional bones, muscles and nerves should have occurred independently in the same population are of course infinitesimally small. And yet in this case there are only three variable factors involved. If we have, say, twenty factors (which is still a modest estimate for the evolution of a complex organ), the odds against their simultaneous alteration by chance alone become absurd, and instead of scientific explanations, we should be trading in miracles.

Let us look at a less primitive example. The vertebrates' conquest of dry land started with the evolution of reptiles from some primitive amphibian form. The amphibians reproduced in the water, and their young were aquatic. The decisive novelty of the reptiles was that, unlike amphibians, they laid their eggs on dry land; they no longer depended on the water and were free to roam over the continents. But the unborn reptile inside the egg still needed an aquatic environment: it had to have water or else it would dry up long before it was born. It also needed a lot of food: amphibians hatch as larvae who fend for themselves, whereas reptiles hatch fully developed. So the reptilian egg had to be provided with a large mass of yolk for food, and also with albumen – the white of egg – to provide the water. Neither the yolk by itself, nor the egg-white itself, would have had any selective value. Moreover, the egg-white needed a vessel to contain it, otherwise its moisture would have evaporated. So there had to be a shell made of a leathery or limey material, as part of the evolutionary package-deal. But that is not the end of the story. The reptilian embryo, because of this shell, could not get rid of its waste products. The soft-shelled amphibian embryo had the whole pond as a lavatory; the reptilian embryo had to be provided with a kind of bladder. It is called the allantois, and is in some respects the forerunner of the mammalian placenta. But this problem having been solved, the embryo would still remain trapped inside its tough shell; it needed a tool to get out. The embryos of some fishes and amphibians, whose eggs are surrounded by a gelatinous membrane, have glands on their snouts: when the time is ripe, they secrete a chemical which dissolves the membrane. But embryos surrounded by a hard shell need a mechanical tool: thus snakes and lizards have a tooth transformed into a kind of tin-opener, while birds have a caruncle – a hard outgrowth near the tip of their beaks which serves the same purpose. In some birds – the honey-guides – which lay their eggs like cuckoos in alien nests, the caruncle serves yet another purpose: it grows into a sharp hook with which the newly hatched invader kills off his foster-brethren, after which it amiably sheds the hook.

All this refers to one aspect only of the evolution of reptiles; needless to say, countless other essential transformations of structure and behaviour were required to make the new creatures viable. The changes could have been gradual – but at each step, however small, *all* the factors involved in the story had to cooperate harmoniously. The liquid store in the egg makes no sense without the shell. The shell would be useless, in fact murderous, without the allantois and without the tin-opener. Each change, taken in isolation, would be harmful, and work *against* survival. You cannot have a mutation A occurring alone, preserve it by natural selection, and then wait a few thousand or million years until mutation B joins it, and so on, to C and D. Each mutation occurring alone would be wiped out before it could be combined with the others. They are all interdependent. The doctrine that their coming together was due to a series of blind coincidences is an affront not only to commonsense but to the basic principles of scientific explanation.

The propounders of the orthodox theory may have been uneasily aware that something essential was missing, and paid occasional lip service to 'unsolved problems', then hurriedly swept them under the carpet. To quote one authority, Sir Peter Medawar (himself not excessively given to tolerance of other people's opinions): 'Twenty years ago it all seemed easy: with mutation as a source of diversity, with selection to pick and choose ... Our former complacency can be traced, I suppose, to an understandable fault of temperament: scientists tend not to ask themselves questions until they can see the rudiments of an answer in their minds. Embarrassing questions tend to remain unasked or, if asked, to be answered rudely ...'[1a]*

A convenient way to evade these embarrassing questions was to concentrate attention on the statistical treatment of mutations in large populations of the fruit fly, *Drosophila melanogaster* – the pet animal of geneticists because it propagates so fast and has only four pairs of chromosomes. The method is based on the measurement of the variations of some isolated, and mostly trivial, characteristic, such as the colour of the eyes or the distribution of bristles on the fly's body. Steeped in the atomistic tradition, the upholders of the theory were apparently unable to see that these mutations of a single factor – virtually all of them deleterious – were quite irrelevant to the central problem of evolutionary progress, requiring simultaneous changes in all the factors affecting the structure and function of a complex organ. The geneticist's obsession with the bristles of the fruit fly, and the Behaviourist's obsession with the bar-pressing of the rat, show a more than superficial analogy. Both derive from a mechanistic philosophy

---

* Compare this with Sir Julian Huxley's *ex cathedra* pronouncement: 'In the field of evolution, genetics has given its basic answer, and evolutionary biologists are free to pursue other problems.'[2]

which regards the living creature as a collection of elementary bits of behaviour (S-R units) and of elementary bits of heredity (Mendelian genes).

Internal Selection

The alternative proposed here is the concept of the open hierarchy. Let us see whether it can be applied to the evolutionary process. I shall start by quoting Waddington's answer to problems of the type posed by the giant panda's finger:

> There are still some of us for whom the orthodox modern explanations do not seem very satisfying. One well-known problem is this: many organs are very complex things, and in order to bring about any improvement in their functioning, it would be necessary to make simultaneous alterations in several different characters ... and that, it might appear, is something which one would not expect to occur under the influence of chance alone.
>
> There have always been, and still are, reputable biologists who feel that such considerations make it doubtful whether random hereditary changes can provide a sufficient basis for evolution. But I believe that the difficulty largely disappears if one remembers that an organ like an eye is not simply a collection of elements, such as a retina, a lens, an iris, and so on, which are put together and happen to fit. It is something which is gradually formed while the adult animal is developing out of the egg; and as the eye forms, the different parts influence one another. Several people have shown that if, by some experimental means, the retina and eyeball are made larger than usual, that in itself will cause a larger lens to appear, of at least approximately the appropriate size for vision. There is no reason, therefore, why a chance mutation should not *affect the whole organ in a harmonious way*; and there is a reasonable possibility that it might improve it ... A random change in a hereditary factor will, in fact, not usually result in an alteration in just one element of the adult animal; it will bring about a shift in the whole developmental system, and may thus alter a complex organ as a whole[3] (my italics).

We remember from the previous chapter that the growing eye-bud of the embryo is an autonomous holon, which, if part of its tissue is taken away, will nevertheless develop into a normal eye, thanks to its self-regulating properties. It is by no means surprising that it should display the same self-regulating powers, or 'flexible strategies' of growth, if the disturbance is caused not by a human agent, but by a mutated gene, as Waddington suggests. The chance mutation merely triggers off the process; the 'pre-natal skills' of the embryo will do the rest, in every successive generation. The enlarged eye has become an evolutionary novelty.*

But embryonic development is a many-levelled hierarchic process; and this leads one to assume that selective and regulative controls operate on several levels to *eliminate* harmful mutations and to *coordinate* the effects of acceptable ones. Various authors† have suggested that this screening process might start at the very base of the hierarchy, on the level of the molecular chemistry of the gene-complex. Mutations are chemical changes, presumably caused by the impact of cosmic radiations and other factors, on the germ cells. The changes consist in alterations in the sequence of the chemical units in the chromosomes – the four letters of the genetic alphabet. Mostly they are the equivalents of misprints. But there seems to be again a hierarchy of correctors and proof-readers at work to eliminate these; 'The struggle for survival of mutations begins at the moment mutation occurs', writes L. L. Whyte. 'It is obvious that entirely arbitrary changes will not be physically, chemically, or functionally stable ... Only those changes which result in a mutated system that satisfies certain stringent physical, chemical and functional conditions will be able to survive ...'⁴ All others will be eliminated,

---

* It should be added that the example of the enlarged mutant eye is typical of the sort of thing a mutating gene will do. Genes regulate chemical reaction rates, including the rates of growth; and one of the most frequent effects of gene mutations is to alter the speed of growth of one part relative to others, and thus to modify the proportions of the organ.

† Von Bertalanffy, Darlington, Spurway, Lima da Faria, L. L. Whyte. See footnote on p 174.

either by the death of the mutated cell and its offspring at an early stage or, as we shall presently see, by the remarkable self-repairing properties of the gene-complex as a whole.

In the orthodox theory, natural selection is entirely due to the pressures of the environment, which kills off the unfit and blesses the fit with abundant progeny. In the light of the preceding considerations, however, before a new mutation has a chance to be submitted to the Darwinian tests of survival in the external environment, it must have passed the tests of *internal selection* for its physical, chemical and biological fitness.

The concept of internal selection, of a hierarchy of controls which eliminate the consequences of harmful gene-mutations and coordinates the effects of useful mutations, is the missing link in orthodox theory between the 'atoms' of heredity and the living stream of evolution. Without that link, neither of them makes sense. There can be no doubt that random mutations do occur: they can be observed in the laboratory. There can be no doubt that Darwinian selection is a powerful force. But in between these two events, between the chemical changes in a gene and the appearance of the finished product as a newcomer on the evolutionary stage, there is a whole hierarchy of internal processes at work which impose strict limitations on the range of possible mutations and thus considerably reduce the importance of the chance factor. We might say that the monkey works at a typewriter which the manufacturers have programmed to print only syllables which exist in our language, but not nonsense syllables. If a nonsense syllable occurs, the machine will automatically erase it.* To pursue the metaphor, we would have to populate the higher levels of the hierarchy with proof-readers and then editors,

* This metaphor is almost literally applicable to mistakes made in the protein manufacture in micro-organisms due to 'nonsense syllables' appearing in the RNA code.[5]

whose task is no longer elimination, but correction, self-repair and coordination – as in the example of the mutated eye.

That was an example of harmonizing the consequences of a potentially *favourable* mutation. Let me now quote another example of evolutionary self-repair after a potentially *harmful* mutation.

The Case of the Eyeless Fly

The fruit fly has a mutant gene which is recessive, ie, when paired with a normal gene, has no discernible effect (it will be remembered that genes operate in pairs, each gene in the pair being derived from one parent). But if two of these mutant genes are paired in the fertilized egg, the offspring will be an eyeless fly. If now a pure stock of eyeless flies is made to inbreed, then the whole stock will have only the 'eyeless' mutant gene, because no normal gene can enter the stock to bring light into their darkness. Nevertheless, within a few generations, *flies appear in the inbred 'eyeless' stock with eyes that are perfectly normal*. The traditional explanation of this remarkable phenomenon is that the other members of the gene-complex have been 'reshuffled and recombined in such a way that they deputise for the missing normal eye-forming gene'.[6] Now re-shuffling, as every poker player knows, is a randomizing process. No biologist would be so perverse as to suggest that the new insect-eye evolved by pure chance, thus repeating within a few generations an evolutionary process which took hundreds of millions of years. Nor does the concept of natural selection provide the slightest help in this case. The recombination of genes to deputize for the missing gene must have been coordinated according to some overall plan *which includes* the rules of genetic self-repair after certain types of damage by deleterious mutations. But such coordinative controls can only operate on levels higher than that of individual genes. Once more we are driven to the conclusion that the genetic code is not an architect's blueprint; that the gene-complex and its internal environment form a remarkably stable, closely knit, self-regulating micro-hierarchy; and that mutated genes in any of its holons are liable to cause corresponding reactions in others, coordinated by higher levels. This micro-hierarchy controls the pre-natal skills of the embryo, which enable it to reach its goal, regardless of the hazards it may encounter during development. But phylogeny is a sequence of ontogenies, and thus we are confronted with the profound question: is the mechanism of phylogeny also endowed with some kind of evolutionary instruction booklet? Is there a strategy of the evolutionary process comparable to the 'strategy of the genes' – to the 'directiveness' of ontogeny (as E. S. Russell has called it)?

Let me recapitulate. The eyes in the normal fruit fly, and the eyes which suddenly appear in the 'eyeless stock', are homologous organs, identical in appearance, and yet produced by a different combination of genes; and this is only one of many similar phenomena. Genetic atomism is dead. Hereditary stability and hereditary change are both based, not on a mosaic of genes, but on the action of the gene-complex 'as a whole'. But this face-saving expression – which is now coming into increased use – is empty, like so many other holistic formulations, unless we interpolate between the gene-complex as a whole, and the individual gene, a hierarchy of genetic sub-assemblies – self-regulating holons of heredity, which control the development of organs, and *also control their possible evolutionary modifications*, by canalizing the effects of random mutations. A hierarchy with its built-in, self-regulatory safeguards is a stable affair. It cannot be pulled in here, pulled out there, like Patou belabouring his model. It is capable of variation and change, but only in coordinated ways *and only in limited directions*. Can we say anything about the general principles which determine that direction?

The Puzzle of Homology

The most fundamental principle of evolutionary strategy, related to the watchmakers' parable, is the *standardization* of sub-assemblies. But since most of us have no very clear idea of the mechanism of our time-pieces, we might look under the hood of a motor car instead. Here the sub-assemblies are easily named: chassis, engine, battery, steering, brakes, differential, and so on to the distributor and heating system. Each of these component parts is a more or less self-contained unit, a mechanical holon in its own right. A V8 engine, or a standard battery, can be taken out of the car and made to function by itself, like an organ *in vitro*. It can be transferred to another type of car, and even to a different species of machine, such as a motor boat. But how do automobiles *evolve*?

The manufacturers know that it does not pay to design a new model from scratch, by starting on the level of elementary components; they make use of already existing, standard components – chassis, brakes, etc – each of which has developed out of long previous experience, and then proceed by relatively small improvements or modifications of some of these – for instance, by re-designing the body-line, or improving the cooling system, or introducing bucket seats.

Similar restraints can be shown to operate in biological evolution. Compare the front wheels of the latest model with those of a pre-war vintage car – they are based on the same principles. Compare the structure of the forelimbs in man, dog, bird and whale, and you find that evolution has retained the same basic design:

FIGURE 6

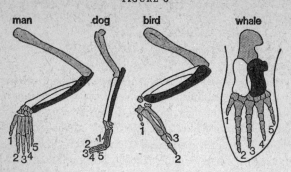

Vertebrate forelimbs (after *Life, An Introduction to Biology*, by G. G. Simpson et al.)

The human arm and the bird's wing are called homologous organs because they show the same structural design – of bones, muscles, blood vessels and nerves – and are descended from the same ancestral organ. The functions of arm and wing are so different that it would be logical to expect each to have a quite different design. In fact, evolution proceeded, just as car manufacturers do, by merely modifying an already existing component (the forelimb of the reptilian ancestor, from which birds and mammalians branched out more than two hundred million years ago), instead of starting from scratch. Once Nature has taken out a patent for manufacturing a component organ, it sticks to it tenaciously: the organ or device has become a stable evolutionary holon.

This principle holds all along the line, from the sub-cellular level to the 'wiring diagram' of the primate brain. The same make of organelles functions in the cells of mice and men; the same make of contractile protein serves the motion of amoeba and of the pianist's fingers; the same four chemical units constitute the alphabet of heredity throughout the animal and plant kingdoms – only the words are different for every creature. The proverbial lavishness of Nature is com-

pensated by its less obvious conservatism and parsimony –
one might almost call it stinginess – of basic homologous
designs, from organelles to brain structures. 'This concept of
homology', wrote Sir Alister Hardy, 'is absolutely fundamental to what we are talking about when we speak of
evolution. Yet in truth', he added wistfully, 'we cannot
explain it at all in terms of present-day biological theory'.[7]

The reason for this failure is, as we have seen, that the
orthodox theory assumed homologous structures in different
species to be due to the same 'atomic' genes inherited from the
common ancestor (though modified by mutation in the course
of their long descent); whereas there is now ample evidence
that homologous structures can be produced by the action of
quite different genes. The only way out of this cul-de-sac
seems to be to substitute for genetic atomism, which has so
drastically broken down, the concept of the genetic micro-
hierarchy, with its own built-in rules, that permit a great
amount of variation, but only in limited directions *on a
limited number of themes*. This really amounts to the revival of
an ancient idea which goes back to Goethe – and even further
to Plato. The point is worth a short historical digression –
which may make it clear why the concept of homology has
such great importance not only for the biologist, but also for
the philosopher.

Archetypes in Biology

Long before Darwin, naturalists were divided into evolutionists (Buffon, Lamarck, St Hilaire, etc), and anti-evolutionists who believed that the Creator had put down the first
giraffe, mosquito and walrus simultaneously as ready-made
products on the earth. But both pro- and anti-evolutionists
were equally struck by the similarity of organs and designs in
otherwise widely different species. The term 'homologue
organ' was actually coined by Geoffroy St Hilaire. His
Philosophie Anatomique, published in 1818, starts with the

question: '... Is it not generally acknowledged that vertebrates are built up on one uniform plan – eg, the forelimb may
be modified for running, climbing, swimming or flying, yet
the arrangement of bones remains the same ...?'[8]

Goethe had become an evolutionist long before that,
through his studies of the morphology (a term which he
coined) of plants and animals. In his *Metamorphosis of Plants*,
published in 1790, he postulated that all existing plants could
be derived from a common ancestor, the *Urpflanze* or arche-
plant; and that all the organs of plants are homologous*
modifications of a single structure, expressed in its simplest
form in the leaf. Though Goethe was already at the height of
his fame, the *Metamorphosis* had a hostile reception (incredible
as it seems, his own publisher in Leipzig rejected it, and he
had to go to Cotta in Gotha); but it had considerable influence on the German *Naturphilosophen*, who combined com-
parative anatomy with transcendental mysticism. These men
were not evolutionists, but they were fascinated by the
universal recurrence of the same basic patterns in the design
of animals and plants; they called them 'archetypes' and
thought that they constituted the key to the Lord's design of
creation.

The idea that all the existing flowers, trees, vegetables and
so on are derived from a single ancestral plant seems to have
occurred to Goethe during his sojourn in Sicily, where he had
spent most of his time in botanizing. After his return, in 1787,
he confided to Herder:

> I have seen the main point, the core of the problem, clearly and
> beyond doubt; everything else I can already see, too, as a whole,
> and only a few details need working out. The ancestral plant will
> turn out to be the most wondrous creation of the world, for which
> Nature herself shall envy me. With the aid of this model and the
> key to unlock it, one can then invent further plants *ad infinitum*
> which, however, must be consistent; that is to say, plants which, if
> they do not exist, yet could exist; which, far from being shadows

* Though he does not use the word.

or glosses of the poet's or painter's fancy, must possess an inherent rightness and necessity. The same law applies to all the remaining domains of the living.[9]

The conditions of 'inherent rightness and necessity', to which all existing and possible forms of life must conform, Goethe was of course unable to define; but his intuition told him that they could not include fanciful, arbitrary patterns created by the unbridled imagination of painters – or science-fiction writers. They must conform to certain archetypal patterns, *limited in their range by the basic structure and chemistry of organic matter*. Evolution cannot be a random process, pulling in bits here, pulling out bits there. It must conform to some orderly design, like 'the stern, eternal laws which guide the wandering planets in their orbits'.*

Goethe's German followers, the *Naturphilosophen*, took up his concept of archetypes, but not his belief in evolution. They regarded the archetypes not, as he did, as ancestral forms out of which the homologue organs had evolved, but as patterns of divine design – *leitmotivs* which, together with all their possible variations, have coexisted since the day of Creation. Much the same beliefs were shared by some great anatomists in Europe at that time, among them Richard Owen. It was Owen who defined 'homologous organs' as 'the *same* organ in different animals under every variety of form and function'. While he tirelessly demonstrated the multitude of such organs in the animal kingdom, he attributed them to the parsimony of the divine Designer – just as Kepler had attributed his planetary laws to the ingenuity of the divine Mathematician.

But whatever the beliefs of these men, the concept of homology came to stay, and became a cornerstone of modern evolutionary theory. Animals and plants are made out of homologous organelles like the mitochondria, homologous organs like gills and lungs, homologous limbs such as arms and wings. They are the stable holons in the evolutionary

* *Faust*, Prologue.

flux. *The phenomena of homology implied in fact the hierarchic principle in phylogeny as well as in ontogeny.* But the point was never made explicit, and the principles of hierarchic order hardly received a cursory glance. This may be the reason why the inherent contradictions of the orthodox theory could pass so long unnoticed.

The Law of Balance

There are manifestations on still higher levels of what I have called the stability of evolutionary holons. Such are the geometrical relations discovered by d'Arcy Thompson, which demonstrate that one species may become transformed into another and yet preserve its own basic design. The drawings below show a porcupine fish (*Diodon*) and the very different

FIGURE 7

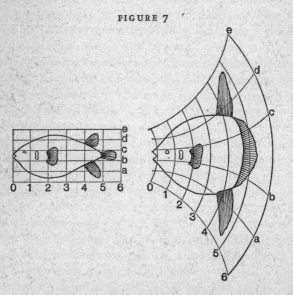

Sun fish and porcupine fish (after D'Arcy Thompson)

looking sun fish (*Orthogoriscus*) as they appear in Thompson's classic, *On Growth and Form*, published in 1917.

I have compared the evolution of homologue organs to the procedure of motorcar manufacturers when they bring out a new model, which differs from the previous one merely in some modifications of this or that component, while the other standardized parts remain unaltered. In the case of the fish, it is not a particular organ that has been modified, but the chassis and body-line as a whole. Yet it has not been arbitrarily re-designed. The pattern has remained the same. It has merely been evenly distorted according to a simple mathematical equation. Imagine the drawing of the porcupine fish and its lattice of Cartesian coordinates imprinted on a rubber sheet. The sheet is thicker at the head end, and therefore more resistant than at the tail end. Now you grip the top and bottom edges of the rubber sheet and stretch it. The result will be the sun fish. Corresponding points of the anatomy of the two fishes will have the same coordinates (the eye, for instance, will have 'longitude' 0,5, and 'latitude' C).

Thompson found that this phenomenon had general validity. Putting the outline drawing of an animal on a grid of coordinates, and then drawing another animal belonging to the same zoological group, he found that he could transform one shape into the other by some simple trick of rubber-sheet-geometry, which can be expressed by a mathematical formula. The next drawing, Figure 8, shows the transformation, by

FIGURE 8

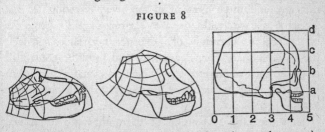

Skulls of baboon, chimpanzee and man (after D'Arcy Thompson)

means of a harmoniously deformed grid of Cartesian co-ordinates, of a baboon's skull into a chimpanzee's and a man's.

These are not idle mathematical games. They provide a realistic insight into the evolutionary workshop. Here are d'Arcy Thompson's own comments:

> We know beforehand that the main difference between the human and the Simian types depends upon the enlargement or expansion of the brain and brain case in man, and the relative diminution or enfeeblement of his jaws. Together with these changes, the facial angle increases from an oblique angle to nearly a right angle in man, and the configuration of every constituent bone of the face and skull undergoes an alteration. We do not know to begin with, and we are not shewn by the ordinary methods of comparison, how far these various changes form part of one harmonious and congruent transformation, or whether we are to look, for instance, upon the changes undergone by the frontal, the occipital, the maxilliary and the mandibular regions as a congeries of separate modifications or independent variables. But as soon as we have marked out a number of points in the gorilla's or chimpanzee's skull, corresponding with those which our co-ordinate network intersected in the human skull, we find that these corresponding points may be at once linked up by smoothly curved lines of intersection, which form a new system of coordinates and constitute a simple 'projection'* of our human skull ... and in short it becomes at once manifest that the modifications of jaws, brain-case, and the regions between, are all portions of one con-tinuous and integral process.[10]

Surely this process is the exact opposite of evolution through random changes 'in all and every direction'. If that were the case we should get what Thompson calls 'a congeries of separate modifications or independent variables'. In fact, the variations are inter-dependent, and must be controlled from the apex of the hierarchy which coordinates the pattern of the whole by harmonizing the relative growth-rates of the various parts.

Thus the rapid expansion of the anthropoid brain was

* In the sense of Projective Geometry.

accompanied by appropriate changes in the other parts of the skull, effected by a simple and elegant geometrical transformation. The eighteenth century was familiar with this kind of phenomenon, which the twentieth took a long time to re-discover. Goethe called it 'Nature's budgeting law', Geoffroy St Hilaire called it *loi du balancement*, the principle of the equilibrium of organs. From the concept of developmental homeostasis there is only one logical step to the concept of *evolutionary homeostasis* – the *loi du balancement* applied to phylogenetic changes. Faithful to Goethe, one might call it the preservation of certain basic, archetypal designs through all changes, combined with the striving towards their optimal realization in response to adaptive pressures.

The Doppelgängers

The last phenomenon to be mentioned in this context is an enigma wrapped in a puzzle. The enigma concerns the marsupials – the class of pouched animals living in Australia. The puzzle is that evolutionists refuse to see the enigma.

Nearly all mammalians are either marsupials or placentals. (The 'nearly' refers to the near-extinct monotremes, such as the duck-billed platypus, a kind of living fossil which lays eggs as reptiles do, but suckles its young.) The marsupials could be called the poor relatives of us 'normal', that is, placental, mammals; they have evolved along a parallel branch of the evolutionary tree. The marsupial embryo, while in the womb, receives hardly any nourishment from its mother. It is born in a very immature state of development, and is reared in an elastic pouch, or bag of skin, on the mother's belly. A newborn kangaroo is really a half-finished job – about an inch long, naked, blind, with hind-legs that are no more than embryonic buds. One might speculate whether the human infant, more developed but still helpless at birth, would be better off in a maternal pouch than in a cot; and also whether this would increase its oedipal inclinations. But whether the marsupial's method of reproduction is better or worse than the placental's, the point is that it is fundamentally different.

The two lines split up at the very beginning of mammalian evolution, in the Age of Reptiles, and have evolved separately, out of some small mouse-like common ancestral creature, over some hundred and fifty million years. The enigma is, why so many species produced by the independent evolutionary line of the marsupials are so startlingly similar to placentals. It is almost as if two artists who had never met, never heard of each other, and never had the same model, had painted a parallel series of nearly identical portraits. Figure 9 shows on the left side a series of placental mammals, and on the right their opposite numbers among marsupials.

Let me repeat: we know that, contrary to all appearances, the two series of animals have evolved independently from each other. Australia was cut off from the Asiatic mainland some time during the late Cretaceous, when the only existing mammals were unpromising-looking tiny creatures, hanging precariously on to existence. The marsupials seem to have evolved earlier than the placentals from a common egg-laying ancestor with part-reptilian, part-mammalian features; at any rate, the marsupials got to Australia before it was cut off, and the placentals did not. These immigrants were, as already said, mouse-like creatures, probably not unlike the still surviving, yellow-footed pouched mouse, but much more primitive. And yet these mice, confined to their island continent, branched out and gave rise to pouched versions of moles, ant-eaters, flying squirrels, cats and wolves – each like a somewhat clumsy copy of the corresponding placentals.* Why, if evolution were a free-for-all, restrained only by selection for fitness, why did Australia not produce some of the bug-eyed monsters of science fiction? The only moder-

* Marsupials have also evolved, again independently, in South America.

FIGURE 9

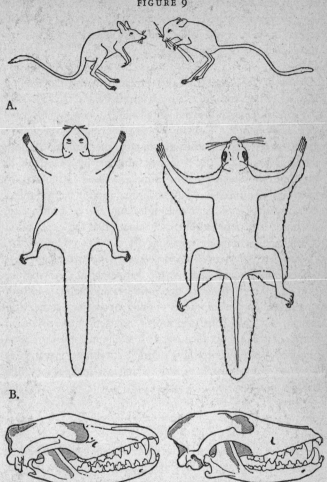

A.

B.

C.

A. Marsupial jerboa and placental jerboa. B. Marsupial flying phalanger and placental flying squirrel (after Hardy). C. Skull of marsupial Tasmanian wolf compared to skull of placental wolf (after Hardy)

ately unorthodox creation of that isolated island in a hundred million years are the kangaroos and wallabies; the rest of its fauna consists of rather poor replicas of more efficient placental types – variations on a limited number of archetypal themes.*

How is the enigma to be explained? The explanation offered by the orthodox theory is summed up in the following passage from an otherwise excellent textbook, that I have repeatedly quoted: 'Tasmanian [ie, marsupial] and true wolves are both running predators, preying on other animals of about the same size and habits. Adaptive similarity [ie, adaptation to similar environments] involves similarity also of structure and function. The mechanism of such evolution is natural selection.'[11] And G. G. Simpson, a leading Harvard authority, discussing the same problem, concludes that the explanation is 'selection of random mutations'.[12]

Once more the *deus ex machina*. Are we really to believe that the condition described by the vague terms 'preying on animals of approximately the same size and habits' – which could be applied to hundreds of different species – sufficiently explains the emergence, twice over, independently from each other, of the almost identical two skulls in Figure 9? One might as well say, with the wisdom of hindsight, that there is only one way of making a wolf, which is to make it look like a wolf.

The Thirty-six Plots

In Chapter VI, I compared the series of scanning and filtering mechanisms through which the intake of our sense-organs must pass before it is admitted to awareness and found worthy to be preserved by memory, to the seventeen gates of the Kremlin. The sense-receptors of eye, ear and skin are exposed

* The reasons for the inferiority of marsupials compared to placentals will be discussed in Chapter XVI.

(in a famous phrase of William James') to a continuous
bombardment by the 'blooming, buzzing confusion' of the
outside world; without careful scrutiny by the sentries
guarding the gates, we should be at the mercy of all random
intruders, and our minds and memories would be all confusion,
unable to make sense of our chaotic sensations.

We can now apply the same metaphor to the alert guar-
dians who protect the gates of heredity against the chaos that
would ensue if random mutations 'in all and every direction'
were given free access. We must assume that mutations –
that is, 'changes' in the original sense of the word – on the
elementary quantum level are occurring constantly under the
impact of radiations and other factors impinging on the
gene-complex. The giant molecules of the chromosome chains
consisting of millions of atoms must also be surrounded by a
'blooming, buzzing confusion' of their own sub-microscopic
universe. Most of these changes would be transitory, quickly
rectified by self-regulatory devices of the gene-complex, or
without noticeable effect on its functioning. The relatively few
mutations potentially capable of affecting heredity would be
submitted to sifting and processing at the gates of successively
higher levels of the hierarchy. I have mentioned several stages
of this processing, for which there is solid evidence: the
elimination of 'mis-spelt' syllables in the genetic code;
'developmental homeostasis' which ensures that mutations
should affect a whole organ in a harmonious way; similar
processes on higher levels (Thompson's transformations, *loi
du balancement*) which preserve the proper equilibrium between organs; the evolution of homologous organs from
different combinations of genes (*drosophila*-eye), and of similar
species of independent evolutionary origin (marsupials).*

The conclusion which emerges from all this is that there
must be unitary laws underlying evolutionary variety,

* I shall not bother the reader with technical terms like 'homeoplasy', 'convergence', 'parallelism', which are merely descriptive, but not explanatory.

permitting unlimited variations on a limited number of themes. Translated into our terminology, this means that the evolutionary process, like all hierarchic operations, is governed by fixed canons, and guided by adaptable strategies. The latter are partly (see below) accounted for by the selective pressures of the environment – predators, competitors, etc; but the laws which confine possible evolutionary advances to certain main avenues cannot be defined in terms of these external factors – which only enter into action *after* a change proposed by mutating genes has been approved and passed muster at the successive Kremlin gates of the organism's internal controls. These internal controls define the 'evolutionary canon'.

Several eminent biologists have in recent years toyed with this idea, but without spelling out its profound implications.* Thus von Bertalanffy wrote: 'While fully appreciating modern selection theory, we nevertheless arrive at an essentially different view of evolution. It appears to be not a series of accidents, the course of which is determined only by the change of environments during earth history and the resulting struggle for existence, which leads to selection within a chaotic material of mutations . . . but is governed by definite laws, and we believe that the discovery of these laws constitutes one of the most important tasks of the future.'[13] Waddington and Hardy have both re-discovered Goethe's notion of archetypal forms; Helen Spurway concluded from the evidence of homology that the organism has only 'a restricted mutation spectrum' which 'determines its possibilities of evolution'.[14]

But what exactly do these authors mean by expressions like 'archetypal selection', 'organic laws co-determining evolution', 'mutation spectrum', or 'moulding influences guiding evolutionary change along certain avenues'?[15] They seem to mean in fact, without saying it in as many words, that given

* For an excellent short critical discussion see L. L. Whyte's *Internal Factors in Evolution*, and W. H. Thorpe's review of the book in *Nature*, May 14th, 1966.

the conditions on our particular planet, the chemistry and temperature of its atmosphere, and the available energies and building materials, life from its inception in the first blob of living slime could only progress in a limited number of directions in a limited number of ways. But this implies that just as the Australian and European wolf were both potentially foreshadowed in the ancestral mouse-like creature, that creature in turn was foreshadowed in the ancestral chordate, and so on back to the ancestral protist, and the first, self-replicating strand of nucleic acid.

If this conclusion is correct, it sheds some additional light on man's status in this universe. It puts an end to the fantasies of science fiction regarding future forms of life on earth. But it does not mean the opposite either: it emphatically does not mean a rigidly determined universe which unwinds like a mechanical clockwork. It means, to revert to one of the *leitmotivs* of this book, that the evolution of life is a game played according to fixed rules which limit its possibilities but leave sufficient scope for a limitless number of variations. The rules are inherent in the basic structure of living matter; the variations derive from adaptive strategies.

In other words, evolution is neither a free-for-all, nor the execution of a rigidly predetermined computer programme. It could be compared to a musical composition whose possibilities are limited by the rules of harmony and the structure of the diatonic scales – which, however, permit an inexhaustible number of original creations. Or it could be compared to the game of chess obeying fixed rules but with equally inexhaustible variations. Lastly, the vast number of existing animal species (about one million) and the small number of major classes (about fifty) and of major phyla or divisions (about ten), could be compared with the vast number of works of literature and the small number of basic themes or plots. All works of literature are variations on a limited number of *leitmotivs*, derived from man's archetypal experiences and conflicts, but adapted each time to a new environment – the costumes, conventions and language of the period. Not even Shakespeare could invent an original plot. Goethe quoted with approval the Italian dramatist Carlo Gozzi,* according to whom there are only thirty-six tragic situations. Goethe himself thought that there were probably even less; but their exact number is a well-kept secret among writers of fiction. A work of literature is constructed out of thematic holons – which, like homologue organs, need not even have a common ancestor.

Three times at least, but probably much more often, eyes with lenses have evolved independently in animals as widely different as molluscs, spiders and vertebrates. Most insects have, unlike the spider, compound eyes, but these are merely modifications of the same optical principle: the smooth-curved surface of the camera lens is broken up into a honeycomb of small corneal lenses, each with its own light-sensitive tube. These are the only two basic types of image-forming eyes† throughout the animal kingdom. But again there are countless variations and refinements, from the 'pinhole eye' of the nautilus which functions on the principle of the *camera obscura*, without lens, through the rudimentary lenses of starfish, up to the precision mechanisms by which various groups of animals achieve accommodation and focussing of the eye on objects of varying distance. Fishes, perhaps because they have more time on their fins, move the whole lens closer to the retina when focussing on distant objects. Mammals, including man, have evolved a more elegant method of focussing by altering the curvature of the lens – flattening it for close objects, thickening it for distant vision. Predatory birds have developed an even more effective strategy for keeping the prey in focus while sweeping down on it:

---

* Author of *Tuurandot* and many other successful works.

† As distinct from primitive, light-sensitive units which respond to differences in light intensity, but do not provide pattern-vision.

instead of adjusting the relatively inert lens, they quickly change the curvature of the more flexible cornea. Another essential refinement, colour vision, also evolved independently several times. Lastly, the gradual shifting of the position of the eyes from the side to the front of the head led to binocular vision – the fusion of the images in each separate eye into a single three-dimensional image in the brain.

The purpose of the preceding paragraph was not to praise the glories of vision, but to point to the remarkable achievements of adaptive strategies making the best of the organism's limited possibilities. The limitations are inherent in the physico-chemical structure of living matter as it exists on earth – and presumably on any planet whose conditions are remotely similar to those on earth. But there is no limit to what an artist can do with Gozzi's meagre list of thirty-six themes.

XI

EVOLUTION CTD: PROGRESS BY INITIATIVE

When you don't know where a road leads, it sure as hell will take you there.

LEO ROSTEN

EXPRESSIONS like 'adaptive strategy' or 'exploiting opportunities' imply an active striving towards an optimal realization of the evolutionary potential.

In recent years it has become once more scientifically respectable to speak of goal-directedness in *ontogeny* – from the canalization of embryonic development to the purposiveness of instinctive and learned behaviour. But not so in *phylogeny*. There the official attitude may still be fairly summarized by the following quotation from G. G. Simpson: 'It does seem that the problem [of evolution] is now essentially solved and that the mechanism of adaptation is known. It turns out to be basically materialistic, with no sign of purpose as a working variable in life history, and with any possible Purposer pushed back to the incomprehensible position of First Cause.' And later on: 'Man is the result of a purposeless and materialistic process that did not have him in mind. He was not planned.'[1]

However, there is no need to engage in philosophical debate over this kind of pronouncement, because it is based on spurious alternatives. According to Simpson, evolution is either 'basically materialistic' (whatever that means in this context) – or else there must be a Purposer, a god; man is either the result of a purposeless process or else he must have been 'planned' from the beginning. But the term 'purpose' in its biological context implies neither a Purposer nor a cut-and-dried image of the ultimate goal to be achieved. The predator setting out on its nightly round does not look for a particular rabbit or hare, he looks for a likely prey; the chess-player cannot generally foresee or plan the ultimate mate situation: he uses his skill to take advantage of the opportunities on the board. Purposiveness means goal-directed instead of random activity, flexible strategies instead of rigid mechanisms, and adaptive behaviour – but on the organism's own terms: it does not 'adapt' to a freezing environment by lowering its body temperature, but by burning up more fuel. In a word, as E. W. Sinnott wrote, purpose is 'the directive activity shown by individual organisms that distinguishes living things from inanimate objects'.[2] Or, to quote the Nobel Laureate H. J. Muller, 'purpose is not imported into nature, and need not be puzzled over as a strange or divine something else that gets inside and makes life go . . . it is simply implicit in the fact of biological organization, and it is to be studied rather than admired or "explained"'.[3]

Let me repeat: to talk of 'directiveness', or purpose in this limited sense, in ontogeny, has become respectable once more; but to apply these terms to phylogeny is still considered heretical (or at least in bad taste). But phylogeny is an abstraction, which only acquires a concrete meaning when we realize that 'phylogeny, evolutionary descent, is a sequence of ontogenies', and that 'the course of evolution is through changes in ontogeny'. The quotations in the previous sentence are actually also by Simpson[4] and contain the answer to his own conundrum about the Purposer behind the purpose. *The Purposer is each and every individual organism, from the inception of life, which struggled and strove to make the best of its limited opportunities.*

Acting Before Reacting

When orthodox evolutionists speak of 'adaptations' they mean, as Behaviourists do when they speak of 'responses', an essentially passive process or mechanism, controlled by the environment. This view may be in keeping with their philosophy, but it is certainly not in keeping with the evidence which shows, to quote G. E. Coghill once more, that 'the organism acts on the environment before it reacts to it'.[5] Coghill has demonstrated that in the embryo the motor-nerve tracts become active, and movements make their appearance, before the sensory nerves become functional. And the moment it is hatched or born the creature lashes out at the environment, be it liquid or solid, with cilia, flagellae, or contractile muscle fibre; it crawls, swims, glides, pulsates; it kicks, yells, breathes, feeds on its surroundings for all it is worth. It does not merely adapt to the environment, but constantly adapts the environment to itself – it eats and drinks its environment, fights and mates with it, burrows and builds in it; it does not merely respond to the environment, but asks questions by exploring it. The 'exploratory drive' is now recognized by the younger generation of animal psychologists to be a primary biological instinct, as basic as the instincts of hunger and sex; it can on occasion be even more powerful than these. Countless experimenters* – starting with Darwin himself – have shown that curiosity, and the 'seeking out of thrills', is an instinctual urge in rats, birds, dolphins, chimpanzees and man; and so is what Behaviourists call 'ludic behaviour' – known to ordinary mortals as playfulness.

The exploratory drive has a direct bearing on the theory of evolution. This was realized by at least two eminent biologists at the turn of the century – Baldwin and Lloyd Morgan – but was promptly and conveniently forgotten. In recent years, however, this so-called 'Baldwin effect' was rediscovered,

* Cf. *Act of Creation*, Book Two, Chapter Eight.

independently, by Hardy and Waddington. Let me explain what is meant by an amusing example which Hardy gave at a meeting of the Linnaean Society in 1956. A few years earlier, some clever blue-tits had noticed that the bottles which the milkman left at the doorstep contained a puzzling white liquid, and they discovered a way of getting at it by removing the tops of the bottles with their beaks. The liquid proved to be rather delicious. So the birds learned to deal with cardboard tops, and soon also with metal tops. This new skill soon spread, apparently by imitation, 'right through the tit population of Europe'.[6]

Never again will our milk bottles be safe. However, Hardy continued, if the bottles were living organisms – a species of clams with an odd cylindrical shell; and if the tits continued to feed on them, then after a while only the 'bottles' with thicker caps would survive, and natural selection would produce a species of 'thick-capped bottles' – but also perhaps a species of tits with 'more specialized, tin-opener-like beaks for dealing with them'.[7]

The emergence of thick-capped 'bottle' creatures would illustrate the *passive*, Darwinian type of evolution through the selective pressure of predators in the environment. But the evolution of tits with more efficient beaks is meant to illustrate a quite different type of evolutionary process, based on the *initiative* of some enterprising individuals in the species. These discover a new method of feeding, a new skill which, spreading by imitation, becomes incorporated into the species' ways of life. The lucky mutation (or re-combination of genes) which produces beaks appropriate to the new skill comes only afterwards, as a kind of genetic endorsement of the discovery. The initial act in the process, the evolutionary pioneer work, so to speak, was done by the tit's exploratory activities, its curiosity which led it to investigate the environment – and not merely submit to its pressures. We have seen that the famous typewriter of the monkey is controlled by internal selection;

now the machine has been further programmed: the monkey merely has to go on trying until he hits a certain pre-specified key.

The example of the tin-opener beak is of course imaginary, but the conclusions are supported by many observations. Thus one of 'Darwin's finches' on the Galapagos Isles, *C. pallidus*, pecks holes or crevices into the tree bark, and 'having excavated, it picks up a cactus spine or twig, one or two inches long, and holding it lengthwise in its beak, pokes it up the crack, dropping the twig to seize the insect as it emerges . . . Sometimes the bird carries a spine or twig about with it, poking it into cracks and crannies as it searches one tree after another. This remarkable habit . . . is one of the few recorded uses of tools in birds' (Hardy[8]).

According to the orthodox theory, we would have to believe that some random mutation, by modifying the shape of the bird's beak (which, however, is not very different from the beaks of other finches) *caused* it to develop its ingenious way of hunting insects. And we would also have to believe that it was the same *deus ex machina* which forced the tit to open milk bottles. Let us rather agree with Hardy that 'the emphasis in the present-day view must be false'; and that the main causative factor of evolutionary progress is *not* the selective pressure of the environment, but the initiative of the living organism, 'the restless, exploring and perceiving animal that discovers new ways of living, new sources of food, just as the tits have discovered the value of the milk bottles . . . It is adaptations which are due to the animal's behaviour, to its restless exploration of its surroundings, to its initiative, that distinguish the main diverging lines of evolution; it is these dynamic qualities which led to the different roles of life that open up to a newly emerging group of animals in that phase of their expansion technically known as adaptive radiation – giving the lines of runners, climbers, burrowers, swimmers and conquerors of the air.'[9]

One might call this the 'progress by initiative', or do-it-yourself theory of evolution. It does not do away with chance mutations, but further narrows down the part played by them in the total picture to that of a lucky hit at a pre-set target, which is sooner or later bound to occur. Once it has occurred the spontaneously acquired habit or skill becomes hereditary, incorporated into the animal's native repertory: it has no longer to be invented or learned, it has become an instinct, endorsed by the gene-complex.* In fact, the range and importance of random mutations has been so much whittled down by the various factors mentioned in this and the previous chapter, that the whole Darwin-Lamarck controversy loses much of its importance.

The point will perhaps become clearer if we draw a parallel between the role of chance in evolution and in scientific discovery. Behaviourists tend to ascribe any original idea to pure chance. But the history of science teaches that most

* In a series of experiments with *Drosophila* Waddington has demonstrated that such 'genetic assimilation' (as he called it) of acquired characters becoming hereditary does indeed occur. This does not necessarily mean, however, that Lamarck was right and that the acquired feature (in this case a change in the fly's wing-structure, produced by exposure of the pupae to heat) was the direct *cause* of the mutation which made it hereditary after a few generations, so that the wing-change occurred even *without* heat-exposure. It could be that a few mutant flies were already present in the stock, and were then selected for survival on a Darwinian basis; it could also be that the appropriate mutation arose by chance in the process. Waddington leaves the question open whether he had produced an experimental confirmation of Lamarck, or an imitation of Lamarckian inheritance by means of a Darwinian mechanism; he concludes that 'it would be unsafe to consider that the occurrence of directed mutation related to the environment can be ruled out of court *a priori*', and that 'it seems wisest to keep an open mind on the subject'.[10] That is a far cry from the almost fanatical attitude of the neo-Darwinian citadel.

Waddington has gone even further by maintaining that if natural selection works primarily in favour of plastic, adaptable behaviour, then the process of canalization during development will become so flexible in itself that it no longer requires any particular gene mutation to endorse the new feature, merely 'some random mutation to take over the switching function of the original environmental stimulus. The type of hereditary change envisaged by Baldwin is, therefore, much more likely than he could have realized.'[11]

discoveries were made by several people independently from each other, at more or less the same time;* and this fact alone (apart from all other considerations) is sufficient to show that when the time is ripe for a given type of invention or discovery, the favourable chance event which sparks it off is bound to occur sooner or later. 'Fortune favours the prepared mind', wrote Pasteur, and we may add: fortunate mutations favour the prepared animal.

A stupid and industrious scholar could indeed write a history of science as a history of lucky hazards: Archimedes' overspilling bath-water, Galileo's swinging chandelier, Newton's apple, James Watt's tea-kettle, Harvey's fish-heart, Gutenberg's wine-press, Pasteur's spoilt culture, Fleming's nose-drip – and so on and so forth, whether apocryphal or true does not matter. But he would have to be very stupid indeed not to realize that if that particular chance event had not occurred, a hundred others might have had the same triggering effect on the prepared mind – or on some other contemporary mind working in the same direction; and only a very perverse historian could fail to see that the primary cause and directing force of scientific progress is the curiosity and initiative of scientists, and not the random appearance of chandeliers, apples, tea-kettles and nose-drips 'in all and every direction'.

Yet it is precisely this perverse view which determines the orthodox interpretation not only of the evolution of new animal forms, but also of new patterns of animal behaviour. The only explanation that neo-Darwinian theory has to offer is that new forms of behaviour, too, arise from chance mutations affecting the nervous system, preserved by natural selection. If, apart from a few tentative studies, the evolution of behaviour (as distinct from the evolution of physical structures) is still an uncharted territory, the reason may

* See *The Act of Creation*, pp 109 ff.

perhaps be an unconscious reluctance to put the already strained theoretical framework of neo-Darwinian genetics to an additional test. To quote a very trivial example: an individual song-bird or jackdaw or sparrow, on spotting a predator, will give an alarm call, warning the whole flock. 'These alarm calls', Tinbergen points out, 'are a clear example of an activity which serves the group but endangers the individual.'[12] Are we really to assume that the 'wiring diagram' in the sparrow's nervous system, which releases the alarm call in response to a stimulus of predatory shape, arose by random mutation *and* was perpetuated by natural selection in spite of its negative survival value for the mutant? The same question could be asked concerning the phylogenetic origin of the ritualized mock-fights in a great variety of animals, including stags, iguanas, birds, dogs, fish. Dogs, for instance, sprawl on their backs as a token of defeat and surrender, exposing their vulnerable bellies and jugular veins to the victor's fangs. One is inclined to call this a rather risky attitude; and what is the *individual* survival value of *not* hitting (or biting, goring) below the belt?

One could add a whole volume of examples of complex, purposeful animal activities that defy any explanation by chance mutation and natural selection; and the list would actually have to start with a single-celled sea animal, a relative to the amoeba, which builds elaborate houses out of the needle-like spiculae of sponges. From this simple protozoan, without eyes or a nervous system, which is but a gelatinous mass of flowing protoplasm, through the architectural skill of spiders and insects, through bottle-raiding birds, tool-making chimpanzees and up to man, we find the same lesson repeated – a display of patterns of instinctive and learned behaviour which cannot be explained by any twist of logic as the result of random changes in bodily structure. To quote Dr Ewer: 'Behaviour will tend to be always a jump ahead of structure and so play a decisive role in the evolutionary process.'[13] In this light, evolution no longer appears as a tale told by an idiot, but rather as an epic recited by a stutterer – at times haltingly and painfully, then precipitating in bursts.

Once More Darwin and Lamarck

There remains a hard core of phenomena that seems to defy explanation by any of the processes discussed so far, and to cry out for a Lamarckian explanation in terms of the inheritance of acquired characters. There is, for example, the hoary problem why the skin on the soles of our feet is so much thicker than elsewhere. If the thickening occurred *after* birth, as a result of stress, wear and tear, there would be no problem. But the skin of the sole is already thickened *in the embryo* which has never walked, bare-foot or otherwise. A similar, even more striking phenomenon are the callosities on the African wart-hog's wrists and forelegs, on which the animal leans while feeding; on the knees of camels; and, oddest of all, the two bulbous thickenings on the ostrich's undercarriage, one fore, one aft, on which that ungainly bird squats. All these callosities make their appearance, as the skin on our feet does, in the embryo. They are inherited characters. But is it conceivable that these callosities should have evolved by chance mutations just exactly where the animal needed them? Or must we assume that there is a causal, Lamarckian connection between the animal's needs and the mutation which provides them? Even Waddington, who does not completely rule out the possibility of Lamarckian inheritance, prefers to invoke the Baldwin effect and developmental canalization – though it is not easy to see how they can satisfactorily explain phenomena of this kind.

But on the other hand, it is equally difficult to see how an acquired callosity could conceivably produce changes in the gene-complex. Difficult, but not entirely impossible. It is true that the germ cells are set apart from other body cells in splendid isolation, but their isolation is not absolute: they are affected by radiation, heat and certain chemicals. It would indeed, as Waddington says, be 'unsafe to rule *a priori* out of court' the possibility that changes in the gene activities of body cells could, under certain circumstances, also cause changes in the gene activities of germ cells by means of hormones or enzymes. Herrick[14] has also kept an open mind on the problem. Waddington has actually produced a tentative model of directive mutation to indicate that at the present stage of biochemistry such a process is conceivable.[15]

It would not serve any useful purpose to rehash the arguments and counter-arguments, which have been repeated over and again. In a few years' time the whole battle might be of merely historical interest, like the Newton-Huyghens controversy on the corpuscular versus the wave theory of light. Darwinian selections operating on chance mutations doubtless occur, but they are not the whole picture, and probably not even a very important part of the picture for two simple reasons: first, because the range within which chance factors can operate is considerably narrowed down by the factors discussed before; and in the second place because in the present form of the orthodox theory the very term 'selection' has become ambiguous. It once meant 'survival of the fittest'; but, to quote Waddington for the last time: 'Survival does not, of course, mean the bodily endurance of a single individual, outliving Methuselah. It implies, in its present-day interpretation, perpetuation as a source for future generations. That individual "survives" best which leaves most offspring. Again, to speak of an animal as "fittest" does not necessarily imply that it is strongest or most healthy or would win a beauty competition. Essentially, it denotes nothing more than leaving most offspring. The general principle of natural selection, in fact, merely amounts to the statement that the individuals which leave most offspring are those which leave most offspring. It is a tautology.'[16]

The Lamarckians, on the other hand, have failed to provide experimental evidence for the inheritance of acquired characters which could *not* be interpreted – or explained away – on a Darwinian basis. That again proves nothing – except that if Lamarckian inheritance occurs, *it must be a rather rare event*. It could not be otherwise, for if every experience of the ancestors left its hereditary trace on the offspring, the result would be a chaos of shapes and a bedlam of instincts. But some of the 'hard-core' cases make it appear at least probable that some well-defined structural adaptations, such as the thickening of the skin on our feet or the ostrich's callosities, which were acquired by generation after generation, did in the end lead to changes in the gene-complex which made them inheritable. Biochemistry does not exclude this possibility; and the almost fanatical insistence on its rejection is but one more example of the intolerance and dogmatism of scientific orthodoxies.

It seems, then, that neo-Darwinian and neo-Lamarckian modes of evolution are extreme cases at opposite ends of a wide spectrum of evolutionary phenomena. I have mentioned a number of these; but there is still one more to be discussed, which has a special significance to man.

XII

EVOLUTION CTD:
UNDOING AND RE-DOING

Who has seen the wind? Neither you nor I.
But when the trees bow down their heads,
The wind is passing by.
CHRISTINA ROSSETTI

THERE have been periods of 'adaptive radiation' – sudden bursts of new forms branching out of the evolutionary tree in a relatively short time. Such was the reptilian outburst in the Mesozoic, or the mammalian outburst in the Paleocene – the first about two hundred, the second about eighty, million years ago. The opposite phenomenon is the decline and extinction of evolutionary branches. It is estimated that for every one of the existing one million species, hundreds must have perished in the past. And, as far as one can judge, most of the lines which have not perished have become stagnant – their evolution came to a standstill at various stages in the long distant past.

Blind Alleys

The principal cause of stagnation and extinction is over-specialization. Take, for example, that charming and pathetic creature the koala bear, which specializes in feeding on the leaves of a particular variety of eucalyptus tree and on nothing else; and which, in lieu of fingers, has hook-like claws ideally suited for clinging to the bark of the tree – and for nothing else. Its human equivalent – minus the charm – is the pedant, the slave of habit, whose thinking and behaviour move in rigid grooves. (Some of our departments of higher learning seem expressly designed for breeding koala bears.)

Some years ago, in the *Yale Review*, Sir Julian Huxley gave the following short summary of the evolutionary process:

> The course followed by evolution appears to have been broadly as follows. From a generalized early type, various lines radiate out, exploiting the environment in various ways. Some of these comparatively soon reach a limit to their evolution, at least as regards major alteration. Thereafter they are limited to minor changes such as the formation of new genera and species. Others, on the other hand, are so constructed that they can continue their career, generating new types which are successful in the struggle for existence because of their greater control over the environment and their greater independence of it. Such changes are legitimately called 'progressive'. The new type repeats the process. It radiates out into a number of lines, each specializing in a particular direction. The great majority of these come up against dead ends and can advance no further: specialization is one-sided progress, and after a longer or shorter time, reaches a biomechanical limit . . .
>
> Sometimes all the branches of a given stock have come up against their limit, and then either have become extinct or have persisted without major change. This happened, for instance, to the echinoderms, which with their sea-urchins, starfish, brittle-stars, sea-lilies, sea cucumbers, and other types now extinct had pushed the life that was in them into a series of blind alleys: they have not advanced for perhaps a hundred million years, nor have they given rise to other major types.
>
> In other cases, all but one or two of the lines suffer this fate, while the rest repeat the process. All reptilian lines were blind alleys save two – one which was transformed into the birds, and another which became the mammals. Of the bird stock, all lines came to a dead end; of the mammals, all but one – the one which became man.[1]

But, having made this point, Huxley drew a conclusion which is much less convincing: 'Evolution', he concluded, 'is seen as an enormous number of blind alleys, with a very occasional path of progress. It is like a maze in which almost all turnings are wrong turnings.'[2]

This sounds just like the Behaviourist's view of the rat in the maze as a paradigm of human learning. In both cases the explicit or tacit assumption is once more that progress is governed by blind chance – chance mutations preserved by natural selection, random tries preserved by reinforcement, and that is all there is to it.

Escape from Specialization

In the three previous chapters I discussed a number of phenomena which reduce the factor of chance to a subordinate role. Now I propose to discuss one more line of escape from the maze, known to students of evolution under the ugly name of *paedomorphosis*, coined by Garstang nearly half a century ago. But although the existence of the phenomenon is recognized, there is little mention of it in the textbooks because – like the Baldwin effect or the marsupial puzzle – it runs against the *Zeitgeist*.* To put it simply, the phenomenon of paedomorphosis indicates that in certain circumstances evolution can retrace its steps, as it were, along the path which led to the dead end, and make a fresh start in a new, more promising direction. The crucial point here is the appearance of some useful evolutionary novelty in the *larval or embryonic* stage of the ancestor, a novelty that may disappear before the ancestor reaches the adult stage, but which reappears and is preserved in the *adult stage of the descendant*. The following example will make this involved process clearer.

There is now strong evidence in favour of the theory, proposed by Garstang as far back as 1928, that the chordates – and thus we, the vertebrates – are descended from the larval stage of some primitive echinoderm, perhaps rather like the

*I am much indebted to Mr D. Lang Stevenson for having called my attention to Garstang's work.

sea urchin or sea cucumber (echinoderm = 'prickly-skinned'). Now an adult sea cucumber would not be a very inspiring ancestor – it is a sluggish creature which looks like an ill-stuffed sausage with leathery skin, lying on the sea bottom. But its free-floating larva is a much more promising proposition: unlike the adult sea cucumber, the larva has bilateral symmetry like a fish; it has a ciliary band – a forerunner of the nervous system – and some other sophisticated features not found in the adult animal. We must assume that the sedentary adult residing on the sea bottom had to rely on mobile larvae to spread the species far and wide in the ocean, as plants scatter their seeds in the wind; that the larvae, which had to fend for themselves, exposed to much stronger selective pressures than the adults, gradually became more fish-like; and that eventually they became sexually mature while still in the free-swimming, larval state – thus giving rise to a new type of animal which never settled on the bottom at all, and altogether eliminated the senile, sedentary cucumber-stage from its life history.

This speeding up of sexual maturation relative to the development of the rest of the body – or, to put it differently, the gradual retardation of bodily development beyond the age of sexual maturation – is a familiar evolutionary phenomenon, known as *neoteny*. Its result is that the animal begins to breed while still displaying larval or juvenile features; and it frequently happens that the fully adult stage is never reached – it is dropped off the life cycle.

This tendency towards a 'prolonged childhood', with the corresponding squeezing out of the final adult stages, amounts to a *rejuvenation and de-specialization* of the race – an escape from the cul-de-sac in the evolutionary maze. As J. Z. Young wrote, adopting Garstang's views: 'The problem which remains is in fact not "how have vertebrates been formed from sea squirts?", but "how have vertebrates eliminated the [adult] sea-squirt stage from their life history?" It is wholly reasonable to consider that this has been accomplished by paedomorphosis.'[3]

Neoteny, in fact, amounts to a rewinding of the biological clock when evolution is in danger of running down and coming to a standstill. Gavin de Beer has compared the classical view of evolution (such as expressed in Huxley's image of the maze) to the classical view of the universe as a mechanical clockwork. 'On this view', he wrote, 'phylogeny would gradually slow down and become stationary. The race would not be able to evolve any further and would be in a condition to which the term "racial senescence" has been applied. It would be difficult to see how evolution was able to produce as much phylogenetic change in the animal kingdom as it has, and it would lead to the dismal conclusion that the evolutionary clock is running down. In fact, such a state of affairs would present a dilemma analogous to that which follows from the view that . . . the universe has been wound up once and that its store of free energy was irremediably becoming exhausted. We do not know how energy is built up again in the physical universe; but the analogous process in the domain of organic evolution would seem to be paedomorphosis. A race may become rejuvenated by pushing the adult stage of its individuals off from the end of their ontogenies, and such a race may then radiate out in all directions . . . until racial senescence due to gerontomorphosis [see below] sets in again.'[4]

Neoteny in itself is of course not enough to produce these evolutionary bursts of adaptive radiations. The 'rejuvenation' of the race merely provides the opportunity for evolutionary changes to operate on the early, malleable phases of ontogeny: hence paedomorphosis, 'the shaping of the young'. In contrast to it, gerontomorphosis (*geras* = old age) is the modification of fully adult structures which are already highly specialized.*

* The word 'gerontomorphosis' was coined by de Beer as a contrast to Garstang's 'paedomorphosis'.

This sounds like a rather technical distinction, but it is in fact of vital importance. Gerontomorphosis cannot lead to radical changes and new departures; it can only carry an already specialized evolutionary line one more step further in the same direction – as a rule into a dead end of the maze. To quote de Beer again:

> The terms gerontomorphosis and paedomorphosis, therefore, express not only the stage in the life history of an animal with which they are concerned, but they also convey the meaning of racial senescence and rejuvenescence. It is interesting to note that as a result of considerations based on a different line of thought, Child[5] had been led to express similar views. 'If evolution is in some degree a secular differentiation and senescence of protoplasm, the possibility of evolutionary rejuvenescence must not be overlooked. Perhaps the relatively rapid rise and increase of certain forms here and there in the course of evolution may be the expression of changes of this sort.'[5a]

Draw Back to Leap

It seems that this retracing of steps to escape the dead ends of the maze was repeated at each decisive evolutionary turning point. I have mentioned the evolution of the vertebrates from a larval form of some primitive echinoderm. Insects have in all likelihood emerged from a millipede-like ancestor – not, however, from adult millipedes, whose structure is too specialized, but from its larval forms. The conquest of the dry land was initiated by amphibians whose ancestry goes back to the most primitive type of lung-breathing fish; whereas the apparently more successful later lines of highly specialized gill-breathing fishes all came to a dead end. The same story was repeated at the next major step, the reptiles, who derive from early, primitive amphibians – not from any of the later forms that we know.

And lastly, we come to the most striking case of paedomorphosis, the evolution of our own species. It is now generally recognized that the human adult resembles more the embryo of an ape than an adult ape. In both simian embryo and human adult, the ratio of the weight of the brain to total body weight is disproportionately high. In both, the closing of the sutures between the bones of the skull is retarded to permit the brain to expand. The back-to-front axis through man's head – ie, the direction of his line of sight – is at right angles to his spinal column: a condition which, in apes and other mammals, is found only in the embryonic, not in the adult stage. The same applies to the angle between backbone and uro-genital canal – which accounts for the singularity of the human way of copulating face to face. Other embryonic – or, to use Bolk's term, *foetalized* – features in adult man are: the absence of brow-ridges; the scantness and late appearance of body hair; pallor of the skin; retarded growth of the teeth, and a number of other features – including 'the rosy lips of man which were probably evolved in the young as an adaptation to prolonged suckling and have persisted in the adult, possibly under the influence of sexual selection' (de Beer).[6]

'If human evolution is to continue along the same lines as in the past', wrote J. B. S. Haldane, 'it will probably involve still greater prolongation of childhood and retardation of maturity. Some of the characters distinguishing adult man will be lost.'[7] There is, incidentally, a reverse of the medal which Aldous Huxley pointed out in one of his later, despairing novels: artificial prolongation of the absolute lifespan of man might provide an opportunity for features of the *adult* primate to reappear in human oldsters: Methuselah would turn into a hairy ape.* But this ghastly perspective does not concern us here.

* Huxley, *After Many a Summer*. Some physical characteristics in the very old seem to indicate that the genes which could produce such a transformation are still present in our gonads, but are prevented from becoming active by the neotenic retardation of the biological timeclock. The obvious conclusion is that prolongation of the human lifespan is only desirable if it can be accompanied by techniques which exert a parallel influence on the genetic clock.

The essence of the process which I have described is an evolutionary *retreat* from specialized adult forms of bodily structure and behaviour, to an earlier or more primitive, but also more plastic and less committed stage – followed by a sudden advance in a new direction. It is as if the stream of life had momentarily reversed its course, flowing uphill for a while, then opened up a new stream-bed. I shall try to show that this *reculer pour mieux sauter* – of drawing back to leap, of undoing and re-doing – is a favourite gambit in the grand strategy of the evolutionary process; and that it also plays an important part in the progress of science and art.

Figure 10 (on the next page) is from Garstang's original paper,[7a] and is meant to represent the progress of evolution by paedomorphosis. Z to Z_9 is the progression of zygotes (fertilized eggs) along the evolutionary ladder; A to A_9 represents the adult forms resulting from each zygote. Thus the black line from Z_4 to A_4, for instance, represents ontogeny, the transformation of egg into adult; the dotted line from A to A_9 represents phylogeny – the evolution of higher forms. But note that the thin lines of evolutionary progress do not lead directly from, say, A_4 to A_5 – that would be gerontomorphosis, the evolutionary transformation of an *adult* form. The line of progress branches off from the unfinished, embryonic stage of A_4. This represents a kind of evolutionary retreat from the finished product, and a new departure towards the evolutionary novelty Z_5–A_5. A_4 could be the adult sea cucumber: then the branching-off point on the line A_4–Z_4 would be its larva; or A_8 could be the adult primate ancestor of man, and the branching-off point its embryo – which is so much more like the A_9 – ourselves.

But Garstang's diagram could also represent a fundamental aspect of the evolution of *ideas*. The emergence of biological novelties and the creation of mental novelties are processes which show certain analogies. It is of course a truism that in mental evolution social inheritance through tradition and written records replaces genetic inheritance. But the analogy goes deeper: neither biological evolution nor mental progress follows a continuous line from A_6 to A_7. Neither of them is strictly cumulative in the sense of continuing to build where the last generation has left off. Both proceed in the zigzag fashion indicated in the diagram. The revolutions in the

FIGURE 10

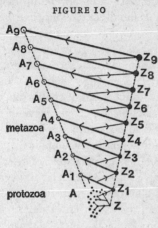

(after Garstang); see text

history of science are successful escapes from blind alleys. The evolution of knowledge is continuous only during those periods of consolidation and elaboration which follow a major breakthrough. Sooner or later, however, consolidation leads to increasing rigidity, orthodoxy, and so into the dead end of overspecialization – to the koala bear. Eventually there is a crisis and a new 'breakthrough' out of the blind alley – followed by another period of consolidation, a new orthodoxy, and so the cycle starts again.

But the new theoretical structure which emerges from the breakthrough is not built on top of the previous edifice; it branches out from the point where progress has gone wrong. The great revolutionary turns in the evolution of ideas have a decidedly paedomorphic character. Each zygote in the diagram would represent the seminal idea, the seed out of which a new theory develops until it reaches its adult, fully matured stage. One might call this the ontogeny of a theory. The history of science is a series of such ontogenies. True novelties are not derived directly from a previous adult theory, but from a new seminal idea – not from the sedentary sea urchin but from its mobile larva. Only in the quiet periods of consolidation do we find gerontomorphosis – small improvements added to a fully grown, established theory.

In the history of literature and art, the zigzag course is even more in evidence: Garstang's diagram could have been designed to show how periods of cumulative progress within a given 'school' and technique end inevitably in stagnation, mannerism or decadence, until the crisis is resolved by a revolutionary shift in sensibility, emphasis, style.*

At first sight the analogy may appear far-fetched; I shall try to show that it has a solid factual basis. Biological evolution is to a large extent a history of escapes from the blind alleys of over-specialization, the evolution of ideas a series of escapes from the bondage of mental habit; and the escape mechanism in both cases is based on the principle of undoing and re-doing, the draw-back-to-leap pattern.

Summary

After this anticipatory excursion, let me return for the last time to our starting point, the monkey at the typewriter. The monkey, according to the orthodox doctrine, is supposed to proceed by hit and miss, just as mental evolution, according to Behaviourist doctrine, is supposed to proceed by trial and error. In both cases, progress is secured by the stick-and-carrot method: the successful tries are rewarded by the carrot of survival or of 'reinforcement'; the harmful ones are weeded

* See *The Act of Creation*, Book One, Chapters X and XXIII.

out by the stick of extinction, or by 'negative reinforcement'.

The alternative view which is here proposed does not deny that trial and error are inherent in all progressive development. But there is a world of difference between the random tries of the monkey at the typewriter, and the various directive processes summarized in preceding chapters – starting with the hierarchic controls and regulations built into the genetic system and culminating in the draw-back-to-leap pattern of paedomorphosis. The orthodox view implies reeling off the available responses in the animal's repertory, or on the Tibetan prayer-wheel of mutations, until the correct one is hit upon by chance. The present view also relies on trial and error – each escape from a blind alley followed by a new departure is just that – but of a more complex, sophisticated and purposive kind: a groping and exploring, retreating and advancing towards higher levels of existence. 'Purpose', to quote H. J. Muller again, 'is not imported into Nature ... It is simply implicit in it.'[8]

Each of the salient facts that I have mentioned has been separately known for some time, but their implications have mostly been ignored by orthodox evolutionists. Yet if these isolated facts and theories are worked into a synthesis, they make the problem of evolution appear in a new light. There may be a monkey hammering away at the typewriter, but that device is organized in such a way as to defeat the monkey. Evolution is a process with a fixed code of rules, but with adaptable strategies. The code is inherent in the conditions of our planet; it restricts progress to a limited number of avenues; while at the same time all living matter strives towards the optimal utilization of the offered possibilities. The combined action of these two factors is manifested on each successive level: in the micro-hierarchy of the gene-complex, the canalization of embryonic development, and its stabilization by developmental homeostasis. Homologue organs – evolutionary holons – and similar animal forms arise from independent origins and provide archetypal unity-in-variety. The initiative of the animal, its curiosity and exploratory drive, act as pacemakers of progress; a quasi-Lamarckian mechanism of inheritance may in rare cases come to its aid; paedomorphosis offers an escape from blind alleys and a new departure in a different direction; and lastly, Darwinian selection operates within its limited scope.

The part played by a lucky chance mutation is reduced to that of the trigger which releases the coordinated action of the system; and to maintain that evolution is the product of blind chance means to confuse the simple action of the trigger with the complex, purposive processes which it sets off. Their purposiveness is manifested in different ways on different levels of the hierarchy; on each level there is trial and error, but on each level it takes a more sophisticated form. Some years ago, two eminent experimental psychologists, Tolman and Krechevsky, created a stir by proclaiming that the rat learns to run a maze by forming hypotheses.[9] Soon it may be permissible to extend the metaphor and to say that evolution progresses by making and discarding hypotheses, in the process of spelling out a roughed-in idea.

XIII

THE GLORY OF MAN

We are all in the gutter, but some of us are looking at the stars
OSCAR WILDE

THE activities of animal and man vary from machine-like automatisms to ingenious improvizations, according to the challenge they face.* Other things being equal, a monotonous environment leads to the mechanization of habits, to stereotyped routines which, repeated under the same unvarying conditions, follow the same rigid, unvarying course. The pedant who has become a slave of his habits thinks and acts like an automaton running on fixed tracks; his biological equivalent is the over-specialized animal – the koala bear clinging to his eucalyptus tree.

On the other hand, a changing, variable environment presents challenges which can only be met by flexible behaviour, variable strategies, alertness for exploiting favourable opportunities. The biological parallel is provided by the evolutionary strategies discussed in previous chapters.

However, the challenge may exceed a critical limit, so that it can no longer be met by the organism's customary skills. In such a major crisis – and both biological evolution and human history are punctuated by such crises – one of two possibilities may occur. The first is *degenerative* – leading to stagnation, biological senescence, or sudden extinction as the case may be. In the course of evolution this happened over and

* See Chapter Eight.

again; to each surviving species there are a hundred which failed to pass the test. Part Three of this book discusses the possibility that our own species is facing a crisis unique in its history, and that it is in imminent danger of failing the test.

The alternative possibility of reacting to a critical challenge is *regenerative* in a broad sense; it involves major reorganizations of structure and behaviour, which result in biological or mental progress. I shall try to show that both are based on the same draw-back-to-leap pattern, activating creative potentials which are dormant or inhibited in the normal routines of existence. In phylogeny, the major advances are due to the activation of embryonic potentials through paedomorphosis. In mental evolution something analogous seems to happen at each major turning point. The connection between the emergence of biological novelties and of mental novelties is provided by one of the basic attributes of living things: their capacity for *self-repair*. It is as fundamental to life as the capacity for reproduction, and in some lower organisms which multiply by fission or budding, the two are often indistinguishable.

Forms of Self-Repair

To understand this connection, we must proceed by a series of steps from primitive to higher animals, and finally to man. Needham has called regeneration 'one of the more spectacular pieces of magic in the repertoire of living organisms'.[1] Its most impressive manifestations are found in lowly creatures like flat-worms and polyps. If a flatworm is cut transversely into two parts, the head-end will grow a new tail, and the tail-end will grow a new head; even if cut into six or more slices, each slice can regenerate a complete animal.

Among higher animals, amphibians are capable of regenerating a lost limb or organ. When a salamander's leg is amputated, the muscle and skeletal tissues near the wound-surface de-differentiate and assume the appearance of embryonic cells.[2] Around the fourth day, a blastema or 'regeneration bud' is formed, similar to the 'organ bud' in the normal embryo; and from then on the process follows closely the growth of limbs in embryonic development. The region of the amputation-stump has regressed to a quasi-embryonic state and displays genetic growth-potentials which are inhibited in normal adult tissues.* I have compared (p 147) the gene-complex in a specialized cell to a piano with most keys inactivated by scotch tape; regenerating tissues have the whole keyboard at their disposal. The 'magic' of self-repair thus has a regressive (catabolic) and a progressive (anabolic) phase; it follows the undoing-re-doing pattern. 'The trauma plays a role similar to that of fertilization in embryonic development' (Hamburger[4]). The shock triggers off the creative reaction.

The replacement of a lost limb or lost eye is a phenomenon of a quite different order from that of adaptive processes in a normal environment. Regeneration could be called a 'meta-adaptation' to traumatizing challenges. But the power to perform such feats manifests itself only when the challenge exceeds a critical limit. The regenerative capacity of a species thus provides it with an additional safety device in the service of survival, which enters into action when normal adaptive measures fail – as the hydraulic shock-absorbers of a motor car enter into action when the limit of elasticity of the suspension springs is exceeded.

But it is more than a safety device: we have seen that the major phylogenetic changes were also brought about by a retreat from adult to embryonic forms. Indeed, the main line of development which led up to our species could be described as a series of operations of *phylogenetic self-repair*: of escapes

* To be accurate, the origin of the material which forms the blastema is still somewhat controversial; according to Hamburger,[3] it is likely that it consists partly of de-differentiated cells, partly of undifferentiated mesenchyme-type connective tissue-cells, which fulfil a function similar to that of the 'reserve' or 'regeneration' cells in primitive organisms.

from blind alleys by the undoing and re-moulding of mal-adapted structures.*

As we move further up the ladder from reptile to mammal, the power of regenerating bodily structures decreases, and is superseded by the increasing powers of the nervous system to reorganize behaviour. (Ultimately, of course, these reorganizations of function must also involve structural changes of a fine-grained nature in the nervous system, and so we are still moving along a continuous line.) More than a century ago, the German physiologist Pflüger demonstrated that even a decapitated frog is not just a reflex automaton. If a drop of acid was put on the back of its left foreleg, it would wipe it off with the hind-leg on the same side – this is the normal spinal reflex. But if the left hind-leg was immobilized, the frog used its *right* hind-leg instead, to wipe off the acid. Thus even the headless creature – a 'spinal preparation' as it is euphemistically called – proved itself capable of improvising when reflex-action was prevented.

In the first half of this century, K. S. Lashley and his collaborators, in a series of classical experiments, demolished the notion of the nervous system as a rigid mechanism. 'The results indicate', Lashley wrote, 'that when habitually used motor-organs are rendered non-functional by removal or paralysis, there is an immediate, spontaneous use of other motor systems which had not been previously associated with, or used in, the performance of the activity.'[5] The frog, using his left leg instead of the right one in the scratch-reflex, is a simple illustration of this; but Lashley showed that the nervous system is capable of incomparably more surprising feats; that brain tissues which normally serve a specialized function can, under certain circumstances, take over the function of other,

---

* Evidently, self-repair by the individual animal produces no evolutionary novelty, it merely restores its capability to function normally in a stable environment; 'phylogenetic self-repair', on the other hand, implies evolutionary changes in a changing environment.

injured brain tissues – much as the foragers in a beehive take over the functions of the kidnapped builders (p 130). To mention one among many examples: Lashley trained rats to choose between two alternative targets always the relatively brighter one. Then he removed the rats' visual cortex, and their discriminatory skill disappeared, as one would expect. But, contrary to what one would expect, the mutilated rats were able to learn the same skill again. Some other brain area, not normally specializing in visual learning, must have taken over this function, deputizing for the lost area.

Moreover, if a rat has learned to find its way through a maze, no matter what parts of its motor cortex are injured, it will still make a correct run; and if the injury renders it incapable of executing a right turn, it will achieve its aim by a three-quarter turn to the left. The rat may be blinded, deprived of smell, partially paralysed in different ways – each of which would throw the chain-reflex automaton, which it is supposed to be, completely out of gear. Yet: 'One drags himself through [the maze] with his forepaws; another falls at every step but gets through by a series of lunges; a third rolls over completely in making each turn, yet avoids rolling into a cul-de-sac and makes an errorless run.'[6]

Higher Forms of Self-Repair

As we arrive at the top of the ladder, we find in man the faculty of physical regeneration reduced to a minimum, but compensated by his unique powers to re-mould his patterns of behaviour – to meet critical challenges by creative responses.

Even on the level of elementary perception, learning to see through spectacles which turn the world upside down (see p 99) testifies to these powers. Experiments which create the same effect have been carried out on animals – reptiles and monkeys – by cutting the optic nerve and letting it grow together after twisting the severed end of the bundle half round the clock. As a result, the animals see the world upside-down, reach leftward when food is shown on the right, and downward if it is offered from above. They never get over the maladjustment. Human subjects, however, fitted with inverting glasses, do get over it. The effect at first is thoroughly upsetting: you see your body upside-down, your feet planted on a floor which has become the ceiling of the room. Or, with left-right inverters, you try to move away from a wall, and bump into it. Yet after a certain time, which may mean several days, the subject becomes adjusted to living in an inverted world, which then appears to him more or less normal again. The retinal image and its projection in the visual cortex are still upside-down; but, thanks to the intervention of some higher echelons in the hierarchy, the mental image has become reorganized. At the present stage of knowledge physiology has no satisfactory explanation for this phenomenon. All one can say is that if our orientation, our postural and motor reactions to the visual field depend on wiring circuits in the brain, living in an inverted world must entail a lot of undoing and re-doing in the wiring diagram.

Inverting spectacles are drastic gadgets; but most of us go through life wearing contact lenses of which we are unaware and which distort our perceptions in more subtle ways. Psychotherapy, ancient and modern, from shamanism down to contemporary forms of analytical or abreaction techniques, has always relied on that variety of undoing-re-doing procedure which Ernst Kris, an eminent practitioner, has called 'regression in the service of the ego'.[6a] The neurotic, with his compulsions, phobias, and elaborate defence-mechanisms, is a victim of rigid, maladaptive specialization – a koala bear hanging on for dear life to a barren telegraph pole. The therapist's aim is to induce a temporary regression in the patient; to make him retrace his steps to the point where they went wrong, and to come up again, metamorphosed, reborn.

The same pattern is reflected in countless variations on the death-and-resurrection motif in mythology. Joseph is thrown into a well; Mohammed goes out into the desert; Jesus is resurrected from the tomb; Jonah is reborn out of the belly of the whale. Goethe's *Stirb und Werde*, Toynbee's Withdrawal and Return, the mystic's dark night of the soul preceding spiritual rebirth, derive from the same archetype: draw back to leap. (The French *reculer pour mieux sauter* is a more expressive phrase for it.)

Self-Repair and Self-Realization

There is no sharp dividing line between self-repair and self-realization. All creative activity is a kind of do-it-yourself therapy, an attempt to come to terms with traumatizing challenges. In the scientist's case the trauma may be the impact of data which shake the foundations of a well-established theory, and make nonsense of his cherished beliefs; observations which contradict each other, problems which cause frustration and conflict. In the artist's case, challenge and response are manifested in his tantalizing struggle to express the inexpressible, to conquer the resistance of his medium, to escape from the distortions and constraints imposed by the conventional styles and techniques of his time.

We can now pick up the thread from the previous chapter: the decisive breakthroughs in science, art or philosophy are successful escapes from blind alleys, from the bondage of mental habits, from orthodoxy and over-specialization. The method of escape follows the same undoing-re-doing pattern as in biological evolution; and the zigzag course of advance in science or art repeats the pattern of Garstang's diagram.

Every revolution has a destructive and a constructive aspect. The destruction is wrought by jettisoning previously unassailable doctrines, and seemingly self-evident axioms of thought. The progress of science, like an ancient desert trail, is strewn with the bleached skeletons of discarded theories which seemed once to possess eternal life. Progress in art involves an equally agonizing reappraisal of accepted values, criteria of relevance, frames of perception. When we discuss the evolution of art and science from the historian's point of view, the undoing and re-doing is taken for granted as a normal, inevitable part of the story. If, however, we focus our attention on the concrete individual who initiated the revolutionary change, we are faced with the psychological problem of the nature of human creativity.

I have discussed that subject at length in *The Act of Creation*, but as it is pertinent to our present theme, I must briefly return to it. Readers acquainted with the earlier book may find that some passages in this chapter have a familiar ring; but they will also find that it carries the discussion a step further.

A quick glance at the evolution of astronomy will make the 'zigzag pattern' clearer. Newton once said that if he could see farther than others it was because he stood on the shoulders of giants. But did he really stand on their shoulders – or on some other part of their anatomy? He adopted Galileo's laws of free fall, but rejected Galileo's astronomy. He adopted Kepler's planetary laws, but demolished the rest of the Keplerian edifice. He did not take as his point of departure their completed 'adult' theories, but retraced their development to the point where it had gone wrong. Nor was the Keplerian edifice built on top of the Copernican edifice. That ramshackle structure of epicycles he tore down; he kept only its foundations. Nor did Copernicus continue to build where Ptolemy had left off. He went back two thousand years to Aristarchus. All great revolutions show, as already said, a notably 'paedomorphic' character. They demand as much undoing as re-doing.

But to undo a mental habit sanctified by dogma or tradition one has to overcome immensely powerful intellectual and emotional obstacles. I mean not only the inertial forces of society; the primary locus of resistance against heretical novelty is inside the skull of the individual who conceives of it. It reverberates in Kepler's agonized cry when he discovered that the planets move not in circular but in elliptical pathways: 'Who am I, Johannes Kepler, to destroy the divine symmetry of the circular orbits!' On a more down-to-earth level the same agony is reflected in Jerome Bruner's[7] experimental subjects who, when shown for a split second a playing card with a *black* queen of hearts, saw it as red, as it should be; and when the card was shown again, reacted with nausea at such a perversion of the laws of Nature. To unlearn is more difficult than to learn; and it seems that the task of breaking up rigid cognitive structures and reassembling them into a new synthesis cannot, as a rule, be performed in the full daylight of the conscious, rational mind. It can only be done by reverting to those more fluid, less committed and specialized forms of thinking which normally operate in the twilight zones of awareness.

Science and the Unconscious

There is a popular superstition, according to which scientists arrive at their discoveries by reasoning in strictly rational, precise, verbal terms. The evidence indicates that they do nothing of the sort.* To quote a single example: in 1945, Jacques Hadamard organized a nation-wide inquiry among eminent mathematicians in America to find out their working methods. The result showed that all of them, with only two exceptions, thought neither in verbal terms, nor in algebraic symbols, but relied on visual imagery of a vague, hazy kind. Einstein was among those who answered the questionnaire; he wrote: 'The words of the language as they are written or spoken do not seem to play any role in my mechanism of thought, which relies on more or less clear images of a visual and some of a muscular type. It seems to me that what you call

* Cf. *The Act of Creation*, Book One, Chapters V–XI.

full consciousness is a limit case which can never be fully accomplished because consciousness is a narrow thing.'[8]

Einstein's statement is typical. On the testimony of those original thinkers who have taken the trouble to record their methods of work, *not only verbal thinking but conscious thinking in general plays only a subordinate part in the brief, decisive phase of the creative act itself.* Their virtually unanimous emphasis on spontaneous intuitions and hunches of unconscious origin, which they are at a loss to explain, suggests that the role of strictly rational and verbal processes in scientific discovery has been vastly over-estimated since the age of enlightenment. There are always large chunks of irrationality embedded in the creative process, not only in art (where we are ready to accept it) but in the exact sciences as well.

The scientist who, facing an obstinate problem, regresses from precise verbal thinking to vague visual imagery, seems to follow Woodworth's advice: 'Often we have to get away from speech in order to think clearly.' Language can become a screen between the thinker and reality; and creativity often starts where language ends, that is, by regressing to pre-verbal levels of mental activity.

Now I do not mean, of course, that there is a little Socratic daemon housed in the scientist's or artist's skull, who does his homework for him; nor should one confuse unconscious mentation with Freud's 'primary process'. The primary process is defined by Freud as devoid of logic, governed by the pleasure-principle, accompanied by massive discharges of affect, and apt to confuse perception and hallucination. It seems that between this very primary process, and the so-called secondary process, governed by the reality-principle, we must interpolate several levels of mental activity which are not just mixtures of 'primary' and 'secondary', but are cognitive systems in their own right, each governed by its own canon of rules. The paranoid delusion, the dream, the daydream, free association, the mentality of children at various ages, and of primitives at various stages should not be lumped together, for each has its own logic or rules of the game. But while clearly different in many respects, all these forms of mentation have certain features in common, since they are ontogenetically, and perhaps phylogenetically, older than those of the civilized adult. They are less rigid, more tolerant, ready to combine seemingly incompatible ideas, and to perceive hidden analogies between cabbages and kings. One might call them 'games of the underground', because if not kept under restraint, they would play havoc with the routines of disciplined thinking. But under exceptional conditions, when disciplined thinking is at the end of its tether, a temporary indulgence in these underground games may suddenly produce a solution – some far-fetched, reckless combination of ideas, which would be beyond the reach of, or seem to be unacceptable to, the sober, rational mind. I have proposed the term 'bisociation' for these sudden leaps of creative imagination, to set them apart from the more pedestrian or associative routines. I shall come back to this in a moment; the point to retain is that the creative act in mental evolution again reflects the pattern of *reculer pour mieux sauter*, of a temporary regression, followed by a forward leap. We can carry the analogy further and interpret the Eureka cry as the signal of a happy escape from a blind alley – an act of mental self-repair.

Association and Bisociation

A convenient definition of associative thinking is given by Humphrey:[9] 'The term "association", or "mental association", is a general name often used in psychology to express the conditions under which mental events, whether of experience or behaviour, arise.' In other words, the term 'association' simply indicates the process by which one idea leads to another.

But an idea has associative connections with many other ideas established by past experiences; and which of these connections will be activated in a given situation depends on the *type* of thinking we are engaged in at the moment. Orderly thinking is always rule-governed, and even dreaming, or daydreaming, has its own rules. In the psychological laboratory, the experimenter lays down the rule 'name opposites'. Then he says 'dark', and the subject promptly says 'light'. But if the rule is 'synonyms', then the subject will associate 'dark' with 'black' or 'night' or 'shadow'. To talk of stimuli as if they were acting in a vacuum is meaningless; what response a given stimulus will evoke depends on the rules of the game we are playing at the time – the *canon* (see Chapter III) of that particular mental skill. But we do not live in laboratories where the rules of the game are laid down by explicit orders; in the normal routines of thinking and talking the rules are implicit and unconscious.

This applies not only to the rules of grammar, syntax, and common-or-garden logic, but also to those which govern the more complex structures we call 'frames of reference', 'universes of discourse' or 'associative contexts'; and to the 'hidden persuaders' which prejudice our reasoning. In *The Act of Creation* I proposed the term 'matrix' as a unifying formula to refer to such cognitive structures, that is to say, to all *mental habits and skills governed by a fixed set of rules but capable of varied strategies in attacking a problem*. In other words, matrices are *cognitive holons* and display all the characteristics of holons discussed in previous chapters. They are controlled by their canons, but guided by feedback from the environment – the distribution of the men on the chessboard, the features of the problem in hand. They range from extremes of pedantic rigidity to liberal open-mindedness – within limits. They are ordered into 'vertical' abstractive hierarchies, which interlace in 'horizontal' associative networks and cross-references.

Let me repeat: all routine thinking is comparable to playing a game according to fixed rules and more or less flexible strategies. The game of chess allows for more varied strategies than draughts, a vaster number of choices among moves permitted by the rules. But there is a limit to them; and there are hopeless situations in chess when the most subtle strategies won't save you – short of offering your opponent a jumbo-sized Martini. Now, in fact, there is no rule in chess preventing you from doing that. But making a person drunk while remaining sober oneself is a different sort of game with a different context. Combining the two games is a bisociation. In other words, associative routine means thinking according to a given set of rules on a single plane, as it were. The bisociative act means combining two different sets of rules, to live on several planes at once.

I do not mean to belittle the value of law-abiding routines. They lend coherence and stability to behaviour, and structured order to thought. But when the challenge exceeds a critical limit, adaptive routines are no longer sufficient. The world moves on and new facts arise, creating problems which cannot be solved within the conventional frames of reference, by applying to them the accepted rules of the game. Then the crisis is on, with its desperate search for a remedy, the unorthodox improvization which will lead to the new synthesis – the act of mental self-repair.

The Latin *cogito* comes from *coagitare*, to shake together. *Bisociation means combining two hitherto unrelated cognitive matrices in such a way that a new level is added to the hierarchy, which contains the previously separate structures as its members.* The motions of the tides were known to man from time immemorial. So were the motions of the moon. But the idea to relate the two, the idea that the tides were due to the attraction of the moon, occurred, as far as we know, for the first time to a German astronomer in the seventeenth century; and when Galileo read about it, he laughed it off as an occult fancy. Moral: the more familiar the previously unrelated structures are, the more striking the emergent synthesis, and the more obvious it looks in the driver's mirror of hindsight. The history of science is a history of marriages between ideas which were previously strangers to each other, and frequently considered as incompatible. Lodestones – magnets – were known in antiquity as a curiosity of Nature. In the Middle Ages they were used for two purposes: as navigators' compasses and as a means to attract an estranged wife back to her husband. Equally well known were the curious properties of amber which, when rubbed, acquired the virtue of attracting flimsy objects. The Greek for amber is *elektron*, but the Greeks were not much interested in electricity; nor were the Middle Ages. For nearly two thousand years, electricity and magnetism were considered as separate phenomena, in no way related to each other. In 1820 Hans Christian Oersted discovered that an electric current flowing through a wire deflected a magnetic compass which happened to be lying on his table. At that moment the two contexts began to fuse into one: electro-magnetism, creating a kind of chain-reaction which is still continuing and gaining in momentum.

The AHA Reaction

From Pythagoras, who combined arithmetic and geometry, to Newton, who combined Galileo's studies of the motion of projectiles with Kepler's equations of planetary orbits, to Einstein, who unified energy and matter in a single sinister equation, the pattern is always the same. The creative act does not create something out of nothing, like the God of the Old Testament; it combines, reshuffles and relates already existing but hitherto separate ideas, facts, frames of perception, associative contexts. This act of cross-fertilization – or self-fertilization within a single brain – seems to be the essence of creativity, and to justify the term 'bisociation'.*

* Similar views have been put forward, among others, by the mathematician Henri Poincaré, who in an oft-quoted lecture explained discovery as the happy

Take the example of Gutenberg, who invented the printing press (or at least invented it independently from others). His first idea was to cast letter-types like signet rings or seals. But how could he assemble thousands of little seals in such a way that they made an even imprint on paper? He struggled with the problem for years, until one day he went to a wine harvest in his native Rhineland, and presumably got drunk. He wrote in a letter: 'I watched the wine flowing, and going back from the effect to the cause, I studied the power of the wine press which nothing can resist . . .' At that moment the penny dropped: seals and the wine press combined gave the letter press.

Gestalt psychologists have coined a word for that moment of truth, the flash of illumination, when bits of the puzzle suddenly click into place – they call it the AHA experience. But this is not the only type of reaction which the bisociative click can produce. A quite different kind of response is aroused by telling a story like the following:

> A Marquis at the court of Louis XV had unexpectedly returned from a journey and, on entering his wife's boudoir, found her in the arms of a bishop. After a moment's hesitation, the Marquis walked calmly to the window, leaned out and began going through the motions of blessing the people in the street.
>
> 'What are you doing?' cried the anguished wife.
>
> 'Monseigneur is performing my functions,' replied the noble-man, 'so I am performing his.'*

---

meeting of 'hooked atoms of thought' in the unconscious mind. According to Sir Frederick Bartlett, 'the most important features of original experimental thinking is the discovery of overlap . . . where formerly only isolation and difference were recognized'.[10] Jerome Bruner[11] considers all forms of creativity as a result of 'combinatorial activity'. McKellar[12] talks of the 'fusion' of perceptions, Kubie[13] of the 'discovery of unexpected connections between things'; and so on, back to Goethe's 'connect, always connect'.

* I have used this particular story in The Act of Creation and am using it again because of its neat pattern. Most anecdotes need lengthy explanations to make their logical structure clear.

Laughter may be called the HAHA reaction.* Let us briefly discuss first the logical, then the emotional, aspect of it.

The HAHA Reaction

The Marquis' behaviour is both unexpected and perfectly logical – but of a logic not usually applied to this type of situation. It is the logic of the division of labour, where the rule of the game is the *quid pro quo*, the give-and-take. But we expected, of course, that his reactions would be governed by a quite different canon, that of sexual morality. It is the interaction between these two mutually exclusive associative contexts which produces the comic effect. It compels us to perceive the situation at the same time in two self-consistent but habitually incompatible frames of reference; it makes us function on two wave-lengths simultaneously. While this unusual condition lasts, the event is not, as is normally the case, perceived in a single frame of reference, but *bisociated* with two.

But this unusual condition does not last for long. The act of discovery leads to a lasting synthesis, a *fusion* of the two previously unrelated frames of reference; in the comic bisociation we have a *collision* between incompatible frames which for a brief moment cross each other's path. However, the difference is not absolute. Whether the frames are compatible or not, whether they will collide or merge, depends on subjective factors – for after all, the colliding or merging takes place in the minds of the audience. In Kepler's mind the motions of the moon and the motions of the tides fused – they became branches of the same causative hierarchy. But Galileo treated Kepler's theory literally as a joke – he called it an 'occult fancy'. The history of science abounds with examples of discoveries greeted with howls of laughter because they

* I am grateful to Dr Brennig James for having suggested this term as a twin to the AHA reaction.

seemed to be a marriage of incompatibles – until the marriage bore fruit and the alleged incompatibility of the partners turned out to derive from prejudice. The humorist, on the other hand, deliberately chooses discordant codes of behaviour, or universes of discourse, to expose their hidden incongruities in the resulting clash. Comic discovery is paradox stated – scientific discovery is paradox resolved.

Looked at from his own point of view, the Marquis' gesture was a truly original inspiration. If he had followed the conventional rules of the game, he would have had to beat up or kill the Bishop. But at the court of Louis XV assassinating a Monseigneur would have been considered, if not exactly a crime, still in very bad taste; it could not be done. To solve the problem, that is, to save his face and at the same time humiliate his opponent – a second frame of reference, governed by different rules of the game, had to be brought into the situation and combined, bisociated, with the first. All original comic invention is a creative act, a malicious discovery.

Laughter and Emotion

The emphasis is on malicious, and this brings us from the *logic* of humour to the *emotional factor* in the HAHA reaction. When the expert storyteller tells an anecdote, he creates a certain tension which mounts as the narrative progresses. But it never reaches its expected climax. The punch-line acts like a guillotine which cuts across the logical development of the situation; it debunks our dramatic expectations, the tension becomes redundant and is exploded in laughter. To put it differently, laughter disposes of emotional tension which has become pointless, is denied by reason, and has to be somehow worked off along physiological channels of least resistance.

If you look at the brutal merriment of the people in a tavern scene by Hogarth or Rawlinson, you realize at once that they are working off their surplus of adrenalin by con-tractions of the face muscles, slapping of thighs and explosive exhalations of breath from the half-closed glottis. The emotions worked off in laughter are aggression, sexual gloat-ing, conscious or unconscious sadism – all operating through the sympathico-adrenal system. However, when you look at a clever *New Yorker* cartoon, Homeric laughter yields to an amused and rarefied smile; the ample flow of adrenalin has been distilled into a grain of Attic salt. Take, for instance, that classic definition: 'What is a sadist? A person who is kind to a masochist . . .' The word 'witticism' is derived from 'wit' in its original sense of ingenuity; the two domains are con-tinuous, without a sharp dividing line. As we move from the coarse towards the subtler forms of humour, the joke shades into epigram and riddle, the comic simile into the hidden analogy; and the emotions involved show a similar transition. The emotive voltage discharged in coarse laughter is aggres-sion robbed of its purpose; the tension discharged in the AHA reaction is derived from an intellectual challenge. It snaps at the moment when the penny drops – when we have solved the riddle hidden in the *New Yorker* cartoon, in a brain-teaser or in a scientific problem.

Let me repeat, the two domains of humour and discovery form a continuum. As we travel across it, from left to centre, so to speak, the emotional climate gradually changes from the malice of the jester to the detached objectivity of the sage. And if we now continue the journey in the same direction, we find equally gradual transitions into the third domain of creativity, that of the artist. The artist, too, hints rather than states, and poses riddles; and so we get a symmetrically reversed transition towards the other end of the spectrum, from highly intellectualized art forms towards the more sensual and emotive, ending in the thought-free beatitude of the mystic.

The AH Reaction

But how does one define the emotional climate of art? How does one classify the emotions which give rise to the experience of beauty? If you leaf through textbooks of experimental psychology, you won't find much of it. When Behaviourists use the word 'emotion', they nearly always refer to hunger, sex, rage and fear, and the related effects of the release of adrenalin. They have no explanations to offer for the curious reaction one experiences when listening to Mozart, or looking at the ocean, or reading for the first time John Donne's *Holy Sonnets*. Nor will you find in the textbooks a description of the physiological processes accompanying the reaction: moistening of the eyes, catching one's breath, followed by a kind of rapt tranquillity, the draining of all tensions. Let us call this the AH reaction – and thus complete the trinity.

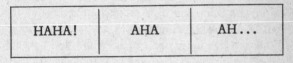

| HAHA! | AHA | AH... |

Laughter and weeping, the Greek masks of comedy and tragedy, mark the extremes of a continuous spectrum; both are overflow reflexes, but in every other respect are physiological opposites. Laughter is mediated by the sympathico-adrenal branch of the autonomic nervous system, weeping by the para-sympathetic branch; the first tends to galvanize the body into action, the second tends towards passivity and catharsis. Watch yourself breathing when you laugh: long deep intakes of air, followed by bursts of exhalatory puffs – ha, ha, ha! In weeping, you do the opposite: short, gasping inspirations – sobs – are followed by long, sighing expirations – a-a-h, aah . . .

In keeping with this, the emotions which overflow in the AH reaction are the direct opposites of those exploded in laughter. The latter belong to the adrenergic, aggressive-defensive type of emotions. In our theory, these are manifestations of the *self-assertive* tendency. Their opposites I shall call the *self-transcending* emotions, derived from the *integrative* tendency. They are epitomized in what Freud called the oceanic feeling: that expansion of awareness which one experiences on occasion in an empty cathedral when eternity is looking through the window of time, and in which the self seems to dissolve like a grain of salt in a lot of water.

Art and Emotion

The polarity between the integrative and self-assertive tendencies is, as we have seen, inherent in all hierarchic order and manifested on every level, from embryonic development to international politics. The *integrative* tendency, which is our present concern, reflects the 'part-ness' of a holon, its dependence on, and belonging to, a more complex whole. It is at work all along the line, from the physical symbiosis of organelles, through the aggregation of herd and flock, up to the cohesive forces in insect states and primate societies.

The single individual, considered as a whole, represents the apex of the organismic hierarchy, but at the same time he is a part, an elementary unit in the social hierarchy. The dichotomy is reflected in his emotional nature. His self-assertion as an autonomous, independent whole is expressed in ambition, competitiveness, aggressive-defensive behaviour, as the case may be. His integrative tendency reflects his dependence, as a part, on family, tribe, society. But – and this is an essential but – participation in a social group is not always sufficient to satisfy the individual's integrative potential; and to some people it provides no satisfaction at all. Every man is a holon, and feels the need to be a part of something that transcends the narrow boundaries of the self; that need is at the root of the 'self-transcending' emotions. It *may* be fulfilled by social identification – to which we shall return in Part Three. But that higher entity to which the individual craves to surrender his identity may also be God, Nature or Art; the magic of form, the ocean of sound, or the mathematical symbols of convergence in the infinite. This is the type of emotion which enters into the AH reaction.

The self-transcending emotions show a wide range of variety. They may be joyous or sad, tragic or lyrical; their common denominator, to repeat this once more, is the feeling of *integrative participation in an experience which transcends the boundaries of the self.*

Self-assertive emotions tend towards bodily activity; the self-transcending emotions are essentially passive and cathartic. The former are manifested in aggressive-defensive behaviour; the latter in empathy, rapport and identification, admiration and wonder. The shedding of tears is an outlet for an excess of the self-transcending emotions, as laughter is for the self-assertive emotions. In laughter, tension is suddenly exploded, emotion debunked; in weeping it is gradually drained away, without breaking the continuity of mood; emotion and thought remain united. The self-transcending emotions do not tend towards action, but towards quiescence. Respiration and pulse rate are slowed down; 'entrancement' is a step towards the trance-like states induced by contemplative mystics; the emotion is of a quality that cannot be consummated by any specific voluntary act. You cannot take the mountain panorama home with you; you cannot merge with the infinite by any exertion of the body; to be 'overwhelmed' by awe and wonder, 'enraptured' by a smile, 'entranced' by beauty – each of these words expresses passive surrender. The surplus of emotion cannot be worked off by any purposeful muscular activity, it can only be consummated in internal – visceral and glandular – processes.

The various causes which may lead to an overflow of tears – aesthetic or religious rapture, bereavement, joy, sympathy, self-pity – all have this basic element in common: a craving to transcend the island boundaries of the individual, to enter into a symbiotic communion with a human being, living or dead, or some higher entity, real or imaginary, of which the self is felt to be a part.

The self-transcending emotions are the step-children of psychology, but they are as basic, and as firmly rooted in biology as their opposites. Freud and Piaget, among others, have emphasized the fact that the very young child does not differentiate between ego and environment. The nourishing breast appears to it as a more intimate possession than the toes of its own body. It is aware of events, but not of itself as a separate entity. It lives in a state of mental symbiosis with the outer world, a continuation of the biological symbiosis in the womb. The universe is focussed on the self, and the self *is* the universe – a condition which Piaget called 'protoplasmic' or 'symbiotic' consciousness.* It may be likened to a fluid universe, traversed by the tidal rise and fall of physiological needs, and by minor storms which come and go without leaving solid traces. Gradually the floods recede, and the first islands of objective reality emerge; the contours grow firmer and sharper; the islands grow into continents, the dry territories of reality are mapped out; but side by side with it the liquid world coexists, surrounding it, interpenetrating it by canals and inland lakes, the vestigial relics of the erstwhile symbiotic communion – the origin of that 'oceanic feeling' which the artist and the mystic strive to recapture on a higher level of development, at a higher turn of the spiral.

It is also at the origin of the sympathetic magic practised by all primitive and not so primitive people. When the medicine man disguises himself as the rain-god, he produces rain. Drawing a picture of a slain bison guarantees a successful hunt. This is the ancient unitary source out of which the ritual

* For a more recent treatment of this subject, see E. G. Schachtel's important work *Metamorphosis* (1963).

dance and song, the mystery plays of the Acheans and the calendars of the Babylonian priest-astronomers were derived. The shadows in Plato's cave are symbols of man's loneliness; the paintings in the Altamira caves are symbols of his magic powers.

We have travelled a long way from Altamira and Lascaux, but the artist's inspirations and the scientist's intuitions are still fed by that same unitary source – though by now we should rather call it an underground river. Wishes do not displace mountains, but in our dreams they still do. Symbiotic consciousness is never completely defeated, merely relegated underground to those primitive levels in the mental hierarchy where the boundaries of the ego are still fluid and blurred – as blurred as the distinction between the actor and the hero whom he impersonates – and with whom the spectator identifies. The actor on the stage is himself and somebody else at the same time – he is both the dancer and the rain-god. Dramatic illusion is the coexistence in the spectator's mind of two universes which are logically incompatible; his awareness, suspended between the two planes, exemplifies the bisociative process in its most striking form. All the more striking because he produces physical symptoms – palpitations, sweating or tears – in response to the perils of a Desdemona whom he *knows* to exist merely as a shadow on the TV screen.

The Creative Trinity

But let Othello get the hiccoughs – and instead of *co-existence* between the two planes juxtaposed in the spectator's mind, you get *collision* between them. Comic impersonation produces the HAHA reaction because the parodist arouses aggression and malice; whereas tragic impersonation achieves the suspension of disbelief, the co-existence of incompatible planes, because the tragedian induces the spectator to identify. It excites the self-transcending and inhibits or neutralizes the self-assertive

emotions. Even when fear and anger are aroused in the spectator, these are *vicarious* emotions, derived from his identification with the hero – which in itself is a self-transcending act.
The vicarious emotions aroused in this manner carry a dominant element of sympathy, which facilitates catharsis – in
conformity with the Aristotelian definition: 'Through inci-
dents arousing horror and pity to accomplish the purgation of
such emotions.' Art is a school of self-transcendence.

We thus arrive at a further generalization. *The HAHA
reaction signals the collision of bisociated contexts, the AHA
reaction signals their fusion, the AH reaction their juxtaposition.**
When you read a poem, two frames of reference interact in
your mind: one governed by meaning, the other by rhythmic
patterns of sound. Moreover, these two matrices operate on
two different levels of awareness – the first in broad daylight,
the other much deeper down, on those archaic levels of the
mental hierarchy which reverberate to the shaman's tom-tom,
and which make us particularly receptive to, and suggestible
by, messages which arrive in a rhythmic pattern or accompanied by such a pattern.†

Routine thinking involves a single matrix, artistic experience always involves more than one. Rhythm and metre,
rhyme and euphony, are not artificial ornaments of language,
but combinations of contemporary, sophisticated frames of
reference with archaic and emotionally more powerful games
of the mind. The same is true of poetic imagery: visual

---

* This difference is reflected in the quasi-cumulative progression of science
through a series of successive mergers, compared to the quasi-timeless character
of art, its continuous restatement of basic patterns of experience in changing
idioms. But I said twice 'quasi' because the difference is a matter of degrees;
because the progress of science is not cumulative in the strict sense – it is moving
in a zigzag course rather than in a straight line; and on the other hand, the
development of a given art form over a period of time often displays a cumulative progression.

† 'In the rhyme', wrote Proust, 'the superimposition of two systems, one
intellectual, the other metric . . . is a primary element of ordered complexity,
that is to say, of beauty.'

thinking is an earlier form of mental activity than thinking in verbal concepts; we dream mostly in pictures. In other words, creative activity always implies a *temporary regression* to these archaic levels, while a simultaneous process goes on in parallel on the highest, most articulate and critical level: the poet is like a skin-diver with a breathing tube.

It has been said that scientific discovery consists in seeing an analogy where nobody has seen one before. When, in the Song of Songs, Solomon compared the Shulamite's neck to a tower of ivory, he saw an analogy which nobody had seen before; when Harvey compared the heart of a fish to a mechanical pump, he did the same; and when the caricaturist draws a nose like a cucumber, he again does just that. In fact, all combinatorial, bisociative patterns are trivalent – they can enter the service of humour, discovery or art, as the case may be.

Man has always looked at Nature by superimposing a second frame on the retinal image – mythological, anthropomorphic, scientific frames. The artist imposes his style by emphasizing contours or surfaces, stability or motion, curves or cubes. So, of course, does the caricaturist; only his motives, and his criteria of relevance, are different. And so does the scientist. A geographical map has the same relation to a landscape as a character-sketch to a face; every diagram or model, every schematic or symbolic representation of physical or mental processes is an unemotional caricature – or stylized portrait – of reality.

In the language of the Behaviourist, we would have to say that Cézanne, glancing at a landscape, receives a stimulus, to which he responds by putting a dab of paint on the canvas – and that is all there is to it. But in fact the two activities take place on two different planes. The stimulus comes from one environment, the distant landscape. The response acts on a different environment, a rectangular surface of ten inches by fifteen. The two environments obey two different sets of laws.

An isolated brush-stroke does not represent an isolated detail in the landscape. There are no point-to-point correspondences between the two planes; each obeys a different rule of the game. The artist's vision is bi-focal, just as the poet's voice is bi-vocal, as he bisociates sound and meaning.

Summary

What I have been trying to suggest in this chapter is that all creative activity – the conscious and unconscious processes underlying the three domains of artistic inspiration, scientific discovery and comic inventiveness – have a basic pattern in common: the co-agitation or shaking together of already existing but previously separate areas of knowledge, frames of perception or universes of discourse. But conscious rational thinking is not always the best cocktail shaker. It is invaluable so long as the challenge does not exceed a certain limit; when that is the case, it can only be met by an undoing and re-forming of the mental hierarchy, a temporary regression culminating in the bisociative act which adds a new level to the open-ended structure. It is the highest form of mental self-repair, of escape from the blind alleys of stagnation, over-specialization and maladjustment; but it is already foreshadowed by analogous phenomena on lower levels of the evolutionary scale, discussed in previous chapters.

The three domains of creativity form a continuum. The boundaries between science and art, between the AH reaction and the AHA reaction, are fluid, whether we consider architecture or cooking or psychiatry or the writing of history. There is nowhere a sharp break where witticism changes into wit, or where science stops and art begins. The emotional climate in the three domains shows equally continuous transitions. At one end of the spectrum the coarse practical joker is motivated by self-assertive malice; the artist at the opposite extreme, by the craving for self-transcendence. The motivation of the scientist operating in the middle region of the continuum is a well-balanced combination of the two: ambition and competitiveness neutralized by self-transcending devotion to his task. Science is the neutral art.

Science, the hoary cliché goes, aims at truth, art at beauty. However, the criteria of truth, such as verification by experiment, are not as hard and clean as we tend to believe. The same experimental data can often be interpreted in more than one way – and that is why the history of science echoes with as many impassioned controversies as the history of literary criticism. Moreover, the verification of a discovery comes *after* the act; the creative act itself is for the scientist, as for the artist, a leap into the dark, where both are equally dependent on their fallible intuitions. And the greatest mathematicians and physicists have confessed that at those decisive moments, when taking the plunge, they were guided not by logic, but by a sense of beauty which they were unable to define. Vice versa, painters and sculptors, not to mention architects, have always been guided, and often obsessed, by scientific or pseudo-scientific theories and criteria of truth – the golden section, the laws of perspective, Dürer's and Leonardo's laws of proportion in representing the human body, Cézanne's doctrine that everything in nature is modelled on the cylinder and sphere, Braque's alternative theory that cubes should be substituted for spheres. And the same is true, of course, for literature, from the formal laws imposed on Greek tragedy to various recent schools, and equally for the rules of harmony and counterpoint in music. In other words, the experience of truth, however subjective, must be present for the experience of beauty to arise; and vice versa: an 'elegant' solution of a problem gives rise in the connoisseur to the experience of beauty. Intellectual illumination and emotional catharsis are complementary aspects of an indivisible process.

I have been trying in this chapter to give an outline of a

theory of creativity which I have developed in earlier work; and to carry it a step further. An outline must necessarily be sketchy; all I can do is to refer the interested reader to the original – and to apologize for having cribbed a few passages from it.

XIV

THE GHOST IN THE MACHINE

The great questions are those an intelligent child asks and, getting no answers, stops asking.

GEORGE WALD

HAVING travelled this far, the reader may protest that it is sacrilegious to call the creation of a Brahms symphony or Newton's discovery of the laws of motion an act of self-repair, and to compare it to the mutation of a sea-squirt larva, the regeneration of a salamander limb, or the rehabilitation of patients by psychotherapy. On the contrary, I believe that this overall view of biological and mental evolution reveals the working of creative forces all along the line towards an optimal realization of the potentials of living matter and living minds – a universal tendency towards 'spontaneously developing states of greater heterogeneity and complexity' (Herrick[1]). These sober words of a great physiologist point to one of the basic facts of life which science had long lost from sight, and is still slow in re-discovering.

The 'Second Law'

The gospel of flat-earth science was Clausius' famous Second Law of Thermodynamics. It asserted that the universe is running down like a clockwork affected by metal fatigue, because its energy is being steadily, inexorably degraded, dissipated into heat, until it will finally dissolve into a single, shapeless, homogeneous bubble of gas of uniform temperature just above absolute zero, inert and motionless – the cosmic *Wärmetod*. Only in recent times did science begin to recover from the hypnotic effect of this nightmare, and to realize that the Second Law *applies only in the special case of so-called 'closed systems'* (such as a gas enclosed in a perfectly isolated container). But no such closed systems exist even in inanimate nature, and whether or not the universe as a whole is a closed system in this sense is anybody's guess. All living organisms, however, are 'open systems', that is to say, they maintain their complex form and functions through continuous exchanges of energies and material with their environment.★ Instead of 'running down' like a mechanical clock that dissipates its energies through friction, the living organism is constantly 'building up' more complex substances from the substances it feeds on, more complex forms of energies from the energies it absorbs, and more complex patterns of information – perceptions, feelings, thoughts – from the input of its receptor organs.

'Hierarchical organization on the one hand, and the characteristics of open systems on the other, are fundamental principles of living nature, and the advancement of theoretical biology will depend mainly on the development of a theory of these two fundamentals.'[2] This was written many years ago by von Bertalanffy, one of the pioneers of the new orientation in biology, but it was not greeted with much enthusiasm. The idea that organisms, in contrast to machines, were primarily *active* instead of being merely *reactive*, that instead of passively adapting to their environment they were 'creative in the sense that new patterns of structure and behaviour are constantly fabricated' (Herrick[3]), was profoundly distasteful to the *Zeitgeist*. These 'open systems' which were capable of maintaining themselves indefinitely in a state of dynamic equili-

★ The term 'open system' in this technical sense is of course quite unrelated to the concept of infinite regress in open-ended hierarchies.

brium sounded suspiciously like perpetual-motion machines – ruled out forever by that implacable Second Law. That this Law did not apply to living matter, and was in a sense *reversed* in living matter, was indeed hard to accept by an orthodoxy still convinced that all phenomena of life could ultimately be reduced to the laws of physics. It was in fact a physicist, not a biologist, the Nobel laureate Erwin Schrödinger, who summed up the position in his celebrated paradox: 'What an organism feeds on is negative entropy.'[4] Now *entropy* ('transformed energy') is the name for degraded energy which has been dissipated by friction and other wasteful processes into the random motion of molecules, and which cannot be retrieved. In other words, entropy is a measure of energy waste, of order degraded into disorder. Clausius' Second Law can be expressed by saying that the entropy of a closed system always tends to increase towards a maximum, when all order will have vanished as in the chaotic motion of gas molecules;* so if the universe is a closed system, it must eventually 'unwind' itself from cosmos into chaos.

Thus entropy became a key-concept of mechanistically orientated science – its alias for Thanatos, the God of Death. 'Negative entropy', then, is a typically perverse way of referring to the power of life to 'build *up*' complex systems out of simpler elements, structured patterns out of shapelessness, order out of disorder. Equally characteristic is the fact that Norbert Wiener, the father of cybernetics (see p 120f) defined information as 'essentially a negative entropy'.[5] In modern communication theory, entropy is equated with 'noise' which causes a waste of information (it may be acoustic noise, like a hum on the radio receiver, or 'visual noise', like the flickering of the TV image). Our perceptions, then, become 'negative noises', knowledge becomes negative ignorance, amusement the absence of boredom, and cosmos the absence of chaos. But whatever the terminology, the fact

* The word 'gas' was actually derived from the Greek *chaos*.

remains that living organisms have the power to build up ordered, coherent perceptions and complex systems of knowledge out of the chaos of sensations impinging on them; life sucks information from the environment as it feeds on its substances and synthesises its energies. The same irrepressible 'building-up' tendency is manifested in phylogenesis, in the phenomena of evolution by initiative, the slow progress towards more complex forms and functions, the emergence of new levels in the organismic hierarchy and of new methods of coordination, resulting in greater independence from, and mastery of, the environment.

We need not be unduly upset about the use of negatives to describe these palpably positive processes, because it merely reflects the scientist's unconscious dread of falling into the heresy of vitalism, of reverting to Aristotle's entelechies, Leibnitz' monads, or Bergson's *élan vital*. There would indeed be nothing to be gained by a romantic revival of concepts which suffer from what Whitehead once called 'misplaced concreteness'. It seems wiser to stick to the more cautious and non-committal formulations of that *élan* by hard-boiled empiricists, who would nevertheless refuse to believe that the earth is flat and that evolution from randomness to order is the work of random events. Let me add to the list of those whom I have already quoted, Herbert Spencer's Law of Evolution as 'an integration of matter . . . from an indefinite, incoherent homogeneity, to a definite, coherent heterogeneity'.[6] The German biologist Woltereck coined the term 'anamorphosis' for the primary and ubiquitous trend in Nature towards the emergence of more complex forms; L. L. Whyte called it 'the fundamental principle of the development of pattern';* Einstein rejected the concept of randomness by

* 'Two major contrasted tendencies are evident in natural processes, towards local order and towards uniformity of general "disorder". The first is displayed in all processes where a region of order tends to differentiate itself from a less ordered environment. This is seen in crystallization, in chemical combination, and in most organic processes. The second tendency is displayed in

his 'refusal to believe that God plays dice with the world'; Schrödinger was led to postulate the existence of an ego which ultimately 'controls the motions of the atoms'.[6b] Lastly, to quote von Bertalanffy again: 'According to the Second Law of Thermodynamics, the general direction of physical events is towards decrease of order and organization. In contrast to this, a direction towards increasing order seems to be present in evolution.'[7]

In the present theory this directive factor is called the Integrative Tendency. I have tried to show that it is inherent in the concept of hierarchic order, and manifested on every level, from the symbiosis of organelles in the cell, to ecological communities and human societies. Every living holon has the dual tendency to preserve and assert its individuality, such as it is, but at the same time to function as an integrated part of an existing whole, or an evolving whole.

This much, I think, one can say with some confidence. Beyond that, the beginnings of the evolutionary story are hidden behind the big bang with which the universe started, if it started that way, or behind the continuous creation of matter out of nothing, if that is the way it is. Evolution, as the cliché goes, is a journey of unknown origin to an unknown destination, a sailing along a vast ocean; but we can at least map the route which has carried us from the sea-cucumber stage to the conquest of the moon; and to deny that there is a wind blowing which makes the sails move is not only a rash hypothesis, but also a sign of metaphysical churlishness.

But whether we say that the wind, coming from a distant past, pushes the boat along, or whether we say that it drags it along into the future, is a matter of convenience. The

---

the processes of radiation and diffusion, and leads towards a uniformity of thermal "disorder". The two tendencies normally work in opposed directions, the first producing regions of differentiated order and the second dispersing them' (Whyte[6a]).

purposiveness of all vital processes – the striving of the blastula to grow into a chicken, regardless of the obstacles and hazards to which it is exposed, the resourceful improvizations of animals and men to reach the target of their endeavours, might lead the unprejudiced observer to the conclusion that the pull of the future is as real, and sometimes more decisive than the pressure of the past. The pressure may be compared to the force exerted by a compressed spring, the pull to that of an expanded spring, threaded on the axis of time. Neither of them is more or less mechanistic than the other. Modern physics is re-thinking its ideas about time. If the future is completely determined in the Laplacian sense, then one description is as valid as the other. If it is indeterminate in the Heisenbergian sense, and there is an unknown factor operating within the air bubbles in the stream of causality, it may be influenced by the future as much as by the past. We ought to try to keep an open mind about causality and finality, even if the Zeitgeist frowns on us.*

The Swing of the Pendulum

In his book *The Concept of Mind* (1949) Professor Gilbert Ryle, an Oxford philosopher of strong Behaviourist leanings, attacked the customary distinction made between physical and mental events by calling the latter ('with deliberate abusiveness', as he said) the 'ghost in the machine'. Subsequently in a BBC broadcast, he elaborated his metaphor, and the ghost in the machine became a horse in a locomotive.[9] Professor Ryle is a prominent representative of the so-called Oxford School of Philosophy, which, in the words of one of its critics, 'treats genuine thought as a disease' (Gellner[10]). This curious philosophical aberration is now on the wane† and to hark back to it would arouse the indignant protests of the SPCDH (see

* It is interesting to note that Waddington in a recent book argues in favour of a 'quasi-finalistic' view.[8]

† See, *inter alia*, Smythies,[11] John Beloff,[12] Gellner[13] and Kneale.[14]

Appendix Two). Regardless of the verbal acrobatics of Behaviourists and their allies, the fundamental problems of mind and matter, of free will versus determinism, are still very much with us, and have acquired a new urgency – not as a subject of philosophical debate, but because of their direct bearing on political ethics and private morals, on criminal justice, psychiatry, and our whole outlook on life. By the very act of denying the existence of the ghost in the machine – of mind dependent on, but also responsible for, the actions of the body – we incur the risk of turning it into a very nasty, malevolent ghost.

Before the advent of Behaviourism, it was the psychologists and logicians who insisted that mental events have special characteristics which distinguish them from material events, whereas the physiologists were by and large inclined to take the materialist view that all mental events can be reduced to the operation of the 'automatic telephone exchange' in the brain. During the last fifty years, however, the situation has been almost reversed. While Oxford dons kept snickering about the horse in the locomotive, those men whose life work was devoted to the anatomy, physiology, pathology and surgery of the brain became increasingly converted to the opposite view. It could be summed up in a sigh of resignation: 'Oh, Brain is Brain, and Mind is Mind, and we don't know how the twain meet.' Let me give an illustration of the type of experiment which led them to that conclusion.

One of the greatest living neurosurgeons is Wilder Penfield of McGill University, who has evolved new techniques of experimenting on the exposed brain of consenting patients undergoing an operation. The patient is conscious; the experiments – which are painless – consist in applying low-voltage currents to selected points on the surface of the cerebral cortex. As the cortex is insensitive, the patient is unaware of the stimulating current, but he is aware of the movements which the current causes him to execute. Penfield reports:

When the neurosurgeon applies an electrode to the motor area of the patient's cerebral cortex causing the opposite hand to move, and when he asks the patient why he moved the hand, the response is: 'I didn't do it. You made me do it.' ... It may be said that the patient thinks of himself as having an existence separate from his body.

Once when I warned such a patient of my intention to stimulate the motor areas of the cortex, and challenged him to keep his hand from moving when the electrode was applied, he seized it with the other hand and struggled to hold it still. Thus, one hand, under the control of the right hemisphere driven by an electrode, and the other hand, which he controlled through the left hemisphere, were caused to struggle against each other. Behind the 'brain action' of one hemisphere was the patient's mind. Behind the action of the other hemisphere was the electrode.[15]

Penfield concluded his memorable paper:*

There are, as you see, many demonstrable mechanisms [in the brain]. They work for the purposes of the mind automatically when called upon ... But what agency is it that calls upon these mechanisms, choosing one rather than another? Is it another mechanism or is there in the mind something of different essence? ... To declare that these two things are one does not make them so. But it does block the progress of research.[16]

It is interesting to compare the reaction of Penfield's patients with the reaction of subjects who are made to carry out a post-hypnotic suggestion – changing chairs, or touching their ankles, or saying 'February' when they hear the word 'three'. In both cases the subject's actions have been caused by the experimenter; but whereas the subject who does not know that he is obeying a post-hypnotic command automatically finds a more or less plausible rationalization why he touched his ankle, Penfield's patients realize that they are obeying a physical compulsion: 'I never had a patient say, "I just wanted to do that anyway!"' One is tempted to say that the hypnotist imposes his will on the subject's mind – the surgeon merely on his brain.

* Delivered at the 'Control of the Mind' Symposium at the University of California Medical Centre in San Francisco, 1961.

Two recent symposia on *Control of the Mind* (1961)[17] and *Brain and Conscious Experience* (1966)[18] were impressive demonstrations of the swing of the pendulum. Sir Charles Sherrington, perhaps the greatest neurologist of the century, was no longer alive, but his approach to the mind-body problem was repeatedly invoked as a kind of *leitmotiv*: 'That our being should consist of *two* fundamental elements offers, I suppose, no greater inherent improbability than that it should rest on one only ... We have to regard the relation of mind to brain as still not merely unsolved, but still devoid of a basis of its very beginning.'[19]

The Stage and the Actors

However, if the flat-earthers have signally failed to demonstrate their contention that the mind-body problem is a pseudo-problem, it would be equally foolish to go to the other extreme and revert to crass Cartesian dualism. Nor would there be much point in going over once more the various theories which have been put forward to bridge the gulf – interaction, parallelism, epiphenomenalism, identity-hypothesis, and so forth.* Let us inquire instead whether the conception of the open-ended hierarchy can shed any new light on this very old problem.

The first, and at the same time decisive, step is to break away from thinking in terms of a two-tiered mind-matter dichotomy, and start thinking in terms of a multi-levelled hierarchy. Matter is no longer a unitary concept; the hierarchy of macroscopic, molecular, atomic, subatomic levels trails away without hitting rock-bottom, until matter dissolves into patterns of energy-concentration, and then perhaps into tensions in space. In the opposite direction we are faced with the

* Apart from the symposia mentioned previously, which approach the problem from the neurophysiological point of view, an excellent philosophical symposium has recently been edited by J. R. Smythies, *Brain and Mind* (1965).

same situation: there is an ascending series of levels, leading from automatic and semi-automatic reactions, through awareness and self-awareness, to the self's awareness of its awareness of itself, and so on, without hitting a ceiling.

The Cartesian tradition to identify 'mind' with 'conscious thinking' is deeply engrained in our habits of thought, and makes us constantly forget the obvious, trivial fact that consciousness is not an all-or-nothing affair but a *matter of degrees*. There is a continuous scale of gradations which extends from the unconsciousness that results from being hit on the head, through the restricted forms of consciousness in dreamless sleep, dreaming, day-dreaming, drowsiness, epileptic automatisms, and so on, up to bright, wide-awake states of arousal. These are the general *states* of consciousness which determine the amount of lighting – darker or brighter – of the stage on which the mental activity takes place. But the lower end of the scale extends far below the human level: ethologists who spend their lives observing animals refuse to draw a lower limit for consciousness, while neurophysiologists talk of 'spinal consciousness' in lower animals, and biologists of the 'protoplasmic consciousness' of protists.* Bergson even asserted that 'the unconsciousness of a falling stone is something different from the unconsciousness of a growing cabbage'.

The states of consciousness in man are easily influenced by drugs which alter the overall functioning of the brain; but also by the type of activity that goes on on the stage – whether, lying in bed, I am thinking of the coming holidays, or counting sheep. Thus we have the paradoxical situation of a feedback loop where the actor's activities automatically brighten or darken the stage-lights – which in turn influence

---

* Such as the *foraminifera*, mentioned before (Chapter XI), which construct microscopic houses out of spicules of dead sponges – houses which Hardy calls 'marvels of engineering skill, as if built to a plan'. Yet these single-celled creatures have of course no nervous system.

the actions of the actors. Dreaming and other 'games of the underground' obey rules of acting different from those of the fully lit stage.

We must distinguish, however, between these *general states of consciousness* – degrees of wakefulness, fatigue, intoxication – and the degree of *awareness of a specific activity*. The first refers to 'being conscious', the second to 'being conscious *of* something'. The first corresponds to the overall lighting of the stage, the second to the beam concentrated on a particular actor. That the two are interrelated we have already seen. But awareness of a particular ongoing activity has its own variable scale. In man, this scale extends from the silent, self-regulating activities of viscerae and glands, of physiological processes of which we are normally unaware, through perceptions on the fringes of awareness, to automatized routines which we perform mechanically like a robot; and finally up to concentrating on a problem by directing on it the beam of focal awareness – one actor singled out on the stage, the rest of which is plunged into darkness.

Shifts of Control

But now we come to an important point. We have seen (in Chapter VIII) that one and the same activity – driving a car, for instance – can be, according to circumstances, either carried out automatically without conscious awareness of one's own actions, or accompanied by varying degrees of awareness. Driving on a familiar quiet road, I can hand over to the 'automatic pilot' in my nervous system, and think about something else. Overtaking other cars on a motorway is mostly a kind of semi-conscious routine; overtaking in a tricky situation requires full awareness of what I am doing. These alternative possibilities apply not only to sensory-motor skills such as driving, bicycling, typing, playing the piano, but also to cognitive skills such as adding up a column of numbers, or 'turning one's mouth loose' to give a lecture – as Lashley's friend did (Chapter II).

There seem to be several factors which determine how much, if any, conscious attention is to be paid to an ongoing activity. First, the acquisition of a skill by learning requires a high degree of concentration, whereas with increasing mastery and practice it can be left 'to look after itself'; which is another way of saying that the rules which govern rule-governed behaviour – the canon of the skill – function unconsciously; and this again applies equally to manipulative, perceptual and cognitive skills. The process of condensation of learning into habit goes on all the time, and amounts to a continual transformation of 'mental' into 'mechanical' activity – of 'mind-processes' into 'machine-processes'.

Thus consciousness may be described in a negative way as the quality accompanying an activity *which decreases in proportion to habit-formation*. The transformation of learning into routine is accompanied by a dimming of the lights of awareness. We expect, therefore, that the opposite process will take place when routine is disturbed: that it will cause a change from 'mechanical' to 'mindful' behaviour. Everyday-experience confirms this; but what are the implications?

Habits and skills are functional holons, each with a fixed canon of rules and flexible strategies. Flexible strategies imply choices between several alternatives. The question is how these choices are made. Automatized routines are self-regulating in the sense that their strategy is automatically guided by feedbacks from their environments, without the necessity of referring decisions to higher levels. They operate by closed feedback loops, like servo-mechanisms or radar-controlled aeroplane landing devices. I have mentioned (p 121) the boy on his bicycle and the tightrope-walker keeping his balance with the aid of a bamboo stick, as examples of such 'kinetic homeostasis'. The tightrope-walker certainly executes very supple, flexible manoeuvres, but they do not require conscious decisions; the visual and kinaesthetic feedback provides all the guidance needed. The same applies to driving a car – so long as nothing unexpected happens, such as a kitten crossing the road. At that moment, a strategic choice has to be made which is beyond the competence of auto-matized routine,* and must be referred to 'higher quarters'. *This shift of control* of an ongoing activity from one level to a higher level of the hierarchy – from 'mechanical' to 'mindful' behaviour – seems to be of the essence of conscious decision-making and of the subjective experience of free will. It is what the patient on the operating table experiences when he consciously tries with his left hand to restrain the machine-like motion of his right hand – and which, as Penfield says, makes him 'think of himself as having an existence separate from his body'.

The Serial View

But at this point we risk once more falling back into simple two-tiered Cartesian dualism. The patient with his brain exposed is, of course, an exceptional and extreme case. The driver, who has to make a fast decision whether to run over the kitten or risk the safety of his passengers, does not think of his ego as leading 'an existence separate from his body'. What happens in the moment of crisis is a sudden shift to a higher level in a many-levelled hierarchy, from a semi-automatic to a more conscious performance – which is a relative, not an absolute, affair. And, whatever the conscious decision, its execution – the 'spelling-out process' – must still rely on the automatized sub-skills (braking, swerving, etc) on lower levels.

'Consciousness', to quote Thorpe, 'is a primary datum of existence and as such it cannot be fully defined . . .[20] The evidence suggests that at the lower levels [of the evolutionary

* In computer language we would have to say: 'for which it has not been programmed'.

scale] consciousness, if it exists, must be of a very generalized kind, so to say unstructured; and that with the development of purposive behaviour and a powerful faculty of attention, consciousness associated with expectation will become more and more vivid and precise.'[21]

What I am suggesting is that such gradings of 'structuring, vividness and precision' are found not only along the ladder of evolution, but also among members of the same species, and within the same individual at different stages of development and in different situations. Each 'upward' shift in the hierarchy leads to more vivid and structured conscious states, each downward shift has the opposite effect. Let me briefly elaborate on this.

Only a fraction of the sensory input to the cerebral cortex reaches consciousness, and again only a fraction of this is highlighted by focal awareness. But inputs which become conscious at all have already been processed and transformed: certain ranges of electro-magnetic waves have taken on the subjective qualities of colours, airwaves the qualities of pitch, and so forth. This is the first step in the serial process of promoting 'physical events' into 'mental events', and some philosophers regard it as the basic mystery, while others are unable to see the problem, and point out that bees, too, for instance, perceive patterns and colours, and dogs have their private universes of smell. I shall deliberately evade this deadlocked controversy, because the *same problem* arises with each shift upward in the hierarchies of perceiving, doing, knowing. Air vibrations do not become music in one single, magic transformation from the physical to the mental, but *by a whole series* of operations, of abstracting patterns in time and assembling them into more comprehensive patterns on higher levels of the hierarchy. The conscious appreciation of music depends on this, and the degree of 'musical awareness' corresponds to the degree of integration of melodic, harmonic, contrapuntal patterns into a coherent whole.

As another example, reverting to the discussion in Chapter II, consider how we convert variations of air pressure into ideas, and back again. Understanding language depends on a constantly repeated series of 'quantum jumps', so to speak, from one level of the speech hierarchy to the next higher one: phonemes can only be interpreted on the level of morphemes, words must be referred to context, sentences to the larger context; and behind the meaning stands the intention, the unverbalized idea, the train of thoughts. But trains need pointsmen to guide them on their course. The pointsmen need instructions. And so on. Infinite regress is not an invention of philosophers. In one of Alfred Hayes' short stories* the heroine reflects on the chain of events which led to the accidental death of her child:

'Because we always think of things as happening in some sort of succession. And then we say: because. Thinking the because explains. And then you examine the because, as I've done, oh, so many times since, and it opens up and inside there's another because, smaller, a because inside the other because, and you keep opening them and they keep disclosing other becauses ...'

Classical dualism knows only a single mind-body barrier. The hierarchic approach implies *a serialistic instead of a dualistic view*. Each in the series of upward shifts in assimilating music or language amounts to the crossing of a barrier from lower to higher states of awareness. The 'spelling out' of an idea is the reverse process: it converts 'airy nothings' into the mechanical motion of the organs of speech. This too is done by a series of steps, each of which triggers off pre-set neural 'mechanisms' of a more and more automatized type. The unverbalized image or idea which sets the process going pertains to a more 'mentalistic', ethereal level than its embodiment in speech; the invisible sentence-generating machinery works unconsciously, automatically, and can be thrown out of gear by damage to well-defined areas of the cortex; and the last step

* *The Beach at Ocean View.*

of articulating the sounds of speech is performed by entirely mechanized muscle contractions. Each step downward entails a handing-over of responsibility to more automatized automatisms; each step upward to more mentalistic processes of mentation. The mind-machine dichotomy is not localized along a single boundary between ego and environment, but is present on every level of the hierarchy. It is, in fact, a manifestation of our old friend, the two-faced god Janus.

To put it in a different way: the 'spelling out' of an intent – whether it is a verbal intent or just the lighting of a cigarette – is a process of *particularization*, of setting sub-routines into motion, functional holons of a subordinate, autonomous part-character. On the other hand, the referring of decisions to higher levels, as well as the interpretation and generalization of inputs, are integrative processes which tend to establish a higher degree of unity and *wholeness* of experience. Thus every upward shift or 'quantum jump' in the hierarchy would represent a quasi-holistic move, every downward shift a particularistic move, the former characterized by heightened awareness and mentalistic attributes, the latter by dimming awareness and mechanistic attributes.

Consciousness in this view is an emergent quality, which evolves into more complex and structured states in phylogeny, as the ultimate manifestation of the Integrative Tendency towards the creation of order out of disorder, of 'information' out of 'noise'. To quote another outstanding neurophysiologist of our time, R. W. Sperry (his italics):

Prior to the first appearance of conscious awareness in evolution, the entire cosmic process, science tells us, was only, as someone has phrased it, 'A play before empty benches', colourless and silent at that because, according to our present physics, prior to the advent of brains there was no *colour* and no *sound* in the universe, nor was there any flavour or aroma and probably rather little sense and no feeling or emotion. Before brains the universe was also free of pain and anxiety . . . There is no more important quest in the whole of science probably than the attempt to understand those very particular events in evolution by which brains worked out that special trick that enabled them to add to the cosmic scheme of things: colour, sound, pain, pleasure, and all the other facets of mental experience.[22]

The Flatworm's Ego

Looking upward – or inward – every man has the feeling that there is in him a personality-core, or apex, 'which controls his thinking and directs the searchlight of his attention' (Penfield), a feeling of wholeness. Looking outward or downward he is only aware of the task at hand, a partial kind of awareness which fades, in descending order, into the dimness of routine, the unawareness of visceral processes, of the growing cabbage and the falling stone.

But in the upward direction the hierarchy is equally open-ended. The self which directs the searchlight of my attention can never be caught in its focal beam. Even the operations which generate language include processes which cannot be expressed by language (p 49). It is a paradox as old as Achilles and the Tortoise, that the experiencing subject can never fully become the object of his experience; at best he can achieve successive approximations. If learning and knowing consist in making oneself a private model of the universe,* it follows that the model can never include a complete model of itself, because it must always lag one step behind the process which it is supposed to represent. With each upward-shift of awareness towards the apex of the hierarchy – the self as an integrated whole – it recedes like a mirage. 'Know thyself' is the most venerable and the most tantalizing command.

On the other hand, even man's limited, incomplete capacity for self-awareness puts him into a category apart from other living beings. Animals as lowly as the flatworm apparently show signs of attentiveness and expectancy which could be

---

* See Craik, The Nature of Explanation (1943), one of the cornerstones of modern communication theory.

called primitive forms of awareness; primates and domestic pets may also have the rudiments of self-awareness; but man nevertheless occupies a lone peak.

Now we have seen (Chapter IV) that if a flatworm is cut transversely into six segments, each of them is capable of regenerating into a complete animal, so that the classical dualist would have to assume that its mind or soul has split into six 'solons' (p 87). In the present theory, however, the self or mind is not regarded as a discrete entity, a whole in an absolute sense; but each of its functional holons in the many-levelled hierarchy – from visceral regulations to cognitive habits – is regarded as having a measure of individuality, with the Janus-faced attributes of partness and wholeness; and the degree of their integratedness into a unified personality varies with circumstances, but is never absolute. Total awareness of selfhood, the identity of the knower and the known, though always in sight, is never achieved. It could only be achieved at the peak of the hierarchy which is always one step removed from the climber.

From this point of view, it is no longer absurd to assume that the flatworm's fragments, whose tissues have reverted to the condition of the growing embryo, have started all over again to build up a mind-body hierarchy, perhaps even with its concomitant dim awareness of selfhood. If consciousness is an emergent quality, the ugly paradox of the 'solon' – implicit in all Eastern and Platonic philosophy – ceases to exist.

The slow emergence of awareness in phylogeny is reflected to some extent in ontogeny. In the preceding chapter I quoted Piaget and Freud on the newborn infant's fluid world of experience, which knows as yet no boundaries between self and not-self. In a series of classic studies Piaget has shown that the establishment of that boundary is a gradual process, and that only around the age of seven or eight does the average child become fully conscious of its own, separate, personal identity.

'That particular ingredient of the ego [self-awareness] must be built up by experience', Adrian commented.[23] But there is no end to that building process.

A Road to Freedom

I have compared its successive stages to an infinite mathematical series converging towards unity,* or to a spiral curve converging towards a centre which it will only reach after an infinite number of involutions.

But the quest for the self is a rather abstract pastime for philosophers and depth-psychologists; for ordinary mortals it assumes importance only where moral decisions or the feeling of responsibility for one's past actions – in other words, the problem of free will – is involved. The puzzle concerning the agency which directs one's thinking, and of the agency behind that agency, bothers one only when one feels guilty about one's silly, or sinful, or idle thoughts – or actions.

I like to imagine a dialogue at high table at an Oxford college, between an elderly don of strictly deterministic persuasion, and a young Australian guest of uninhibited temperament. The Australian exclaims:

'If you go on denying that I am free in my decisions, I'll punch your nose!'

The old man gets red in his face: 'I deplore your unpardonable behaviour.'

'I apologize. I lost my temper.'

'You really ought to control yourself.'

'Thank you. The experiment was conclusive.'

It was indeed. 'Unpardonable', 'ought to', and 'control yourself' are all expressions which imply that the Australian's behaviour was *not* determined by heredity-cum-environment, that he was free to choose whether to be polite or rude.

* The simplest series of this kind is: $S = (\frac{1}{2} + \frac{1}{4} + \frac{1}{8} + \frac{1}{16} + \cdots \frac{1}{n})$, where n has to approach infinity for the sum S to approach unity.

Whatever one's philosophical convictions, in everyday life it is impossible to carry on without the implicit belief in personal responsibility; and responsibility implies freedom of choice.

If I may quote what I wrote much earlier on – when I was still primarily interested in the political implications of the problem:

> It is now six o'clock in the evening, I have just had a drink and I feel a strong temptation to have a couple more and then go and dine out instead of writing this essay. I have fought myself over this issue for the last quarter of an hour and finally I have locked the gin and the vermouth in the cupboard and settled down to my desk, feeling very satisfied with myself. From a deterministic point of view this satisfaction is entirely spurious, since the issue was already settled before I started fighting myself; it was also settled that I should feel this spurious satisfaction and write what I write. Of course in my heart of hearts I do not believe that this is so, and I certainly did not believe it a quarter of an hour ago. Had I believed it, the process which I call 'inner struggle' would not have taken place, and fatality would have served me as a perfect excuse for going on drinking. Thus my disbelief in determinism must be contained in the set of factors which determine my behaviour; one of the conditions for fulfilling the prearranged pattern is that I should not believe that it is prearranged. Destiny can only have its way by forcing me to disbelieve in it. Thus the very concept of determinism condemns a man to live in a world where the rules of conduct are based on *As Ifs* and the rules of logic on *Becauses*.
>
> This paradox is not confined to scientific determinism; the Moslem, living in a world of religious determinism, displays the same mental split. Though he believes, in the words of the Koran, that 'every man's destiny is fastened on his neck', yet he curses his enemy and himself when he blunders, as if all were masters of their choice. He behaves on his own level exactly like old Karl Marx who taught that man's mental make-up is a product of his environment, yet showered invectives on everybody who, in obedience to his environmental conditioning, couldn't help disagreeing with him.[24]

The subjective experience of freedom is as much a given datum as the sensation of colour, or the feeling of pain. It is the feeling of making a not enforced, not inevitable, choice.

It seems to be working from inside outward, originating in the core of the personality. Even psychiatrists of the deterministic school agree that the abolition of the experience of having a will of his own leads to collapse of the patient's whole mental structure. Is that experience nevertheless based on an illusion?

The majority of participants at the symposium on 'Brain and Conscious Experience', mentioned above, were of the opposite opinion. One of the speakers, Professor MacKay, a communication theorist and computer expert, whom one would expect to incline towards a mechanistic outlook, concluded his paper as follows (his italics): 'Our belief that we are normally free in making our choices, so far from being contradictable, *has no valid alternative* from the standpoint even of the most deterministic pre-Heisenberg physics . . .'[25]

MacKay based his argument partly on the indeterminacy of modern physics, but mainly on a logical paradox to which I have already alluded: determinism implies predictability of behaviour, which means that an ideal computer, given all the relevant data about me, could predict what I am going to do; but these data would have to include my belief that I am free, which would have to be fed into the computer. At this point the argument becomes highly technical, and I must refer the reader to the original paper.

But arguments from logic and epistemology seem to me rather less convincing than the hierarchic approach. The fixed canons which govern the activities of a holon leave it a number of alternative choices. On the visceral level these choices are decided by the closed feedback-loops of homeostatic regulations. But on higher levels, the variety of choices increases with increasing complexity; and the decisions depend less and less on closed loops and stereotyped routines. Com-

* Heisenberg's Uncertainty Principle, one of the foundations of modern physics, suggests that on the quantum level strict determinism no longer applies.

pare playing noughts and crosses with playing chess. In both cases, my choice of the next move is 'free' in the sense of not being determined by the fixed rules of the game. But while noughts and crosses offers only a few alternative choices, determined by simple, almost automatic strategies, the competent chess-player is guided in his decisions by strategic precepts on a much higher level of complexity; and these precepts have an even larger margin of uncertainty. They form a delicate, precarious web of pros and cons. It is this upward shift to higher levels which makes the choice into a *conscious* choice; and it is the delicate balance of pros and cons which lends it the subjective flavour of *freedom*.

From the objective point of view the decisive factor seems to me to be that the 'degrees of freedom', in the physicist's sense, *increase* in ascending order. Thus the higher the level to which decision-making is referred, the less predictable the choices; and the ultimate decisions rest with the apex – but the apex itself does not rest. It goes on receding. The self, which has ultimate responsibility for a man's actions, can never be caught in the focal beam of his own awareness – and consequently its actions can never be predicted by the perfect computer, however much data it is fed: because the data will of necessity always be incomplete.* In the end, they will again lead to an infinitely regressing series of loops within loops, and becauses inside becauses.

A Sort of Maxim

If we reverse our steps and move downward in the hierarchy, decision-making is taken over by semi-automatic, then by

---

* This is related to MacKay's arguments and also to Karl Popper's[26] proposition that no information system (such as a computing machine) can embody within itself an up-to-date representation of itself, *including that representation*. A somewhat similar argument has been advanced by Michael Polanyi on the indeterminacy of the boundary conditions of physico-chemical systems.[27]

fully automatic, routines, and with each shift of control to lower levels the subjective experience of freedom diminishes, accompanied by a dimming of awareness. Habit is the enemy of freedom; the mechanization of habits tends towards the 'rigor mortis' of the robot-like pedant (Chapter VIII). Machines cannot become like men, but men can become like machines.

The second enemy of freedom is passion, or more specifically, the self-assertive, hunger-rage-fear-rape class of emotions. When they are aroused, the control of decisions is taken over by those primitive levels of the hierarchy which the Victorians called 'the Beast in us', and which are in fact correlated to phylogenetically older structures in the nervous system (see below, Chapter XVI). The loss of freedom resulting from this downward shift of controls is reflected in the legal concept of 'diminished responsibility', and in the subjective feeling of acting under a compulsion: 'I couldn't help it . . .', 'I lost my head', 'I must have been out of my mind'. It is once more the Janus principle. Facing upward or inward, towards that unattainable core from which my decisions seem to emanate, I feel free. Facing the other way, there is the robot – or the beast.

It is at this point that the moral dilemma of judging others arises. How am I to know whether or to what extent his responsibility was diminished when he acted as he did, and whether he could 'help it'? Compulsion and freedom are opposite ends of a graded scale; but there is no pointer attached to the scale that I could read. The safest hypothesis is to assign a minimum of responsibility to the other, and a maximum to oneself. There is an old French adage, *Tout comprendre c'est tout pardonner* – to understand all is to forgive all. On the above hypothesis it should be altered to: *Tout comprendre, ne rien se pardonner* – understand all, forgive yourself nothing. It sounds like moral humility combined with intellectual arrogance. But it is relatively safe.

The Open-Ended Hierarchy

While the self-assertive emotions *narrow* the field of consciousness (passion is not 'blind', but blinkered), the self-transcending emotions *expand* it, until the self seems to dissolve in the 'oceanic feeling' of mystic contemplation or aesthetic entrancement. The self-assertive emotions tend to constrict freedom of choice, the self-transcending emotions tend towards freedom *from* choice in the peace that passeth all understanding.

This un-selfing of the self seems to be the opposite of the quest for total self-awareness. In the literature of mysticism, however, they appear to be closely related. The aim of Hatha Yoga, for instance, is to attain a higher level of self-awareness by getting viscera and individual muscles under voluntary control. But these practices are considered as only a means towards the end of attaining to a state of 'pure consciousness, without object or content other than consciousness itself'.* In this state, the transient individual self is thought to enter into a kind of spiritual osmosis with the Atman, the universal spirit – and to merge into it. Other mystic schools attempt to reach the same end by different routes; but all seem to agree that the conquest of the self is a means towards transcending it.

I am aware that in this chapter I have indulged in some momentous question-begging. I did not attempt to *define* consciousness which, being the precondition of all mental activity, cannot be defined by that activity; and I agree with MacKay that 'my own consciousness is a primary datum, which it would be nonsense to doubt because it is the platform on which my doubting is built'.[28]

We cannot say what consciousness is, but we can say whether there is more or less of it, and also whether it is of

* See *The Lotus and the Robot*, Part One.

a coarse or refined texture. It is an emergent quality which evolves towards higher levels of complexity, and is inseparably married to the activities of the brain. Classical dualism regarded mental and bodily activities as different categories, enlightened monists regard them as complementary aspects of the same process; but this still leaves us with the problem how the two are related. The hierarchic approach turns this absolute distinction into a relative one, it replaces the dualistic (or double-aspect) theory by a serialistic hypothesis, in which 'mental' and 'mechanical' are relative attributes, the dominance of one or the other deriving from a change of levels. This still leaves a host of problems unanswered, but at least it poses a few new questions. It could, for instance, provide a new approach to the phenomena of extra-sensory perception as an emergent level of supra-individual consciousness – or, alternatively, as an earlier version of 'psychosymbiotic' awareness, preceding self-awareness, which evolution has abandoned in favour of the latter. But this is a subject outside the scope of this book.

The related concepts of the 'open-ended hierarchy' and of 'infinite regress' have been a recurrent *leitmotiv* in these pages. Some scientists dislike the concept of infinite regress because it reminds them of the little man inside the little man inside the little man, and of the tiresome paradoxa of logic, like the Cretan liar. But there is another way of looking at it. Consciousness has been compared to a mirror in which the body contemplates its own activities. It would perhaps be a closer approximation to compare it to the kind of Hall of Mirrors where one mirror reflects one's reflection in another mirror, and so on. We cannot get away from the infinite. It stares us in the face whether we look at atoms or stars, or at the becauses behind the becauses, stretching back through eternity. Flat-earth science has no more use for it than the flat-earth theologians had in the Dark Ages; but a true science of life must let infinity in, and never lose sight of it. In two earlier books[29] I have tried to show that throughout the ages the great innovators in the history of science had always been aware of the transparency of phenomena towards a different order of reality, of the ubiquitous presence of the ghost in the machine – even such a simple machine as a magnetic compass or a Leyden jar. Once a scientist loses this sense of mystery, he can be an excellent technician, but he ceases to be a *savant*. One of the greatest of all times, Louis Pasteur, has summed this up in one of my favourite quotations:

> I see everywhere in the world the inevitable expression of the concept of infinity . . . The idea of God is nothing more than one form of the idea of infinity. So long as the mystery of the infinite weighs on the human mind, so long will temples be raised to the cult of the infinite, whether it be called Brahmah, Allah, Jehovah or Jesus . . . The Greeks understood the mysterious power of the hidden side of things. They bequeathed to us one of the most beautiful words in our language – the word 'enthusiasm' – *en theos* – a god within. The grandeur of human actions is measured by the inspiration from which they spring. Happy is he who bears a god within, and who obeys it. The ideals of art, of science, are lighted by reflection from the infinite.[30]

It is a credo one is happy to share, and a fitting conclusion for this part of the book.

I have tried to explain in it the general principles of a theory of Open Hierarchic Systems (OHS), as an alternative to current orthodox theories. It is essentially an attempt to bring together and shape into a unified framework three existing schools of thought – none of them new. They can be represented by three symbols: the tree, the candle and the helmsman. The tree symbolizes hierarchic order. The flame of a candle, which constantly exchanges its materials, and yet preserves its stable pattern, is the simplest example of an 'open system'. The helmsman represents cybernetic control. Add to these the two faces of Janus, representing the dichotomy of partness and wholeness, and the mathematical sign of the infinite (a horizontal figure of eight), and you have a picture-strip version of OHS theory. Readers less given to the pictur-esque are again referred to the summary of principles in Appendix One.

We must now turn from order to disorder – to the predica-ment of man, and attempt to diagnose its causes.

PART THREE

DISORDER

XV

THE PREDICAMENT OF MAN

All our Righteousness are as filthy rags.
ISAIAH *lxiv*

THE postulated polarity of integrative versus self-assertive potentials in biological and social systems is fundamental to the present theory. It follows logically from the concept of hierarchic order – that venerable truism which seems so self-evident and turns out to be so fertile if we take the trouble to work out its implications.

The integrative potential of a holon makes it tend to behave as a part of a larger, more complex unit; its self-assertive potential makes it tend to behave as if it were itself a self-contained, autonomous whole. In every type of hierarchy that we have discussed, and on every level of each hierarchy, we have found this polarity reflected in a *coincidentia oppositorum*. This sometimes manifests itself in apparently paradoxical phenomena which have caused bitter controversies among biologists, because it depended on the conditions of the experiment which of the opposite tendencies would be more in evidence. In embryonic development, for instance, a cell tissue may show 'regulative' and 'mosaic' properties at different stages. In social bodies, the dichotomy between cooperation and competition is all too obvious – from ambivalent tensions in the family, to the agonized coexistence of the United Nations. We must now turn to its paradoxical and profoundly disturbing effects on the emotive behaviour of the individual.

The Three Dimensions of Emotion

Emotions are mental states accompanied by intense feeling and involving bodily changes of a widespread character. They have also been described as 'over-heated drives'. A conspicuous feature of all emotions is the feeling of pleasantness or unpleasantness attached to them, usually called their '*hedonic tone*'. Freud thought that pleasure is derived from 'the diminution, lowering or extinction, of psychic excitation' and 'un-pleasure [*Unlust*, discomfort, as distinct from physical pain] from an increase of it'.[1]

This is, of course, true in so far as the satisfaction or frustration of urgent biological needs is concerned. But it is patently untrue of the type of experience which we call pleasurable excitements or thrills. The preliminaries which precede the sexual act certainly cause an 'increase in the quantity of excitation' and should therefore be unpleasurable, but the evidence indicates that they are not. There is no satisfactory answer anywhere in Freud's works to this embarrassingly banal objection.* In the Freudian system the sexual drive is essentially something *to be disposed of* – by consummation or sublimation; pleasure is derived not from its pursuit, but from getting rid of it.

The Behaviourist school, from Thorndike to Hull, took a similar attitude; it recognized only one basic type of motivation, and that a negative one: 'drive-reduction' – ie, the diminution of tensions derived from biological needs. In fact, however, research on 'stimulus-deprivation' (undertaken to study the reaction of space-travellers to long hours in monotonous environments) has revealed that the organism needs a continuous flow of stimulation, that its hunger for experience and thirst for excitation are probably as basic as hunger and

* For a detailed discussion of Freud's attitude to pleasure, see Schachtel.[2]

thirst themselves are. As Berlyne has summed it up: 'Human beings and higher animals spend most of their time in a state of relatively high arousal and ... expose themselves to arousing stimulus situations with great eagerness.'[3] After bread, the circus games always came next on the list.

In fact, *Unlust* – discomfort, frustration, etc, – is not caused by an increase of excitation as such; it arises when a drive finds its outlets blocked; or when its intensity is so increased that the normal outlets are insufficient; or for both reasons. A moderate amount of over-heating may be experienced as pleasurable excitement while anticipating or imagining the act of consummation. The physical discomforts of strenuous sports are readily accepted in the pleasurable anticipation of the reward – which may be nothing more substantial than a sense of achievement. Frustration changes into relief the moment it is realized that the target is within reach, that is, long before the actual process of satisfying the drive has started. Moreover, there are *vicarious emotions*, derived from partial identification with another person, or the heroine on the screen, which are satisfied by *vicarious rewards*; the consummatory act is lived out in fantasy, in internalized, instead of overt, behaviour. Thus the 'hedonic tone' depends on several factors, and could be described as *a feedback report on the progress or otherwise of the drive towards its real, anticipated, or imaginary target.*

Emotions can be classified according to their source, ie, the nature of the drive which gives rise to them – hunger, sex, curiosity, care of the offspring, and so on. A second factor to be taken into account is their pleasure–unpleasure rating. To use a coarse but helpful analogy, let us compare our emotional set-up with a tavern, in which there is a variety of taps, each serving a different kind of brew; these are turned on and off as the need arises. Then each tap would represent a different *drive*, and the pleasure-rating would be represented by the *rate of flow* – which can be nice and smooth, or impeded by air-locks, or by too much or too little pressure behind it.

Now we come to a third factor: the degree of toxicity of each brew. The self-assertive, aggressive-defensive tendency which enters into a given emotion shall be symbolized by its toxic alcohol content; the self-transcending tendency by its content of soothing, neutral liquid. We thus arrive at a three-dimensional view of emotions. The first factor is the nature of its source, represented by a particular tap; the second its hedonic tone – rate of flow; the third is its ratio of self-assertion to self-transcendence. It is with this third aspect that we shall be mainly concerned.

One of the difficulties besetting this subject is that we rarely experience a pure emotion. The barman tends to mix the contents of the taps: sex may be combined with curiosity, and with virtually any other drive. The hedonic tone also tends towards ambivalence; anticipation may make actual discomfort pleasurable, and the unconscious component of the drive may give rise to feelings which change a plus into a minus sign; the pain felt by the masochist on one level of awareness may be experienced as pleasure on another level. But we are concerned with a third type of ambiguity. Leaving aside the extremes of blind rage at one end, and mystic trance at the other end of the spectrum, most of our emotional states show paradoxical combinations of the two basic tendencies.

Take an instinct-drive like *care for the offspring*, shared by virtually all mammalians and birds. Whatever the emotions to which this instinct gives rise in animals (and some of their manifestations are rather paradoxical), in man they certainly take an often disastrously ambivalent form. The child is regarded by its parent as its own 'flesh and blood' – a biological bond which transcends the frontiers of the self; at the same time, over-protective mothers and domineering fathers are classic examples of self-assertiveness.

If we turn from parental to *sexual love*, we again find both tendencies present – on the one hand, impulses towards aggression, domination, subjugation; on the other, towards empathy and identification. The mixture varies from rape to platonic worship, according to its degree of toxicity.

Hunger is an apparently simple biological drive, which one would hardly expect to give rise to complex, ambivalent emotions. The teeth are symbols of aggression; biting, snapping, attacking and wolfing one's food are single-minded, crude manifestations of self-assertiveness. But there is another side to the act of feeding, related to magic and primitive religion. It could be called empathy by ingestion. By partaking of the flesh of the slain animal, man or god, an act of transubstantiation takes place; the virtues and wisdom of the victim are ingested and a kind of mystic communion is established. The costumes and rituals varied; but the principle always involved the transfer of some kind of spiritual substance between god, animal and man, whether the people in question were primitive Australian savages, highly civilized Mexican Aztecs, or Greeks at the height of the Dionysian cult. In the most telling version of the legend, Dionysius is torn to pieces and eaten by the evil Titans, who in turn are slain by Zeus' thunderbolt; man is born out of their ashes, heir to their wickedness, but also to the divine flesh. Transmitted through the Orphic mystery cult, the tradition of partaking of the torn god's flesh and blood entered in a sublimated and symbolic form into the rites of Christianity. Even in the sixteenth century, men were excommunicated from the Lutheran church because they denied the doctrine of ubiquity – the physical presence of the blood and body of Christ in the consecrated host. To the devout, Holy Communion is the supreme experience of self-transcendence; and no offence is meant by pointing to the unbroken tradition which connects ingestion with transubstantiation as a means of breaking down the ego's boundaries.

Echoes of this ancient communion survive in the various rites of commensality – baptismal and funeral meals, the symbolic offering of bread and salt, the Indian taboo on sharing meals with people of different caste. Oral eroticism and quaint expressions like 'devouring love', which occur in most languages, are further reminders that even while eating, man does not live by bread alone; and that *even the seemingly simplest act of self-preservation may contain a component of self-transcendence.*

And vice versa, caring for the sick or the poor, protecting animals against cruelty, serving on committees, and devoting one's time to social work, are admirably altruistic pursuits – and often wonderful outlets for bossiness and self-assertion, even if unconscious. The family likeness between hospital matrons and sergeant majors, surgeons and star performers, do-gooders and hockey-team captains, testifies to the endless variety of combinations into which the integrative and self-assertive tendencies may enter.

To avoid possible confusion, I should point out that according to the three-dimensional theory of emotions outlined above, self-assertion and self-transcendence are not specific emotions but tendencies which enter into *all* emotions and modify their character according to which of the two dominates. For the sake of brevity, however, it is sometimes convenient to talk loosely of 'self-transcending emotions' instead of 'emotions in which the self-transcending tendencies dominate'.

The Perils of Aggression

To recapitulate: the single individual, considered as a whole, represents the apex of the organismic hierarchy; considered as a part, he is the lowest unit of the social hierarchy. On this boundary-line between physiological and social organization, the two opposite potentials which we have encountered on every level manifest themselves in the form of emotive behaviour. So long as all goes well, the self-assertive and integrative tendencies of the individual are more or less evenly balanced in his emotional life; he lives in a kind of dynamic equilibrium with his family, tribe or society, and also with the universe of values and beliefs which constitutes his mental environment.

A certain amount of self-assertiveness, 'rugged individualism', ambition, competitiveness, is as indispensable in a dynamic society as the autonomy and self-reliance of its holons is indispensable to the organism. A well-meaning but woolly ideology, which has become fashionable on the rebound from the horrors of the last decades, would proclaim aggressiveness in all its forms as altogether damnable and evil. Yet without a moderate amount of aggressive individualism there could be no social or cultural progress. What John Donne has called man's 'holy discontent', is an essential motive force of the social reformer, the satirist, artist and thinker. We have seen that creative originality in science or art always has a constructive and a destructive side – destructive, that is to say, to established conventions of technique, style, dogma or prejudice. And since science is made by scientists, the destructive aspect of scientific revolutions must reflect some element of destructiveness in the scientist's mind, a preparedness to go recklessly against accepted beliefs. The same, of course, is true of the artist – even if he is not a 'fauve'. Thus aggression is like arsenic: in small doses a stimulant, in large doses a poison.

We are now concerned with the latter, the poisonous aspect of the self-assertive emotions. Under conditions of stress, an over-excited organ tends to escape its restraining controls and to assert itself to the detriment of the whole, or even to monopolize the functions of the whole. The same happens if the coordinating powers of the whole are so weakened – by senescence or central injury – that it is no longer able to control its parts.* In extreme cases, this can lead to pathological

* In the terminology of C. M. Child, the part becomes 'physiologically isolated' from the whole.[4]

changes of an irreversible nature, such as malignant growths with untramelled proliferation of tissues that have escaped from genetic control. On a less extreme level, practically any organ or function may get temporarily and partially out of control. In pain, the injured part tends to monopolize the attention of the whole organism; as a result of emotional or other stresses, the digestive juices may attack the stomach walls; in rage and panic, the sympathico-adrenal apparatus takes over from the higher centres which normally coordinate behaviour; and when sex is aroused, the gonads seem to take over from the brain.

Not only parts of the body can, under conditions of stress, assert themselves in harmful ways, but mental structures as well. The *idée fixe*, the obsession of the crank, are cognitive holons running riot. There is a whole gamut of mental disorders in which some subordinate part of the mental hierarchy exerts its tyrannical rule over the whole; from the relatively harmless infatuation with some pet theory, to the insidious domination over the mind of 'repressed' complexes (characteristically called 'autonomous complexes' by Freud because they are beyond the ego's control), and so to the clinical psychoses in which large chunks of the personality seem to have 'split off' and lead a quasi-independent existence. In the hallucinations of the paranoiac, not only the cognitive but also the perceptual hierarchy has fallen under the sway of the unleashed mental holon, which imposes its peculiar rules of the game on it.

However, clinical insanity is merely an extreme manifestation of tendencies which are potentially present, but more or less under restraint in the normal mind – or what we call by that name. Aberrations of the human mind are to a large extent due to the obsessional pursuit of some part-truth, treated as if it were a whole truth – of a holon masquerading as a whole. Religious, political, philosophical fanaticisms, the stubbornness of prejudice, the intolerance of scientific orthodoxies and of artistic cliques, all testify to the tendency to build 'closed systems' centred on some part-truth, and to assert its absolute validity in the teeth of evidence to the contrary. In extreme cases, a cognitive holon which has got out of control can behave like a cancerous tissue invading other mental structures.

If we turn from individuals to social holons – professional classes, ethnic groups, etc, – we again find that, so long as all is well, they live in a kind of dynamic equilibrium with their natural and social environment. In social hierarchies, the physiological controls which operate inside of organisms are of course replaced by institutional controls which restrain the self-assertive tendencies of these groups on all levels, from whole social classes down to the individual. Once more, the ideal of frictionless, pacific cooperation, without competition, without tensions, is based on a confusion of the desirable and the possible. Without a moderate amount of self-assertiveness of its parts, the body social would lose its individuality and articulation; it would dissolve into a kind of amorphous jelly. However, under conditions of stress, when tensions exceed a critical limit, some social holon – the army, the farmers or the trade unions – may get over-excited and tend to assert itself to the detriment of the whole, just like an over-excited organ. Alternatively, the decline of the integrative powers of the whole may lead to similar results, as the collapse of empires indicates on a grandiose scale.

The Pathology of Devotion

Thus the self-assertive tendencies of the individual are a necessary and constructive factor – so long as they do not get out of hand. On this view the more sinister manifestations of violence and cruelty can be written off as pathological extremes of basically healthy impulses which, for one reason or another, have been denied their normal gratifications. Provide the young with harmless outlets for aggression – games, competitive sports, adventure, sexual experimentation – and all will be well.

Unfortunately, neither of these remedies, though often tried, has ever worked. For the last three or four thousand years, Hebrew prophets, Greek philosophers, Indian mystics, Chinese sages, Christian preachers, French humanists, English utilitarians, German moralists, American pragmatists, have discussed the perils of violence and appealed to man's better nature, without much noticeable effect. There must be a reason for this failure.

The reason, I believe, lies in a series of fundamental misconceptions concerning the main causes which compelled man to make such a mess of his history, which prevented him from learning the lessons of the past, and which now put his survival in question. The first of these misconceptions is putting the blame for man's predicament on his selfishness, greed, etc; in a word, on the aggressive, self-assertive tendencies of the individual. The point I shall try to make is that selfishness is not the primary culprit; and that appeals to man's better nature were bound to be ineffectual because the main danger lies precisely in what we are wont to call his 'better nature'. In other words, I would like to suggest that the *integrative tendencies of the individual are incomparably more dangerous than his self-assertive tendencies*. The sermons of the reformers were bound to fall on deaf ears because they put the blame where it did not belong.

This may sound like a psychological paradox. Yet I think most historians would agree that the part played by impulses of selfish, individual aggression in the holocausts of history was small; first and foremost, the slaughter was meant as an offering to the gods, to king and country, or the future happiness of mankind. The crimes of a Caligula shrink to insignificance compared to the havoc wrought by Torquemada. The number of victims of robbers, highwaymen, rapers, gangsters and other criminals at any period of history is negligible compared to the massive numbers of those cheerfully slain in the name of the true religion, just policy, or correct ideology. Heretics were tortured and burnt not in anger but in sorrow, for the good of their immortal souls. Tribal warfare was waged in the purported interest of the tribe, not of the individual. Wars of religion were fought to decide some fine point in theology or semantics. Wars of succession, dynastic wars, national wars, civil wars, were fought to decide issues equally remote from the personal self-interest of the combatants.* The Communist purges, as the word 'purge' indicates, were understood as operations of social hygiene, to prepare mankind for the golden age of the classless society. The gas chambers and crematoria worked for the advent of a different version of the millennium. Heinrich Eichmann (as Hannah Ahrendt, reporting on his trial, has pointed out)[5] was not a monster or a sadist, but a conscientious bureaucrat, who considered it his duty to carry out his orders and believed in obedience as the supreme virtue; far from being a sadist, he felt physically sick on the only occasion when he watched the Zircon gas at work.

Let me repeat: the crimes of violence committed for selfish, personal motives are historically insignificant compared to those committed *ad majorem gloriam Dei*, out of a self-sacrificing devotion to a flag, a leader, a religious faith or a political conviction. Man has always been prepared not only to kill but also to die for good, bad or completely futile causes. And what can be a more valid proof of the reality of the self-transcending urge than this readiness to die for an ideal?

No matter what period we have in view, modern, ancient, or prehistoric, the evidence always points in the same direction: the tragedy of man is not his truculence, but his proneness to delusions. 'The worst of madmen is a saint run mad':

---

* Rape and plunder in war was no doubt an incentive to a minority of mercenaries and adventurers; but theirs was not the making of decisions.

Pope's epigram applies to all major periods of history – from the ideological crusades of the totalitarian age down to the rites which govern the life of primitives.

The Ritual of Sacrifice

Anthropologists have paid far too little attention to the earliest, ubiquitous manifestation of the delusionary streak in the human psyche: the institution of human sacrifice, the ritual killing of children, virgins, kings and heroes to placate and flatter the gods. It is found at the dawn of civilization in every part of the world; it persisted through the height of antique civilizations and pre-Columbian cultures, and is sporadically still being practised in remote corners of the world. The usual attitude is to dismiss this subject as a sinister curiosity belonging to the dark superstitions of the past; but this attitude begs the question of the universality of the phenomenon, ignores the clue that it provides to the delusional streak in man's mental structure, and its relevance to the problems of the present.

Let me insert at this point a personal anecdote. In 1959, I stayed as a guest with my late friend Dr Verrier Elwin at his house in Shillong, Assam. Dr Elwin was the leading authority on Indian tribal life, Chief Adviser to the Indian Government on Tribal Affairs, and had married a beautiful girl from an Orissa tribe. One day, one of his three sons, a quiet, intelligent little boy of ten, asked to accompany me on my morning walk. At the point where we lost sight of the house the boy became worried and insisted on turning back. I complied, asked him what the matter was, and after hedging for a while, he confessed that he was afraid of meeting some bad men, Khasis, who killed little boys.

Later on, I mentioned the matter to Verrier, who explained that the child had indeed acted on his instructions not to venture out of sight of the house. The Khasis are an Assam tribe who were suspected of still secretly practising human sacrifice. From time to time there were rumours about the disappearance of a small child. The risks of meeting marauding Khasis on the outskirts of Shillong were remote, but still ... Then he explained that the Khasis' traditional method of sacrifice had been to push two sticks up the nostrils into the child's brain; the more it cried and bled, the more pleased the gods.

I mention this story to give an instance of what the abstract notion 'human sacrifice' meant in concrete terms. Surely these Khasis must have been insane? That is precisely the point: the act indicates mental derangement. But it was a universal form of mental derangement, cutting across the frontiers of races and cultures. To quote a recent author on the subject, G. Hogg:

> Sacrifice, of course was a gesture: the supreme gesture, if you will. There is no part of the world, however remote, in which sacrifice in one form or another has not played an essential part in the way of life of the people ... Sacrifice, and often as not human sacrifice, was an integral part of the priestly rites, and immolation was very extensively associated with the consuming of human flesh ... The practice of cannibalism, as such, is almost certainly less of an established institution than human sacrifice, or immolation. Nevertheless, except in the case of the Fijians and certain other Melanesian tribes, among whom the sheer lust for human flesh seems to have predominated over all other considerations, the basic ritualistic motive is virtually identical. Both in the sacrifice of human beings, and in the partaking of portions of their flesh before or after the sacrifice, there is always the underlying principle of the transfer of 'soul-substance' ... In Mexico, sacramental rites probably reached a higher degree of complexity than anywhere else. Human flesh was considered the only food likely to be acceptable to the principal gods who had to be propitiated. Therefore human beings, carefully selected, were looked upon as representations of such gods as Quetzalcoatl and Tetzcatlipoca and, with most elaborate ceremonial rites, were eventually sacrificed to those gods whom they in fact represented, the onlookers being invited to share portions of the flesh in order thus to identify themselves with the gods to whom sacrifice had been made.[6]

All this has nothing to do with the seven deadly sins – pride, covetousness, lust, anger, gluttony, envy, sloth – against which the sermons of the moralists are chiefly directed. The eighth sin, deadlier than all – self-transcendence through misplaced devotion – is not included in the list.

But where is the jury who decides whether devotion is of the 'right' or the 'misguided' kind? As we are on the subject of the Aztecs, let me quote a passage from Prescott, which provides a hint of the relevance of their madness to our own times. Prescott estimates that the number of young men, virgins and children sacrificed *annually* throughout the Aztec empire was between twenty and fifty thousand; then continues:

> Human sacrifices have been practised by many nations, not excepting the most polished nations of antiquity; but never by any, on a scale compared with those in Anahuac. The amount of victims immolated on its accursed altars would stagger the faith of the most scrupulous believer ... Strange that, in every country, the most fiendish passions of the human heart have been those kindled in the name of religion! ...
>
> In reflecting on the revolting usages recorded in the preceding pages, one finds it difficult to reconcile their existence with anything like a regular form of government, or an advance in civilization. Yet the Mexicans had many claims to the character of a civilized community. One may, perhaps, better understand the anomaly, by reflecting on the condition of some of the most polished countries in Europe in the sixteenth century, after the establishment of the modern Inquisition; an institution which yearly destroyed its thousands, by a death more painful than the Aztec sacrifices; which armed the hand of brother against brother, and, setting its burning seal upon the lip, did more to stay the march of improvement than any other scheme ever devised by human cunning.
>
> Human sacrifice, however cruel, has nothing in it degrading to its victim. It may be rather said to ennoble him by devoting him to the gods. Although so terrible with the Aztecs, it was sometimes voluntarily embraced by them, as the most glorious death, and one that opened a sure passage into paradise. The Inquisition, on the other hand, branded its victims with infamy in this world, and consigned them to everlasting perdition in the next.[7]

Prescott then devotes a paragraph to the cannibalistic rites accompanying the Aztec sacrifices; but immediately afterwards performs a remarkable mental somersault:

> In this state of things, it was beneficently ordered by Providence that the land should be delivered over to another race, who would rescue it from the brutish superstitions that daily extended wider and wider, with extent of empire. The debasing institutions of the Aztecs furnish the best apology for their conquest. It is true, the conquerors brought along with them the Inquisition. But they also brought Christianity, whose benign radiance would still survive, when the fierce flames of fanaticism should be extinguished; dispelling those dark forms of horror which had so long brooded over the fair regions of Anahuac.[8]

Prescott must have known, though, that shortly after the Mexican conquest, the 'benign radiance' of Christianity manifested itself in the Thirty Years War, which killed off a goodly proportion of Europe's population.

The Observer from Mars

The Scientific Revolution and the Age of Enlightenment seemed to signal a new departure for man. They did, in so far as the conquest, and subsequent rape, of Nature are concerned; but they did not solve, on the contrary they deepened, his predicament. Religious wars were superseded by patriotic, then by ideological, wars, fought with the same self-immolating loyalty and fervour. The opium of revealed religion was replaced by the heroin of secular religions, which commanded the same bemused surrender of the individuality to their doctrines, and the same worshipful love offered to their prophets. The devils and succubi were replaced by a new demonology: sub-human Jews, plotting world domination; bourgeois capitalists promoting starvation; enemies of the people, monsters in human shape were surrounding us, ready to pounce. In the thirties and forties the paranoid streak exploded with unprecedented vehemence in the two most powerful nations of Europe. In the two decades following the last great war forty minor wars and civil wars have been fought. At the time of writing, Roman Catholics, Buddhists and Dialectical Materialists are waging another civil war within a war, to impose the only True Belief on the people of an Asian nation; while monks and schoolgirls douse themselves with petrol and burn alive to the clicking of Press cameras, in a new ritual of self-immolation *ad majorem gloriam*.

In one of the early chapters of Genesis, there is an episode which has inspired countless religious painters. It is the scene where Abraham ties his son to a pile of wood and prepares to cut his throat with a knife, then burn him for the love of Jehovah. We all disapprove of cutting a child's throat for personal motives; the question is why so many have for so long approved of the insane gesture of Abraham. To put it vulgarly, we are led to suspect that there is somewhere a screw loose in the human mind, and always has been. To put it into more scientific language, we ought to give serious consideration to the possibility that somewhere along the line something has gone seriously wrong with the evolution of the nervous system of *homo sapiens*. We know that evolution can lead into a blind alley, and we also know that the evolution of the human brain was an unprecedentedly rapid, almost explosive, process. I shall come back to this in the chapter that follows; for the moment, let us merely note as a possible hypothesis that the delusional streak which runs through our history may be an endemic form of paranoia, built into the wiring circuits of the human brain.

It is certainly not difficult to imagine that an objective observer on an alien, more advanced planet, after studying the human record, would come to this diagnosis. We are of course always willing and ready to go along with such science-fiction fantasies, so long as we do not have to take the conclusions literally, and apply them to the reality around us. But let us try to do just that, and to imagine the observer's reaction when he discovers that for nearly two thousand years, millions of otherwise intelligent people were convinced that the vast majority of our species who did not share their particular creed and did not perform its rites were consumed by flames through eternity by order of a loving god. This observation, I realize, is not exactly new. But to dismiss such singular phenomena simply as indoctrination or superstition means to beg the question, which is at the very core of the human predicament.

The Cheerful Ostrich

Before going further, let me try to forestall a frequently met objection. When you mention, however tentatively, the hypothesis that a paranoid streak is inherent in the human condition, you will promptly be accused of taking a one-sided, morbid view of history; of being hypnotized by its negative aspects; of picking out the black stones in the mosaic, and neglecting the triumphant achievements of human progress. Why not select the white stones instead – the Golden Age of Greece, the monuments of Egypt, the marvels of the Renaissance, Newton's equations, the conquest of the moon?

True enough, this way offers a more cheerful view. Personally speaking, having written such a lot about the creative side of man, I can hardly be accused of belittling his achievements. However, the question is not one of choosing, according to temperament or mood, the brighter or the darker side; but of perceiving both together, of noticing the contrast, and inquiring into its causes. To dwell on the glories of man and ignore the symptoms of his possible insanity is not a sign of optimism, but of ostrichism. It could be compared to the attitude of that jolly physician who, a short time before Van Gogh committed suicide, declared that he could not be insane because he painted such beautiful pictures. A number of authors, with whose attitude I am otherwise in sympathy, seem to be writing in the same jolly vein when they discuss the future prospects of man: C. G. Jung and his followers; Teilhard de Chardin, and the so-called Evolutionary Humanists.

A more balanced approach to human history might be to view it as a symphony with a rich orchestration, played against a background of persistent drumming by a savage horde of shamans. At times a scherzo would make us forget it, but in the long run the monotonous beating of the tom-toms always gains the upper hand and tends to drown every other sound.

Integration and Identification

Poets have always said that man is mad; and their audiences always nodded delightedly because they thought it was a cute metaphor. But if the statement were taken literally, there would seem to be little hope: for how can a madman diagnose his own madness? The answer is that he can, because he is not entirely mad the entire time. In their periods of remission, psychotics have written astonishingly sane and lucid reports of their illness; even in the acute phases of phychoses artificially induced by drugs like LSD, the subject, while experiencing vivid delusions, knows them to be delusions.

Any attempt at a diagnosis of the predicament of man must proceed in several cautious steps. In the first place, let us remember that all our emotions consist of 'mixed feelings' in which both the self-assertive and the self-transcending tendencies participate. But they can interact in various ways – some beneficial, some disastrous.

The most common and normal interaction is mutual restraint: the two tendencies counterbalance, equilibrate each other. Competitiveness is restrained by acceptance of the rules of civilized conduct. The self-assertive component in sexual desire seeks only its own satisfaction, but in a harmonious relationship it is combined with the equally strong need to provide pleasure and satisfaction to the other. Irritation, caused by a person's obnoxious behaviour, is mitigated by empathy – by understanding the motives of that behaviour. In the creative scientist or artist, ambition is balanced by self-transcending immersion in the task. In an ideal society, both tendencies would be harmoniously combined in its citizens – they would be saintly and efficient, yogis and commissars at the same time. But let tensions wax or integration wane, and competition turns into ruthlessness, desire into rape, irritation into rage, ambition into ego-mania, the commissar into a terrorist.

However, on the historic scale, the ravages caused by the excesses of individual self-assertion are, as already suggested, relatively small compared to those which result from mis-placed devotion. Let us inquire a little closer into the causative processes behind it.

The integrative tendencies of the individual operate through the mechanisms of empathy, sympathy, projection, intro-jection, identification, worship – all of which make him feel that he is a *part* of some larger entity which transcends the boundaries of the individual self (p 220). This psychological urge to belong, to participate, to commune, is as primary and real as its opposite. The all-important question is the *nature* of that higher entity of which the individual feels himself a part. In early infancy, symbiotic consciousness unites the self and the world in an indivisible unit. Its reflection survives in the sympathetic magic of primitives, the belief in transub-stantiation, the mystic bonds which unite a person with his tribe, his totem, his shadow, his effigy, and later with his god. In the major Eastern philosophies, the 'I am thou and thou art me', the identity of the 'Real Self' with the Atman, the all-one, has been preserved throughout the ages. In the West it only survived in the tradition of the great Christian mystics; European philosophy and science, from Aristotle onward, made every man an island. It could not tolerate those vestiges of symbiotic awareness which survived in other cultures; the urge for self-transcendence had to be sublimated and canalized.

One way of achieving this was through the transformation of magic into art and science. This made it possible for the happy few to achieve self-transcendence on a higher turn of the spiral, by that sublime expansion of awareness which Freud called the oceanic feeling, which Maslow[9] calls 'the peak experience', and which I called the AH-reaction. But only a minority qualifies for it. For the others, there are only a few traditional outlets open to transcend the rigid boundaries of the ego. Historically speaking for the vast majority of mankind, the only answer to its integrative cravings, its longing to belong and to find meaning in existence, was identification with tribe, caste, nation, church or party – with a social holon.

But now we arrive at a crucial point. The psychological process, by means of which this identification was achieved, was mostly of the primitive, infantile kind of projection which populates heaven and earth with angry father-figures, fetishes to be worshipped, demons to be execrated, dogmas to be blindly believed. This crude form of *identification* is something quite different from *integration* into a well-ordered social hierarchy. It is a regression to an *infantile* form of self-transcendence; and in extreme cases almost a shortcut back to the womb. To quote Jung for a change: 'Not only do we speak of Mother Church, but even of the "womb of the Church" ... Catholics call the baptismal font "*immaculata divini fontis uterus*".'[10] However, we need not go to these extremes to realize that mature, sublimated expressions of the integrative tendency are the exception rather than the rule in human society. In looking at the historic record, men at all times seem to have behaved like Konrad Lorenz' 'imprinted' geese, which forever follow the keeper in misguided devotion because he was the first moving object they saw after hatching, cunningly substituted for the mother goose.

As far as we can look back on history, human societies have always been fairly successful in enforcing the sublimation of the *self-assertive* impulses of the individual – until the howling little savage in its cot became transformed into a more or less law-abiding and civilized member of society. But at the same time they singularly failed to induce a similar sublimation of the *self-transcending* impulses. Accordingly, the longing to belong, left without appropriately mature outlets, manifested itself mostly in primitive or perverted forms. The cause of this important contrast between the development of the two basic tendencies will, I hope, become apparent later on. But first, let us have a closer look at its psychological and social consequences.

The Perils of Identification

How does identification work? Let us consider the simplest case, where only two individuals are involved. Mrs Smith and Mrs Brown are friends. Mrs Brown has lost her husband in an accident; as Mrs Smith sheds compassionate tears, she participates in her friend's sorrow, becomes partially identified with her by an act of empathy, projection or introjection – whatever you like to call it. A similar process takes place when the other person is not a real individual but a heroine on the screen or in the pages of a novel. It is essential, however, that we make a clear distinction between two different emotional processes involved in the event, although they are experienced at the same time. The first is the act of identification itself, characterized by the fact that the subject has, for the moment, more or less forgotten her own existence and participates in the existence of another person, who may even live at another place in another time. This is clearly a self-transcending, gratifying and cathartic experience for the simple reason that, while it lasts, Mrs Smith has quite forgotten her own worries, jealousies and grudges against Mr Smith. The act of identification temporarily *inhibits* the self-asserting tendencies.

But there is a second process involved which may have the opposite effect: the process of identification may lead to the arousal of *vicarious emotions*. When Mrs Smith is 'sharing Mrs Brown's sorrow', the process of *sharing* (the first process) instantly leads to the second: the experience of *sorrow*. But the second process may also be the feeling of anxiety or anger. You commiserate with young Oliver Twist; as a result you feel like strangling Fagin with your own hands. The sharing is a self-transcending, cathartic experience. But it may act as a *vehicle* for anger – anger as a vicarious emotion, experienced on behalf of another, but genuinely felt.

The anger felt at the machinations of the perfidious villain on the screen – whom Mexican audiences have been known to riddle with bullets – is genuine anger. When we watch a thriller, we develop the physical symptoms of acute anxiety – palpitations, tense muscles, sudden jumps of alarm. Here, then, is the paradox – and the predicament. We have seen, on the one hand, that the self-transcending impulses of projection, participation, identification *inhibit* self-assertion, purge us of our selfish worries and desires. But on the other hand, the process of identification may *stimulate* the surge of anger, fear and vengefulness – which, although experienced *on behalf of another person*, nevertheless express themselves in the well-known adreno-toxic symptoms. The physiological mechanisms that enter into action are essentially the same whether the threat or offence is directed at oneself or the person or group with whom one identifies. They are self-assertive, although the self has momentarily changed its address – by being, for instance, projected into the guileless hero on the screen; or the local soccer team; or into 'my country, right or wrong'.

Art is a school of self-transcendence; but so is a patriotic rally, a voodoo session, a war dance. It is a triumph of the imaginative powers of our minds that we are capable of shedding tears over the death of an Anna Karenina who only exists as printer's ink on paper, or as a shadow on a screen. The illusions of the stage are ultimately derived from sympathetic magic – from the partial identification of spectator, actor and the god or hero whom he impersonates. But this magic is highly sublimated; the process of identification is tentative, partial, a momentary suspension of disbelief; it does not impair the critical faculties, does not undermine personal identity. But the voodoo session or Nuremberg rally does just that. The films shown by the Ministry of Truth in Orwell's *Nineteen Eighty-Four* aim at regressing the audience to a primitive level, and trigger off orgies of collective hatred. The spectators, nevertheless, are experiencing vicarious emotions of an unselfish kind; a righteous indignation whose manifestations are the more savage because it is impersonal, self-transcending and can be indulged in with a clean conscience.

Thus the glory and the tragedy of the human condition *both derive from our powers of self-transcendence*. It is a power which can be harnessed to creative or destructive purpose; it is equally capable of turning us into artists or killers, but more likely into killers. It can restrain selfish impulses, but also arouse violent emotions experienced on behalf of the entity with whom the identificatory rapport has been established. Injustices, or pretended injustices, inflicted on that entity are likely to generate more fanatical behaviour than the sting of a personal insult. Jenkins' ear may have become a comic cliché, but at the time it was a major contributary cause for the declaration of war on Spain. The execution of Nurse Edith Louisa Cavell in World War I caused more spontaneous indignation against Teutonic brutality than the mass executions of Jews in World War II. It is easy to identify oneself with a heroic Red Cross nurse, whereas persecuted Jews may arouse pity, but not impulses of identification.

Hierarchic Awareness

The mechanism which I have discussed – self-transcendence serving as an instrument, or vehicle, for emotions of the opposite class – finds its most disastrous expression in group psychology.

I have repeatedly stressed that the selfish impulses of man constitute a much lesser historic danger than his integrative tendencies. To put it in the simplest way: the individual who indulges in an excess of aggressive self-assertiveness incurs the penalties of society – he outlaws himself, he contracts *out* of the hierarchy. The true believer, on the other hand, becomes more closely knit *into it*; he enters the womb of his church, or party, or whatever the social holon to which he surrenders his identity. For identification in this primitive form always entails a certain impairment of individuality, an abdication of the critical faculties and of personal responsibility. The priest is the good shepherd of his flock, but we also use the same metaphor in a derogatory way when we speak of the masses following a demagogue, like sheep; both expressions, one approving, one pejorative, express the same truth.

This leads us back to the essential difference between primitive *identification*, resulting in a homogeneous flock, and mature forms of *integration* in a social hierarchy. In a well-balanced hierarchy, the individual retains his character as a social holon, a part-whole, who *qua* whole, enjoys autonomy within the limits of the restraints imposed by the interests of the community. He remains an individual whole in his own right, and is even expected to assert his holistic character by originality, initiative, and above all, personal responsibility. The same criteria of value apply to the larger social holons – professional groups, trade unions, social classes – on the higher echelons of the hierarchy. They are expected to display the virtues implied in the Janus principle: to be self-regulating autonomous wholes, but also conform to national – or international – interests. An ideal society of this kind could be said to possess 'hierarchic awareness', where every holon on every level is conscious both of its rights as a whole and its duties as a part.

However, the phenomena usually designated by the terms 'group mentality' or 'psychology of the masses' (*Massenpsychologie*) reflect a fundamentally different attitude. It is based – to say it once more – not on *integrated* interaction, but on *identificatory* rapport. Integration in a social hierarchy preserves the personal identity and responsibility of its holons; identification, while it lasts, implies a partial or total surrender of both.

We have seen that this surrender can take varied forms, some beneficial, some harmful. In mystic or aesthetic entrancement, the self dissolves in the oceanic feeling; one of the French expressions for the orgasm is *la petite mort*; if passion is blind, true love blurs the view; a visit to the theatre is an escape from the self. Self-transcendence always entails a surrender; but the amount and quality of the sacrifice depends on the degree of sublimation and the nature of the outlets. In the more sinister phenomena of mass psychology, sublimation is minimal and all the outlets are *gleichgeschaltet* – aligned in a single direction.

Induction and Hypnosis

Among the harmless manifestations of group psychology are such trivial phenomena as infectious laughter, infectious yawning, infectious fainting. The infection, say in a girl's classroom or dormitory, seems to be transmitted by some subtle germ which fills the air, or by a kind of mutual induction: 'Whenever I looked at Sally Anne or Sally Anne at me, we started giggling again, we couldn't stop it. In the end we all got hysterical.' Not only adolescent girls, but guardsmen lined up on parade, too, are prone to such phenomena: one six-footer happens to faint, and others topple over like nine-pins. At revivalist meetings, and the like occasions, the symptoms are more lively: once the first devotee has started to holler, jump, quake or spin, others are seized by an irresistible urge to follow suit. The next step leads to more uncanny manifestations: the tarantula dancers of the Dark Ages, the collective hallucinations of the nuns of Loudun rolling on the floor in the embrace of obscene devils; the lynching crowds of all races and denominations; the revelries on Hanging Days at Newgate; the jolly French *commères* turned into drooling *tricoteuses*; and, by way of contrast, the rigidly disciplined, ritualized Nuremberg rallies and Red Square parades. Or, for another contrast, the hordes of screaming teenage Bacchantae mobbing Pop-stars, and the leering teenage Narcissi coiffured like cockroaches.

All these phenomena – some harmless, some sinister, some grotesque – have one basic element in common: the people participating in them have to some extent surrendered their independent individualities, become more or less de-personalized; while their impulses have to the same extent become synchronized, aligned in the same direction like magnetized files of iron. The force which binds them together is variously called 'social infection', 'mutual induction', 'collective hysteria', 'mass hypnosis', etc; the common element of all is identification with the group at the price of relinquishing part of one's personal identity. Immersion in the group mind is a kind of poor man's self-transcendence.

It has also been compared by Freud and others to a semi-hypnotic, or quasi-hypnotic, state.

The hypnotic state is easy to demonstrate, but difficult to define or explain. That, and the uncanny powers it confers on the hypnotist, may be the main reason why it has for so long been treated with scepticism and distrust by Western science – whereas in tribal societies, and in the advanced civilizations of the East, it was used for both benevolent and malevolent purposes. Mesmer produced spectacular cures with its help, but he had no idea how it worked; his spurious explanations in terms of animal magnetism, combined with showmanship, brought hypnotism into further disrepute. In the course of the nineteenth century several eminent English surgeons carried out major operations painlessly under hypnosis, but their reports met with scepticism and hostility. Orthodox medicine refused to accept the reality of a phenomenon which could easily be demonstrated, and even for a while became a parlour game. Prejudice wore down only gradually; Charcot and his school in France, and Freud in his early period, produced hypnotic phenomena as a matter of routine, and used them as a therapeutical tool. But it was the Scottish physician James Baird who, in 1841, coined the word 'hypnotism', which sounded a little more respectable than the earlier terms – mesmerism, magnetism or somnambulism.* At present, qualified medical hypnotists are employed in growing numbers by dental surgeons in lieu of anaesthetists, and the use of hypnotism in childbirth, psychotherapy and dermatology has become commonplace. So much so that we are apt to forget to wonder how it works. For, as already said, it is a phenomenon easy to produce but difficult to explain – particularly in terms of flat-earth psychology.

An explanation, or at least description, as good as any other was given half a century ago by Kretschmer: 'In the hypnotic state the functions of the ego seem to be suspended, except those which communicate with the hypnotizer as though through a narrow slit in a screen.'[11] The slit focusses the beam of the hypnotic rapport. The rest of the hypnotized subject's world is screened off or blurred.

A more recent description by an Oxford experimental

* The last expression was coined by the Marquis Chastenay de Puysegur, a follower of Mesmer, who had noticed that his patients when in trance seemed to move and act like sleepwalkers.

psychologist, Dr Oswald, leads to essentially similar conclusions:

> The human hypnotic trance [as distinct from cataleptic states induced in animals] has a name that grew out of a resemblance to sleep-walking. The human hypnotic trance is not a state of sleep. Nor, let it be emphasized, is it a state of unconsciousness ... It is not possible to categorize it in a manner that would be universally acceptable. It remains a very definite puzzle. It is certainly a state of inertia, but only in respect of spontaneous actions. In response to the hypnotist's commands, vigorous activity may ensue without disrupting the trance, or destroying the rapport. It is this rapport that is so characteristic. The hypnotized individual's own initiative is subservient to that of the hypnotist. Alternatives to that which the hypnotist suggests simply do not seem to arise. If you ask your friend to go and shut the door he may quietly do so, or he may comment that, since he sees no reason for you to be so idle, you might as well go and do it yourself. The hypnotized person just gets on and does it.[12]

Lastly, *Drever's Dictionary of Psychology*: 'Hypnosis: artificially induced state, similar in many respects to sleep, but specially characterized by exaggerated suggestibility, and the continuance of contact or rapport with the operator.'[13]

Freud in his book on *Group Psychology and the Analysis of the Ego* took the hypnotic state as his starting point. He regarded hypnotizer and hypnotized as a 'group formation of two', and thought that the hypnotic trance provided the clue to 'the profound alteration in the mental activities of individuals subjected to the influence of a group'.[14] Indeed, the 'hypnotic effect' of prophets and demagogues on their 'spellbound' followers has become so much of a cliché that one tends to overlook its literal, pathological relevance. Le Bon's classic analysis of the mentality of the heroic, murderous mobs of the French Revolution (which Freud and others took as their text) remains as true as it was a century and a half ago. As in the hypnotized subject, so in the individual subjected to the influence of the crowd, personal initiative is relinquished in favour of the leader and 'the functions of the ego seem to be suspended', except those which are 'in rapport with the operator'. This entails a state of mental inertia, a mild form of somnambulism or 'spellboundness' which, however, may at any moment burst into violent activity at the leader's command. Crowds tend to behave in a 'fanatical' (or 'heroic'), that is, *single-minded* way, because the individual differences between its members are temporarily suspended, their critical faculties anaesthetized; the whole mass is thus intellectually *reduced* to a primitive common denominator, a level of communication which all can share: single-mindedness must be simple-minded. But at the same time, the emotional dynamism of the crowd is *enhanced* by mutual induction between its members, and by the fact that the slits in the screen – or blinkers – are all aligned in the same direction. It is a kind of resonance effect, which makes the members of the crowd feel that they are part of an irresistible power; moreover, of a power which *ex hypothesi cannot do wrong*. Identification absolves from individual responsibility; as in the hypnotic rapport, initiative and responsibility for the subject's actions are surrendered to the hypnotizer. This is the exact opposite of 'hierarchic awareness', of the consciousness of individual freedom within the limitations of a rule-governed hierarchy. Hierarchic awareness shows the two faces of Janus; crowd mentality is like a single, blinkered profile.

It not only implies the suspension of personal responsibility, but also of the self-assertive tendencies of the individual. We have met this paradox before. The total identification of the individual with the group makes him unselfish in more than one sense. It makes him indifferent to danger and less sensitive to physical pain – again a mild form of hypnotic anaesthesia. It makes him perform comradely, altruistic, heroic actions – to the point of self-sacrifice – and at the same time behave with ruthless cruelty towards the enemy or victim of the group. But the brutality displayed by the members of a fanatic crowd is impersonal and unselfish; it is exercised in the interest or the supposed interest of the whole; and it entails the readiness not only to kill but also to die in its name. In other words, *the self-assertive behaviour of the group is based on the self-transcending behaviour of its members*, which often entails sacrifice of personal interests and even of life in the interest of the group. To put it simply: *the egotism of the group feeds on the altruism of its members*.

This becomes less paradoxical when we realize that the social group is a holon with its own specific structure and canon of rules – which differ from the rules that govern the individual behaviour of its members (cf pp 71 f.). A crowd is of course a very primitive holon – the human equivalent of a herd or flock. But it remains nevertheless true that the crowd as a whole is not simply the sum of its parts, and that it displays characteristic features not found on the level of its individual parts.*

Needless to say, once the fury of the group is unleashed, its individual members can give their aggressive impulses free rein. But this is a secondary kind of aggressiveness, catalized by a previous act of identification, as distinct from primary aggressiveness, based on personal motives. The physical manifestations of such secondary aggressiveness may be indistinguishable from those of primary aggression – just as the anger aroused by the villain in the film produces the physical

---

* In a recent paper (in press) on 'The Evolution of Systems of Rules of Conduct' Professor F. A. von Hayek defines as his aim 'to distinguish between the systems of rules of conduct which govern the behaviour of the individual members of a group (or of the elements of any order) and the order or pattern of actions which results from this for the group as a whole ... That [they] are not the same thing should be obvious as soon as it is stated, although the two are in fact frequently confused.'[15]

At times the rules which govern individual and group behaviour may even be in direct opposition. Years ago, when I wrote novels, I made one character – a Roman lawyer in the first century BC – write a treatise which bore the title: 'On The Causes Which Induce Man To Act Contrary To The Interests Of Others When Isolated, And To Act Contrary To His Own Interests When Associated In Groups Or Crowds'.[16]

symptoms of anger directed at a real person. But in both cases we are dealing with aggression as a secondary process derived from identification – with the group in the first case, with the screen-hero in the second.

Sociologists who regard war as a manifestation of man's repressed aggressive urges make one feel at once that they have never served in the ranks, and have no idea of the mentality of private soldiers in war time. There is waiting – somebody has said that it occupies ninety per cent of a soldier's time; there is grumbling and grousing, much preoccupation with sex, inter-mittent fear, and, above all, the fervent hope that it will soon be over, followed by the return to civvy street – but *hating* does not enter into the picture. In modern warfare, the enemy is mostly invisible, and 'fighting' is reduced to the impersonal manipulation of long-range weapons. In classical warfare, attacks were carried out by units – that is groups – against positions held by other groups; the features of individual enemies whom one had killed or may have killed were hardly ever perceived; trying to kill them was under the circumstances a *sine qua non* of survival, but primary aggression played no significant part in the picture. Nor did 'defence of home and family'. Soldiers do not fight at their homesteads, but at places hundreds or thousands of miles away, to defend the homes, families, territory, etc, of the *group* of which they are a part. The professed and occasionally real hatred of *Boches* or Wops, Fascists or Reds, is again not a matter of personal primary aggression; it is directed against a group, or rather against the common denominator which all members of the group share. The individual victim of such hatred is punished not as an individual, but as a symbolic representative of that common denominator.

In the First World War soldiers in opposite trenches were capable of fraternizing during Christmas, and of starting shooting at each other once Boxing Day was over. War is a ritual, a deadly ritual, *not the result of aggressive self-assertion, but of self-transcending identification*. Without loyalty to tribe, church, flag or ideal, there would be no wars; and loyalty is a noble thing. I do not mean, of course, that loyalty must necessarily be expressed in group violence – merely that it is a precondition of it; that self-transcending devotion, all through history, has acted as a catalyst for secondary aggression.

Sweet Caesar's Wounds

Shakespeare has expressed this seemingly abstract point with a persuasiveness which no psychological treatise can hope to achieve. In Mark Antony's oration to the throng of Roman citizens there is a decisive moment, when he deliberately quells their first, superficial resentment against the conspirators. He makes his audience form a ring about the corpse of Caesar – not yet appealing for revenge, but arousing first their pity:

> *Ant.* If you have tears, prepare to shed them now.
> You all do know this mantle; I remember
> The first time ever Caesar put it on,
> 'Twas on a summer's evening in his tent,
> That day he overcame the Nervii:
> Look, in this place ran Cassius' dagger through . . .
> And in his mantle muffling up his face,
> Even at the base of Pompey's statue
> (Which all the while ran blood) great Caesar fell.
> O what a fall was there, my countrymen!
> Then I, and you, and all of us fell down. . . .

Having thus identified 'I' and 'you' and 'all of us' with the dead leader, and shown them 'sweet Caesar's wounds, poor, poor, dumb mouths, and bid them speak for me', he has got the crowd into exactly the mood he wanted:

> O now you weep, and I perceive you feel
> The dint of pity: these are gracious drops.
> Kind souls, what, weep you, when you but behold
> Our Caesar's vesture wounded? Look you here,
> Here is himself, marr'd as you see with traitors.

1.*C.* O piteous spectacle!
2.*C.* O noble Caesar!
3.*C.* O woeful day!
4.*C.* O traitors, villains!
1.*C.* O most bloody sight!
2.*C.* We will be reveng'd!
All. Revenge! About! Seek! Burn! Fire! Kill!
    Slay! Let not a traitor live!

And so mischief is afoot once more, wing'd by the noblest sentiments.

The Structure of Beliefs

A mob in action displays an extreme form of group mentality. But to be affected by it, a person need not be physically present in a crowd; mental identification with a group, nation, church or party is often quite sufficient. If our imagination can produce all the physical symptoms of emotions in reaction to the perils of personae which exist merely as printer's ink, how much easier, then, to have the experience of belonging, of being part of a group, though it is not physically present. One can be a victim of group mentality even in the privacy of one's bath.

A mob in action needs a leader. Religious or political movements need leaders to get under way; once established, they still benefit, of course, from efficient leadership, but the primary need of a group, the factor which lends it cohesion as a group, is a creed, a shared system of beliefs, a faith that transcends the individual's personal interests. It may be represented by a symbol – the totem or fetish which provides a mystic sense of union among the members of the tribe. It may be the conviction that one belongs to a Chosen Race whose ancestors made a covenant with God; or to a Master Race whose ancestors were equipped with a gene-complex of special excellence; or whose Emperors were descended from the sun. It may be the conviction that observance of certain rules and rites qualifies one for membership in a privileged élite in after-life; or that manual work qualifies for membership in the élite class of history.

How do these powerful collective belief-systems come into being? When the historian attempts to trace them back to their origin, he inevitably ends up in the twilight of mythology. If a belief carries a strong emotive power, it can always be shown to spring from archaic sources. Beliefs are not invented; they seem to materialize as the humidity in the atmosphere condenses into clouds, which subsequently undergo endless transformations of shape.

Rational arguments have little impact on the true believer, for the creed to which he is emotionally committed can be contradicted by evidence without losing its magic power. From prehistoric days until quite recent times, that magic was derived from religious beliefs. To dispense with God was unthinkable even to the Founding Fathers of modern science: Copernicus was an orthodox Thomist, Kepler a Lutheran mystic, Galileo called God the Chief Mathematician of the Universe; Newton believed, with Bishop Usher, that the world was created in 4004 BC. The movements towards social reform were just as firmly based on the ethics of Christianity.

The Age of Enlightenment, culminating in the French Revolution, was a decisive turning-point in the history of man. It was dramatized by Robespierre's symbolic gesture of deposing God and enthroning the Goddess of Reason in the vacant chair. She proved to be a dismal failure. The Christian mythos had a continuous ancestry which can be traced back, through Greece, Palestine and Babylon, to the myths and rites of neolithic man; it provided an archetypal mould for man's self-transcending emotions, his craving for the absolute. The progressive trends and ideologies of the nineteenth century proved to be a poor substitute. From the point of view of material welfare, public health and social justice, the last hundred and fifty years of secular reforms certainly brought more tangible improvements in the lot of the common man than fifteen hundred years of Christianity had done; yet their reflection in the group mind was a different matter. Religion may have been opium to the people, but opium addicts are not given to much enthusiasm for a rational, healthy diet. Among the intellectual élite, the rapid advance of science created a rather shallow optimistic belief in the infallibility of Reason, in a clear, bright, crystalline world with a transparent atomic structure, with no room for shadows, twilights and myths. Reason was thought to be in control of emotion, as the rider controls the horse – the rider representing enlightened, rational thought, the horse representing what the Victorians called 'the dark passions' and 'the beast within us'. Nobody foresaw, no pessimist ventured to guess, that the Age of Reason would end in the greatest emotional stampede in history, which left the rider crushed under the hoofs of the beast. Yet once more the beast was motivated by the noblest ideals – by the secular messianism of the Classless Society and of the Millennial Reich; and once more we are apt to forget that the vast majority of men and women who fell under the totalitarian spell was activated by unselfish motives, ready to accept the role of martyr or executioner, as the cause demanded.

Both the Fascist and the Soviet myths were not synthetic constructions, but revivals of archetypes, both capable of absorbing not only the cerebral component but the total man; both provided emotional saturation.

The Fascist myth is undisguised and explicit. The opium is doled out to the masses quite openly. The archetypes of Blood and Soil, of the dragon-slaying Superman, the deities of Walhalla and the satanic powers of the Jews are systematically called up for national service. One half of Hitler's genius consisted in hitting the right unconscious chords. The other half was his alert eclecticism, his flair for hypermodern avant-garde methods in Economy, Architecture, Technology, Propaganda and Warfare. The secret of Fascism is the revival of archaic beliefs in an ultra-modern setting.

The Nazi edifice was a skyscraper fitted with hot water pipes which drew on underground springs of volcanic origin.[17]

The Soviet myth had an equally profound appeal to a large section of humanity. The classless Communist society was to be a revival of the Golden Age of mythology at the highest, ultimate turn of the dialectical spiral. It was a secular version of the Promised Land, the Kingdom of Heaven. One of the salient features of this archetypal myth is that the advent of the Millennium must be preceded by violent upheaval: the ordeal of forty years in the desert, the Apocalypse, the Last Judgement. Their secular equivalent is the liquidation of the Bourgeois world through Revolutionary Terror. Some of the early Russian and contemporary Chinese literature extolling Revolutionary Justice being done to a 'putrefied and gangrened Capitalist society' reminds one indeed of the Last Judgements of Grünewald or Hieronymus Bosch. The true believer has a genuine horror of the 'Reformist' heresy, the belief in a bloodless transition towards socialism (which caused the Communists to denounce Socialists, and later the Chinese to denounce the Russians, as traitors to the cause). No apocalypse, no kingdom come.

The Split

Fascist propaganda did not take much trouble to harmonize emotion with reason; it dismissed logical objections to its doctrines as 'destructive criticism'. Göring's epigram 'When I hear the word "culture" I reach for my gun' was a frank declaration of war on the intellect: the rider must obey the horse. The Leninist theory of Scientific Socialism, on the other hand, was an offspring, in the line of direct descent, of the Age of Enlightenment. It was an eminently rationalist credo, based on a materialist conception of history, which derided all emotionalism as 'petit-bourgeois sentimentality'. How is it to be explained that millions of adherents of this rationalist doctrine – including progressive intellectuals all over the world – accepted the logical absurdities of the 'Stalin personality cult', the show trials, purges, the alliance with the Nazis; and that those who lived outside Russia accepted them voluntarily, in self-imposed discipline, without pressure from Big Brother? The Stalin regime is a matter of the past, but its lethal rites are being faithfully repeated in China and elsewhere, meeting with the same approval of a new generation of well-meaning sympathizers. At the time of writing, the end of 1966, China is convulsed by another of the mass purges which are endemic in the system; and I have before me a recent cutting with the comments by the official New China agency on a swim which President Mao Tse-tung, 'the radiant sun that lights the minds of the world's revolutionary people', took in the Yangtze river:

> His cross-Yangtze swim was a great encouragement to the Chinese people and revolutionaries throughout the world, and a heavy blow to imperialism, modern revisionism and the monsters and freaks who are opposed to socialism and Mao Tse-tung's thought.[18]

I have spoken of the paranoid streak that runs through History. Modern man may be quite willing to admit that such a streak has indeed existed among the Aztecs or at the time of the witch-burning mania. He is perhaps less willing to admit that a comparable delusional element was present in 'the doctrine that nearly all mankind, including all the babies who die unbaptized, are to receive for ever tortures more severe than any earthly expert can contrive to inflict, with the corollary that to watch the tortures eternally is one of the delights of the blessed'.[19] Yet this doctrine (the Abominable Fancy, as Dean Farrar called it) was part of the collective belief-system of the majority of Europeans well to the end of the seventeenth century, and for many considerably longer. However, even those who appreciate to its full extent the mental disorder underlying such fancies are apt to dismiss them as phenomena of the past. It is not easy to love humanity and yet to admit that the paranoid streak is as much in evidence in contemporary history as it was in the distant past but more devastating in its consequences; and that, as the record shows, it is not accidental, but endemic – inherent in man's condition.

No matter how much the symptoms vary, the pattern of the disorder is the same: a mentality split between faith and reason, between emotion and intellect.* Faith in a shared belief-system is based on an act of emotional commitment; it rejects doubt as something evil; it is a form of self-transcendence which demands the partial or total surrender of the critical faculties of the intellect, comparable to the hypnotic state.

> Newton wrote not only the *Principia* but also a treatise on the topography of Hell. Up to this day we all hold beliefs which are not only incompatible with observable facts, but with facts actually observed by ourselves. The hot steam of belief and the iceblock of reasoning are packed together inside our skulls, but as a rule they do not interact; the steam does not condense and the ice does not melt. The human mind is basically schizophrenic, split into two mutually exclusive planes ... The Primitive knows that his idol is a piece of carved wood, and yet he believes in its power to make rain; and though our beliefs underwent a gradual refinement, the dualistic pattern of our minds remained basically unchanged.[20]

Up to the Revival of Learning in the thirteenth century, this dualism seems to have caused no particular problem, because it was taken for granted that the intellect played the subordinate role of *ancilla fidei*, the hand-maid of faith. But the situation changed when St Thomas Aquinas recognized the 'Light of Reason' as an independent source of knowledge beside the 'Light of Grace'. Reason was promoted from the

---

* Schizophrenia ('split-mindedness') is usually defined as a state of mental disorder in which there is dissociation between intellectual and affective processes. Paranoid schizophrenia is characterized by persistent, systematized delusions.

status of a hand-maid to that of the 'bride' of faith. As a bride, she was of course still bound to obey her spouse; nevertheless she was henceforth recognized to exist in her own right. And with that, the conflict became inevitable. From time to time it reached a dramatic peak: in the burning of Servetius, the Galileo scandal, the clash between Darwinians and fundamentalists, the stubborn opposition of the Catholic Church to birth control. In such climactic moments the smouldering conflict is brought into the open; they provide the split mind with an opportunity to become conscious of its split, and to overcome it by taking sides. Such open confrontations, however, are rare; the normal way of living with a split mind was and is to patch it up with rationalizations and subtle techniques of pseudo-reasoning. These were obligingly provided at all times by dialecticians of various brands, from theologians to Marxian Evangelists. Thus a *modus vivendi* is achieved, based on self-deception, perpetuating the delusive streak. This applies of course not only to the Western world, but to Hindus, Moslems and militant Buddhists as well; Asian history has been as bloody, holy and cruel as ours.

The Comforts of Double-Think

To recapitulate: without a transcendental belief, each man is a mean little island. The need for self-transcendence through some form of 'peak experience' (religious or aesthetic) and/or through social integration is inherent in man's condition. Transcendental beliefs are derived from certain ever-recurrent archetypal patterns which evoke instant emotive responses.*
But once they become institutionalized as the collective property of a group, they degenerate into rigid doctrines which, without losing their emotive appeal to the true believer,

---

* William James' *The Varieties of Religious Experience* is still the classic in this field. A more recent treatment is offered by Alister Hardy in his *The Divine Flame*.

potentially offend his reasoning faculties. This leads to the split: emotion responds to the piercing call of the Muezzin, the intellect shrinks from it. To eliminate the dissonance, various forms of double-think have been designed at various times – powerful techniques of self-deception, some crude, some extremely sophisticated. Secular religions – political ideologies – too, have their ancient origins in the utopian craving for an ideal society; but when they crystallize into a movement or party, they can be distorted to such an extent that the actual policy pursued is the direct opposite of the professed ideal. The reason why idealistic movements – whether religious or secular – show this apparently inevitable tendency to degenerate into their own caricatures can be derived from the peculiarities of the group mind: its tendency towards intellectual oversimplification combined with emotional arousal, and its quasi-hypnotic suggestibility by leader-figures or belief-systems.

I can speak of this with some first-hand experience, based on seven years (1931–8) of membership in the Communist Party during Stalin's terror regime. In writing about that period, I have described the operations of the deluded mind in terms of elaborate manoeuvrings to defend the citadel of faith against the hostile incursions of doubt. There are several concentric rings of defences protecting the fortress. The outer defences are designed to ward off unpalatable facts. For the simple-minded this is made easy by official censorship, the banning of all literature liable to poison the mind; and by implanting a fear of contamination, or of guilt by association, through contact with suspected heretics. Crude as these methods are, they quickly produce a blinkered, sectarian outlook on the world. Avoidance of forbidden information, first imposed from the outside, soon becomes a habit – an emotive revulsion against the dirty packs of lies offered by the enemy. For the majority of believers, this is quite enough to ensure unswerving loyalty; the more sophisticated are frequently forced to fall back on the inner defence positions. In 1932–3, the years of the great famine which followed the forced collectivization of the land, I travelled widely in the Soviet Union, writing a book which was never published. I saw entire villages deserted, railway stations blocked by crowds of begging families, and the proverbial starving infants – but they were quite real, with stick-like arms, puffed up bellies and cadaverous heads.

I reacted to the brutal impact of reality on illusion in a manner typical of the true believer. I was surprised and bewildered – but the elastic shock-absorbers of my Party training began to operate at once. I had eyes to see, and a mind conditioned to explain away what they saw. This 'inner censor' is more reliable and effective than any official censorship ... It helped me to overcome my doubts and to re-arrange my impressions in the desired pattern. I learnt to classify automatically everything that shocked me as 'the heritage of the past' and everything I liked as 'the seeds of the future'. By setting up this automatic sorting machine in his mind, it was still possible in 1933 for a European to live in Russia and yet to remain a Communist. All my friends had that automatic sorting machine in their heads. The Communist mind has perfected the techniques of self-deception in the same manner as its techniques of mass propaganda. The inner censor in the mind of the true believer completes the work of the public censor; his self-discipline is as tyrannical as the obedience imposed by the regime; he terrorizes his own conscience into submission; he carries his private Iron Curtain inside his skull, to protect his illusions against the intrusion of reality.[20a]

Behind the curtain there is the magic world of double-think. 'Ugly is beautiful, false is true, and also conversely.' This is not Orwell; it was written, in all seriousness, by the late Professor Suzuki, the foremost propounder of modern Zen, to illustrate the principle of the identity of opposites.[21] The perversions of Pop-Zen are based on juggling with the identity of opposites, the Communist's on juggling with the dialectics of history, the Schoolman's on a combination of Holy Scripture with Aristotelian logic. The axioms differ, but the delusional process follows much the same pattern. Facts and

arguments which succeed in penetrating the outer defences
are processed by the dialectical method until 'false' becomes
'true', tyranny the true democracy, and a herring a racehorse:

> Gradually I learnt to distrust my preoccupation with facts, and to
> regard the world around me in the light of dialectic interpretation.
> It was a satisfactory and indeed blissful state; once you had assimi-
> lated the technique, the so-called facts automatically took on the
> proper colouring and fell into their proper place. Both morally and
> logically, the Party was infallible: morally, because its aims were
> right, that is, in accord with the Dialectic of History, and these
> aims justified all means; logically, because the Party was the van-
> guard of the proletariat, and the proletariat the embodiment of the
> active principle in History . . . I now lived in a mental world which
> was a 'closed system', comparable to the self-contained universe of
> the Middle Ages. All my feelings, my attitudes to art, literature and
> human relations, became reconditioned and moulded to the
> pattern.[22]*

The most striking feature of the paranoiac's delusional
system is its inner consistency, and the patient's uncanny
persuasiveness in expounding it. Much the same applies to any
'closed system' of thought. By a closed system I mean a
cognitive matrix, governed by a canon, which has three
main peculiarities. Firstly, it claims to represent a truth of
universal validity, capable of explaining all phenomena, and
to have a cure for all that ails man. In the second place, it is a
system which cannot be refuted by evidence, because all
potentially damaging data are automatically processed and
reinterpreted to make them fit the expected pattern. The
processing is done by sophisticated methods of casuistry,

---

* This was written in 1952. Fifteen years later the scene has shifted, but the
pattern repeats itself: 'According to the Chinese Press, quoted in the *Literary
Gazette*, Shakespeare's plays are "fundamentally opposed to socialist realism"
. . . As for the composer Bizet, his opera *Carmen* is decried as an attempt "to
sell sex and individualism". The trouble with Beethoven's Ninth Symphony
was that it was infused with a concept of "bourgeois humanist love". Interest
in bourgeois classical music can only "paralyse revolutionary resolution".
Chinese critics also discerned a "revisionist outlook" in Tolstoy's *Anna
Karenina*[23]'.

centred on axioms of great emotive power, and indifferent to the rules of common logic; it is a kind of Wonderland croquet, played with mobile hoops. In the third place, it is a system which invalidates criticism by shifting the argument to the subjective motivation of the critic, and deducing his motivation from the axioms of the system itself. The orthodox Freudian school in its early stages approximated a closed system: if you argued that for such and such reasons you doubted the existence of the so-called castration complex, the Freudian's prompt answer was that your argument betrayed an unconscious resistance indicating that you yourself have a castration complex; you were caught in a vicious circle. Similarly, if you argued with a Stalinist that to make a pact with Hitler was not a nice thing to do, he would explain that your bourgeois class-consciousness made you unable to understand the dialectics of history. And if a paranoiac lets you in on the secret that the moon is a hollow sphere filled with aphrodisiac vapours which the Martians have put there to bewitch mankind; and if you object that the theory, though attractive, is based on insufficient evidence, he will at once accuse you of being a member of the world conspiracy to suppress truth.

A closed system is a cognitive structure with a distorted, non-Euclidian geometry in curved space, where parallels intersect and straight lines form loops. Its canon is based on a central axiom, postulate or dogma, to which the subject is emotionally committed, and from which the rules of processing reality are derived. The amount of distortion involved in the processing is a matter of degrees, and an important criterion of the value of the system. It ranges from the scientist's involuntary inclination to juggle with data as a mild form of self-deception, motivated by his commitment to a theory, to the delusional belief-systems of clinical paranoia. When Einstein made his famous pronouncement 'if the facts do not fit the theory, then the facts are wrong' he spoke with his tongue in his cheek; but he nevertheless expressed a profound feeling of the scientist committed to his theory. As we have seen, an occasional suspension of strict logic in favour of a temporary indulgence in the games of the underground is an important factor in scientific and artistic creativity. But geniuses are rare. And if geniuses sometimes indulge in these non-Euclidian games where reasoning is guided by emotional bias, it is an individual bias, a hunch of their own making; whereas the group mind receives its emotional beliefs ready-made from its leaders or from its catechism.

Let me repeat, however, that the amount of logical distortion needed to keep the deluded mind happy in its faith is a factor of decisive importance. Here lies the answer to that ethical relativism which cynically proclaims that all politicians are corrupt, all ideologies eyewash, all religion designed to befuddle the masses. The fact that power corrupts does not mean that all men in power are equally corrupt.

The Group Mind as a Holon

Earlier in this chapter I referred to the tendency of over-excited organs to assert themselves to the detriment of the whole, and then went on to the pathology of cognitive structures getting out of control: the *idée fixe* of the crank, obsessions running riot, closed systems centred on some part-truth pretending to represent the whole truth. We now find similar symptoms on a higher level of the hierarchy, as pathological manifestations of the group mind. The difference between these two kinds of mental disorder is the same as that between the primary aggressiveness of the individual and the secondary aggressiveness derived from his identification with a social holon. The individual crank, enamoured of his own pet theory, the patient in the mental home convinced that there is a sinister conspiracy aimed at his person, are disowned by society; their obsessions serve some unconscious private purpose. In contrast to this, the collective delusions of the crowd or group are based, not on individual *deviations* but on the individual's tendency to *conform*. Any single individual who would today assert that he has made a pact with the Devil and had intercourse with succubi, would promptly be sent to a mental home. Yet not so long ago, belief in such things was a matter of course – and approved by 'common-sense' in the original meaning of the term, ie, consensus of opinion.*

I have suggested that the evils of mankind are caused, not by the primary aggressiveness of individuals, but by their self-transcending identification with groups whose common denominator is low intelligence and high emotionality. We now come to the parallel conclusion that the delusional streak running through history is not due to individual forms of lunacy, but to the collective delusions generated by emotion-based belief-systems. We have seen that the cause underlying these pathological manifestations is the split between reason and belief – or more generally, insufficient coordination between the emotive and discriminative faculties of the mind. Our next step will be to inquire whether we can trace the cause of this faulty coordination – this disorder in the hier-archy – to the evolution of the human brain. Should con-temporary neurophysiology, though still in its infancy, be able to provide some indication of the causes of the trouble, we would have made a first step towards a frank diagnosis of our predicament – and thereby gain some inkling of the direction in which the search for a remedy must proceed.

Summary

The considerations set out in earlier chapters led us to distin-guish three factors in emotion: nature of the drive, hedonic

---

* 'Philosophy of commonsense; accepting primary beliefs of mankind as ultimate criterion of truth' (The Concise Oxford Dictionary).

tone, and the polarity of the self-assertive and self-transcending tendencies.

Under normal conditions the two tendencies are in dynamic equilibrium. Under conditions of stress the self-assertive tendency may get out of control and manifest itself in aggressive behaviour. However, on the historical scale, the damages wrought by individual violence for selfish motives are insignificant compared to the holocausts resulting from self-transcending devotion to collectively shared belief-systems. It is derived from primitive identification instead of mature social integration; it entails the partial surrender of personal responsibility and produces the quasi-hypnotic phenomena of group-psychology. The egotism of the social holon feeds on the altruism of its members. The ubiquitous rituals of human sacrifice at the dawn of civilization are early symptoms of the split between reason and emotion-based beliefs, which produces the delusional streak running through history.

XVI

THE THREE BRAINS

I have no inclination to keep the domain of the psychological floating as it were in the air, without any organic foundation . . . Let the biologists go as far as they can and let us go as far as we can. Some day the two will meet.

FREUD

LET me recapitulate: when one contemplates the streak of insanity running through human history, it appears highly probable that *homo sapiens* is a biological freak, the result of some remarkable mistake in the evolutionary process. The ancient doctrine of original sin, variants of which occur independently in the mythologies of diverse cultures, could be a reflection of man's awareness of his own inadequacy, of the intuitive hunch that somewhere along the line of his ascent something has gone wrong.

Mistakes in Brain-Making

The strategy of evolution, like any other strategy, is subject to trial and error. There is nothing particularly improbable in the assumption that man's native equipment, though superior to that of any known animal species, nevertheless may contain some serious fault in the circuitry of his most precious and delicate instrument – the central nervous system.

Whether a skylark is happier than a rainbow trout is a nice debating point; both are stagnant species, but well adapted to their ways of life, and to call them evolutionary mistakes because they have not got the brains to write poetry would be the height of hubris. When the biologist talks of evolutionary mistakes, he means something more tangible and precise: some obvious deviation from Nature's own standards of engineering efficiency, a construction fault which deprives an organ of its survival value – like the monstrous antlers of the Irish elk. Some turtles and insects are so top-heavy that if in combat or by misadventure they fall on their back, they cannot get up again, and starve to death – a grotesque error in construction which Kafka turned into a symbol of the human predicament. But before talking of man, I must discuss briefly two earlier evolutionary mistakes in brain-building, both of which had momentous consequences.

The first concerns the brain development of the arthropods which, with more than seven hundred thousand known species, constitute by far the largest phylum of the animal kingdom. They range from microscopic mites through centipedes, insects and spiders to ten-foot giant crabs; but they all have this in common, that *their brains** *are built around their gullets*. In vertebrates, the brain and spinal cord are both dorsal – at the back of the alimentary canal. In invertebrates, however, the main nerve chain runs *ventrally* – on the belly side of the animal. The chain terminates in a ganglionic mass *beneath* the mouth. This is the phylogenetically older part of the brain; whereas the newer and more sophisticated part of it developed *above* the mouth, in the vicinity of the eyes or other distance-receptors. Thus the alimentary tube passes through the midst of the evolving brain-mass, and this is very bad evolutionary strategy because, if the brain is to grow and expand, the alimentary tube will be more and more compressed (see Figure 11). To quote Gaskell's *The Origin of Vertebrates*:

> Progress on these lines must result in a crisis, owing to the inevitable squeezing out of the food-channel by the increasing

* In lower forms the ganglionic masses which are precursors of the brain.

nerve-mass ... Truly, at the time when vertebrates first appeared, the direction and progress of variation in the Arthropoda was leading, owing to the manner in which the brain was pierced by the oesophagus, to a terrible dilemma – either the capacity for taking in food without sufficient intelligence to capture it, or intelligence sufficient to capture food and no power to consume it.[1]

FIGURE II

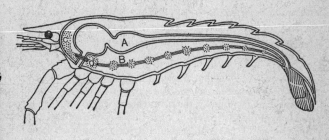

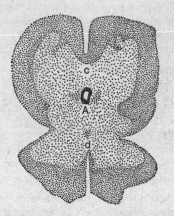

Top: relation between the alimentary canal (A) and nervous system (B) of an invertebrate. The upper brain mass (c) and the lower brain mass (d) constrict the alimentary canal (after Wood Jones and Porteus). Bottom: section across the brain of a scorpion-like invertebrate. The upper and lower brain masses (c and d) constrict the narrow alimentary tube (A) in the centre of the brain (after Gaskell)

The dilemma seems to have been particularly acute for 'the highest scorpion and spider-like animals, whose brain-mass has grown round and compressed the food-tube so that nothing but fluid pabulum can pass through into the stomach; the whole group have become blood-suckers. These kinds of animals – the sea-scorpions – were the dominant race when the vertebrates first appeared ... Further upward evolution demanded a larger and larger brain with the ensuing consequence of a greater and greater difficulty of food supply.'[2] Another authority, Wood Jones, comments:

> To become a blood-sucker is to become a failure. Phylogenetic senility comes with the specialization of blood-sucking. Phylogenetic death is sure to follow. Here, then, is an end to the progress in brain building among the invertebrates. Faced with the awful problem of the alternatives of intellectual advance accompanied by the certainty of starvation, and intellectual stagnation accompanied by the inability of enjoying a good square meal, they must perforce elect the latter if they are to live. The invertebrates made a fatal mistake when they started to build their brains around the oesophagus. Their attempt to develop big brains was a failure ... Another start must be made.[3]

The failure is reflected by the fact that even in the highest forms of invertebrates – the social insects – behaviour is almost entirely governed by instinct; learning by experience plays a relatively small part. And since all members of the beehive are descended from the same pair of parents with no discernible varieties in heredity, they have little individuality: insects are not persons. Admiration for the marvellous organization of the beehive should not blind us to this fact. In vertebrates, on the other hand, as we ascend the evolutionary ladder, individual learning plays an increasing role compared to instinct – thanks to the increase in size and complexity of the brain, which was free to grow without imposing on us a diet of porridge.

The second cautionary tale concerns our old friends, the marsupials. I have called them the poor cousins of us placentals, because each species of pouched animal, from mouse to wolf, is of an inferior 'make' compared to its opposite number in the placental series. Wood Jones (himself an Australian) comments regretfully: '... They are failures. Wherever marsupial meets higher mammal, it is the marsupial that is circumvented by superior cunning and forced to retreat or to succumb. The fox, the cat, the dog, the rabbit, the rat and the mouse are all ousting their parallels in the marsupial phylum.'[4]

The reason is simple: the brains of the marsupials are not only smaller, but of a vastly inferior construction. The ringtailed opossum and the bush-baby lemur are both arboreal and nocturnal animals with certain similarities in size, appearance and habits. But in the opossum, a marsupial, about one-third of the cerebral hemispheres is given to the sense of smell – sight, hearing and all higher functions are crowded together in the remaining two-thirds. The placental lemur, on the other hand, has not only a larger brain, though its body is smaller than the opossum's, but the area devoted to smell in the lemur's brain has shrunk to relative insignificance, giving way, as it should, to areas serving functions that are more vital to an arboreal creature.

When the marsupials took to the trees, smell ought to have become unimportant to them compared to the distance receptors, sight and hearing, and their nervous system ought to have reflected the change. But in contrast to our ancestors, the placental tree-dwellers, this change failed to take place in the marsupials. Moreover, an important component is lacking in the brain of the higher marsupials, the so-called *corpus callosum*. This is a conspicuous nerve tract which, in placentals, connects the 'new' (non-olfactory) areas of the right and left cerebral hemispheres. It obviously plays a vital integrative part, though the details of its functioning are still somewhat problematical,* and its absence from the marsupial brain

* Some humans were found at autopsies to have been born without a true *corpus callosum* – yet were apparently none the worse for it.

seems to have been a principal factor in their arrested development.

The point where that development comes to an end is the koala bear. It is, to quote Wood Jones again, 'the largest and most perfectly adapted tree-dwelling marsupial. In bulk we may compare it with the Patas monkey.'[5] But, compared to the monkey, the koala cuts a very poor figure: 'In the koala the tree-climber has become a tree-clinger. Hands have turned into hooks; and fingers are not used for plucking fruit or leaves or testing novel objects, but for fixing the animal, by virtue of the long curved claws, to the tree upon which it clings.'[6]

It cannot do otherwise because its principal sense is still smell, which is of little use in an arboreal creature. Like Quoodle, the koala thinks with his nose. His brain weighs only one-seventh of the monkey's; and most of it is occupied by the smell area which in the monkey has virtually vanished; while the non-smell areas of the koala have no *corpus callosum* to connect them. The koala is the end of the marsupial line of evolution, left behind clinging to his eucalyptus tree like a discarded hypothesis – while his monkey cousin is only the beginning of the evolution from primate to man. It is a fascinating speculation whether, if the marsupials had been equipped with a *corpus callosum*, they would have evolved into a pouched parallel to man, as they have evolved into pouched parallels of the flying squirrel and the wolf.

'A Tumorous Overgrowth'

But before congratulating ourselves on having such a superior brain which does not strangle our oesophagus or condemn us to live by smell, we ought to pause and examine the possibility that man, too, might carry a constructional fault inside his skull, perhaps even more serious than the arthropod and marsupial precedents; a constructional error which potentially threatens his extinction – but which might still be corrected by a supreme effort of self-repair.

The first reason for this suspicion is the extraordinary rapidity of the evolutionary growth of the human brain – a feat, as we know, unique in evolutionary history. To quote Professor Le Gros Clark: 'It now appears from the fossil record that the hominid brain did not begin to enlarge significantly before the beginning of the Pleistocene, but from the middle Pleistocene [*circa* half a million years ago] onwards it expanded at a most remarkable speed – greatly exceeding the rate of evolutionary change which had so far been recorded in any anatomical character in lower animals ... The rapidity of the evolutionary expansion of the brain during the Pleistocene is an example of what has been termed "explosive evolution".'[7]

Next, let me quote from Judson Herrick's *The Evolution of Human Nature*:

> The history of civilization is a record of slow but dramatic enrichment of human life interspersed with episodes of wanton destruction of all the accumulated riches of property and spiritual values. These episodic reversions to bestiality seem to be increasing in virulence and in the magnitude of the resulting disasters until now we are threatened with the loss of everything that has been won in our struggle for the better life.
>
> In view of this record it has been suggested that the enlargement of the human brain has gone so fast and so far that the result is actually pathological. Normal behaviour depends upon the preservation of a balanced interplay between integrating and disintegrating factors and between the total pattern and local partial patterns. So, it is claimed, the human cortex is a sort of tumorous overgrowth that has got so big that its functions are out of normal control and 'race' erratically like a steam engine that has lost its governor.
>
> This ingenious theory was published by Morley Roberts and quoted with apparent approval by Wheeler.[8] Their arguments seem to be plausible in view of the past history of wars, revolutions, and crumbled empires, and the present worldwide turmoil that threatens total destruction of civilization. But the theory is neurological nonsense.[9]

In the form stated here it certainly is. It cannot be the *size* of the cortex alone which 'puts its function out of normal control'. We must look for a more plausible cause.

The cause which contemporary research seems to indicate is not increase in size, but *insufficient coordination* between archicortex and neocortex – between the phylogenetically old areas of our brain, and the new, specifically human areas which were superimposed on it with such unseemly haste. This lack of coordination causes, to use a phrase coined by P. MacLean, a kind of 'dichotomy in the function of the phylogenetically old and new cortex that might account for differences between emotional and intellectual behaviour'.[10] While 'our intellectual functions are carried on in the newest and most highly developed part of the brain, our affective behaviour continues to be dominated by a relatively crude and primitive system. This situation provides a clue to understanding the difference between what we "feel" and what we "know" . . .'[11]

Let us look a little closer at what is implied in these statements by an eminent contemporary neurophysiologist.

The Physiology of Emotion

The distinction between 'knowing' and 'feeling', between reason and emotion, goes back to the Greeks. Aristotle in *De Anima* pointed to visceral sensations as the *substance* of emotion and contrasted them with the *form*, ie, the ideational content of the emotion. The intimate connection between emotion and the viscerae is a matter of common experience, and has always been taken for granted by laymen and physicians alike: we know that emotional arousal affects heartbeat and pulse; that fear stimulates the sweat glands, grief the tear glands, and the respiratory, digestive, not to mention the reproductive, systems are all involved in the experience of emotion. So much so that the word 'visceral' was originally used to refer to strong emotional feelings, including fear ('he has no guts') and pity ('the bowels of mercy').

Well into the eighteenth century, the medical profession adhered to the Galenic doctrine, according to which thoughts circulated in the brain, emotions circulated in the vessels of the body. At the beginning of the nineteenth century, this ancient dualism yielded to a more modern version: in his immensely influential books, *Anatomie Générale* and *Recherches Physiologiques sur la Vie et la Mort*, Xavier Bichat drew a fundamental distinction between the *cerebro-spinal nervous system*, including the brain and spinal cord, which looked after all the *external* transactions of the animal with its environment; and the 'ganglionic', now called *autonomic nervous system*, which controlled all organs serving *internal* functions. The first was governed by a single centre, the brain; but the second, Bichat thought, was governed by a great number of 'little brains', such as the solar plexus, in various parts of the body. The cerebro-spinal nervous system was held to be responsible for all voluntary action; the autonomic, governing the viscera, was beyond voluntary control; and so were the passions or emotions which all belonged to the visceral domain.

Bichat's doctrine reigned for a whole century; it was proved wrong in many, if not most, details; but the distinction he made between the functions of the two systems, and their correspondence with the ancient dualism between thought and emotion, is still valid in broad outlines. Nobody, of course, believes any longer that the experience of emotion is located in 'little brains' in the vicinity of the heart and bowels. All experience is centralized in the brain, including the control of the autonomic system which looks after visceral function. As one would expect, the viscera are controlled by a phylogenetically very ancient structure in the brain-stem, the region of the hypothalamus (thalamus: Greek for inner chamber or woman's apartment). This is the crucial area, in close proximity to the pituitary gland and to the vestiges of the primitive smell-brain, which regulates visceral and glandular functions beyond voluntary control, and is intimately connected with emotional experience.

But we must not jump to the conclusion that the hypothalamus itself is the 'seat' of emotion. That would leave out of account the ideational aspect, and would reduce emotion to 'nothing but' visceral reactions. William James came in fact very close to this position when, in 1884, he published an article that launched the famous James-Lange theory of emotions. In a nut-shell, the theory said that in those situations which require visceral reactions to cope with them (eg, accelerated heartbeat for running away from danger), the feeling that one's heart races *is* the emotion. The heart does not race because we are frightened; we are frightened because the heart races; and we do not weep because we feel sad, we feel sad because we weep. It is the perception of one's own visceral reactions which lends emotional colouring to experience. The visceral reaction itself is automatic and unconscious, either innate or acquired by past experience.

The James-Lange theory gave rise to endless controversies which even today, eighty years after its launching, have not completely died down. In 1929 Walter Cannon – a pioneer in this field – seemed to have given the *coup de grâce* to it, when it was shown that emotional behaviour persists even after the connections between viscera and brain had been severed. This and other experimental evidence brought the theory into disrepute.* James' doctrine that emotions are 'nothing but'

---

* Nevertheless, quite recently Mandler has shown that even the seemingly decisive evidence (Cannon's famous 'five points') is open to a different interpretation: 'Although visceral changes are essential for the initial establishment of emotional behaviour, on later occasions the emotional behaviour may prove to have been conditioned to external stimuli, and may occur both without visceral support and – in some form – prior to it . . . Cannon's argument that emotional behaviour may be present in the absence of visceral activity will

visceral reactions has certainly proved untenable; but the very fact that the doctrine was so hard to kill shows that it contained a hard core of truth – the fact, driven home by common, everyday observation, that diffuse bodily sensations from internal processes which are not under voluntary control form an essential component of all emotional experience. Cannon's own theory of emotions (the Cannon-Bard theory) laid decisive emphasis on the bodily changes in 'emergency reactions' to hunger, pain, rage and fear, mediated by adrenal hormones and the autonomic nervous system. But he shifted the focus of attention from the visceral to the cerebral mechanisms in the hypothalamus which control them, and regarded the bodily changes as *expressions* rather than causes of emotional feeling.

The Cannon-Bard theory was in its turn criticized by Lashley and others; but at this point the subject becomes too technical. To sum up, we may safely conclude that emotions are 'overheated drives' (due to internal and/or external stimulations) which are temporarily – or even permanently – deprived of an adequate outlet; the dammed-up excitement stimulates visceral and glandular activity, affecting circulation digestion, muscle-tone, etc; and 'the reverberations of the total organism can then register centrally as felt emotion' (Herrick[13]). Or, to quote Mandler's more recent survey of the subject: 'As far as the physical background of emotion is concerned, we can agree with commonsense that some sort of internal, visceral response accompanies the production of emotional behaviour.'[14] And there is further evidence that these visceral responses depend on archaic structures in the brain whose fundamental pattern has undergone but little

---

probably have to be restricted to saying that it will only be present when intact visceral structures and responses have previously mediated the link between environmental conditions and emotional behaviour ... Visceral response is important for the establishment, but not for the maintenance, of emotional behaviour.'[12]

change in the whole course of evolution 'from mouse to man' (MacLean).

The Three Brains

After this historical excursion, let us return to the question how these archaic structures, and the archaic feelings to which they give rise, get along with the brand-new structures and functions in our brains. The following excerpts lead straight into the problem; they are from a medical paper by Professor Paul MacLean, who fathered the so-called Papez-MacLean theory of emotions:

> Man finds himself in the predicament that Nature has endowed him essentially with three brains which, despite great differences in structure, must function together and communicate with one another. The oldest of these brains is basically reptilian. The second has been inherited from lower mammals, and the third is a late mammalian development, which in its culmination in primates, has made man peculiarly man.
>
> Speaking allegorically of these three brains within a brain, we might imagine that when the psychiatrist bids the patient to lie on the couch, he is asking him to stretch out alongside a horse and a crocodile. The crocodile may be willing and ready to shed a tear and the horse to neigh and whinny, but when they are encouraged to express their troubles in words, it soon becomes evident that their inability is beyond the help of language training. Little wonder that the patient who has personal responsibility for these animals and who must serve as their mouthpiece is sometimes accused of being full of resistances and reluctant to talk . . .[15] The reptilian brain is filled with ancestral lore and ancestral memories and is faithful in doing what its ancestors say, but it is not a very good brain for facing up to new situations. It is as though it were neurosis-bound to an ancestral superego.
>
> In evolution one first sees the beginning of emancipation from the ancestral superego with the appearance of the lower mammalian brain, which Nature builds on top of the reptilian brain . . . Investigations of the last twenty years have shown that the lower mammalian brain plays a fundamental role in emotional behaviour. It has a greater capacity than the reptilian brain for learning new

approaches and solutions to problems on the basis of immediate experience. But like the reptilian brain, it does not have the ability . . . to put its feelings into words.[16]

In the remainder of this chapter I shall lean heavily on Mac-Lean's experimental work and theoretical conclusions (though deviating from the latter in minor details). The great attraction of the theory is its consistently hierarchic approach, in the sense in which this term is used in the present book. 'In its evolution', he writes, 'the brain of man retains the hierarchical organization of the three basic types which can be conveniently labelled as reptilian, paleo-mammalian and neo-mammalian. The limbic system [see below] represents the paleo-mammalian brain, which is an inheritance from lower mammals. Man's limbic system is much more highly structured than that of lower animals, but its basic organization, chemistry, etc, are very similar. The same may be said of the other two basic types. And there is ample evidence that all three types have their own special subjective, cognitive (problem-solving) memory and other parallel functions.'[17] We can paraphrase this by saying that each functions as a relatively autonomous holon on its own level.

I shall not burden the reader with a disquisition on brain anatomy, but a few remarks about the evolution of the brain may be helpful at this point. The ancient anatomists compared the brain to a fruit like an orange: the central part is like the pulp, the outer like the rind; so the former was named medulla, the latter cortex. The medulla is a prolongation of the spinal cord, and is further prolonged into the *brain-stem*. Inside or near to it are clusters and structures of cell masses such as the hypothalamus, the reticular system, the basal ganglia. This is the phylogenetically oldest part of the brain, its core or chassis, roughly corresponding to the basic structures of the reptile's brain. It contains the essential apparatus for internal (visceral and glandular) regulations, for primitive activities based on instincts and reflexes, and also the centres for arousing the animal's vigilance or putting it to sleep. The cortex or rind, on the other hand, is the apparatus for 'intelligent' behaviour, from the capacity to acquire new responses by whatever primitive form of learning, up to conceptual thought. The cortex emerges at the stage of evolutionary history when the amphibians began to turn into reptiles; the first promising cortical divisions are found in the turtle. The cortex is the surface-layer of the *cerebral hemispheres* which grow out of the brain-stem and fold around it like a cloak or mantle (hence 'pallium'). It consists of the outer, 'grey' cortical layer of cell bodies, and the white fibres underlying it. The human cortex is about a tenth of an inch thick and contains about ten thousand million neurons densely packed together, covering an area of about three square feet, crammed into the *gyri* and *sulki*, convolutions and invaginations of the crinkled sheet. Truly a staggering feat of circuitry – and yet . . .

The old anatomists' analogy of the orange helps one to get a rough idea of the basic structure of the brain; but beyond that it becomes misleading. The cortex, unlike the rind of the orange, is not homogeneous. Different types of nerve cells dominate in different functional areas; and more than a hundred different areas have been mapped, numbered or named according to their microscopic structure and other criteria. But although the details of these classifications are controversial, there is general agreement that, judged by their evolutionary history and by their distinctive texture, the cortex has three basic sub-divisions. The older anatomists called them archipallium, paleopallium and neopallium; MacLean calls them archicortex, mesocortex and neocortex, co-ordinated respectively with the reptilian, primitive mammalian and neo-mammalian brain. But the spatial arrangement of these three main cortical divisions inside our skulls is not easy to explain or visualize; MacLean proposed a simplified model in the form of an inflatable toy balloon with three distinct segments (Figure 12).[18]

A, M and N stand for archi, meso, and neo cortex. 'The uninflated balloon represents the situation found in the amphibian. With the appearance of the reptile, there is a ballooning out of the archicortex and a considerable expansion of the mesocortex. During the phylogeny of the mammal, one of the most striking events of all evolution occurs. This is the

FIGURE 12

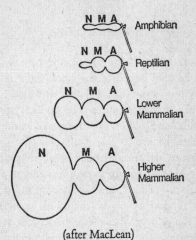

(after MacLean)

great ballooning out of the neocortex. In the process, the archicortex and the greater part of the mesocortex are folded like two concentric rings into the limbic lobe and are relegated, as it were, to the cellar of the brain' (Figure 13).[19]

The result of this folding-in process is shown in Figure 13, where (a) is a side-view, and (b) a vertical cross-section of a monkey's brain. The two in-folded rings together form a large convolution, the so-called *limbic lobe* of the cerebral cortex, shown in black. 'Limbic' means 'hemming in', 'forming a border around' the term was coined in 1878 by the great brain-mapper, Broca, because the limbic convolution surrounds the brain-stem — the central core (not shown on the

FIGURE 13

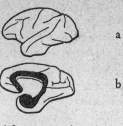

a

b

(after MacLean)

diagram). In fact, the limbic cortex is so closely connected to the brain-stem that together they constitute a functionally integrated system – the '*limbic system*' with its 'reptilian' and 'primitive-mammalian' features. The limbic system may thus be loosely called the 'old brain', in contrast to the 'neocortical system' or 'new brain'.

Already Broca had demonstrated that 'the great limbic lobe is found as a kind of common denominator in the brains of all mammals ... The faithful preservation of this cortex through the phylogeny of the mammals contrasts with the rapid evolution and growth of the neocortex around it, the latter representing the growth of intellectual function ... The limbic cortex is structurally primitive compared to the neocortex; it shows essentially the same degree of development and organization throughout the mammalian series. This would suggest that it functions on an animalistic level in both animal and man.'[20]

Emotion and the Ancient Brain

This is surely an odd state of affairs. If the evidence had not taught us the contrary, we would expect an evolutionary development which gradually transformed the primitive old brain into a more sophisticated instrument – as it transformed claw into hand, gill into lung. Instead, evolution *superimposed a new, superior structure on an old one*, with partly overlapping functions, and *without providing the new with a clear-cut, hierarchic control over the old* – thus inviting confusion and conflict. Let us have a closer look at this dichotomy between the limbic and neocortical systems.

MacLean compares the cortex with a television screen that gives the animal a combined picture of the outside and inside worlds. This is a useful analogy for the limited purpose for which he employs it. But to avoid misunderstandings I would like, before making use of it, to point out its limitations. Of all parts of the body the cerebral cortex is the most intimately connected with awareness and self-awareness; but it would be wrong to call it – as is sometimes done – the *seat* of awareness. To quote that wise mechanist, Judson Herrick: 'The search for a *seat* of consciousness in general or of any particular kind of conscious experience is a pseudo-problem because the conscious act has properties that are not definable in terms of the spatial and temporal units which are employed in the measurement of the objects and events of our objective world. What we search for and find by objective inquiry is the apparatus which *generates* awareness. This mechanism has locus in space and time, but the awareness as such is not located in any particular part of the mechanism' (my italics).[21]

In this sense, then, the cerebral cortex is probably the principal 'apparatus which generates awareness'. The ancient structures in the brain-stem may be said to provide the 'raw material' of awareness: the reticular formation 'arouses' the animal; the hypothalamic structures contribute the visceral component; but ultimately 'the cerebral cortex is to the brain what the television screen is to the television set and what a radar screen is to the pilot'.[22] If this is the case, we must face the paradox that evolution has provided us with at least two such screens, one ancient, one new.

The ancient, limbic screen has, as we have seen, three

principal characteristics: (a) its microscopic structure is coarse and primitive compared to the neocortex; (b) its basic pattern is still essentially the same as in the lower mammals; (c) in contrast to the new cortex, the limbic system is intimately connected by two-way neural pathways – fibres as thick as a pencil – with the hypothalamus and other centres in the brain-stem concerned with visceral sensations and emotional reactions – including sex, hunger, fear and aggression; so much so that the limbic system once bore the name 'the visceral brain'.* The term was changed because it gave the impression that it was *only* concerned with the viscera; whereas in fact the ancient, limbic cortex, as we shall presently see, also has its own mental processes: it emotes and *thinks* – though not in verbal concepts.

The limbic system may be compared to a primitive television screen which combines, and often confuses, projections from the internal, visceral environment with the external environment. 'Such a cortex must have offered some of the confusion of a twice-exposed film. In any event, it could not have been altogether satisfactory, because when Nature proceeded to develop the neo-mammalian brain, she constructed progressively a bigger and finer type of screen, which gave predominantly a picture of the outside world made up of impressions from the eye, the ear and the surface of the body ... But Nature in her frugality did not discard the old screen. Since it seemed adequate for smelling, tasting and feeling what is going on inside the body, she has kept the filaments in the tube of the old screen glowing night and day.'23

However, the old brain is not merely concerned with taste, smell and visceral sensations, leaving the new to turn its gaze outward: that would be an idyllic distribution of labour. The 'Papez theory of emotions' originated in the study of pathological conditions in which the 'old tube' interferes with the

* Even earlier the limbic cortex was called the rhinencephalon, ie, smell brain, because it was thought to be exclusively concerned with smell.

new, and tends to usurp its functions. Papez noted that damage to the limbic system caused a variety of symptoms which primarily affected the emotional behaviour of animal and man. An extreme case is the terrible disease of rabies, whose virus appears to have a predilection for the limbic system, and in which 'the patient is subject to paroxysms of rage and terror'.[24] Less extreme but equally telling are the emotional states in the 'sacred disease', epilepsy. Hughlin Jackson, one of the pioneers of neurology, described the epileptic aura preceding the attack as the 'dreamy state', a kind of 'double consciousness', in which the patient is aware of the reality around him, but as if it were a dream, or a repetition of something that happened before (*déjà vu*). During the actual fit of psycho-motor epilepsy, the 'animal-istic' brain seems to take over the personality. Biting, chewing and grinding the teeth, terror or furore are well-known distressing accompaniments of the fit, of which as a rule the sufferer retains no memory. All the clinical evidence points in these cases to the limbic system as the focus of the epileptic discharge.[25] Typical of the clinical material is, for instance, the case of a nymphomaniac woman of fifty-five 'who, for more than ten years, complained of a persistent "passionate feeling". Later she developed convulsions. It is notable that perfume was thought to exaggerate her symptoms'[26] – smell is the most 'visceral' of the senses. She underwent brain surgery, and the operation revealed a lesion affecting the limbic lobe.

The human clinical material is limited, and electro-encephalography is a recent invention; thus most of the evidence is provided by experimentation on animals. They are basically of two kinds: electrical or chemical excitation of the brain, and surgical elimination of certain areas of it. Let me quote MacLean again:

> From animal experimentation on limbic epilepsy (induced by electrical stimulation) it has become evident that seizure-discharges induced in the limbic lobe tend in their spread to be confined to the

limbic system. Seldom do the discharges, analogous to stampeding bulls, burst out of this corral and jump the fence into the neo-mammalian brain. Such experiments provide the most striking evidence available of a dichotomy of function (or what has been called a 'schizophysiology' of the limbic and neocortical systems). Patients with smouldering limbic epilepsy may manifest all the symptoms of schizophrenia; the schizophysiology in question is possibly relevant to the pathogenesis of this disease . . .

From the standpoint of the patient lying on the couch, the schizophysiology under consideration is significant because it indicates that the lower mammalian brain is able to some degree to function independently, to make up its own mind. The primitive, crude screen provided by the limbic cortex might be imagined as portraying a confused picture of the inside world and the outside world. This may partly account for the manifest confusion that has been described in psychosomatic conditions – the confusion, for example, in which food or other edibles serve as representations of something in the external world that is desired to be assimilated into the self or mastered and destroyed like a prey or enemy.* One finds descriptions of the patient who eats presumably because of the need for love, because of anxiety or nervousness, or because of the need to chew up or get rid of what arouses his anger and hate.[27]

More recent methods of experimentation with implanted electrodes which permit low-voltage stimulation of precisely defined points of the monkey's brain, produced even more striking results. Stimulation of certain *loci* in the limbic system caused penile erection or ejaculation in males; stimulation of other points caused feeding reactions – chewing and salivation; yet other areas elicited exploratory, aggressive-defensive or fearful behaviour. (It should be pointed out that these experiments are painless, and that monkeys with implanted electrodes in the so-called 'pleasure centres' quickly and willingly learn to stimulate themselves by pressing a lever which activates the current.) However, excitement of one kind readily spills over to adjacent points which arouse emotions of another kind. Thus oral activity – chewing, sniffing, salivation – may combine with aggression; aggressive display with sex; sex

* The relevance of this to the phenomena discussed on pp 262 f is obvious.

with oral activity. Feeding often produces erection in babies and dogs; and some other aspects of doggy behaviour also fall far below Victorian standards.

'Schizophysiology'

Here again, the contrast between old and new cortex provides an unexpected clue, and an added dimension to the psycho-analytical approach. On the new TV screen (the sensory cortex) the body is represented in the well-known form of a little homunculus, shown in all textbooks, on which the mouth and the anal-genital region are placed correctly at opposite ends of the projection area. In the old, lower mam-malian brain, however, 'nature apparently found it necessary to bend the limbic lobe upon itself in order to afford the olfactory sense close participation in both oral and anogenital functions'.[28]

This is a truly unexpected vindication of Freud's theory of infantile sexuality. It is at the same time a reminder that the survival of the lower mammalian brain in our heads is not metaphor but fact. In the sexual, as in all other contexts, maturation seems to mean a transition from the domination of the old brain towards the domination of the new. But quite apart from emotional upsets and pathological conditions, the transition even in the normal person can never be complete. *The schizophysiology is built into our species.*

In surgical ablation experiments, the effects are more drastic. After excision of certain parts of the limbic lobe, monkeys of previously savage temperament seem to lose the instinctive reactions necessary for survival. They become docile, show neither fear nor anger, do not fight back when provoked, do not learn to avoid painful situations. They also lose their instinctive feeding habits: a monkey which normally lives on fruit will now eat raw meat or fish, and show a compulsive tendency to put every object into its mouth: nails, faeces, burning matches. Lastly, the sexual and maternal instincts also go haywire: male cats will try to copulate with chickens, and mother rats will let their litter die.[29]

However, the old brain is not merely concerned with affect; it also perceives, remembers and 'thinks' in its own, quasi-independent ways. In primitive animals, the limbic system is the highest integrative centre for the drives of hunger, sex, fight and flight; and the anatomical and physiological evidence indicates that it continues to serve these functions in higher animals, including man. It occupies, as already mentioned, a strategically central position for correlating internal sensations with perceptions from the outside world, and for initiating appropriate action according to its own lights. Though dominated by instinct, it is clearly capable of learning simple lessons: a monkey will taste a burning match only once, if its limbic system is intact; if it is damaged, it will burn its mouth over and again. 'One can hardly imagine a more useless brain than one that sat around by itself all day generating nothing but emotions and not participating in cognitive, memory and other functions.'[30] But it functions all the same in a phylogenetically old-fashioned way – in a way which psychiatrists call infantile or primitive.

On the basis of the foregoing observations one might infer that [the old cortex] could hardly deal with information in more than a crude way, and was possibly too primitive a brain to analyse language. Yet it might have the capacity to participate in a non-verbal type of symbolism. This would have significant implications as far as symbolism affects the emotional life of the individual. One might imagine, for example, that though the visceral brain could never aspire to conceive of the colour red in terms of a three-letter word or as a specific wave-length of light, it could associate the colour symbolically with such diverse things as blood, fainting, fighting, flowers, etc – correlations leading to phobias, obsessive-compulsive behaviour, etc. Lacking the help and control of the neocortex, its impressions would be discharged without modification into the hypothalamus and lower centres of affective behaviour. Considered in the light of Freudian psychology, the old brain would have many of the attributes of the unconscious *id*. One might argue, however, *that the visceral brain is not at all unconscious (possibly not even in certain stages of sleep), but rather eludes the grasp of the intellect because its animalistic and primitive structure makes it impossible to communicate in verbal terms.* Perhaps it were more proper to say, therefore, it was an animalistic and illiterate brain. (MacLean[31]; italics in the original.)

A Taste of the Sun

Our emotions are indeed notoriously inarticulate, incommunicable in verbal terms. The novelist's main difficulty is to describe what his characters *feel* – as distinct from what they think or do. We can describe intellectual processes in the most intricate detail, but have only the crudest vocabulary even for the vital sensations of bodily pain – as both physician and patient know to their sorrow. Suffering is 'dumb'. Love, anger, guilt, mourning, joy, anxiety command a vast rainbow spectrum of emotions of varied colour and intensity which we are unable to convey verbally, except for trite clichés – 'broken hearts' and 'pangs of despair'; or else by the indirect method of invoking visual imagery and the hypnotic effect of rhythm and euphony, which 'lull the mind into a waking trance'.

Poetry could thus be said to achieve a synthesis between the sophisticated reasoning of the neocortex and the more primitive emotional ways of the old brain. This *reculer pour mieux sauter*, draw-back-to-leap process, which seems to underlie all creative achievement, may reflect a temporary regression from over-concrete, neocortical thinking to more fluid and 'instinctive' modes of limbic thinking – a 'regression to the id in the service of the ego'. We also remember that sometimes 'we have to get away from speech to think clearly' – and speech is a monopoly of the new cortex. In a similar way, other phenomena discussed in the chapters on creativity and on memory can be interpreted in terms of hierarchic levels in the evolution of the brain. Thus, for instance, the distinction we have made between abstractive memory, on the one hand, and the emotionally significant 'picture-strip' on the other (Chapter VI), seems to reflect the characteristic distinction between the new and ancient brain.*

The consequences of the innate 'schizophysiology' of man thus range from the creative to the pathological. If the former is a *reculer pour mieux sauter*, the latter is a *reculer sans sauter*. Its forms vary from what we regard as more or less normal behaviour, where unconscious emotional bias distorts reasoning only to a moderate extent, in socially approved or tolerated ways, through the open or smouldering conflicts of neurosis, to psychosis and psychosomatic disease. In extreme cases, the distinction between the outer and inner world can become blurred – not only by hallucinations, but also in other ways; the patient seems to regress to the magic universe of the primitive: 'The impression is gained clinically that [these] patients ... show an exaggerated tendency to regard the external world as though it were part of themselves. In other words, internal feelings are blended with what is seen, heard or otherwise sensed in such a way that the outside world is experienced as though it were inside. In this respect there is a resemblance to children and primitive peoples.'[32] An example of such confusion is the remark of a girl suffering from epilepsy about her first seizure – which occurred when, as a child, she walked into the bright sunlight: 'I had a funny taste in my mouth of the sun.' A poet might have written that line; but unlike the poor child, he would have been aware of his own confusion.

'Knowing with one's Viscera'

We all can sometimes feel the taste of the sun in the mouth; but our major confusions arise, not from such visceral interference with our *perceptions*, but with our *convictions* and

* Cf also Kluever's three levels of visual memory[31a] (p 112).

beliefs. Irrational beliefs are anchored in emotion; they are *felt* to be true. Believing has been described as 'knowing with one's viscera'. More correctly we should say that it is a type of knowing which is *dominated* by the influence of the inarticulate old brain, even if it is *formulated* in articulate verbal terms. At this point, these neurophysiological considerations merge with the psychological phenomena discussed in the previous chapter. The schizophysiology of the brain provides a clue to the delusional streak in the history of man.

A closed system, as defined in the previous chapter, is a cognitive matrix with a distorted logic, the distortion being caused by some central axiom, postulate or dogma, to which the subject is emotionally committed, and from which the rules of processing the data are derived. Cognitive systems are, of course, not exclusive products of the reptilian or paleomammalian or neo-mammalian brain, but of their combined efforts. The amount of distortion varies according to which level dominates, and to what extent. Without some contribution from the ancient levels concerned with internal, bodily sensations, the experience of our own reality would probably be absent – we should be like 'disembodied spirits' (MacLean[33]). Without the neocortex, we should be at the mercy of affect, and our thinking would be like the monkey's or infant's. But detached, rational thought is a new and fragile acquisition; it is affected by the slightest irritation of the old brain which, once aroused, tends to dominate the scene.

However, we know that in between the 'disembodied spirit' of pure abstract reasoning, and the passionate neighings in the old cortex, there is a series of intermediary levels. As already said (pp 210 f), it would be a gross oversimplification to distinguish only two types of mentation, such as Freud's 'primary' and 'secondary' process, the first governed by the pleasure principle, the second by the reality principle. In between these two, we have to interpolate several methods of cognition, as we find them in primitive societies at various stages of development, in children at various ages, and in adults in various states of consciousness – such as dreaming, day-dreaming, hallucinating, etc. Each of these systems of thought has its own canon, its particular 'rules of the game', which reflect – in a manner we are at a loss to explain – the complex interactions of various levels and structures in the brain. The old and new levels must interact all the time – even if their coordination is inadequate, and deficient in the controls which lend stability to a well-balanced hierarchy.

One of the consequences of this is that verbal symbols become associated with emotive values and visceral reactions – as the psychogalvanic lie-detector so dramatically shows. And that applies, of course, not only to single words or single ideas; complex doctrines, theories, ideologies are apt to acquire a similar emotional saturation – not to mention fetishes, leader-figures and Causes. Unfortunately, we cannot apply a lie-detector to measure the irrationality of our belief-systems, or the visceral component in our rationalizations. The true believer moves in a vicious circle inside his closed system: he can prove to his satisfaction everything that he believes, and he believes everything he can prove.

Janus Revisited

MacLean distinguishes two basic motivational drives, each giving rise to its appropriate types of emotion: *self-preservation* and *preservation of the species*. His experimental work on monkeys led him to a tentative localization of the first in the lower, of the second in the upper half of the limbic system. The emotions derived from the self-preserving drives are the classic trinity of hunger, rage and fear. They depend on the sympathetic division of the autonomic nervous system and on the galvanizing effect of adrenal hormones released into the bloodstream. If we include the aggressive and oral components of sexual behaviour into this group (and we have seen how electric stimulation of one of these responses spills over into another), we get a fairly complete inventory of what we have called the *self-assertive* tendencies.

The other of MacLean's basic drives, preservation of the species, is a less clear-cut category. He includes in it the care of the young, the grooming habits and other forms of friendly social behaviour in monkeys; but he seems to regard them in the Freudian tradition, as derivatives from the sexual drive:

> Concern for the welfare and preservation of the species is based on sexuality, and in man it reflects itself in a multiplicity of ways. It is a concern that leads to courtship and the eventual rearing of the family. It is a concern that permeates our songs, our poetry, our novels, art, theatre, architecture. It is a concern that preoccupies us in planning for the higher education of our children. It is a concern that promotes the building of libraries, institutes of research and hospitals. It is a concern that inspired medical research to prevent suffering and dying of patients ... It is a concern that makes us think in terms of rockets, travel in outer space, and the possibility of immortal life in some other world.[34]

By the time we have travelled from the first sentence of this quotation to the last, the connection with sexuality has become more and more tenuous – unless we subscribe to the doctrine that all social, artistic and scientific activities are sublimations or substitutions for sexuality. It is equally difficult to see how the 'magnetic force', as Konrad Lorenz has called it, which holds a herd or a shoal of ocean fish together – an attraction which seems to increase in geometrical proportion with the size of the shoal and to depend on no other factor[35] – could be based on sexuality. The same consideration applies to the division of labour in the beehive, with its vast proportion of sexless workers. Even though the most powerful of drives, sexuality is not the only, and perhaps not even the primary, bond which holds animal and human societies together, and which ensures the preservation and welfare of the species – including the spiritual and artistic welfare of our own. It seems therefore more appropriate to include the sexual instinct, together with the other forces of social cohesion, in the more general category of our 'integrative tendencies'. Sex, as we have seen, is a relative late-comer on the evolutionary stage; whereas the polarity of self-assertive versus integrative tendencies is inherent in all hierarchic order, and present on every level of living organisms and social organizations.

In the animal kingdom, of course, MacLean's term 'preservation and welfare of the species' (as distinct from self-preservation) covers practically all manifestations of what we call the integrative tendencies; and if MacLean is correct in localizing them in the upper half of the limbic system, and the drives of self-preservation in the lower half, we cannot ask for a better confirmation of the postulated polarity.

Thus as long as we confine the discussion to monkeys, the question of terminology is reduced to a semantic quibble. But when we come to man, the integrative tendency may assume a variety of forms, including the self-transcending emotions which enter into religious and artistic experience, but have little bearing on preservation of the species. They too must have their neurophysiological correlates, but here the subject becomes rather technical, and the general reader may safely skip the next two paragraphs.

We have seen that a close correlation exists between the aggressive-defensive emotions and the sympathetic division of the autonomic nervous system. It would be tempting to assume a symmetrical correlation between the self-transcending emotions and the other division of the autonomic system – the parasympathetic. There is some evidence in favour of this view, although it is not conclusive. In general (but there are, as we shall presently see, important exceptions) the action of the two divisions is mutually antagonistic: they equilibrate each other. The sympathetic division prepares the animal for emergency reactions under the stress of hunger, pain, rage and fear. It accelerates the pulse, increases blood-pressure, provides added blood-sugar as a source of energy. The parasympathetic division does in almost every respect the opposite: it lowers blood-pressure, slows the heart, neutralizes excesses of blood-sugar, facilitates digestion and the disposal of body wastes; activates the tear-glands – it is generally calming and cathartic. Characteristically, laughter is a sympathetic, weeping a parasympathetic, discharge.

Both divisions of the autonomic nervous system are controlled by the limbic brain (the hypothalamus and adjacent structures). Different authors have described their functions in different terms. *Allport*[36] related the pleasurable emotions to the parasympathetic, the unpleasant ones to the sympathetic. *Olds*[36a] distinguishes between 'positive' and 'negative' emotive systems, activated respectively by the parasympathetic and sympathetic centres in the hypothalamus. From a quite different theoretical approach, *Hebb* also arrived at the conclusion that a distinction should be made between two categories of emotion, 'those in which the tendency is to maintain or increase the original stimulating conditions (pleasurable or integrative emotions)' and 'those in which the tendency is to abolish or decrease the stimulus (rage, fear, disgust)'.[36b] *Pribram* has made a similar distinction between 'preparatory' (warding-off) and 'participatory' emotions.[36c] *Hess* and *Gellhorn* distinguish between an ergotropic (energy-consuming) system operating through the sympathetic division to ward off threatening stimuli, and a trophotropic (energy-conserving) system which operates through the parasympathetic in response to peaceful or attractive stimuli.[37] Gellhorn has summarized the emotional effects of two different types of drugs: on the one hand the 'pep pills', such as benzedrine, and on the other the tranquillizers, such as chlorpromazine. The former activates the sympathetic, the latter the parasympathetic, division. When administered in small doses, the tranquillizers cause 'slight shifts in the hypothalamic balance to the parasympathetic side, resulting in calm and contentment, apparently similar to the state before falling asleep, whereas more marked alterations lead to a depressive mood'.[38] The benzedrine-type drugs, on the other hand, activate the sympathetic division, cause increased aggressiveness in animals, and in man in small doses alertness and euphoria, in larger doses over-excitation and manic behaviour. Lastly, *Cobb* has summoned up the implicit contrast in a pointed form: 'Rage is called the most adrenergic, and love the most cholinergic [characteristically parasympathetic] reaction.'[39]

What this short survey indicates is, in the first place, a general trend among authorities in this field to distinguish between *two basic categories of emotion* – though the definitions of the categories differ, and are mixed up with the hedonic tone (which, in the present theory, is an independent variable of either category; cf pp. 261f). In the second place, there is a general feeling that the two categories are 'somehow' correlated to the two divisions of the autonomic nervous system.

But the correlation is not a simple and clear-cut one. Thus, for instance, according to MacLean, 'erection is a parasympathetic phenomenon, whereas ejaculation depends on sympathetic mechanisms'[40] – which, as far as categories are concerned, is neither here nor there. Moreover, strong parasympathetic stimulation may cause nausea or vomiting which, though cathartic (that is, 'cleansing' in the literal sense), can hardly be called an act of psychological self-transcendence. In a word, the functioning of the autonomic nervous system is one of the most intriguing physiological aspects of man's emotional life; and in fairness to the general reader I ought to point out that, while there is ample evidence that the self-assertive emotions are mediated by the sympathico-adrenal division, there is no conclusive proof for the symmetrical correlation suggested here. Such proof can be forthcoming only when human emotions outside the hunger-rage-fear class will be recognized as a worthwhile object of study by experimental psychology – which at present is not the case.

In conformity with the *Zeitgeist*, the self-transcending emotions are still the stepchildren of psychology, in spite of their evident reality. Weeping, for instance, is certainly an observable behavioural phenomenon (the Behaviourist could even measure the amount of lachrymation in milligrams per second). But it is almost completely ignored in psychological literature.*

Some additional facts about the autonomic nervous system are pertinent to our theme. In strongly emotional or pathological conditions, the mutually antagonistic, ie, equilibrating action of the two divisions no longer prevails; instead they may mutually *reinforce* each other, as in the sexual act; or over-excitation of one division may lead to a temporary *rebound* or over-compensatory 'answering effect' by the other;[41] lastly, the parasympathetic may act as a *catalyst* that triggers its antagonist into action.[42]

The first of these three possibilities is relevant to our emotional state in listening to rhapsodic music – a Wagner opera for instance – where relaxed, cathartic feelings seem to be paradoxically combined with euphoric arousal. The second possibility is reflected in 'emotional hangovers' of one kind or another. The third possibility is the most relevant to our theme: it shows in concrete physiological terms how one type of emotional reaction can act as a vehicle for its opposite – as self-transcending identification with the hero on the screen releases vicarious aggressiveness against the villain; as identification with a group or creed releases the savagery of mob-behaviour. The rationalizations for it are formulated in the language-symbols of the new cortex; but the emotive dynamism is generated by the old brain, and conveyed to viscera and glands by the autonomic nervous system.

This is another point where neurophysiological research begins to merge with psychology, to provide clues to its

* For a discussion of the subject, and a bibliography of weeping, see *The Act of Creation*, Chapters XII–XIV and pp 725–8.

paradoxes – and perhaps a first inkling of an answer to the human predicament.

Summary

The evolution of arthropods and marsupials shows that mistakes in brain building do occur. The strategy of evolution is subject to trial and error, and there is nothing particularly improbable in the assumption that in the course of the explosive growth of the human neocortex evolution erred once more. The Papez-MacLean theory offers strong evidence for the dissonant functioning of the phylogenetically old and new cortex, and the resulting 'schizophysiology' built into our species. This would provide a physiological basis for the paranoid streak running through human history, and point the direction of the search for a cure.

XVII

A UNIQUE SPECIES

I cannot but conclude the bulk of your natives to be the most pernicious race of little odious vermin that nature ever suffered to crawl upon the surface of the earth.

SWIFT, *Voyage to Brobdingnag*

The Unsolicited Gift

IN ONE of his essays,[1] Sir Julian Huxley made a list of the characteristics which are unique to the species man: language and conceptual thought; the transmission of knowledge by written records; tools and machinery; biological dominance over all other species; individual variability; the use of the forelimb for manipulating purposes only; all-year-round fertility; art, humour, science, religion and so on. But the most striking feature of man from the evolutionist's point of view is not included in the list – nor have I read a serious discussion of it by any other leading biologist.

It could be called 'the paradox of the unsolicited gift'; I shall try to convey it by a parable. There was once an illiterate shopkeeper in an Arab bazaar, called Ali, who, not being very good at doing sums, was always cheated by his customers – instead of cheating them, as it should be. So he prayed every night to Allah for the present of an abacus – that venerable contraption for adding and subtracting by pushing beads along wires. But some malicious djin forwarded his prayers to the wrong branch of the heavenly Mail Order Department, and so one morning, arriving at the bazaar, Ali found his stall transformed into a multi-storey, steel-framed building, housing the latest IBM computer with instrument panels covering all the walls, with thousands of fluorescent oscillators, dials, magic eyes, etc, and an instruction book of several hundred pages – which, being illiterate, he could not read. However, after days of useless fiddling with this or that dial, he flew into a rage and started kicking a shiny, delicate panel. The shocks disturbed one of the machine's millions of electronic circuits, and after a while Ali discovered to his delight that if he kicked that panel, say, three times and afterwards five times, one of the dials showed the figure eight! He thanked Allah for having sent him such a pretty abacus, and continued to use the machine to add up two and three – happily unaware that it was capable of deriving Einstein's equations in a jiffy, or predicting the orbits of planets and stars thousands of years ahead.

Ali's children, then his grandchildren, inherited the machine and the secret of kicking that same panel; but it took hundreds of generations until they learned to use it even for the purpose of simple multiplication. We ourselves are Ali's descendants, and though we have discovered many other ways of putting the machine to work, we have still only learned to utilize a very small fraction of the potentials of its estimated hundred thousand million circuits. For the unsolicited gift is of course the human brain. As for the instruction book, it is lost – if it ever existed. Plato maintains that it did once – but that is hearsay.

The comparison is less far-fetched than it may seem. Evolution, whatever the driving force behind it, caters for the species' immediate adaptive needs; and the emergence of novelties in anatomical structure and function is by and large guided by these needs. It is entirely unprecedented that evolution should provide a species with an organ *which it does not know how to use*; a luxury organ, like Ali's computer, far exceeding its owner's immediate, primitive needs; an organ which will take the species millennia to learn to put to proper use – if it ever does.

All the evidence indicates that the earliest representative of *homo sapiens* – Cro-Magnon man, who emerges on the scene some fifty to a hundred thousand years ago – was already endowed with a brain which in size and shape was the same as ours. But he made hardly any use of it; he remained a cave-dweller, and never grew out of the Stone Age. From the point of view of his immediate needs, the explosive growth of the neocortex overshot the mark by a time factor of astronomic magnitude. For several tens of thousands of years, our ancestors went on manufacturing bows and arrows and spears, while the organ which tomorrow will take us to the moon was already there, ready for use, inside their skulls.

When we say that mental evolution is a specific characteristic of man and absent in animals, we confuse the issue. The learning potential of animals is automatically limited by the fact that they make full use – or nearly full use – of all organs of their native equipment, including their brains. The capacities of the computer inside the reptilian and mammalian skull are exploited to the full, and leave no scope for further learning. But the evolution of man's brain has so wildly overshot man's immediate needs that he is still breathlessly catching up with its unexploited, unexplored possibilities. The history of science and philosophy is, from this point of view, the slow process of *learning to actualize the brain's potentials*. The new frontiers to be conquered are mainly in the convolutions of the cortex.

Looking in Utter Darkness . . .

But why was this process of *learning to use our brains*, in a quite literal sense, so slow, spasmodic and beset with reverses? Here is the crux of the problem. The answer, as suggested before, is inadequate coordination between the old brain and the new brain – the old brain getting in the way of the new; the passionate neighing of affect-based beliefs preventing us from listening to the voice of reason. Hence the mess we made of our social history; but the progress of 'dispassionate' science laboured under the same curse. We are in the naïve habit of visualizing it as a steady, cumulative process, where each epoch adds some new item to the knowledge of the past, where each generation of Ali's descendants is learning to make better use of Allah's present, thus nicely progressing from the magic-ridden, myth-addicted infancy of civilization, through the pangs of adolescence, to detached, rational maturity.

In fact, however, progress was neither steady nor continuous:

The philosophy of nature evolved by occasional leaps and bounds alternating with delusional pursuits, regressions, periods of blindness and amnesia. The great discoveries which determined its course were sometimes the unexpected by-products of a chase after quite different hares. At other times, the process of discovery consisted merely in the cleaning away of the rubbish that blocked the path. The mad clockwork of Ptolemy's epicycles was kept going for two thousand years; and Europe knew less geometry in the fifteenth century AD than in Archimedes' time.

If progress had been continuous and organic, all that we know, for instance, about the theory of numbers, or analytical geometry, should have been discovered within a few generations after Euclid. For this development did not depend on technological advances or the taming of nature: the whole corpus of mathematics is potentially there in the ten billion neurons of the computing machine inside the human skull ... The jerky and basically irrational progress of knowledge is probably related to the fact that evolution has endowed *homo sapiens* with an organ which he was unable to put to proper use. Neurologists have estimated that even at the present stage we are only using two or three per cent of the potentialities of its built-in 'circuits'.[2]

If one takes a kind of bird's-eye view of the history of science, the first thing that strikes one is its discontinuity. About tens of thousands of years of human prehistory we know very little. Then, in the sixth century BC, we find suddenly, as if sprung from nowhere, a galaxy of Philosophers in Miletus and Elea and Samos, discussing the origins and evolution of the universe, searching for the ultimate principles underlying all diversity. The Pythagoreans attempted the first grand synthesis: they tried to weave the separate threads of mathematics, music, astronomy and medicine into a single carpet with an austere geometrical design. That carpet is still in the making, but its pattern was laid down in the three centuries of the Heroic Age of Greek science. However, after the Macedonian conquest, there followed a period of orthodoxy and decline.

Aristotle's categories became the grammar of existence, his animal spirits ruled the world of physics, everything worth knowing was already known, and everything inventable already invented. The Heroic Age was guided by the example of Prometheus stealing the fire of the gods; the philosophers of the Hellenistic period dwelt in Plato's cave, drawing epicycles on the wall, their backs turned to the daylight of reality.

After that there came a period of hibernation lasting for fifteen centuries. During that time the march of science was not only halted, but its direction reversed. A contemporary philosopher of science, Dr Pyke, wrote about 'the inability of science to go backwards – once the neutron has been discovered it remains discovered'.[3] Does it? In the fifth century BC the educated classes knew that the earth was a spherical body floating in space and spinning round its axis; a thousand years later they thought that it was a flat disc.[4]

In St Augustine's *City of God*, all the treasures of ancient Greek learning, beauty and hope were banned, for all pagan knowledge was 'prostituted with the influence of obscene and filthy devils. Let Thales depart with his water, Anaximenes with the air, the Stoics with their fire, Epicurus with his atoms . . .' And depart they did. To fiddle with the dials of the unsolicited gift became taboo. The revival of learning in the twelfth century was followed by the disastrous marriage of Aristotle's physics with the theology of St Thomas Aquinas, and by another three centuries of sterility, stagnation and scholastic philosophy – 'looking', as Erasmus cried, 'in utter darkness for that which has no existence whatsoever'.

The only periods in the whole of Western history in which there was a truly cumulative growth of knowledge are the three great centuries of Greece, and the last three centuries before the present. Yet the apparatus to generate that knowledge was there all the time during the intervening two thousand years – and also during the thirty thousand years or so which separate us from Altamira and Lascaux. But it was not allowed to generate that knowledge. The affect-inspired phantasmagorias of totem and taboo, dogma and doctrine, guilt and fear, drove back again and again the 'filthy devils' of knowledge. For most of the time throughout human history, the marvellous potentials of the new cortex were only permitted to exert their powers in the service of old emotional beliefs: in the magic-motivated paintings of the Dordogne caves; in the translation of archetypal imagery into the language of mythology; in the religious art of Asia or of the European Middle Ages. Reason's task was to act as the hand-maid of faith – whether it was the faith of medicine-men, theologians, scholastics, dialectical materialists, devotees of President Mao or King Mbo-Mba. The fault, dear Brutus, is not in our stars; it is in the crocodile and the horse that we carry in our skulls. Of all the uniquenesses of man this seems to be the foremost.

The Peaceful Primate

It is characteristic of the conventional biologist's touching optimism that Huxley's list contains only positive, desirable properties. That other terrible uniqueness of our species, intra-specific warfare,* is not even mentioned in passing –

---

* That is, warfare *within* the species, as distinct from the *inter*-specific pursuit of the prey which belongs to a different species.

although in a separate essay in the same volume, on 'War as a Biological Phenomenon', Huxley points out that 'there are only two kinds of animals that habitually make war – man and ants. Even among ants war is mainly practised by one group, comprising only a few species among the tens of thousands that are known to science.'[5] In fact, however, rats, too, wage group or clan warfare. The members of the rat clan, as those of the insect state, do not 'know' each other individually, only by the characteristic smell of their shared nest, hive or locality. The stranger, although of the same species but from a different clan, is instantly recognized by his different smell – he 'stinks'. So he must be ferociously attacked, and if possible killed.

But man and rats are exceptions. As a rule, throughout the whole animal kingdom, fighting with intent to kill only occurs between predator and prey. The law of the jungle sanctions only one legitimate motive for murder, the feeding drive; but the prey must of course be of a different species. Within the same species, powerful instinctual safeguards prevent serious fighting between individuals or groups. These inhibitory mechanisms – instinct-taboos – against killing or seriously injuring con-specifics are as powerful in most animals as the drives of hunger, sex or fear. The unavoidable and necessary self-assertive tendencies among the higher social animals are thus compensated by inhibitory mechanisms which turn fighting between sexual competitors into a more or less symbolic duel, fought according to formal rules, but hardly ever to a lethal finish. The contest is instantly terminated by some specific gesture of surrender by the weaker contestant – the dog rolling on its back, exposing its belly and throat; the defeated stag slinking away. Similarly, the defence of territory is assured nearly always without bloodshed, by strictly ritualized threat-behaviour, mock attacks and the like. Lastly, order of rank in wild animal societies, from birds to monkeys, is established and maintained with a minimum of bullying and fuss.

In the course of the last twenty years, field observations on the life of monkey societies in the wild have led to a complete reversal of our previous ideas about the mentality of our primate ancestors. The earlier studies – such as Solly Zuckerman's in the late 1920s – were based on the behaviour of monkeys confined in the unnatural, crowded conditions of the zoo. These studies yielded important psychological results, in the sense in which studies of human behaviour in prisons and concentration camps do: they reveal the picture of a neurotic society labouring under abnormal stresses, whose members are bored and irritable, constantly bickering and fighting, obsessed by sex, and exposed to the rule of tyrannical, sometimes murderous, leaders. On the strength of this picture, one could only wonder how monkey societies in the wild survived at all.

But since the Second World War a new generation of field observers, whose patient studies often extended over many years, has completely and dramatically reversed the picture. W. M. S. Russell has summed up the result as follows:

> ... After the Second World War the field study of monkeys and apes suddenly mushroomed. The reports of the field observers are virtually unanimous. Carpenter ... reported that fighting is rare in wild gibbons and apparently absent in wild howler monkeys. Washburn and Devore saw signs of internal violence in only one in seven of their bands of wild East African baboons; and no fighting at all between bands. Southwick took over the study of wild howlers in the fifties, and never saw one fight, within or between bands. Jay gives a similar report on wild langur bands, and Imanishi on wild Japanese monkeys. Goodall saw little evidence of fighting in wild chimpanzees, nor Hall in wild bands of the very baboon species that Zuckerman had studied in the zoo. And Emlen and Schaller saw not the slightest trace of aggression within wild gorilla bands; and relations between bands were so friendly that, when two bands met, they might bed down together for the night, and individuals could come visiting for as long as they liked.
>
> These unanimous reports are even more impressive than they first appear, for many of the observers were expecting the reverse.

The early zoo findings had made such a deep impression that at first each field worker assumed that his or her species must be unusual ... We can now see that they were wrong: all monkey and ape species are peaceful in the wild ... A healthy wild primate society shows no trace of serious fighting, either within or between bands. It is now undeniable that primates can live without any violence at all ... Putting together the field and zoo reports, we now know that aggressiveness is not an innate feature of individuals, appearing in some primate species and not in others. All primate species are peaceful in some conditions and violent in others. Violence is a property of societies exposed to stress ...[6]

What conclusions are we to draw from this picture of primate behaviour?

First, that primates (and all other mammals) in the wild show a complete absence of Freud's destructive instinct. In the normal baboon or rhesus monkey society, the self-assertive tendencies of the individual are counter-balanced by its integrative ties with family, leader and clan. Aggression makes its appearance only when tensions of one kind or another upset the balance.

All this is entirely in keeping with the conclusions we arrived at in earlier chapters. But it provides us with only a few limited and somewhat trivial clues to the origins of the human predicament. That stresses caused by shortage of food, overcrowding of territory, natural catastrophes and so on, upset the social equilibrium and produce pathological behaviour – agreed. So do the zoo-like conditions in prisons, the enforced idleness of unemployment, the boredom of the welfare state. This is the kind of stuff social psychologists like to emphasize over and again in their discussions of the perils of modern life in the crowded megalopolis – and they are, of course, quite right. But these are modern phenomena which have little relevance to the core of the problem: the emergence of the unique, murderous, delusional streak in our prehistoric ancestors. They did not suffer from overcrowding, there was no shortage of territory, they did not lead an urban existence; in a word, we cannot lay the blame on stresses of the type to which captive monkeys, or the citizens of contemporary New York, are subjected. To become hypnotized by the specific pathology of the twentieth century narrows one's vision and blinds one to the much older, much more fundamental problem of the chronic savagery of human civilizations, ancient and modern. We are so preoccupied with the social ravages done to the occupants of contemporary Negro ghettoes in America, that we quite forget the horrors of African history when Negroes were free – or the horrors of European or Asian history. To lay the blame for man's pathological condition on the environment means to beg the question. Climatic changes and other environmental pressures are, of course, an immensely powerful factor in biological evolution and human history; but most wars, civil wars and human holocausts were motivated by other reasons.

Where else, then, shall we look for the causes of the Fall – that is to say, for the unique characteristic of our species to practise intra-specific homicide, individually or in groups?

The Harmless Hunter

It has occasionally been suggested that the Fall occurred when our ancestors turned from a vegetarian to a carnivorous diet. Both zoologists and anthropologists have a conclusive answer to this suggestion. The zoologist will point out that hunting the prey which belongs to a different species is a biological drive strictly separate from aggression against con-specifics. To quote Konrad Lorenz:

> The motivation of the hunter is basically different from that of the fighter. The buffalo which the lion fells provokes his aggression as little as the appetising turkey which I have just seen hanging in the larder provokes mine. The differences in these inner drives can clearly be seen in the expressive movements of the animal: a dog about to catch a hunted rabbit has the same kind of excitedly happy expression as he has when he greets his master or awaits some

longed-for treat. From many excellent photographs it can be seen that the lion, in the dramatic movement before he springs, is in no way angry. Growling, laying the ears back, and other well-known expression movements of fighting behaviour are seen in predatory animals only when they are very afraid of a wildly resisting prey, and even then the expressions are only suggested.[7]

The Russells arrive at the same conclusion: 'There is certainly no evidence from mammalian behaviour that social aggression is more prevalent or intense among carnivores than among herbivores.' And as for humans: 'There is certainly no evidence that social violence has been more prevalent or intense in carnivorous hunting than in vegetarian agricultural societies. Hunting people have sometimes been extremely war-like; but no human group has produced more peaceful communities than some of the Eskimos, who have been carnivorous hunters, presumably, since the Old Stone Age.'[8] The Samurai, on the other hand, were strict vegetarians; and so were the Hindu mobs in India which massacred their Moslem brethren whenever given a chance. It was not the eating of reindeer-steaks which caused the Fall.

Lorenz, whom I have just quoted, has a more sophisticated theory. The following extract (compressed) conveys the gist of it:

> The inhibitions controlling aggression in various social animals, preventing it from injuring or killing fellow members of the species, are most important and consequently most highly differentiated in those animals which are capable of killing living creatures of about their own size. A raven can peck out the eye of another with one thrust of its beak, a wolf can rip the jugular vein of another with a single bite. There would be no more ravens and no more wolves if reliable inhibitions did not prevent such actions. Neither a dove nor a hare nor even a chimpanzee is able to kill its own kind with a single peck or bite. Since there rarely is, in Nature, the possibility of such an animal seriously injuring one of its own kind, there is no selection pressure at work to breed inhibitions against killing. One can only deplore the fact that man has definitely not got a carnivorous mentality! All his trouble arises from his being a basically harmless, omnivorous creature, lacking

in natural weapons with which to kill big prey, and, therefore, also devoid of the built-in safety devices which prevent 'professional' carnivores from abusing their killing power to destroy fellow-members of their own species. No selection pressure arose in the prehistory of mankind to breed inhibitory mechanisms preventing the killing of con-specifics until, all of a sudden, the invention of artificial weapons upset the equilibrium of killing potential and social inhibitions. When it did, man's position was very nearly that of a dove which, by some unnatural trick of Nature, has suddenly acquired the beak of a raven. Whatever his innate norms of social behaviour may have been, they were bound to be thrown out of gear by the invention of weapons.[9]

One could pick various holes in this argument, as the critics of Lorenz' book (myself included[10]) have done, and never-theless concede that it contains an element of truth. Without losing ourselves in technicalities, we can reformulate Lorenz' argument by saying that, from the very beginning of the manufacture of weapons, *man's instinct and intellect fell out of step*. The *invention* of weapons and tools was an intellectual creation, the combined achievement of brain and hand – of the marvellous powers of the neocortex to coordinate the manipulative skill of the fingers with the perceptions of the perfected eye, and both with memory and planning. But the *use* to which the weapons were put, was dependent on the motivational drives, on instinct and emotion – on the old brain. The old brain was lacking in the necessary equipment, the inhibitory mechanisms, to deal with man's newly acquired powers; while the new brain had insufficient control over his emotions. What Lorenz' argument boils down to is once more: *inadequate coordination between the all too rapidly grown modern, and the ancient structures of the nervous system*.

However, the awareness of power, which the wielding of spear and bow lends to the hunter, need not necessarily increase aggressivity towards his fellows; it may, as the example of the Eskimos and other hunting communities show, even have the opposite effect. In so far as the purely self-assertive tendencies of individuals are concerned, there is no obvious reason why primitive man should not have learned to come to terms with the added power that weapons gave him, by developing moral responsibilities – a superego as effective in its way as the instinct-taboos against the killing of con-specifics in other hunting animals. And, to judge by the anthropological evidence, such taboos did indeed develop – but they only prevented aggression against the individual's own tribe or social group. To other members of the species the taboo did not apply. *It was not individual aggression which got out of hand, but devotion to the narrow social group with which the individual identified himself to the hostile exclusion of all other groups.* It is the process we have discussed before: the integrative tendency, manifested in primitive forms of identification, serving as a vehicle for the aggressive self-assertiveness of the social holon.

To put it in a different way: to man, *intra-specific differences have become more vital than intra-specific affinities*; and the inhibitions which in other animals prevent intra-specific killing, work only within the group. In the rat it is the smell which decides who is friend or foe. In man, there is a terrifyingly wide range of criteria, from territorial possession through ethnic, cultural, religious, ideological differences, which decide who stinks and who does not.

The Curse of Language

There are other factors which contributed to the tragedy. The first is the enormous range of intra-specific differences between human individuals, races and cultures; a diversity without parallel among other species. In Huxley's list of man's biological 'uniquenesses', this wide range of variety in physical appearance and mental attributes actually occupies the first place. How it arose does not concern us here; Huxley has some interesting things to say on the subject in the essay from which I have quoted. What matters in our context is that these differences and contrasts were a powerful factor of mutual repellence between groups; with the result that *the disruptive forces have always dominated the forces of cohesion in the species as a whole*. To quote Lorenz once more:

> It is no daring speculation to assume that the first human beings who really represented our own species, those of Cro Magnon, had roughly the same instincts and natural inclinations as we have ourselves. Nor is it illegitimate to assume that the structure of their societies and their tribal warfare was roughly the same as can still be found in certain tribes of Papuans and in central New Guinea. Every one of their tiny settlements is permanently at war with the neighbouring villages; their relationship is described by Margaret Mead as one of mild reciprocal head-hunting, 'mild' meaning that there are no organized raids for the purpose of removing the treasured heads of neighbouring warriors, but only the occasional taking of the heads of women and children encountered in the woods.[11]

The people of the neighbouring village were simply not considered as con-specifics; as the stammering barbarians were denied full human status by the Greeks, the pagans by the Church, the Jews by the Nazis. *A priori*, one would imagine that the dawn of abstract, conceptualized thought, its communication by language, and its preservation by cumulative records – the beginning of Teilhard's Noosphere – would have counteracted these fratricidal, species-disrupting tendencies. In actual fact, the cliché about the unifying power of verbal communication represents only half of the truth, and perhaps less than half. In the first place, there is the trivial fact that, while language facilitates communication within the group, it also crystallizes cultural differences, and actually heightens the barriers between groups. The admirable field-observations of monkey societies, which I have just mentioned, have revealed that Primate groups of the same species inhabiting different localities also tend to develop different traditions and 'cultures' – but this differentiation never goes so far as to lead to conflict: mainly, one supposes, because of the absence of separative linguistic barriers. Among humans, however, the separative, group-estranging forces of language are active on every level: nations, tribes, regional dialects, the exclusive vocabularies and accents of social classes; professional jargons. Among the two million aborigines of New Guinea, to whom Margaret Mead refers in the quotation above, seven hundred and fifty different languages are spoken. Ever since the Stone Age, the Tower of Babel has remained a valid symbol. Is it not remarkable that at a time when Hertzian waves and communication satellites have transformed the population of our whole planet into a single audience, no serious effort is being made by responsible bodies (except a few undaunted Esperantists) to propagate a universal *lingua franca*; yet at the same time people are killed in language riots over the primacy of Maharati or Gujurati in India, Flemish or French in Belgium, French or English in Canada. An emotionally maladjusted species, we have the uncanny power of turning every blessing, including language, into a curse.

The main danger of language, however, lies not in its separative, but in its magic, hypnotic, emotion-arousing powers. Words can serve to crystallize thought, to give articulateness and precision to vague images and hazy intuitions. They can also serve to rationalize irrational fears and desires, to give the semblance of logic to the wildest superstitions, to lend the vocabulary of the new brain to the phantasmagorias and delusions of the old. Lastly, words can be used as explosive charges to set off the chain-reactions of group psychology. Ali's computer is just as capable of producing Kant's *Critique of Pure Reason* as the screams of Hitler. Without a language to formulate religious and ideological doctrines, closed belief-systems, slogans and manifestoes, we should be as unable to fight intra-specific wars as the poor baboons. Thus the various blessings which make for the uniqueness of man form at the same time a tragic mesh with one common pattern underlying all – schizophysiology.

The Discovery of Death

A further factor, which provides one of the main threads in the pattern, is the discovery of death – and the refusal to accept it.

The discovery originates in the new brain, the refusal in the old. Instinct takes existence implicitly for granted, and defends it against threats in anger and fear; but it cannot conceive of its change into non-existence. This refusal is one of the *leitmotivs* of history, perpetuating the conflict between faith and reason. In the oldest primitive cultures, among Australian aborigines or Papuans as they were in the last century, 'nobody ever dies a natural death. Even in the case of old people they maintain that death is due to wizardry, and it is the same thing in all misfortunes that may occur. Has a man had a fatal fall? A wizard made him fall. Has another been wounded by a wild boar or bitten by a snake? It was a wizard again. He, too, working from a distance, can make a woman die in childbed, and so on' (Lévy-Bruhl[12]).

The refusal to accept death either as a natural or as a final phenomenon populated the world with witches, ghosts, ancestral spirits, gods, demi-gods, angels and devils. The air became saturated with invisible presences, as in a mental home.* Most of them were malevolent and vengeful, or at least capricious, unpredictable, insatiable in their demands. They had to be worshipped, cajoled, propitiated, and if possible, coerced. Hence the insane gesture of Abraham, the ubiquity of human sacrifice at the bloody dawn of civilization, the holy massacres which have continued ever since. In all

* Thus a contemporary authority, F. M. Berger,[13] writes: 'It is often stated that there is much more anxiety in modern Western society than there is among the more primitive people in the less developed parts of the globe. [In fact however] Randal (1965) reports that, in the Congo and other undeveloped parts of Africa, anxiety is the most common and crippling psychiatric disorder. The Papuans of the Waghi Valley of Central New Guinea who have not progressed beyond a Stone Age culture suffer from more anxiety than any modern industrial civilisation. They also have the highest incidence of peptic ulcers ever found in any community (Montague, 1960).'

mythologies, that dawn is steeped in fear, anxiety and guilt, dramatized by the fall of angels, the fall of man, by floods and catastrophes; but also in comforting promises of eternal survival; until even that consolation was poisoned with the fear of everlasting tortures. And all along reason played the willing handmaid to perverse beliefs, spawned by the visceral brain.

There is, of course, another side to the picture. The refusal to believe in the finality of death made pyramids and temples rise from the sand; it was one of the main inspirations of art, from the Greek tragedy to the paintings of the Renaissance, the music of Bach and the Holy Sonnets of Donne. But what a terrible price to pay for these splendours! There is a hoary belief that the horrors and the splendours are inseparable, that one is the precondition of the other, that to paint like Van Gogh you have to cut off your ear. But this belief itself is symptomatic of the anxiety-ridden mind, which never catches up on the arrears due to the heavenly tax-collector.

Summary

The rise of the human neocortex is the only example of evolution providing a species with an organ which it does not know how to use.

The actualization of its reasoning potentials has been obstructed, throughout prehistory and history, by the affect-based activities of the phylogenetically older structures in the nervous system. Inadequate coordination between the old and new structures made man's instinct and intellect fall out of step. The wide range of intra-specific differences between individuals, races and cultures became a source of mutual repellence. Language increased cohesion within groups, and heightened the barriers between groups. The discovery of death by the intellect, and its rejection by instinct became a paradigm of the split mind.

XVIII

THE AGE OF CLIMAX

I come from a country which does not yet exist.
J. CRAVEIRINHA

The Hinge of History

'THE present generation is the hinge of history ... We may now be in the time of the most rapid change in the whole evolution of the human race, either past or to come ... The world has now become too dangerous for anything less than Utopia.'[1]

This was written by a contemporary American biophysicist, J. R. Platt. We have heard such warnings before – Isaiah, Jeremiah, Cassandra, St John of the Apocalypse, and so on down the centuries through Augustine, the prophets of the Millennium, to Lenin and Oswald Spengler. In every century there was at least one generation which flattered itself to be 'the hinge of history', to live at a time such as never was before, awaiting the blow of the last trumpet or some secular equivalent of it. And there was also James Thurber's unforgettable 'Get-ready man', who wandered barefoot in his nightshirt through the dark streets of his home town, waking people with the blood-curdling cry: 'Get ready, get rready, the wurrld is coming to an end.'

So one ought to be cautious with pronouncements about the uniqueness of one's own time. Nevertheless there are at least two good reasons which justify the view that humanity is going through a crisis unprecedented in its nature and magnitude in the whole of its past history. The first is quantitative, the second qualitative.

The first is the upsetting of the ecological balance. Its consequences have been summed up by Sir Gavin de Beer in an article commemorating the bicentenary of Malthus: 'If we go back a million years to the hominids, or even 250,000 years to Swanscombe Man and his Missus, the curve of population is like an aircraft taking off: for most of that time it just skims along the time axis; then, about AD 1600, the undercarriage is raised and it begins to soar; today it is rising almost vertically, more like a rocket off its pad. A million years to reach 3,250 million; thirty or so to double it!'[2]

To be a little more specific: historians have estimated that the world's population at the beginning of the Christian era was around 250 million. By the middle of the seventeenth century it had doubled, rising to about 500 million. By the middle of the nineteenth it had doubled again and reached the first billion mark.* It is at this point that Pasteur, Lister and Semmelweiss took a hand and changed the ecological balance of our species by declaring war on the micro-organisms in its environment – a change more drastic and far-reaching than all the technical inventions of James Watt, Edison and the Wright brothers put together. But the disaster they unwittingly initiated made itself felt only a century later. By 1925 the population had doubled again, to two billion. By 1965 it was well over three billion, and the doubling period had shrunk from 1,500 years to about 35 years.[3]

This figure is based on an average global growth rate of 2 per cent per annum – 1.6 to 1.8 in industrialized countries, 3 per cent or more in a number of low-income nations. Thus India, which in 1965 had a population of 450 million, at the present growth rate will have 900 million mouths to feed in AD 2000. Even for the short period of fifteen years, 1965–80, to keep up with the estimated population-growth would

* I am following US usage: 1,000 million = one billion.

require an increase of yield per acre of existing farmland by at least 50 per cent; and L. R. Brown of the US Department of Agriculture has calculated 'that an additional 24 million tons of fertilizer a year must be applied to achieve this performance, but the entire world production of fertilizer is only 28.6 million tons a year'.[4] As for China, with a population of 750 million in 1966, it will, if the present trend continues, at the end of the century equal the total population of the earth as it was in 1900.

The explosion is accompanied by the implosion of migrants from rural areas to the cities, 'not inspired by the call of employment but by the desperate hope that some menial job or government relief will be available there ... Kingsley Davies estimates that in the year 2000, the largest Indian city, Calcutta, will contain between 36 and 66 million people. Calcutta sprawling for hundreds of square miles, with a population of 66 million inadequately employed people, suggests a concentration of misery that can only have explosive consequences.'[5]

Returning to the planet as a whole, the prospect is: 7 billion people in 2000; 14 billion in 2035; 25 billion a hundred years from now (see Figure 14). 'But,' as a sober Ford Foundation report says, 'but long before then, in the face of such population pressure, it is inevitable that the Four Horsemen will take over.'[6]

How many people can our planet nourish? According to Colin Clark, one of the leading authorities in this field, 12 to 15 billion – but only on condition that the methods of cultivation and soil preservation in the whole world are brought up to the high standard of the Netherlands. This, of course, is nothing short of Utopia; yet even under these optimum conditions the total population would outpace the total supply in the first decades of the next century.

It will be objected that predictions based on existing population trends are notoriously unreliable. That is our main hope; but since the last war, this unreliability has worked steadily in favour of the pessimists: the factual increase surpasses all maximal predictions. Besides, the great surprises – such as the stabilization of the Japanese population around 1949 by the legalization of abortion – which play havoc with the statistician's predictions have always occurred in highly developed countries, which took family planning more or less for granted long before modern contraceptives came on the market, and were thus able to break the predicted pattern by adapting the number of their babies to economic and psychological trends. In contrast to Japan – the only Asiatic country with a Western level of literacy – fifteen years of intense birth-control propaganda in India has yielded practically no results. The fast breeders in Asia, Africa and Latin America are by nature the least amenable to disciplined family planning. They are the three-quarters of the earth's population which set the pace.

All this has often been said, and repetition tends to blunt rather than sharpen our awareness. The public is aware that there is a problem; it is not aware of the magnitude and the urgency of the problem; it is not aware that we are moving towards a climax which is not centuries, but only a few decades ahead – that is, well within the lifetime of the present generation of teenagers. What I am trying to prove is not that the situation is hopeless, but that it is indeed unique, unprecedented in man's history. De Beer's parable of the aeroplane which skims along the runway for thousands of miles, but within a mile or two from takeoff changes into a rocket, shooting straight up into the sky, is meant to illustrate what the mathematician calls an 'exponential curve' (Figure 14).

The curve should be extended to the left – into the past – for miles on end, along which its rise would only be discernible through a microscope. Then comes the critical moment when Pasteur et al. took the brakes off. The brakes, of course, symbolize the high mortality rate which, balancing

FIGURE 14

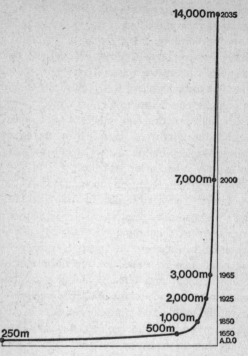

Population curve from the beginning of the Christian era extrapolated to AD 2035

the 'lift' of the birth rate, kept the population curve nearly horizontal. It took about a century – half an inch on our scale – until the consequences became apparent; from then onward the curve rises steeper and steeper, until, in the second half of our century, it starts rocketing towards the sky. It took our species something like a hundred thousand years to spawn its first billion. Today we are adding a further billion to the total every twelve years. In the first few decades of the next century, if the present trend continues, we shall add a billion every six years. After that, every three years; and so on. But long before that de Beer's crazy aeroplane is bound to crash.

An exponential curve reflects a process with the brakes off, which has got out of hand. Even the draughtsman attempting to extend the curve into the future will be defeated because, as the curve gets steeper and steeper, he must run out of paper – as the world must run out of food, of *Lebensraum*, of beaches and river shores, of privacy, of smiles.

The uncanny properties of exponential curves reflect the uniqueness of our time – not only the population explosion, but also the explosion in power, communications and specialized knowledge.

To take the last item first, Dr Ian Morris of University College writes: 'As measured by manpower, number of periodicals or number of scientific papers, science is growing exponentially with a doubling time of about fifteen years. Figure 1 shows the increase of scientific journals since they began in 1665 ...' The figure shows a curve similar to the one above, indicating that the number of scientific journals in 1700 was less than ten, in 1800 around a hundred, in 1850 around a thousand, in 1900 more than ten thousand, after the First World War around a hundred thousand, and by AD 2000 is expected to reach the one million mark. 'The same picture is obtained if the number of scientists or scientific papers is measured, and appears to be comparable for widely different scientific disciplines. During the past fifteen years, the same number of scientists were produced as existed during the entire previous period of science. Thus because the average working life of a research scientist is about forty-five years, seven out of every eight scientists who have ever lived are alive now. Similarly, almost *ninety per cent* of all scientific endeavour has been undertaken during the past fifty years.'[7] The United States National Education Authority sets the doubling time since 1950 even lower: ten years.[8]

Take power next. Again we have that long flat stretch of

the curve from Cro Magnon to about five thousand years ago. With the invention of the lever, the pulley and other simple mechanical devices, the muscular strength of man would appear multiplied, say, five- or tenfold; then the curve would again remain nearly horizontal until the invention of the steam engine and the Industrial Revolution, just two hundred years ago. From then on, it is the same story as before: take-off, steeper and steeper climb to the rocket-like stage. The exponential increase in the speed of communications, or in the range of penetration into the depths of the universe by optical and radio telescopes, is too well known to need stressing; but the following illustration is perhaps less familiar.

At the end of the nineteen twenties we could impart to atomic particles about half a million electron-volts of energy; in the 1930s we could accelerate them to twenty million electron-volts; by 1950 to five hundred million; and at the time of writing, an accelerator of fifty thousand million electron-volts is under construction. But more bemusing than all these figures is to me an episode in 1930, when I nearly lost my job as a science editor because of indignant protests against an article I wrote on the progress in rocketry, in which I predicted space travel 'in our lifetime'. And a year or two before the first Sputnik was launched, Britain's Astronomer Royal made the immortal statement: 'Space travel is bilge'. Our imagination is willing to accept that things are changing, but unable to accept the *rate* at which they are changing, and to extrapolate into the future. The mind boggles at an exponential curve as Pascal's mind boggled when, in the Copernican universe, infinity opened its gaping jaws: '*Le silence éternel de ces espaces infinis m'effraie.*'

That is the position in which we find our ourselves today. We dare no longer extrapolate into the future, partly because we are frightened, mainly because of the poverty of our imagination.

Two Curves

But at least we can look back over our shoulders into the past, and compare the chart which we have just discussed, showing the explosive increase in people, knowledge, power and communications, with another type of chart indicating the progress of social morality, ethical beliefs, spiritual awareness and related values. This chart will yield a curve of quite different shape. It, too, will show a very slow rise during the nearly flat prehistoric miles; then it will oscillate with inconclusive ups and downs through what we call civilized history; but shortly after the exponential curves get airborne, the 'ethical curve' shows a pronounced downward trend, marked by two World Wars, the genocidal enterprises of several dictators, and new methods of terror combined with indoctrination, which can hold whole continents in their grip.

The contrast between these two curves gives certainly an over-simplified, but not an over-dramatized view of our history. They represent the consequences of man's split mind. The exponential curves are all, in one way or another, the work of the new cortex; they show the explosive results of learning at long last how to actualize its potentials which, through all the millennia of our prehistory, have been lying dormant. The other curve reflects the delusional streak, the persistence of misplaced devotion to emotional beliefs dominated by the archaic paleo-mammalian brain.

To quote v. Bertalanffy once more:

> What is called human progress is a purely intellectual affair, made possible by the enormous development of the forebrain. Owing to this, man was able to build up the symbolic worlds of speech and thought, and some progress in science and technology during the 5,000 years of recorded history was made.
>
> Not much development, however, is seen on the moral side. It is doubtful whether the methods of modern warfare are preferable to the big stones used for cracking the skull of the fellow-Neanderthaler. It is rather obvious that the moral standards of Laotse and

Buddha were not inferior to ours. The human cortex contains some ten billion neurons that have made possible the progress from stone axe to airplanes and atomic bombs, from primitive mythology to quantum theory. There is no corresponding development on the instinctual side that causes man to mend his ways. For this reason, moral exhortations, as proffered through the centuries by the founders of religion and great leaders of humanity, have proved disconcertingly ineffective.[9]

As a further illustration of the gulf between our intellectual and emotional development, take the contrast between communication and cooperation. Progress of the means of communication is again reflected by an exponential curve: crowded within a single century are the invention of steamship, railway, motor car, airship, aeroplane, rocket, spaceship; of telegraph, telephone, gramophone, radio, radar; of photography, cinematography, television, telstar . . . The month I was born, the Wright brothers in Kitty Hawk, North Carolina, managed for the first time to stay in the air for one entire minute in their flying machine; the chances are that before I die we shall have reached the moon and perhaps Mars. *No generation of man ever before has witnessed in its lifetime such changes.*

Within that lifetime, our planet has shrunk to Lilliputian proportions, so that instead of Jules Verne's Eighty Days, it can be orbited in eighty minutes. But as to the second curve – the bridging of the distance between nations did not bring them 'closer' to each other – rather the opposite. Before the communications-explosion travel was slow, but there existed no Iron Curtain, no Berlin Wall, no minefields in no-man's-lands, and hardly any restrictions on immigration or emigration; today about one-third of mankind is not permitted to leave its own country. One could almost say that progress in cooperation varied in inverse ratio to progress in communications. The conquest of the air transformed limited into total warfare; the mass media became the demagogue's instruments of fomenting hatred; and even between close neighbours like England and France, the increase in tourist traffic has hardly increased mutual understanding. There have been some positive advances such as the European Common Market; they are minute compared to the gigantic cracks which divide the planet into three major and countless minor, hostile, isolated camps.

The point of labouring these obvious facts is to make them fall into the general pattern. Language, the outstanding achievement of the neocortex, became a more dividing than unifying factor, increasing intra-specific tensions; progress in communications followed a similar trend of turning a blessing into a curse. Even from the aesthetic point of view we have managed to contaminate the luminiferous ether as we have contaminated our air, rivers and seashores; you fiddle with the dials of your radio and from all over the world, instead of celestial harmonies, the ether disgorges its musical latrine slush.

Of all exponential curves, that referring to progress in destructive power is the most spectacular and the best known. To sum it up as briefly as possible: after the First World War, statisticians calculated that on the average ten thousand rifle bullets or ten artillery shells had been needed to kill one enemy soldier. The bombs dropped from flying machines weighed a few pounds. By the Second World War, the block-busters had acquired a destructive power equal to twenty tons of TNT. The first atomic bomb on Hiroshima equalled twenty thousand tons of TNT. Ten years later, the first hydrogen bomb equalled twenty million tons. At the time of writing, we are stockpiling bombs the equivalent of one hundred million tons of TNT and there are rumours of a 'gigaton bomb' – a 'nuclear weapon packing the power of a billion tons of TNT that could be detonated a hundred miles off the US coastline and still set off a fifty-foot tidal wave that would sweep across much of the entire American continent ... or a cobalt bomb that would send a deadly cloud sweeping forever about the earth.'[10]

The New Calendar

I have said that there are two reasons which entitle us to call our time 'unique'. The first is quantitative, expressed by the exponential increase of populations, communications, destructive power, etc. Under their combined impact, an extraterrestrial intelligence, to whom centuries are as seconds, able to survey the whole curve in one sweep, would probably come to the conclusion that human civilization is either on the verge of, or in the process of, exploding.

The second reason is qualitative, and can be summed up in a single sentence: before the thermonuclear bomb, man had to live with the idea of his death as an individual; from now onward, mankind has to live with the idea of its death as a species.

The bomb has given us the power to commit genosuicide; and within a few years we should even have the power to turn our planet into a *nova*, an exploding star. Every age has had its Cassandras and Get-Ready Men, and mankind has managed to survive regardless of their sinister prophecies. But this comforting argument is no longer valid, as no past age, however convulsed by war and pestilence, had possessed our newly acquired power over life on the planet *as a whole*.

The full implications of this fact have not yet sunk into the minds of even the noisiest pacifists. We have always been taught to accept the transitoriness of individual existence, while taking the survival of our species axiomatically for granted. This was a perfectly reasonable belief, barring some unlikely cosmic catastrophe. But it has ceased to be a reasonable belief since the day when the possibility of engineering a catastrophe of cosmic dimensions was experimentally tested and proven. It pulverized the assumptions on which all philosophy from Socrates onward was based: the potential immortality of our species.

But new insights of a revolutionary nature cannot be assimilated at once. There are periods of incubation. The Copernican theory of the earth's motion had to wait eighty years before it took root. The unconscious mind has its own clock, and its own ways of digesting what the conscious mind has rejected as indigestible. The leaders of the French Revolution were well aware of this fact; to hasten the process of assimilation, they introduced a new calendar, starting on the day of the proclamation of the Republic: September 22nd, 1792, became the 1st of Vendémiaire of the year 1. It would perhaps not be a bad idea if we all kept a second calendar, at least in our minds, starting with the year when the new Star of Bethlehem rose over Hiroshima. Calendars imply convictions about the fundamental importance of certain events: the first Olympiad, the founding of the city of Rome, the birth of Jesus, the flight of Mohammed from Mecca. The positing of a year zero provides a time scale, a measure of an age, of the distance covered from the real or assumed starting point of a given civilization.

Thus I am writing this in the year 22 pH – post Hiroshima. For there can be little doubt that in that year a new era started. The human race is facing a challenge unprecedented in its history – which can only be met by taking action of an equally unprecedented nature. The first half of the preceding sentence is now more or less generally accepted, but the second is not. Even the thinking minority still believes that a peril unique in its novelty can be averted by time-worn traditional remedies, by appeals to sweet reason and commonsense. But such appeals are powerless against the militant ideologies of closed systems, whose true believers are convinced – as a professor at Peking University wrote recently – that 'respect for facts and for other people's opinions must be exterminated from man's soul like vermin'.[11]

All efforts of persuasion by reasoned argument rely on the implicit assumption that *homo sapiens*, though occasionally blinded by emotion, is a basically rational animal, aware of the motives of his own actions and beliefs – an assumption which is untenable in the light of both historical and neurological evidence. All such appeals fall on barren ground; they could take root only if the ground were prepared by a spontaneous change in human mentality all over the world – the equivalent of a major biological mutation. Then, and only then, would mankind as a whole, from its political leaders down to the lonely crowd, become receptive to reasoned argument, and willing to resort to those unorthodox measures which would enable it to meet the challenge.

It is highly improbable that such a mental mutation will occur spontaneously in the foreseeable future; whereas it is highly probable that the spark which initiates the chain-reaction will be ignited sooner or later, deliberately or by accident. As the devices of atomic and biological warfare become more potent and simpler to produce, their spreading to young and immature, as well as old and over-ripe, nations is inevitable. An invention, once made, cannot be dis-invented; the bomb has come to stay. Mankind has to live with it forever: not merely through the next crisis and the next one, but forever; not through the next twenty or two hundred or two thousand years, but forever. It has become part of the human condition.

In the first twenty years of the post-Hiroshima era – 1946–66 according to the conventional calendar – men had fought, as already mentioned, forty 'minor' wars and civil wars tabulated by the Pentagon.[12] More than half of them were fought between Communists and non-Communists (China, Greece); the others were either 'anti-colonial' wars (Algeria, Indo-China), 'imperialist adventures' (Suez, Hungary, Bay of Pigs), or 'classical' wars between neighbours (India–Pakistan, Israel–Arabs). But this Pentagon list does not include crises like the Berlin blockade of 1950, and *coups d'état* like the defenestrations in Prague, 1948. As a French diplomat has put it: 'There are no longer such things as war and peace, just different levels of confrontations.'

These wars and civil wars were fought with conventional arms, mostly by nuclear have-nots. But at least on two occasions – Berlin, 1950 and Cuba, 1962 – we were on the brink of nuclear war; and all this in the first two decades since the year zero pH. If one extrapolates from these data into the future, the probability of disaster approaches statistical certainty.

A further aggravating factor is that nuclear devices, like other gadgets, will undergo the process of progressive miniaturization: they will become smaller and easier to make, so that in the long run effective global control of their manufacture will become impracticable on these grounds alone; in the foreseeable future they will be made and stored in large quantities, from windswept Alaska to sunny Stanleyville. It is as if a gang of delinquent children had been locked in a room filled with inflammable material, and provided with matchboxes – accompanied by the warning not to use them. Some social scientists have indeed estimated (to quote J. R. Platt again), that

> our 'half-life'* under these circumstances – that is, the probable number of years before these repeated confrontations add up to a 50–50 chance of destroying the human race forever – may be only about ten to twenty years. Obviously this is not an objectively testable number. Nevertheless the idea is clear. This is the first time in the history of the human race that babies – all babies everywhere, forever – have had such a slim chance of survival.[13]

There is indeed no convincing reason which could lead us to believe that the conflicts, crises, confrontations and wars of the past will not be repeated in varying parts of the world in the years, decades and centuries to come. Ever since the Second

---

* The term is borrowed from atomic physics: 'half-life' is the time taken for half the atoms of a radioactive isotope to disintegrate.

World War, the ideological, racial, ethnic tensions have been on the increase in Africa, Asia, Latin America. In the United States, in spite of all genuine efforts to find a solution, the racial problem is becoming more intractable; even Israel, prime victim of racial persecution, has its own underprivileged majority of coloured Jews. The lessons of the past have been wasted; history not only repeats itself, it seems to be labouring under a neurotic compulsion to do so. Thus in 1920 a town named Danzig on the eastern fringes of Europe was made into an enclave which could only be reached by a narrow corridor through foreign territory. This absurd arrangement became the pretext for World War Two. While it was still on, a town named Berlin, in the heart of Europe, was made into an enclave which could only be reached by a narrow corridor through foreign territory. This absurd repetition became the pretext which has already once brought us to the brink of war, and will in all probability do so again. Hegel wrote: 'What experience and history teach us is this – that people and governments have never learned anything from history, or acted on principles deduced from it.'

It has been said that the blood of martyrs fertilizes the earth. In fact it has been running down into the sewers, with a monotonously gurgling sound, as far as man can remember; and at whatever part of the world we look, there is scant evidence which would encourage us to hope that the gurgling will diminish or stop. If we discard the comforts of wishful thinking, we must expect that the motives and *loci* of potential conflict will continue to drift across the globe like high-pressure areas over a meteorological chart. And our only precarious safeguard against the ballooning of local into total conflict, mutual deterrence, will always remain dependent on uncontrollable psychological factors – the restraint or reckless-ness of fallible key individuals. Russian roulette is a game which cannot be played for long.

So long as we believed that our species as such was virtually immortal, with an astronomical lifespan before it, we could afford to wait patiently for that change of heart which, gradually or suddenly, would make love, peace and sweet reason prevail. But we no longer have that assurance of immortality, nor the unlimited time to wait for the moment when the lion will lie down with the lamb, the Arab with the Israeli, and the Commissar with the Yogi.

The conclusions, if we dare to draw them, are quite simple. Our biological evolution to all intents and purposes came to a standstill in Cro-Magnon days. Since we cannot in the foreseeable future expect the necessary change in human nature to arise by way of a spontaneous mutation, that is, by natural means, we must induce it by artificial means. We can only hope to survive as a species by developing techniques which supplant biological evolution. We must search for a cure for the schizophysiology inherent in man's nature, and the resulting split in our minds, which led to the situation in which we find ourselves.

'Tampering with Human Nature'

I believe that if we fail to find this cure, the old paranoid streak in man, combined with his new powers of destruction, must sooner or later lead to genosuicide. But I also believe that the cure is almost within reach of contemporary biology; and that with the proper concentration of efforts it might be produced within the lifetime of the generation which is now entering on the scene.

I am aware that this sounds over-optimistic, in contrast to the seemingly over-pessimistic views just expressed on the prospect ahead of us if we persist in carrying on in our paranoiac ways. I do not think these apprehensions are exaggerated, and I do not think that the idea of a cure for *homo sap.* is utopian. It is not inspired by science fiction, but based on a realistic assessment of the recent advances in several convergent branches of the life sciences. They do not provide a cure, but they indicate the area of research that may produce it.

I am also aware that any proposal which involves 'artificial tampering with human nature' is bound to provoke strong emotional resistances. These are partly based on prejudice, but partly on a healthy aversion against further intrusions into the privacy and sanctity of the individual by the excesses of social engineering, character engineering, various forms of brain-washing, and other threatening aspects of the air-conditioned nightmare surrounding us. On the other hand, ever since the first hunter wrapped his shivering frame into the hide of a dead animal, man has been tampering with his own nature, creating for himself an artificial environment which gradually transformed the face of the planet, and an artificial mode of existence without which he can no longer survive. There is no turning back on housing, clothing, artificial heating, cooked food; nor on spectacles, hearing aids, forceps, artificial limbs, anaesthetics, antiseptics, prophylactics, vaccines, and so forth.

We start tampering with human nature almost from the moment a baby is born, for one of the first routine measures is the universal practice to drop a solution of silver nitrate into the baby's eyes to protect it against *ophthalmia neonatorum*, a form of conjunctivitis frequently leading to blindness, caused by gonococci which, unknown to her, may have lurked in the mother's genital tract. This is followed, later on, by preventive vaccinations, compulsory in most civilized countries, against smallpox, typhoid and so on. To appreciate the value of these tamperings with the course of Nature, let us remember that the prevalence of smallpox among Red Indians was one of the main causes which made them lose their continent to the white man. In the seventeenth and eighteenth centuries it constituted a hazard to which everybody was exposed. Its ravages might have been even worse but for that intrepid lady,

Mary Wortley Montagu who learnt the ancient oriental practice of 'inoculation' from the Turks, and introduced it to England at the beginning of the eighteenth century. It consisted in infecting the person to be immunized with matter taken from mild smallpox cases – a rather dangerous procedure, but with a much lower fatality rate than 'natural' smallpox (the risk vanished only when Jenner discovered that vaccination with the attenuated virus of *cowpox* gave immunity against smallpox).

A less well-known case of tampering is the prevention of goitre and of a certain variety of cretinism associated with it. When I was a child, and was taken for the holidays to the Alps, the number of inhabitants of mountain valleys who had monstrous swellings in front of their necks, and the number of cretinous children in their families, was quite frightening. Today there is not a single case of goitre in the Tyrolean village where I spend part of the year, nor in the neighbouring valleys. It has been found that goitre is associated with a deficiency of iodine in the thyroid gland, and that the water in regions where the disease used to be endemic was hard and poor in iodine. Thus iodine was periodically added in small quantities to the drinking water or diet of the children, and goitre became virtually a thing of the past.

Evidently, man, or a certain breed of man, was biologically not equipped to live in environments with iodine-poor water, or to cope with the virus of smallpox, and the deadly micro-organisms of malaria or sleeping sickness. If we reverse the situation, we find that some microbes are equally ill-equipped for resisting other species of micro-organisms which we call antibiotics. Now microbes seem to have an enormous mutation rate (or some other method of hereditary adaptation), for, within a few years, they have evolved new drug-resistant strains. We humans cannot perform such evolutionary feats. But we can *simulate* major adaptive mutations by adding iodine to the drinking water, or by putting drops into the eyes of the newborn, to protect them from enemies against which our natural defences are inadequate.

In recent years biologists have discovered that every animal species which they studied – from flower beetles through rabbits to baboons – is equipped with instinctive behaviour-patterns which put a brake on excessive breeding, and keep the population-density in a given territory fairly constant, even when food is plentiful. When the density exceeds a certain limit, crowding produces stress-symptoms which affect the hormonal balance; rabbits and deer begin to die off from 'adrenal stress' without any sign of epidemic disease; the females of rats stop caring for their young, which perish, and abnormal sexual behaviour makes its appearance. Thus the ecological equilibrium in a given area is maintained not only by the relative distribution of animals, plants and micro-organisms, of predators and prey, but also by a kind of intra-specific feedback mechanism which adjusts the rate of breeding so as to keep the population at a stable level. The population of a given species in a given territory behaves in fact as a self-regulating social holon, governed by the in-stinctive canons of 'keeping distance' and maintaining average density.

But in this respect man is again unique – except perhaps for the suicidal lemmings. It seems almost as if in human popula-tions the ecological rule were reversed: the more crowded they are in slums, ghettoes and poverty-stricken areas, the faster they breed. In the past, the stabilizing factor was not the type of feedback mechanism which regulates the rate of breeding in animals, but the death-harvests of war, pestilence and infant mortality. However, already in biblical days, as we learn from the story of Onan, man compensated to some extent for the absence of instinctive breeding-controls by voluntary birth-control through *coitus interruptus* and other practices. Then, a century ago, when Louis Pasteur initiated the 'take-off' of the population curve, Charles Goodyear, rubber manufacturer and inventor (after whom the famous tyre company is named) invented the first artificial contraceptives. The modern methods of birth-control by intra-uterine coils and oral contraceptives represent a much more radical tampering with Nature on a more vital level. They interfere in a permanent (and yet by all indications non-injurious) manner with the physiological processes governing the oestrous cycle. Applied on a worldwide scale – as they must be if the impending catastrophe is to be prevented – they would amount to an *artificially simulated, adaptive mutation*.

Our species became a biological freak when somewhere on the way it lost the instinctual controls which in animals regulate the rate of breeding. It can only survive by inventing methods which imitate evolutionary mutation. We can no longer hope that Nature will provide the corrective remedy. We must provide it ourselves.

Prometheus Unhinged

Mutatis mutandis, can we invent a similar remedy for the schizophysiology of our nervous system, for the paranoid streak in man which made such an appalling mess of our history? And not only of the history of *homo sapiens*, but apparently of his near-human predecessors as well. Let us go back to Lorenz:

> Obviously instinctive behaviour mechanisms failed to cope with the new circumstances which culture unavoidably produced even at its very dawn. There is evidence that the first inventors of pebble tools, the African Australopithecines, promptly used their new weapons to kill not only game, but fellow members of their species as well. Peking Man, the Prometheus who learned to preserve fire, used it to roast his brothers: beside the first traces of the regular use of fire lie the mutilated and roasted bones of *Sinanthropus Pekinenis* himself.[14]

The Promethean myth has acquired an ugly twist: the giant reaching out to steal the lightning from the gods is insane. By all indications the trouble started with the sudden mush-rooming of the neocortex at a rate 'unprecedented in evolutionary history' (p 311). If we compress the whole history of life on earth, from its beginnings some 2,000 million years ago to the present, into a single day from midnight to midnight, then the age of mammals would begin about 11 PM; and the evolution from *Pithecantropus* (Java ape-man) to *Homo sapiens* – that is, the evolution of the human neocortex – would have taken place in the last forty-five seconds. The growth of the cortex, too, followed an exponential curve. Is it unreasonable to assume that at this explosive rate of the brain's development, which so widely overshot its mark, something may have gone wrong? More precisely, that the lines of communication between the very old and the brand-new structures were not developed sufficiently to guarantee their harmonious interplay, the hierarchic coordination of instinct and intelligence. Remembering the mistakes which occurred in the evolution of earlier versions of nervous systems – the arthropod brain choking its alimentary canal, the marsupial brain without adequate connections between the right and left hemispheres – we cannot help suspecting that something similar may have happened to us; and the combined evidence from neurophysiology, psychopathology and human history seems to support this hypothesis.

The neurophysiological evidence indicates, as we have seen, a dissonance between the reactions of neocortex and limbic system. Instead of functioning as integral parts in a hierarchic order, they lead a kind of agonized coexistence. To revert to an earlier metaphor: the rider has never gained complete control of the horse, and the horse asserts its whims in the most objectionable ways. We have also seen that the horse – the limbic system – has direct access to the emotion-generating, viscerally orientated centres in the hypothalamus; but the rider has no direct access to them. Moreover, the stirrups and reins by which the rider is meant to control the horse are inadequate. To quote MacLean once more: 'On the basis of neuronographic studies there appear to be no extensive "associational" connections between the limbic and the neocortex.'* There is no anatomical evidence for the intricate 'loops within loops' of feedbacks, of the delicate interplay of excitation and inhibition, which characterizes the nervous system in general. 'Both horse and man are very much alive to one another and to their environment, yet communication between them is limited. Both derive information and act upon it in a different way.'[15]

Here, then, is the anatomical substratum of the 'divided house of faith and reason' whose tenants are condemned to live in a state of 'controlled schizophrenia' – as the atomic spy Klaus Fuchs described it.

To go on preaching sweet reason to an inherently unreasonable species is, as history shows, a fairly hopeless enterprise. Biological evolution has let us down; we can only hope to survive if we develop techniques which supplant it by inducing the necessary changes in human nature. We may be able to prevent the demotic apocalypse by interfering with woman's oestrous cycle. We cannot cure our paranoic disposition by putting additional wiring circuits into our brains. But we may be able to achieve a cure, or at least a significant improvement, by directing research into the required channels.

---

* The article continues: 'This would indicate that the two depend almost entirely on vertical, rather than horizontal, lines of communication. The so-called diffuse projection system of the diencephalon offers one such possible relating system, but the evidence in this regard is still conflicting. There is ample justification, however, for assuming another system of connections through the reticular system of the midbrain. This part of the brain, which has been shown by Magoun and others to be essential to a state of wakefulness, has been found electrophysiologically to bear a reciprocal relationship to both the limbic and the neocortex. In addition there is anatomical and electrophysiological evidence that the central gray, which lies as a core within this reticulum and which plays a dynamogenous role in emotion, is related to the archicortex.'[15] This is what one means by 'inadequate' coordination.

Mutating into the Future

In 1961 the University of California San Francisco Medical Center organized a symposium on *Control of the Mind*. At the first session, Professor Holger Hydén of Goeteborg University made headlines in the San Francisco press, although the title of his highly technical paper – 'Biochemical Aspects of Brain Activity' – was hardly designed to appeal to the popular press. Hydén is one of the leading authorities in that field. The passage which created the sensation is quoted below (the reference to me is explained by the fact that I was a participant of the symposium):

> In considering the problem of control of the mind, the data give rise to the following question: would it be possible to change the fundamentals of emotion by inducing molecular changes in the biologically active substances in the brain? The RNA,* in particular, is the main target for such a speculation, since a molecular change of the RNA may lead to a change in the proteins being formed. One may phrase the question in different words to modify the emphasis: do the experimental data presented here provide means to modify the mental state by specifically induced chemical changes? Results pointing in that direction have been obtained; this work was carried out using a substance called tricyano-amino-propene.
>
> ... The application of a substance changing the rate of production and composition of RNA and provoking enzyme changes in the functional units of the central nervous system has both negative and positive aspects. There is now evidence that the administration of tricyano-aminopropene is followed by an increased suggestibility in man. This being the case, a defined change of such a functionally important substance as the RNA in the brain could be used for conditioning. The author is not referring specifically to tricyano-aminopropene, but to any substance inducing changes of biologically important molecules in the neurons and the glia and affecting the mental state in a negative direction. It is not difficult to imagine the possible uses to which a government in a police-

---

* Ribosenucleic acid, a key substance in the genetic apparatus.

controlled state could put this substance. For a time they would subject the population to hard conditions. Suddenly the hardship would be removed, and at the same time, the substance would be added to the tap water and the mass-communications media turned on. This method would be much cheaper, and would create more intriguing possibilities, than to let Ivanov treat Rubashov individually for a long time, as Koestler described in his book. On the other hand, a counter-measure against the effect of a substance such as tricyano-aminopropene is not difficult to imagine either.[16]

Leaving technical details aside, the implications are clear. Like any other human science, biochemistry can serve the powers of light or of darkness. Its dangers are terrifying; but we are now concerned with its beneficial possibilities. Let me quote another pertinent passage from Dean Saunders, of the San Francisco Medical School, at the *Control of the Mind* symposium:

> The great technological skill and ingenuity of the modern chemist has provided the medical scientist and the physician with an abundant array of new chemical compounds of varying and diverse structure which influence the central nervous system to distort, accelerate or depress the mental state and behavioural characteristics of the individual. The conference emphasized that many of these chemical agents possess a highly selective action on particular and discrete parts of the nervous system – so much so as to permit from an examination of their actions in man and animals an arrangement in order and rank. Those chemical agents thus offer, by a consideration of the relationships between chemical structure and biological action, the possibility of providing a vast array of drugs influencing the specific activity of the brain. Indeed, since such agents may either potentiate or attenuate one another, exhibit overlap in their actions, and demonstrate polarity in their effects on the brain, the very strong possibility is suggested of a full spectrum of chemical agents which can be used for the control of the mind in the majority of its activities.
>
> ... Here at our disposal, to be used wisely or unwisely, is an increasing array of agents that manipulate human beings ... It is now possible to act directly on the individual to modify his behaviour instead of, as in the past, indirectly through modification of the environment. This, then, constitutes a part of what Aldous Huxley has called 'The Final Revolution' ...[17]

I must comment on the last paragraph in this quotation. Huxley was haunted by the fear that this 'Final Revolution', brought about by the combined effect of drugs and the mass media, could create 'within a generation or so for entire societies a sort of painless concentration camp of the mind, in which people will have lost their liberties in the enjoyment of a dictatorship without tears'.[18] In other words, the state of affairs described in *Brave New World*. As an antidote, Huxley advocated the use of mescalin and other psychodelic drugs, to guide us along the eightfold path towards cosmic consciousness, mystic enlightenment and artistic creativity.

I have been for a long time an admirer of Huxley's personality and work, but in his last years I profoundly disagreed with him; and the points of disagreement will help to clarify the issue.

In *Heaven and Hell*, praising the benefits of mescalin, Huxley offered this advice to modern man in search of his soul: 'knowing as he does ... what are the chemical conditions of transcendental experience, the aspiring mystic should turn for technical help to the specialists in pharmacology, in biochemistry, in physiology and neurology ...'

Now this is precisely what I do *not* mean by the positive uses of psychopharmacology. In the first place, experimenting with mescalin or with LSD 25 does involve serious risks. But quite apart from this, it is fundamentally wrong, and naïve, to expect that drugs can present the mind with gratis gifts – put into it something which is not already there. Neither mystic insights, nor philosophic wisdom, nor creative power can be provided by pill or injection. The psycho-pharmacist cannot *add* to the faculties of the brain – but he can, at best, *eliminate* obstructions and blockages which impede their proper use. He cannot aggrandize us – but he can, within limits, normalize us; he cannot put additional circuits into the brain, but he can, again within limits, improve the coordination between existing ones, attenuate conflicts, prevent the blowing of fuses, and ensure a steady power supply. That is all the help we can ask for – but if we were able to obtain it, the benefits to mankind would be incalculable; it would be the 'Final Revolution' in a sense opposite to Huxley's – the breakthrough from maniac to man.

The 'we' in the previous sentence is not meant to refer to patients in the psychiatric ward or on the therapist's couch. Psychopharmacology will no doubt play an increasing part in the treatment of mental disorders in the clinical sense;* but that is not the point. What we are concerned with is a cure for the paranoic streak in what we call normal people, ie, mankind as a whole: an artificially simulated, adaptive mutation to bridge the rift between the phylogenetically old and new brain, between instinct and intellect, emotion and reason. If it is within our reach to increase man's suggestibility, it will be soon within our reach to do the opposite, to counteract misplaced devotion and that militant enthusiasm, both murderous and suicidal, which we see reflected in the pages of the daily newspaper. The most urgent task of biochemistry is the search for a remedy in the 'increasing range', as Saunders put it, 'of the spectrum of chemical agents which can be used for the control of the mind'. It is not utopian to believe that it can and will be done. Our present tranquillizers, barbiturates, stimulants, anti-depressants and combinations thereof, are merely a first step towards a more sophisticated range of aids to promote a coordinated, harmonious state of mind. Not the unruffled ataraxia sought by the Stoics, not the ecstasy of the dancing dervish, nor the Pop-Nirvana created by Huxley's 'soma' pills – but a state of dynamic equilibrium in which thought and emotion are reunited, and hierarchic order is restored.

* As this book goes to press, the American journal, *Archives of General Psychiatry*, reports experiments at Tulane University which suggest the possibility of a chemical cure for schizophrenia (Gould, D., 'An Antibody in Schizophrenics'. London: *New Scientist*, 2.2.1967.)

A Plea to the Phantom Reader

I am aware that 'control of the mind' and 'manipulating human beings' have sinister undertones. Who is to control the controls, manipulate the manipulators? Assuming that we succeed in synthetizing a hormone which acts as a mental stabilizer on the lines indicated – how are we to propagate its global use to induce that beneficial mutation? Are we to ram it down people's throats, or put it into the tap water?

The answer seems obvious. No legislation, no compulsory measures were needed to persuade Greeks and Romans to partake of 'the juice of the grape that gives joy and oblivion'. Sleeping pills, pep pills, tranquillizers have, for better or worse, spread across the world with a minimum of publicity or official encouragement. They have spread because people liked their effect, and even accepted unpleasant or harmful after-effects. A mental stabilizer would produce neither euphoria, nor sleep, nor mescalin visions, nor cabbage-like equanimity – it would in fact have no noticeably specific effect, except promoting cerebral coordination and harmonizing thought and emotion; in other words, restore the integrity of the split hierarchy. Its use would spread because people like feeling healthy rather than unhealthy in body or mind. It would spread as vaccination has spread, and contraception has spread, not by coercion but by enlightened self-interest.

The first noticeable result would perhaps be a sudden drop in the crime and suicide rate in certain regions and social groups where the new Pill became fashionable. From here on the developments are as unpredictable as the consequences of James Watt's or Pasteur's discoveries had been. Some Swiss canton might decide, after a public referendum, to add the new substance to the chlorine in the water supply,* for a

* Incidentally, even the Don't-Tamper-with-Nature Brigade no longer seriously objects to chlorine or other antiseptics being put into tap water.

trial period, and other countries might follow their example. Or there might be an international fashion among the young, replacing weirdy-beards and purple hearts. In one way or the other, the mutation would get under way.

It is possible that totalitarian countries would try to resist it. But today even Iron Curtains have become porous; hot jazz, mini skirts, discotheques and other bourgeois inventions are spreading irresistibly. When the ruling élite started experimenting with the new medicine, and discovered that it made them see things in an altogether different light – then, and only then, would the world be ripe for a global disarmament conference which is not a sinister farce. And should there be a transitional period during which one side alone went ahead with the cure, while the other persisted in its paranoid ways, there would be none of the risks of unilateral disarmament involved; on the contrary, the mutated side would be stronger because more rational in its long-term policies, less frightened and less hysterical.

I do not think this is science fiction; and I am confident that the type of reader to whom this book is addressed will not think so either. Every writer has a favourite type of imaginary reader, a friendly phantom but highly critical, whose opinion is the only one that matters, with whom he is engaged in a continuous, exhausting dialogue. I feel sure, as I said, that my friendly phantom reader has sufficient imagination to extrapolate from the recent, breathtaking advances of biology into the future, and to concede that the solution outlined here is in the realm of the possible. What worries me is that he will not like it; that he might be repelled and disgusted by the idea that we should rely for our salvation on molecular chemistry instead of a spiritual rebirth. I share his distress, but I see no alternative. I hear him exclaim: 'By trying to sell us your Pills, you are adopting that crudely materialistic attitude and naïve scientific hubris, which you pretend to oppose.' I still oppose it. But I do not believe that it is 'materialistic' to take a realistic view of the condition of man; nor is it *hubris* to feed thyroid extracts to children who would otherwise grow into cretins. To use our brain to cure its own shortcomings seems to me a brave and dedicated enterprise. Like the reader, I would prefer to set my hopes on moral persuasion by word and example. But we are a mentally sick race, and as such deaf to persuasion. It has been tried from the age of the prophets to Albert Schweitzer; and the result has been, as Swift said, that 'we have just enough religion to make us hate, but not enough to love each other'. That applies to all religions, theistic or secular, whether taught by Moses or Marx or Mao Tse Tung; and Swift's anguished cry: 'not die here in a rage, like a poisoned rat in a hole' has acquired an urgency as never before.

Nature has let us down, God seems to have left the receiver off the hook, and time is running out. To hope for salvation to be synthesized in the laboratory may seem materialistic, crankish, or naïve; but, to tell the truth, there is a Jungian twist to it – for it reflects the ancient alchemist's dream to concoct the *elixir vitae*. What we expect from it, however, is not eternal life, nor the transformation of base metal into gold, but the transformation of *homo maniacus* into *homo sapiens*. When man decides to take his fate into his own hands, that possibility will be within reach.

APPENDIX I

GENERAL PROPERTIES OF OPEN
HIERARCHICAL SYSTEMS (OHS)

1. The Janus Effect

1.1　The organism in its structural aspect is not an aggregation of elementary parts, and in its functional aspects not a chain of elementary units of behaviour.

1.2　The organism is to be regarded as a multi-levelled hierarchy of semi-autonomous sub-wholes, branching into sub-wholes of lower order, and so on. Sub-wholes on any level of the hierarchy are referred to as *holons*.

1.3　Parts and wholes in an absolute sense do not exist in the domain of life. The concept of the holon is intended to reconcile the atomistic and holistic approaches.

1.4　Biological holons are self-regulating open systems which display both the autonomous properties of wholes and the dependent properties of parts. This dichotomy is present on every level of every type of hierarchic organization, and is referred to as the *Janus Effect* or Janus principle.

1.5　More generally, the term 'holon' may be applied to any stable biological or social sub-whole which displays rule-governed behaviour and/or structural Gestalt-constancy. Thus organelles and homologous organs are evolutionary holons; morphogenetic fields are ontogenetic holons; the ethologist's 'fixed action-patterns' and the subroutines of acquired skills are behavioural holons; phonemes, morphemes, words, phrases are linguistic holons; individuals, families, tribes, nations are social holons.

2. Dissectibility

2.1   Hierarchies are 'dissectible' into their constituent branches, on which the holons form the nodes; the branching lines represent the channels of communication and control.

2.2   The number of levels which a hierarchy comprises is a measure of its 'depth', and the number of holons on any given level is called its 'span' (Simon).

3. Rules and Strategies

3.1   Functional holons are governed by fixed sets of rules and display more or less flexible strategies.

3.2   The rules – referred to as the system's *canon* – determine its invariant properties, its structural configuration and/or functional pattern.

3.3   While the canon defines the permissible steps in the holon's activity, the strategic selection of the actual step among permissible choices is guided by the contingencies of the environment.

3.4   The canon determines the rules of the game, strategy decides the course of the game.

3.5   The evolutionary process plays variations on a limited number of canonical themes. The constraints imposed by the evolutionary canon are illustrated by the phenomena of homology, homeoplasy, parallelism, convergence and the *loi du balancement*.

3.6   In ontogeny, the holons at successive levels represent successive stages in the development of tissues. At each step in the process of differentiation, the genetic canon imposes further constraints on the holon's developmental potentials, but it retains sufficient flexibility to follow one or another alternative developmental pathway, within the range of its competence, guided by the contingencies of the environment.

3.7   Structurally, the mature organism is a hierarchy of parts within parts. Its 'dissectibility' and the relative autonomy of its constituent holons are demonstrated by transplant surgery.

3.8   Functionally, the behaviour of organisms is governed by 'rules of the game' which account for its coherence, stability and specific pattern.

3.9 Skills, whether inborn or acquired, are functional hierarchies, with sub-skills as holons, governed by sub-rules.

4. Integration and Self-Assertion

4.1 Every holon has the dual tendency to preserve and assert its individuality as a quasi-autonomous whole; and to function as an integrated part of an (existing or evolving) larger whole. This polarity between the Self-Assertive (S-A) and Integrative (INT) tendencies is inherent in the concept of hierarchic order; and a universal characteristic of life.

The S-A tendencies are the dynamic expression of the holon's wholeness, the INT tendencies of its partness.

4.2 An analogous polarity is found in the interplay of cohesive and separative forces in stable inorganic systems, from atoms to galaxies.

4.3 The most general manifestation of the INT tendencies is the reversal of the Second Law of Thermodynamics in open systems feeding on negative entropy (Schrödinger), and the evolutionary trend towards 'spontaneously developing states of greater heterogeneity and complexity' (Herrick).

4.4 Its specific manifestations on different levels range from the symbiosis of organelles and colonial animals, through the cohesive forces in herds and flocks, to the integrative bonds in insect states and Primate societies. The complementary manifestations of the S-A tendencies are competition, individualism, and the separative forces of tribalism, nationalism, etc.

4.5 In ontogeny, the polarity is reflected in the docility and determination of growing tissues.

4.6 In adult behaviour, the self-assertive tendency of functional holons is reflected in the stubbornness of instinct rituals (fixed action-patterns), of acquired habits (handwriting, spoken accent), and in the stereotyped routines of thought; the integrative tendency is reflected in flexible adaptations, improvizations, and creative acts which initiate new forms of behaviour.

4.7 Under conditions of stress, the S-A tendency is manifested in the aggressive–defensive, adrenergic type of emotions, the INT tendency in the self-transcending (participatory, identificatory) type of emotions.

4.8   In social behaviour, the canon of a social holon represents not only constraints imposed on its actions, but also embodies maxims of conduct, moral imperatives and systems of value.

5. Triggers and Scanners

5.1   Output hierarchies generally operate on the trigger-release principle, where a relatively simple, implicit or coded signal releases complex, pre-set mechanisms.

5.2   In phylogeny, a favourable gene-mutation may, through homeorhesis (Waddington) affect the development of a whole organ in a harmonious way.

5.3   In ontogeny, chemical triggers (enzymes, inducers, hormones) release the genetic potentials of differentiating tissues.

5.4   In instinctive behaviour, sign-releasers of a simple kind trigger off Innate Releasive Mechanisms (Lorenz).

5.5   In the performance of learnt skills, including verbal skills, a generalized implicit command is spelled out in explicit terms on successive lower echelons which, once triggered into action, activate their sub-units in the appropriate strategic order, guided by feedbacks.

5.6   A holon on the n level of an output-hierarchy is represented on the (n + 1) level as a unit, and triggered into action as a unit. A holon, in other words, is a system of relata which is represented on the next higher level as a relatum.

5.7   In social hierarchies (military, administrative), the same principles apply.

5.8   Input hierarchies operate on the reverse principle; instead of triggers, they are equipped with 'filter'-type devices (scanners, 'resonators', classifiers) which strip the input of noise, abstract and digest its relevant contents, according to that particular hierarchy's criteria of relevance. 'Filters' operate on every echelon through which the flow of information must pass on its ascent from periphery to centre, in social hierarchies and in the nervous system.

5.9   Triggers convert coded signals into complex output patterns. Filters convert complex input patterns into coded signals. The former may be compared to digital-to-analogue converters, the latter to analogue-to-digital converters (Miller, Pribram et al).

5.10   In perceptual hierarchies, filtering devices range from habituation and the efferent control of receptors, through the constancy phenomena, to pattern-recognition in space or time, and to the decoding of linguistic and other forms of meaning.

5.11   Output hierarchies spell, concretize, particularize. Input hierarchies digest, abstract, generalize.

6. Arborization and Reticulation

6.1   Hierarchies can be regarded as 'vertically' arborizing structures whose branches interlock with those of other hierarchies at a multiplicity of levels and form 'horizontal' networks: arborization and reticulation are complementary principles in the architecture of organisms and societies.

6.2   Conscious experience is enriched by the cooperation of several perceptual hierarchies in different sense-modalities, and within the same sense-modality.

6.3   Abstractive memories are stored in skeletonized form, stripped of irrelevant detail, according to the criteria of relevance of each perceptual hierarchy.

6.4   Vivid details of quasi-eidetic clarity are stored owing to their emotive relevance.

6.5   The impoverishment of experience in memory is counteracted to some extent by the cooperation in recall of different perceptual hierarchies with different criteria of relevance.

6.6   In sensory-motor coordination, local reflexes are shortcuts on the lowest level, like loops connecting traffic streams moving in opposite directions on a highway.

6.7   Skilled sensory-motor routines operate on higher levels through networks of proprioceptive and exteroceptive feedback loops within loops, which function as servo-mechanisms and keep the rider on his bicycle in a state of self-regulating, kinetic homeostasis.

6.8   While in S-R theory the contingencies of environment determine behaviour, in OHS theory they merely guide, correct and stabilize pre-existing patterns of behaviour (P. Weiss).

6.9   While sensory feedbacks guide motor activities, perception in its turn is dependent on these activities, such as the various scanning motions of the eye, or the humming of a tune in aid of its auditory recall. The perceptual and motor hierarchies are so intimately co-operating on every level that to draw a categorical distinction between 'stimuli' and 'responses' becomes meaningless; they have become 'aspects of feedback loops' (Miller, Pribram et al).

6.10   Organisms and societies operate in a hierarchy of environments, from the local environment of each holon to the 'total field', which may include imaginary environments derived from extrapolation in space and time.

7. Regulation Channels

7.   The higher echelons in a hierarchy are not normally in direct communication with lowly ones, and vice versa; signals are transmitted through 'regulation channels', one step at a time, up or down.

7.1   The pseudo-explanations of verbal behaviour and other human skills as the manipulation of words, or the chaining of operants, leaves a void between the apex of the hierarchy and its terminal branches, between thinking and spelling.

7.2   The short-circuiting of intermediary levels by directing conscious attention at processes which otherwise function automatically, tends to cause disturbances ranging from awkwardness to psychosomatic disorders.

8. Mechanization and Freedom

8.   Holons on successively higher levels of the hierarchy show increasingly complex, more flexible and less predictable patterns of activity, while on successive lower levels we find increasingly mechanized, stereotyped and predictable patterns.

8.1   All skills, whether innate or acquired, tend with increasing practice to become automatized routines. This process can be described as the continual transformation of 'mental' into 'mechanical' activities.

8.2   Other things being equal, a monotonous environment facilitates mechanization.

8.3   Conversely, new or unexpected contingencies require decisions to be referred to higher levels of the hierarchy, an upward shift of controls from 'mechanical' to 'mindful' activities.

8.4   Each upward shift is reflected by a more vivid and precise consciousness of the ongoing activity; and, since the variety of alternative choices increases with the increasing complexity on higher levels, each upward shift is accompanied by the subjective experience of freedom of decision.

8.5   The hierarchic approach replaces dualistic theories by a serialistic hypothesis in which 'mental' and 'mechanical' appear as relative attributes of a unitary process, the dominance of one or the other depending on changes in the level of control of ongoing operations.

8.6   Consciousness appears as an emergent quality in phylogeny and ontogeny, which, from primitive beginnings, evolves towards more complex and precise states. It is the highest manifestation of the Integrative Tendency (4.3) to extract order out of disorder, and information out of noise.

8.7   The self can never be completely represented in its own awareness, nor can its actions be completely predicted by any conceivable information-processing device. Both attempts lead to infinite regress.

9. Equilibrium and Disorder

9.1   An organism or society is said to be in dynamic equilibrium if the S-A and INT tendencies of its holons counterbalance each other.

9.2   The term 'equilibrium' in a hierarchic system does not refer to relations between parts on the same level, but to the relation between part and whole (the whole being represented by the agency which controls the part from the next higher level).

9.3   Organisms live by transactions with their environment. Under normal conditions, the stresses set up in the holons involved in the transaction are of a transitory nature, and equilibrium will be restored on its completion.

9.4   If the challenge to the organism exceeds a critical limit, the balance may be upset, the over-excited holon may tend to get out of control, and to assert itself to the detriment of the whole, or monopolize its functions – whether the holon be an organ, a cognitive structure (idée fixe), an individual, or a social group. The same may happen if the coordinative powers of the whole are so weakened that it is no longer able to control its parts (Child).

9.5   The opposite type of disorder occurs when the power of the whole over its parts erodes their autonomy and individuality. This may lead to a regression of the INT tendencies from mature forms of social integration to primitive forms of identification, and to the quasi-hypnotic phenomena of group-psychology.

9.6   The process of identification may arouse vicarious emotions of the aggressive type.

9.7   The rules of conduct of a social holon are not reducible to the rules of conduct of its members.

9.8   The egotism of the social holon feeds on the altruism of its members.

10. Regeneration

10.1   Critical challenges to an organism or society can produce degenerative or regenerative effects.

10.2   The regenerative potential of organisms and societies manifests itself in fluctuations from the highest level of integration down to earlier, more primitive levels, and up again to a new, modified pattern. Processes of this type seem to play a major part in biological and mental evolution, and are symbolized in the universal death-and-rebirth motive in mythology.

NB.   The concept of the Holon, and of the Open Hierarchic System, attempts to reconcile atomism and holism. Some of the propositions listed above may appear trivial, some rest on incomplete evidence, others will need correcting and qualifying. They are merely intended to provide a basis for discussion among kindred spirits in both cultures, in search of an alternative to the robot image of man.

The controversial issues discussed in Part Three of this volume were not included in this list.

ON NOT FLOGGING DEAD HORSES*

The initials SPCDH stand for 'Society for the Prevention of Cruelty to Dead Horses'. It is a secret society with international ramifications and with a considerable influence on the intellectual climate of our time. I must mention a few examples of its activities.

The German Government during the war killed six million civilians in its death factories. This was at first kept secret; when the facts seeped through, the SPCDH took the line that to keep harping on them and bringing those responsible to trial was unfair and in bad taste – flogging a dead horse.

The Soviet Government, during the years of Stalin's rule, committed barbarities on an equal scale, though in a different style. If you tried to call public attention to them in the progressive circles of the West, you were denounced as a cold warrior, slanderer and maniac. When the facts were officially admitted by Stalin's successor, the issue was instantly classified by the SPCDH as a dead horse, although it went on ravaging other countries from Peking to Berlin.

English insularism, class distinctions, social snobbery, trial-by-accent, are all declared to be dead horses, and the inane neighings that fill the air must be emanating from ghosts. The same applies to American dollar-worship, materialism, conformism. You can continue the list as a parlour game.

In the Sciences, the SPCDH is particularly active. We are constantly assured that the crudely mechanistic nineteenth-century conceptions in biology, medicine, psychology are dead, and yet one constantly comes up against them in the columns of textbooks, technical journals, and in lecture rooms. In all this, Behaviourist

* See p 18, etc.

psychology occupies a strategic key-position. This is the case not only in the United States, where the Watson-Hull-Skinner tradition is still immensely powerful and keeps an invisible stranglehold (by 'negative reinforcements') on academic psychology. In England, Behaviourism has entered into an alliance with logical positivism and linguistic philosophy; but perhaps its most ominous influence is on clinical psychiatry. 'Behaviour therapy', as practised for instance at Maudsley Hospital, is symptom-therapy in its crudest form, based on Pavlovian and Skinnerian conditioning. The philosophy behind it is summed up in the slogan of our leading Behavioural therapist, H. J. Eysenck:*
'There is no neurosis underlying the symptoms, only the symptom itself.' (In a memorable attack on Eysenck, Kathleen Nott remarked that 'a "symptom" is always *of* something', and pointed out the preposterous implications of the slogan.[1])

But how is it to be explained that while Behaviourism is still floating like a dense smog over the landscape, so many scientists of the younger generation, who are almost stifled by it, keep pretending that the sky is blue, and Behaviourism a matter of the past? Partly, I think, for the reasons mentioned earlier on page 18 though they honestly believe that they have outgrown the sterile orthodoxy of their elders, its terminology and jargon have got into their bloodstream, and they cannot get away from thinking in terms of stimulus, response, conditioning, reinforcement, operants, and so on. Sidney Hook once wrote that 'Aristotle projected the grammar of the Greek language on the cosmos', and it is hardly an exaggeration to say that Pavlov, Watson and Skinner achieved a similar feat when they injected their reflex-philosophy into the sciences of life. Academics, brought up in that tradition, may reject the more obvious absurdities of Watson and Skinner, but nevertheless continue to employ their terminology and methodology, and thus remain unconsciously tied to the axioms implied in them.

A personal experience – one among many, and of a quite harmless sort – may serve as an illustration. When the American edition of *The Act of Creation* was published, Professor George A. Miller of Harvard University wrote an article-review about it in that excellent monthly,

---

* Professor in Psychology in the University of London, and Director of the Psychological Department at the Institute of Psychiatry (Maudsley and Bethlehem Royal Hospitals).

the *Scientific American*. It went on for nine columns, so there could be no misunderstanding due to shortage of space. It is not my intention to bore the reader by answering Miller's criticism of the theory proposed in the book – which would be out of place here; I am only concerned with his attitude to Behaviourism. This attitude is known, from his books and writings, as one of almost passionate rejection of Skinner, S-R theory, and the flat-earth approach in general. And yet, after referring to the attack on the Behaviourist position in *The Act of Creation*, Miller continued (his italics):

> Attacks on stimulus-response theories (which represent modern associationism) are of course nothing new. When one attacks strict stimulus-response Behaviourism these days, one is on the side of the big battalions. Yet Koestler writes as though it were still the 1930s and Behaviourism were in its prime. In 1964 most psychologists who still work in this tradition have introduced hypothetical mechanisms to mediate between stimulus and response. *They* think they are working on exactly the kind of processes Koestler calls bisociation; they are sure to be angered by Koestler's sarcastic misrepresentation of the current situation, and I cannot say that I blame them.[2]

Now I mentioned earlier on page 38 that the 'hypothetical mechanism' which the Behaviourists introduced 'to mediate between stimulus and response' are (as the term itself betrays) no more than face-saving devices. Even Behaviourists had to admit that the same stimulus S (eg, the fall of an apple) may produce a variety of different responses (eg, the theory of universal gravity); and that there must be something happening in the person's head between the S and the R, which they had left out of account. So they decided to call that something – which should be the principal concern of any psychology worth its name – 'hypothetical mechanisms' (or 'intervening variables'); and then promptly swept it under the carpet so that they might return, with a clean conscience, to their rat experiments. It was a naïvely transparent manoeuvre of evasion, and Professor Miller is of course fully aware of this. In his most thought-provoking book (which I have repeatedly quoted[3]) there is no mention whatsoever of 'hypothetical mechanisms which mediate between S and R', because he rejects the whole S-R concept with justified scorn as an anachronism (p 124 n). He is not only 'on the side of the winning battalions', but even a sort of battalion commander. Two columns after rising to the defence of Behaviourism against my 'sarcastic misrepresentations' he declares that, as regards the philosophical background 'I can admire Koestler's courageous attempt to clean out what obviously seem to him the Augean Stables of psychology. I share most of his prejudices and approve most of his aims.' Yet another column further down, at the end of the article, he concludes that perhaps, after all, the Behaviourists today are right (dead horses in Augean Stables?).

I have mentioned this episode because it beautifully exemplifies that ambivalence I have been talking about. Behaviourism was the milk which this generation of scientists imbibed in their cradle; and even if it was bottle-fed and made of dry powder, *you* may criticise your mum, but if a stranger does it, beware. Dissident Catholics, Marxists, Freudians, are liable to the same deep-rooted ambivalence. They may be doubters or rebels, but when the faith which they have abandoned is attacked from outside, they must rise to its defence; and as a last resort they will pretend that it is dead anyway, and not worth bothering about. Hence the SPCDH.

A Jesuit priest, whom I much admire, was once taken to task about the temperature and other conditions in Hell. He obviously resented these crude remarks, but replied with a sweet smile that though Hell exists, it is kept permanently empty by a loving God; so why revive this outdated controversy? . . . Yet millions and millions of believers have lived, loved and died poisoned by mortal fear of everlasting Hell.

I believe that the ultimate effects of ratomorphic philosophy are no less pernicious, though it acts in more indirect and devious ways. I shall conclude with another quotation from v. Bertalanffy, with whose views on this subject I strongly sympathize:

Let us face the fact: a large part of modern psychology is a sterile and pompous scholasticism which, with the blinkers of preconceived notions or superstitions, doesn't see the obvious; which covers the triviality of its results and ideas with a preposterous language bearing no resemblance to normal English or sound theory, and which provides modern society with the techniques for the progressive stultification of mankind. It has been justly said that American positivist philosophy – and the same even more applies to psychology – has achieved the rare feat of being both extremely boring and frivolous in its unconcern with human issues.

Basic for interpretation of animal and human behaviour was the stimulus-response scheme. So far as it is not innate or instinctive, behaviour is said to be shaped by outside influences that have met the organism in the past: classical conditioning after Pavlov, reinforcement after Skinner, early childhood experience after Freud. Hence training, education and human life in general are essentially responses to outside conditions: beginning in early childhood with toilet training and other manipulations whereby socially acceptable behaviour is gratified, undesirable behaviour blocked; continuing with education which is best carried through according to Skinnerian principles of reinforcement of correct responses and by means of teaching machines; and ending in adult man where affluent society makes everybody happy conditioning him, in a strictly scientific manner, by the mass media into the perfect consumer. Hypothetical mechanisms, intervening variables, auxiliary hypotheses have been introduced – without changing the basic concepts or general outlook. But what we need are not some hypothetical mechanisms better to explain some aberrations of the behaviour of the laboratory rat; what we need is a new conception of man.

I don't care a jot whether Professor A, B or C have modified Watson, Hull and Freud here and there and have replaced their blunt statements by more qualified and sophisticated circumlocutions. I do care a lot that the spirit is still all-pervading in our society; reducing man to the lower aspects of his animal nature, manipulating him into a feeble-minded automaton of consumption or a marionette of political power, systematically stultifying him by a perverse system of education, in short, dehumanising him ever farther by means of a sophisticated psychological technology.

It is the expressed or implicit contention that there is no essential difference between rat and man which makes American psychology so profoundly disturbing. When the intellectual élite, the thinkers and leaders, see in man nothing but an overgrown rat, then it is time to be alarmed.[4]

REFERENCES

PREFACE

1, Hardy (1965). 2, Thorpe (1966A). 3, Lorenz (1966).

PART ONE: ORDER

I. THE POVERTY OF PSYCHOLOGY

1, Watson (1913) pp 158–67. 2, Watson (1928) p 6. 3, Loc. cit. 4, Burt (1962) p 229. 5, Skinner (1953) pp 30–1. 6, Harlow (1953) pp 23–32. 7, Skinner (1953) p 150. 8, Hull (1943) p 56. 9, Skinner (1953) pp 108–9. 10, Skinner (1938) p 22. 11, Watson (1928) p 6. 12, Skinner (1938) p 21. 13, Ibid, p 62. 14, Skinner (1953) p 65. 15, Chomsky (1959). 16, Skinner (1957) p 163. 17, Ibid, p 438. 18, Ibid, p 439. 18a, Ibid, p 150. 19, Ibid, p 206. 19a, Watson (1928) pp 198 ff. 20, Skinner (1953) p 252. 21, Watson (1928) pp 3–6. 22, Sherrington (1906) p 8. 23, Herrick (1961) pp 253–4. 24, Watson (1928) p 11.

II. THE CHAIN OF WORDS AND THE TREE OF LANGUAGE

1, Calvin, ed. (1961). 2, Op cit, pp 376–8. 3, Skinner, quoted by Chomsky (1959) p 548. 4, Liberman, Cooper et al. (1965). 5, Lashley (1951) p 116. 6, McNeill (1966). 7, Brown (1965). 8, McNeill, op cit. 9, Ibid. 10, Quoted by Lashley (1951) p 117. 11, Popper (1959) p 280. 12, James (1890) Vol I, p 253. 13, Skinner (1957). 14, Miller (1964A).

III. THE HOLON

1, Needham, J. (1932). 2, Simon (1962). 3, Jacobson (1955). 4, Simon, op cit. 5, Jenkins (1965).

IV. INDIVIDUALS AND DIVIDUALS

1, Simon, op cit. 2, Sager (1965). 3, v. Bertalanffy (1952) pp 48, 50.
4, Dunbar (1946). 5, Weiss and Taylor (1960). 6, Pollock (1965).

V. TRIGGERS AND FILTERS

1, Thorpe (1956) pp 37–8. 2, Bartlett (1958). 3, Gregory (1966) Chapter
11. 4, Kottenhoff (1957). 5, Lashley (1951) p 128.

VI. A MEMORY FOR FORGETTING

1, Koestler and Jenkins (1965A). 2, Koestler (1964) pp ·24–5. 3, Jaensch
(1930), Kluever (1931). 4, Drever (1962). 5, Simon, op cit.

VII. THE HELMSMAN

1, Coghill (1929). 2, Cannon (1939). 3, Wiener (1948) pp 113–14. 4,
Weiss (1951) p 141. 5, v. Bertalanffy (1952) p 119. 6, Miller et al. (1960)
pp 18, 30.

VIII. HABIT AND IMPROVIZATION

1, Thorpe (1956) p 19. 1a, Baehrends (1941). 2, Hingston (1926–7),
quoted by Thorpe (1956) p 39. 3, Thorpe (1956) p 262. 4, Tinbergen
(1953) p 116. 5, v. Bertalanffy (1952) pp 17–18.

PART TWO: BECOMING

IX. THE STRATEGY OF EMBRYOS

1, Huxley, J. (1954) p 14. 1a, Kuhn (1962). 2, Clayton (1964) p 70.
3, Simpson, Pittendrigh and Tiffany (1957) p 330. 4, Bonner (1965)
p 136. 5, Ibid, p 142.

X. EVOLUTION: THEME AND VARIATIONS

1, Waddington (1952). 1a Medawar (1960) p 62. 2, Huxley, J. (1954)
p 12. 3, Waddington (1952). 4, Whyte (1965) p 50. 5, Gorini (1966).
6, de Beer (1940) p 148 and Hardy (1965) p 212, 7, Hardy (1965) p 211.
8, St Hilaire, quoted by Hardy (1965) p 50. 9, Goethe. Editor's Preface

(1872) pp xii–xiii. 10, Thompson (1942) pp 1082–4. 11, Simpson, Pitten-drigh and Tiffany (1957) p 472. 12, Simpson (1949) p 180. 13, v. Bertalanffy (1952) p 105. 14, Spurway (1949), quoted by Whyte (1965). 15, Whyte (1965).

XI. EVOLUTION CTD: PROGRESS BY INITIATIVE

1, Simpson (1950), quoted by Hardy (1965) p 14. 2, Sinnott (1961) p 45. 3, Muller (1943), quoted by Sinnott (1961) p 45. 4, Simpson et al (1957) p 354. 5, Coghill (1929). 6, Hardy (1965) p 170. 7, Ibid, p 178. 8, Ibid, p 176. 9, Ibid, pp 172, 192, 193. 10, Waddington (1957) p 182. 11, Ibid, pp 166–7. 12, Tinbergen (1953) p 55. 13, Ewer (1960), quoted by Hardy (1965) p 187. 14, Herrick (1961) p 117 f. 15, Waddington (1957) pp 180 seq. 16, Ibid, pp 64–5.

XII. EVOLUTION CTD: UNDOING AND RE-DOING

1, Huxley (1964) pp 12–13. 2, Ibid, p 13. 3, Young (1950) p 74. 4, de Beer (1940) p 118. 5, Child (1915) p 467. 5a, de Beer, op cit, p 119. 6, Ibid, p 72. 7, Haldane (1932) p 150. 7a, Garstang (1922). 8, Muller (1943) p 109. 9, Krechevsky (1932).

XIII. THE GLORY OF MAN

1, Needham, A. E. (1961). 2, See, eg, Hamburger (1955). 3, Ibid. 4, Ibid. 5, Lashley (1960) p 239. 6, Lashley (1929). 6a, Kris (1964). 7, Bruner and Postman (1949). 8, Quoted by Hadamard (1949). 9, Humphrey (1951) p 1. 10, Bartlett (1958). 11, Bruner and Postman (1949). 12, McKellar (1957). 13, Kubie (1958).

XIV. THE GHOST IN THE MACHINE

1, Herrick (1961) p 51. 2, v. Bertalanffy (1952) p 128. 3, Herrick (1961) p 47. 4, Schrödinger (1944) p 72. 5, Wiener (1948) pp 76–8. 6, Spencer (1862). 6a, Whyte (1949) p 35. 6b, Schrödinger (1944) p 88. 7, v. Bertalanffy (1952) p 112. 8, Waddington (1961). 9, Ryle (1950). 10, Gellner (1959). 11, Smythies (1965). 12, Beloff (1962). 13, Gellner (1959). 14, Kneale (1962). 15, Penfield (1961). 16, Ibid. 17, Farber and Wilson, eds. (1961). 18, Eccles, ed. (1966). 19, Sherrington (1906). 20, Thorpe (1966B) p 542. 21, Ibid, p 495. 22, Sperry (1960) p 306. 23, Adrian (1966) p 245. 24, Koestler (1945) pp 205–6. 25, MacKay (1966) p 439. 26, Popper (1950). 27, Polanyi (1966). 28, MacKay (1966) pp 252-3. 29, Koestler (1959) and (1964). 30, Quoted by Dubos (1950) p 391 f.

PART THREE: DISORDER

XV. THE PREDICAMENT OF MAN

1, Freud (1920) pp 3-5. 2, Schachtel (1963). 3, Berlyne (1960) p 170. 4, Child (1924). 5, Arendt (1963). 6, Hogg (1961) pp 44-5. 21. 7, Prescott (1964) pp 59, 60, 61. 8, Ibid, p 62. 9, Maslow (1962). 10, Jung (1928) p 395. 11, Kretchmer (1934). 12, Oswald (1966) pp 118-19. 13, Drever (1962). 14, Freud (1922). 15, v. Hayek (1966). 16, Koestler (1940) p 119. 17, Koestler (1945) pp 127-8. 18, *The Times*, London, 27.7.66. 19, Empson (1964). 20, Koestler (1945) p 121. 20a, Koestler (1954). 21, Suzuki (1959) p 33. 22, Koestler (1950) pp 42-3 and (1954) p 26. 23, *The Times*, London, 10.8.66.

XVI. THE THREE BRAINS

1, Gaskell (1908) pp 65-7. 2, Ibid, p 66. 3, Wood Jones and Porteous (1929) pp 27-8. 4, Ibid, p 117. 5, Ibid, p 103. 6, Ibid, p 112. 7, Le Gros Clark (1961). 8, Wheeler (1928) p 46. 9, Herrick (1961) pp 398-9. 10, MacLean (1958) p 613. 11, MacLean (1956) p 351. 12, Mandler (1962) pp 273-4 and 326. 13, Herrick (1961) p 316. 14, Mandler (1962) p 338. 15, MacLean (1962) p 289. 16, MacLean (1964) p 2. 17, MacLean (private communication). 18, MacLean (1958). 19, Ibid, p 615. 20, Ibid, pp 614-15. 21, Herrick (1961) p 429. 22, MacLean (1958) p 614. 23, MacLean (1964) p 3. 24, MacLean (1956) p 339. 25, MacLean (1956) p 341 and (1958) p 619. 26, MacLean (1956) p 341. 27, MacLean (1964) pp 10-11. 28, MacLean (1962) p 296. 29, Miller et al. (1960) p 206. 30, MacLean (private communication). 31, MacLean (1956) p 348. 31a, Kluever (1911). 32, MacLean (1961) p 1737. 33, MacLean (1958) p 619. 34, MacLean (1962) p 292. 35, Lorenz (1966) p 120. 36, Allport (1924). 36a, Olds (1960). 36b, Hebb (1949). 36c, Pribram (1966). 37, Gellhorn (1963). 38, Ibid. 39, Cobb (1950). 40, MacLean (1962) p 295. 41, Pribram (1966) p 9. 42, Gellhorn (1957).

XVII. A UNIQUE SPECIES

1, Huxley, J. (1963) pp 7-28. 2, Koestler (1959) 513-14. 3, Pyke (1961) p 215. 4, Koestler (1964) p 227. 5, Huxley J. (1964) p 192. 6, Russell,

W. M. S., in *The Listener*, London, 5.11.64 and 12.11.64. 7, Lorenz (1966) p 19. 8, Russell, W. M. S. and C., in *The Listener*, London, 3.12.64. 9, Lorenz (1966) pp 206–8. 10, Koestler (1966B). 11, Lorenz (1966) p 215. 12, Lévy-Bruhl (1923) p 63. 13, Berger (1967).

XVIII. THE AGE OF CLIMAX

1, Platt (1966) pp 195, 196 and 200. 2, de Beer (1966). 3, National Research Council Report (1962). 4, Harkavy (1964). 5, Ibid, p 8. 6, Eastman (1965). 7, Morris (1966). 8, *Time*, New York, 29.1.65. 9, v. Bertalanffy (1956). 10, *Time*, New York, 25.9.64. 11, Lindquist (1966). 12, *Time*, New York, 24.9.65. 13, Platt (1966) p 192. 14, Lorenz (1966) p 205. 15, MacLean (1961) pp 1738–9. 16, Hydén (1961). 17, Saunders (1961) p xi f. 18, Huxley, A. (1961).

APPENDIX II. ON NOT FLOGGING DEAD HORSES

1, Nott (1964). 2, Miller (1964B). 3, Miller et al. (1960). 4, v. Bertalanffy (1967).

BIBLIOGRAPHY

The dates given refer to the editions that I have consulted.

ADRIAN, E. D., in *Brain and Conscious Experience*. See Eccles, J. C., ed., 1966.

ALLPORT, F. H., *Social Psychology*. New York, 1924.

ARENDT, H., *Eichmann in Jerusalem*. London, 1963.

BAERENDS, G. P., 'Fortpflanzungsverhalten und Orientierung der Grabwespe' in *Ammophila campestris. Jur. Tijd. voor Entom. 84*, 71–275, 1941.

BARTLETT, F., *Thinking*. London, 1958.

de BEER, G., *Embryos and Ancestors*. Oxford, 1940.

de BEER, G., in *New Scientist*. London, 17.2.66.

BELOFF, J., *Existence of Mind*. London, 1962.

BERGER, F. M., in *Am. Scientist*, 55, 1, March 1967.

BERLYNE, D. E., *Conflict, Arousal and Curiosity*. New York, 1960.

v. BERTALANFFY, L., *Problems of Life*. New York, 1952.

v. BERTALANFFY, L., in *The Scientific Monthly*, January 1956.

v. BERTALANFFY, L., *Psychology in the Modern World*. Heinz Werner Memorial Lectures. New York, 1967 (in press).

BICHAT, X., *Recherches Physiologiques sur la Vie et la Mort*. Paris, 1800.

BICHAT, X., *Anatomie Générale*. Paris, 1801.

BONNER, J., *The Molecular Biology of Development*. Oxford, 1965.

Brain and Conscious Experience. See Eccles, J. C., ed., 1966.

Brain and Mind. See Smythies, J. R., ed., 1965.

BROWN, R., *Social Psychology*. Glencoe, Ill., 1965.

BRUNER, J. S. and POSTMAN, L., in *J. of Personality*, XVIII, 1949.

BURT, C., in *B. J. of Psychol.*, 53, 3, 1962.

CALVIN, A. D., ed., *Psychology*. Boston, Mass., 1961.

CANNON, W. B., *The Wisdom of the Body*. New York, 1939.

CHILD, C. M., *Physiological Foundations of Behaviour*. New York, 1924.

CHOMSKY, N., 'A Review of B. F. Skinner's *Verbal Behaviour*' in *Language* 35, No. 1, 26–58, 1959.

CLARK, W. E. LE GROS, in *The Advancement of Science*. London, September, 1961.

CLAYTON, R. M., in *Penguin Science Survey 1949B*. Harmondsworth, Middlesex, 1964.

COBB, S., *Emotions and Clinical Medicine*. New York, 1950.

COGHILL, G. E., *Anatomy and the Problem of Behaviour*. Cambridge, 1929.

Control of the Mind. See Farber, S. M., and Wilson, R. H. L., eds., New York, 1961.

COOPER, F. S., See Liberman et al., 1965.

CRAIK, K. J. W., *The Nature of Explanation*. Cambridge, 1943.

DARWIN, C. R., *The Origin of Species*. London, 1873 (6th ed.).

DREVER'S *A Dictionary of Psychology*. Harmondsworth, Middlesex, 1962.

DUBOS, R. J., *Louis Pasteur*. Boston, Mass., 1950.

DUNBAR, H. F., *Emotions and Bodily Changes*. New York, 1946.

EASTMAN, N. J., in *Fertility and Sterility*, Vol. 15, No. 5, September–October 1965, reprinted by the Ford Foundation, 1965.

ECCLES, J. C., ed., *Brain and Conscious Experience*. New York, 1966.

EMPSON, W., 'The Abominable Fancy' in *New Statesman*. London, 21.8.64.

EWER, R. F., 'Natural Selection and Neoteny' in *Acta Biotheoretica*. Leiden, 1960.

FARBER, S. M. and WILSON, R. H. L., eds., *Control of the Mind*. New York, 1961.

FORD, E. B. See Huxley, J., 1954.

FREUD, SIGMUND, *Jenseits des Lustprinzips*, 1920.

FREUD, SIGMUND, *Group Psychology and the Analysis of the Ego*, 1922.

FREUD, SIGMUND, *Gesammelte Werke*, Vols. I–XVIII. London, 1940–52.

GALANTER, E. See Miller, G. A., 1960.

GARSTANG, W., 'The Theory of Recapitulation: A Critical Restatement of the Biogenetic Law' in *J. Linnean Soc. London, Zoology*, 35, 81, 1922.

GARSTANG, W., 'The Morphology of the Tunicata, and its Bearings on the Phylogeny of the Chordata' in *Quarterly J. Microscopical Sci.*, 72, 51, 1928.

GASKELL, W. H., *The Origin of Vertebrates.*, 1908.

GELLHORN, E., *Autonomic Imbalance and the Hypothalamus*. Minneapolis, 1957.

GELLHORN, E. and LOOFBOURROW, G. N., *Emotions and Emotional Disorders*. New York, 1963.

GELLHORN, E., *Principles of Autonomic-Somatic Integrations*. Minneapolis, 1967.

GELLNER, E., *Words and Things*. London, 1959.

GOETHE, *Die Metamorphose der Pflanzen*. Gotha, 1790.

GOETHE, *Sämtliche Werke*, Vol. XIV, Editor's Preface. Stuttgart, 1872.

GORINI, L., in *Scientific American*, April 1966.

GREGORY, R. L., *Eye and Brain*. London, 1966.

HADAMARD, J., *The Psychology of Invention in the Mathematical Field*. Princeton, 1949.

HALDANE, J. B. S., *The Causes of Evolution*. London, 1932.

HAMBURGER, V., article on 'Regeneration' in *Encyclopaedia Britannica*, 1955 ed.

HARDY, A. C., 'Escape from Specialization' in Huxley, Hardy and Ford, eds., 1954.

HARDY, A. C., *The Living Stream*. London, 1965.

HARDY, A. C., *The Divine Flame*. London, 1966.

HARKAVY, O., 'Economic Problems of Population Growth'. New York: The Ford Foundation, 1964.

HARLOW, H. F., in *Psychol. Rev.*, 60, 23–32, 1953.

v. HAYEK, F. A., 'The Evolution of Systems of Rules of Conduct' in *Studies in Philosophy, Politics and Economics*. London, 1967 (in press).

HEBB, D. O., *Organization of Behaviour*. New York, 1949.

HERRICK, C. J., *The Evolution of Human Nature*. New York, 1961.

HILGARD, E. R., *Introduction to Psychology*. London, 1957.

HINGSTON, R. W. G., in *J. Bombay Nat. Hist. Soc.*, 31, 1926–7.

Hixon Symposium. See Jeffress, L. A., ed., 1951.

HOGG, G., *Cannibalism and Human Sacrifice*. London, 1961.

HULL, C. L., *Principles of Behaviour*. New York, 1943.

HULL, C. L., *A Behaviour System*. New York, 1952.

HUMPHREY, G., *Thinking*. London, 1951.

HUNTER, W. S., article on 'Behaviourism' in *Encyclopaedia Britannica*, 1955 ed.

HUXLEY, A., *Brave New World*. London, 1932.

HUXLEY, A., *After Many a Summer*. London, 1939.

HUXLEY, A., *The Doors of Perception*. London, 1954.

HUXLEY, A., *Heaven and Hell*. London, 1956.

HUXLEY, A., in *Control of the Mind*. New York, 1961.

HUXLEY, J., HARDY, A. C. and FORD, E. B., eds., *Evolution as a Process*. New York, 1954.

HUXLEY, J., *Man in the Modern World*. New York, 1964.

HYDÉN, H., in *Control of the Mind*. See Farber, S. M. and Wilson, R. H. L., eds., 1961.

JACOBSON, H., in *Am. Scientist*, 43: 119–27, January 1955.

JAENSCH, E. R., *Eidetic Imagery*. London, 1930.

JAMES, W., 'What is Emotion?' in *Mind*, 9, 188–205, 1884.

JAMES, W., *The Principles of Psychology*. New York, 1890.

JAMES, W., *The Varieties of Religious Experience*. London, 1902.

JEFFRESS, L. A., ed., *Cerebral Mechanisms in Behaviour – The Hixon Symposium*. New York, 1951.

JENKINS, J., 'Stanford Seminar Protocols' 1965 (unpublished).

JENKINS, J. See Koestler (1965A).

JUNG, C. G., *Psychology of the Unconscious*. New York, 1919.

JUNG, C. G., *Contributions to Analytical Psychology*. London, 1928.

JUNG, C. G., *Modern Man in Search of his Soul*. London, 1933.

JUNG, C. G., *The Integration of Personality*. London, 1940.

KLUEVER, H., 'The Eidetic Child' in *A Handbook of Child Psychology*. Chicago, 1931.

KNEALE, W., *On Having a Mind*. Cambridge, 1962.

KOESTLER, A., *The Gladiators*. London, 1940.

KOESTLER, A., *The Yogi and the Commissar*. London, 1945.

KOESTLER, A., *Insight and Outlook*. London, 1949.

KOESTLER, A. (with others), *The God That Failed*. London, 1950.

KOESTLER, A., *The Invisible Writing*. London, 1954.

KOESTLER, A., *The Sleepwalkers*. London, 1959.

KOESTLER, A., *The Lotus and the Robot*. London, 1960.

KOESTLER, A., *The Act of Creation*. London, 1964.

KOESTLER, A. and JENKINS, J., 'Inversion Effects in the Tachistoscopic Perception of Number Sequences' in *Psychon. Sci.*, Vol. 3, 1965A.

KOESTLER, A., 'Biological and Mental Evolution' in *Nature*, 208, No. 5015, 1033–6, 11.12.65B.

KOESTLER, A., 'Evolution and Revolution in the History of Science' in *The Advancement of Science*, March, 1966A.

KOESTLER, A., 'Of Geese and Men' in *The Observer*, London, 18.9.66B.

KOTTENHOF, H., in *Acta Psychologica*, Vol. XIII, No. 2 and Vol. XIII, No. 3, 1957.

KRECHEVSKY, I., in *Psychol. Rev.*, 39, 1932.

KRETSCHMER, E., *A Textbook of Medical Psychology*. London, 1934.

KRIS, E., *Psychoanalytic Explorations in Art*. New York, 1964.

KUBIE, L. S., *Neurotic Distortion of the Creative Process*. Lawrence, Kansas, 1958.

KUHN, T., *The Structure of Scientific Revolutions*. Chicago, 1962.

LASHLEY, K. S., in *Hixon Symposium*. See Jeffress, L. A., ed., 1951.

LASHLEY, K. S., *The Neuro-Psychology of Lashley* (Selected Papers). New York, 1960.

LASLETT, P., ed., *The Physical Basis of Mind*. Oxford, 1950.

LÉVY-BRUHL, L., *Primitive Mentality*. London, 1923.

LIBERMAN, A. M., COOPER, F. S., et al., 'Some Observations on a Model for Speech Perception', 1965. To appear in Proceedings of the

Symposium on Models for the Perception of Speech and Visual Form.

Life – An Introduction to Biology. See Simpson, G. G., et al., 1957.

LINDQUIST, S., China and Crisis. London, 1966.

LOOPBOURROW, G. N. See Gellhorn, 1963.

LORENZ, K. L., On Aggression. London, 1966.

MACKAY, D. M., in Brain and Conscious Experience. See Eccles, J. C., ed., 1966.

McKELLAR, P., Imagination and Thinking. London, 1957.

MACLEAN, P., 'Psychosomatic Disease and the "Visceral Brain"' in Psychosom. Med., 11, 338–53, 1949.

MACLEAN, P., 'Contrasting Functions of Limbic and Neocortical Systems of the Brain and their Relevance to Psycho-physiological Aspects of Medicine' in Am. J. of Med., Vol. XXV, No. 4, 611–26, October 1958.

MACLEAN, P., 'Psychosomatics' in Handbook of Physiology – Neurophysiology III, 1961.

MACLEAN, P., 'New Findings Relevant to the Evolution of Psychosexual Functions of the Brain' in J. of Nervous and Mental Disease, Vol. 135, No. 4, October 1962.

MACLEAN, P., 'Man and his Animal Brains' in Modern Medicine, 95–106, 3.2.64.

McNEILL, D., in Discovery. London, July 1966.

MANDLER, G., 'Emotion' in New Directions in Psychology. New York, 1962.

MASLOW, A. H., Toward a Psychology of Being. Princeton, 1962.

MEDAWAR, P., The Future of Man. London, 1960.

MILLER, G. A., GALANTER, E. and PRIBRAM, K. H., Plans and the Structure of Behaviour. New York, 1960.

MILLER, G. A., in Encounter. London, July 1964A.

MILLER, G. A., in Scientific American, December 1964B.

MONTAGUE, J. F., 'Ulcers in Paradise', Clin. Med., 7, 677 ff, 1960.

MORRIS, I., in New Scientist. London, 25.8.66.

MULLER, H. J., Science and Criticism. New Haven, Conn., 1943.

NATIONAL RESEARCH COUNCIL REPORT on 'Natural Resources'. Washington, D.C., 1962.

NEEDHAM, A. E., in New Scientist. London, 2.11.61.

NEEDHAM, J., Order and Life. New Haven, Conn., 1936.

NOTT, K., in Encounter. London, September 1964.

OLDS, J., in Psychiatric Research Reports of the American Psychiatric Association. January 1960.

ORWELL, G., Nineteen Eighteen-Four. London, 1949.

OSWALD, I., *Sleep*. Harmondsworth, Middlesex, 1966.

PAVLOV, I. P., *Conditioned Reflexes*. Oxford, 1927.

PENFIELD, W., in *Control of the Mind*. See Farber, S. M. and Wilson, R. H. L., eds., 1961.

PITTENDRIGH, C. S., See Simpson, G. G., 1957.

PLATT, J. R., *The Step to Man*. New York, 1966.

POLANYI, M., *Personal Knowledge*. London, 1958.

POLANYI, M., *The Tacit Dimension*. New York, 1966.

POLLOCK, M. R., in *New Scientist*. London, 9.9.65.

POPPER, K. R., in *Br. J. Phil. Sci.*, I, Part I, 117–33; Part II, 173–95, 1950.

POPPER, K. R., *The Logic of Scientific Discovery*. London, 1959.

PORTEUS, S. D. See Wood Jones, F., 1929.

POSTMAN, L. See Bruner, J., 1949.

PRESCOTT, W. H., *The Conquest of Mexico* (Bantam ed.). New York, 1964.

PRIBRAM, K. H. See Miller, G. A., 1960.

PRIBRAM, K. H., *Emotion: The Search for Control*, 1967 (in press).

PYKE, M., *The Boundaries of Science*. London, 1961.

RANDAL, J., in *Harper's Magazine*, 231, 56–61, 1965.

RUSSELL, W. M. S. and RUSSELL, C., in *The Listener*. London, 3.12.64.

RUSSELL, W. M. S., in *The Listener*. London, 5.11.64.

RUSSELL, W. M. S., in *The Listener*. London, 12.11.64.

RYLE, G., *The Concept of Mind*. London, 1949.

RYLE, G., in *The Physical Basis of Mind*. See Laslett, P., ed., 1950.

SAGER, R., in *Scientific American*, January 1965.

ST HILAIRE, G., *Philosophie Anatomique*. Paris, 1818.

SAUNDERS, J. B. de C. M., in *Control of the Mind*. See Farber, S. M. and Wilson, R. H. L., eds., 1961.

SCHACHTEL, E. G., *Metamorphosis*. London, 1963.

SCHRÖDINGER, E., *What is Life?* Cambridge, 1944.

SEMON, R., *The Mneme*. London, 1921.

SHERRINGTON, C., *Integrative Action of the Nervous System*. New York, 1906.

SIMON, H. J., 'The Architecture of Complexity' in *Proc. Am. Philos. Soc.*, Vol. 106, No. 6, December 1962.

SIMPSON, G. G., *The Meaning of Evolution*. New Haven, Conn., 1949.

SIMPSON, G. G., PITTENDRIGH, C. S. and TIFFANY, L. H., *Life: An Introduction to Biology*. New York, 1957.

SINNOTT, E. W., *Cell and Psyche – The Biology of Purpose*. New York, 1961.

SKINNER, B. F., *The Behaviour of Organisms*. New York, 1938.

SKINNER, B. F., *Science and Human Behaviour*. New York, 1953.

SKINNER, B. F., *Verbal Behaviour*. New York, 1957.

SMYTHIES, J. R., ed., *Brain and Mind*. London, 1965.

SPENCER, H., *First Principles*. London, 1862.

SPERRY, R. W., in *Brain and Conscious Experience*. See Eccles, J. C., ed., 1966.

SPURWAY, H., 'Remarks on Vavilov's Law of Homologous Variation' in *Supplemento. La Ricerca Scientifica (Pallanza Symposium) 18*. Cons. Naz. delle Ricerche. Rome, 1949.

SUZUKI, D. T., *Zen and Japanese Culture*. London, 1959.

TAYLOR, A. C. See Weiss, P., 1960.

THOMPSON, D. W., *On Growth and Form*. Cambridge, 1942.

THORPE, W. H., *Learning and Instinct in Animals*. London, 1956.

THORPE, W. H., in *Nature*. London, 14.5.1966A.

THORPE, W. H., in *Brain and Conscious Experience*. See Eccles, J. C., 1966B.

TIFFANY, L. H. See Simpson, G. G., 1957.

TINBERGEN, N., *The Study of Instinct*. Oxford, 1951.

TINBERGEN, N., *Social Behaviour in Animals*. London, 1953.

TOLMAN, E. C. See Krechevsky. 1932.

WADDINGTON, C. H., in *The Listener*. London, 13.11.52.

WADDINGTON, C. H., *The Strategy of the Genes*. London, 1957.

WADDINGTON, C. H., *The Nature of Life*. London, 1961

WATSON, J. B., in *Psychol. Rev.*, 20, 158–67, 1913.

WATSON, J. B., *Behaviourism*. London, 1928.

WEISS, P., in *Hixon Symposium*. See Jeffress, L. A., ed. 1951.

WEISS, P. and TAYLOR, A. C., 'Reconstitution of Complete Organs from Single-Cell Suspensions of Chick Embryos in Advanced Stages of Differentiation' in Proc. of *Nat. Academy of Sciences*, Vol. 46, No. 9, 1177–85, September, 1960.

WHEELER, W. M., *Emergent to Volution*. New York, 1928.

WHYTE, L. L., *The Unitary Principle in Physics and Biology*. London, 1949.

WHYTE, L. L., *Internal Factors in Evolution*. New York, 1965.

WIENER, N., *Cybernetics*. New York, 1948.

WILSON, R. H. L. See Farber, S. M., 1961.

WITTGENSTEIN, L., *Tractatus, Logico Philosophicus*. London, 1922.

WOOD JONES, F. and PORTEUS, S. D., *The Matrix of the Mind*. London, 1929.

YOUNG, J. Z., *The Life of Vertebrates*. Oxford, 1950.

ACKNOWLEDGEMENTS

The author and publishers wish to thank the following for permission to quote from various works: The Macmillan Co., New York (*Science and Human Behaviour*, by B. F. Skinner, © 1953 by The Macmillan Co); Allyn and Bacon, Boston (*Psychology*, ed. A. D. Calvin, © 1961 by Allyn and Bacon); Penguin Books Ltd, Harmondsworth ('Differentiation', by R. M. Clayton in *Penguin Science Survey 1964B*); Routledge and Kegan Paul Ltd, London, and Harcourt, Brace and World, Inc, New York (*Life: An Introduction to Biology*, by G. G. Simpson, C. S. Pittendrigh and L. H. Tiffany, © 1957 by Harcourt, Brace and World, Inc, and Routledge and Kegan Paul); *The Listener*, London ('How Do Adaptations Occur?', by C. H. Waddington); Chatto and Windus, London (*Man in the Modern World*, by J. Huxley); Cambridge Univ. Press (*On Growth and Form*, by D. W. Thompson); Edward Arnold Ltd, London (*The Matrix of the Mind*, by F. Wood Jones and S. D. Porteus); Robert Hale Ltd, London (*Cannibalism and Human Sacrifice*, by G. Hogg); Methuen and Co. Ltd, London (*On Aggression*, by K. L. Lorenz, tr. M. Latzke); *The Listener*, London ('The Wild Ones' and 'The Affluent Crowd', by W. M. S. Russell); McGraw Hill, New York (J. B. de C. M. Saunders in *Control of the Mind*).

INDEX

Eidetic images, 112
Einstein, A., 209–10, 214, 232, 301
Elwin, Dr Verrier, 270
Embryo—
    eye-bud of, 145, 156
    morphogenesis of, 142–6
    resemblance of ape to man, 195
Embryonic development, 87–8, 92, 151
Embryonic tissue—
    determination of, 144
    docility of, 144
Emergency reactions, 315
Emotion—
    ancient brain and, 320–5
    and irrational beliefs, 328–30
    and laughter, 217–18
    art and, 219–23
    autonomic nervous system and, 334
    novelists and, 327
    physiology of, 312–16
    three dimensions of, 260–4
    two basic categories of, 334
Emotional commitment, 296, 301
Emotions—
    aggressive-defensive, 332
    classification of, 261
    James-Lange theory of, 314
    overheated drives, 315
    Papez-Maclean theory of, 316 et seq.
    participatory, 333
    preparatory, 333
    self-assertive, 252
    self-transcending, 252, 332
    vicarious, 261
Encounter, 26 n
Encyclopaedia Britannica, 29
Entropy, 231
    negative, 231
Environment—
    hierarchy of, 149, 388
    influence on behaviour, 134–5
    interpretation of, 125–6
    man and, 17
Epigenetic landscape, 150
Epilepsy and the limbic system, 323–4
Equilibrium, dynamic, 389
Erasmus of Rotterdam, 342
Ergotropic system, 333

Ethnic tensions, 368
Euphony, 224
European Common Market, 363
Evolution, 11–12, 152–77
    biological, 17
    by paedomorphosis, 191–200
    explosive, 311
    homology and, 161–6
    internal selection, 156–9
    Law of, 232
    mental, 17
    of brain, 316–20
    of ideas, 196–8
    progress by initiative, 178–88
    random mutation, 152, 155
    retracing of steps in, 194–8
    sex a late-comer in, 332
    strategy of, 305
    superimposition of new on old brain, 321
    the law of balance and, 166–9
Evolution of Human Nature, The, 311
Evolutionary holons, stability of, 166
Evolutionary homeostasis, 169
Evolutionary Humanists, 276
Evolutionary maze, 192
Evolutionary mistakes, 306
Evolutionist doctrines, 140
Ewer, R. F., 185
Exploratory drives, 180
Explosive evolution, 311
Extra-sensory perception, 253
Eye, compound, 176
Eye-bud of embryo, 156–7
Eye-cup of embryo, 143
Eye lenses, 176
Eysenck, H. J., 392

FAINTING, infectious, 283
Faith—
    emotional commitment, 296
    reason and, 296–7
Fall, doctrine of the, 11
Faria, Lima da, 157
Farrar, Dean, 295
Fascism, 293–5
Faust, 165 n
Feedbacks, 59, 119–23, 128, 143, 146, 148–50, 238, 387 ff
Fetish, 291

LEONARD COTTRELL

THE BULL OF MINOS 25p

The thrilling story of the great archaeological discoveries in Crete and Greece made by Heinrich Schliemann and Sir Arthur Evans.

SEEING ROMAN BRITAIN 30p

'A thoroughly practical guidebook intended for the walker, cyclist and motorist – or the fireside reader who has an interest in our country's past.' – BRISTOL EVENING POST

THE GREAT INVASION 30p

An evocative reconstruction of the Roman invasion of Britain, brings to life the armies and their bitter forty-year campaign. The soldiers and their equipment, the battles that were fought and won all provide fascinating parallels with modern methods of warfare.

THE LOST PHARAOHS 25p

'Leonard Cottrell proves that the antiquities of the Nile are not merely inexhaustible in number, but in fascination as well' – NEW YORK TIMES

DIGS AND DIGGERS 40p

With infectious and informed enthusiasm, Leonard Cottrell tells the story of archaeology and how the early beginnings of simple treasure hunting and a romantic approach have developed into a specialized science.

THE LION GATE 30p

A fascinating inquiry into the extent to which this heroic world, described by Homer in the *Iliad* and the *Odyssey*, actually corresponds to the ancient world discovered and reconstructed by archaeologists.

A SELECTION OF POPULAR PAN NON-FICTION

These and other PAN books are obtainable from all booksellers and newsagents. If you have any difficulty please send purchase price plus 5p postage to P.O. Box 11, Falmouth, Cornwall. While every effort is made to keep prices low, it is sometimes necessary to increase prices at short notice. PAN Books reserve the right to show new retail prices on covers which may differ from those advertised in the text or elsewhere.